Aru Shah
AND THE SONG OF DEATH

Aru Shah
AND THE SONG OF DEATH
THE

A PANDAVA NOVEL
BOOK TWO

ROSHANI CHOKSHI

RICK RIORDAN PRESENTS

SCHOLASTIC INC.

ISBN 978-1-338-60608-9

12 11 10 9 8 7 6 5 4 3   21 22 23 24 25

Printed in the U.S.A.   40

First Scholastic printing, February 2020

This book is set in Athenaeum Pro, FCaslon Twelve ITC Std, Teethreedee Std. Front,
Clairvaux Lt Std/Monotype; Adorn Roman, Goudy Trajan Pro, Jenson Recut/Fontspring

Designed by Mary Claire Cruz

For my grandparents—
Vijya, Ramesh, Apolonia, and Antonio—
who carried so much in the crossing of oceans.
I love you.

CONTENTS

ONE

New Demon Who Dis?

Aru Shah had a gigantic lightning bolt, and she really wanted to use it.

But if she used it now, she risked attracting the herd of zombies currently swarming through the Night Bazaar.

"This is the worst Saturday *ever*," moaned Mini, clutching her celestial weapon like a teddy bear.

While Aru's soul father—the god of thunder—had gifted her a lightning bolt named Vajra, Mini's soul father—the god of death—had given her an enchanted *danda* stick named Dee Dee.

The two of them crouched beneath a table by the Frozen Yogurt and Dreams stand, watching through the gaps in the wood as Otherworld citizens ran screaming, dropping grocery bags, or, in the case of one bull-headed *rakshasa*, walloping a zombie over the head with a tote full of tomatoes.

Overhead, a loud announcement blared:

"ATTENTION, ATTENTION! WE HAVE LOCATED AN UNWANTED DEMONIC PRESENCE IN THE

AREA. PLEASE EVACUATE THE NIGHT BAZAAR.
ATTENTION, ATTENTION…"

Aru hated sitting still. But their job here wasn't to fight, but
to *find*…because somewhere in the Night Bazaar was a thief
who had raised the Otherworld alarm and probably let in all
these zombies.

Unfortunately, that thief was also her newest Pandava sister.

Which meant that, just like Aru and Mini, she was the reincarnation of one of the five legendary demigod brothers from
Hindu mythology. Hours ago, they'd seen her carrying a giant
bow and arrow just as Boo, their pigeon mentor, had said, *That
was your sister.*

"Aru!" whispered Mini.

"Shh! A zombie might find us—"

"I think…I think one already has…" said Mini.

Aru turned around just in time to see a pair of pale hands
flip over the table they were under. Bright sunlight and moonlight washed over them from the half-day-half-night sky overhead. Aru blinked against the sudden brightness. She couldn't
get a good read on the zombie's features, even as it snapped
off a table leg (the stand howled, "HOW *DARE* YOU!") and
brandished it at them.

Aru probably should've been scared, but she had a fearsome
weapon, and she knew how to wield it.

She flung Vajra as if it were a javelin. The lightning bolt
zapped the wooden peg out of the zombie's hand, and he pulled
his arm back, stung. The entire yogurt stand tipped over on
top of him.

"Run!" said Mini.

Vajra zoomed back into Aru's hands and she took off.

Around them, the Night Bazaar had fallen into chaos. Storefronts had been toppled, and while most of the shop owners had evacuated, the displays kept fighting. An enchanted flower stall turned its pumpkin vines into a row of exploding jack-o'-lanterns, and the kitchen appliances section summoned an army of wooden spoons to beat a group of zombies over the head. When some of the intruders spilled a bowl of glass beads and started slipping and sliding on them, a *yaksha* storeowner hollered, "YOU'LL PAY FOR THAT! NO SATURDAY DISCOUNT, EITHER!"

"That zombie is chasing us!" Mini yelled at Aru.

Aru glanced over her shoulder. Sure enough, the same zombie stalked after them, shoving aside the feral grocery carts that were anxiously zooming through the Night Bazaar.

"Why do *all* zombies lurch?" asked Aru. "Is that, like, a universal zombie thing?"

She cast Vajra like a net, thinking that would stop him, but the electrified mesh slipped right off, and he stepped over it. Aru frowned. Maybe her aim wasn't as good when she was running…but Vajra had never failed as a net before. Vajra bounded back to her, transforming into a bracelet that wound around her wrist.

Mini skidded to a halt in front of the entrance to the frozen pizza and enchantments aisle. A herd of grocery carts, packed tightly together in fear, blocked their way.

"There she is!" said Mini.

At the end of the aisle, Aru caught sight of the other Pandava girl. The *thief*. She had shifted into a blue wolf and was carrying the large bow and arrow in her mouth as she ran.

"Hey! *Stop!*" yelled Mini.

But they couldn't chase after her. In front of them, the grocery carts hissed and zoomed back and forth like a pack of angry cats. Behind them, the zombie lurched ever closer.

"Can you make us invisible?" asked Aru. "Maybe we can slip past him?"

Casting a shield of invisibility with Dee Dee was one of the new powers Mini had learned in Pandava training. Except she wasn't that good at it yet. Mini waved her danda stick in an arc, creating a force field around the two of them—but it immediately flickered and died.

Beyond the grocery carts, the Pandava thief slipped away before Aru could try to ensnare her.

A low growl erupted behind them. Aru turned slowly, willing Vajra to turn back into a lightning bolt. For the first time, she could take a good look at the zombie. He was tall and wore a white coat open over a bare chest, and there was a strange pale scar right above his heart. Not so much a wound as the center of a spiderweb, which looked like frost creeping out over the skin. And then she noticed something even more bizarre. The coat's buttons were enamel pins in the shape of teeth. Embroidered words next to the left lapel read:

DR. ERNST WARREN, DDS
OPEN WIDE!

"The zombie is a dentist?" said Aru.
"My aunt's a dentist," said Mini. "She said it's soul-crushing."
"Makes sense."

As if highly affronted, the zombie let out a guttural cry and charged at them.

Weeks of training kicked in immediately. In a split second, both girls stood back-to-back, their weapons out before them. The zombie roared and raised his hands. Mini swung Dee Dee at his ankles, knocking him over. Aru spun Vajra in her hands until it became a rope. Then she threw it at the zombie, binding his wrists and ankles.

Mini beamed at Aru, but a second later her smile fell.

"Don't panic," said Aru. "Two against one worked fine!"

"What about two against two *dozen*?"

Aru followed Mini's gaze. Panic zipped through her heart as she watched twenty zombies step out from behind the wreckage of storefronts. All of them wore the same slack-faced expression and ripped shirts that revealed identical frostlike wounds right over their hearts. Froyo Zombie shucked off the lightning rope a moment later, and Vajra whipped back into Aru's hands. Beside her, Mini cast another force field, but it blinked and fizzled out.

"Our weapons aren't working..." said Mini.

Aru didn't want to admit it, but Mini was right. It should've been impossible. Celestial weapons usually overcame everything except, well, *other* celestial weapons.

Just then, a shadow crossed over them. Both girls looked up in time to see Boo careening their way. He carried a small gray vial in his talons.

"Those are *my* Pandavas!" he squawked at the zombies.

He dove in front of the girls, smashing the vial on the ground. Plumes of smoke shot up, obscuring the zombies' view. Flapping quickly, Boo did a U-turn and said, "No time to waste, girls. Go after your sister!"

Some sister, thought Aru. That other Pandava, whoever she was, had landed them in this mess.

"But what about you?" asked Mini worriedly.

"*I* am a pigeon capable of mass annoyance." Boo puffed out his chest. "Don't worry about me. Just find her!"

Aru and Mini turned to face the crowd of angry grocery carts. The cart nearest to her gnashed its metal grate, then reared up on its hind wheels.

Aru swung Vajra the rope above her head and lassoed the cart. It bucked angrily, but the lightning lariat held tight. Aru clambered into the carriage and pulled Mini in after her.

"Giddyup!" yelled Aru, now using Vajra as reins.

The grocery cart snorted, reared back, and then charged through the rest of the herd and down the frozen-food aisle. Mini leaned out of the cart, knocking hundreds of boxes onto the floor to stop the zombies in their tracks.

"I'll be paying for this out of my allowance for years!" she cried.

Aru tugged the reins to the right, steering the cart toward the last place they'd seen the Pandava girl. At the end of the aisle, a dirt path led to an arena where she knew some students trained. Aru and Mini had never met any of the other kids who, because of their lineage, were entitled to study in the Otherworld. Aru liked to think that she and Mini were kept separate from them because, as *Pandavas*, they needed *exclusive* lessons. But Mini suspected it was really because the two of them were in remedial classes....

Once they reached the arena, Aru spotted a pair of girls fighting for control of a golden bow and arrow. One was the Pandava sister they had seen before—the shape-shifter. She had chestnut skin and brown hair with gold highlights. She was also ridiculously tall, and though she had long limbs, they weren't gangly like Aru's, but thick and sturdy, and covered in metal bracelets.

And the other girl? Aru felt as if the wind had been knocked out of her lungs.

"How is that possible?" whispered Mini.

Because the person the Pandava was fighting was...

Aru.

TWO

Keeping Up with the Pandavas

"Isn't that . . . you?" said Mini, the tiniest amount of uncertainty flickering in her voice.

Real Aru pointed at Fake Aru, who was currently unleashing a powerful uppercut against the other Pandava girl. The bow and arrow were on the ground behind them.

"Would I *ever* wear denim on denim?!" demanded Aru.

"Good point," said Mini. She pushed her glasses up on her nose.

The Pandava girl, Aru realized begrudgingly, had some serious moves. She darted ridiculously fast, dodging blows and kicking up dirt. At one point, she transformed into a massive blue jaguar (which was *so* unfair) and attacked Fake Aru, but Fake Aru held her own. With a final powerful blow, Fake Aru sent the Pandava girl–jaguar flying back against a wall, where she slid to the floor, unconscious. In a flash of blue light, the big cat turned back into a girl.

Fake Aru dragged her arm over her mouth, breathing heavily, and picked up the bow and arrow. Then she snapped her fingers. The zombies, who had continued running rampant through the Night Market, immediately went still.

Aru's eyes widened. Fake Aru was *controlling* the zombies. But how?

"She has to be a rakshasi," whispered Mini.

Aru recalled from Pandava class that some rakshasas, beings with animal heads, could take on the appearance of gods, demons, and humans. Including, it would seem, Arus. But why would a rakshasi decide to look like her?

"She must be an evil one," said Aru, brandishing Vajra. "That outfit says it all."

The lightning bolt flared to life. Dee Dee turned into a violet spear. But just as the two of them rushed toward Fake Aru, a burst of white light threw them back. Fake Aru turned to face Real Aru and Mini.

The rakshasi wiggled her fingers in a hello, which was not only really *rude*, but seemed to cause the zombies to perk up and lurch into attack mode again. In a flash, Fake Aru disappeared with the bow and arrow . . . but not without leaving something behind:

A massive fire.

Searing flames erupted in a circle all around Mini and Aru. Black smoke choked off any sight of the zombies.

"Boo!" shouted Mini. "Help us!"

Aru looked up. The skies were empty. Their pigeon mentor was gone. The other Pandava girl was still slumped on the ground.

Right above her head, Aru heard wind ripping through the air and felt the *whump* of vast wings. She shielded her eyes, squinting up as several Guardians—the celestial beings who protected each generation's Pandavas—started to descend from the sky. Aru felt relief and annoyance twinned inside her. Why couldn't they have shown up thirty seconds earlier?

There was Hanuman, the monkey demigod, who appeared as a giant version of himself. His cheeks looked strangely full. Beside him was Urvashi, the stunning *apsara*, wearing a black tank top that read DANCE IS MY SUPERPOWER. Behind them, Aru could see two other figures from the Council of Guardians: a gigantic bear wearing a crown, and an old, scowling woman with the lower body of a snake.

Something about her was even scarier than the zombies.

"SHIELD EACH OTHER!" shouted Boo, swooping overhead.

Aru cast a wide net over herself, Mini, and—though she probably didn't deserve it—the unconscious Pandava girl. Then Mini blasted a force field of violet light around them— successfully this time. The magical shields had barely materialized before jets of water, as if from a bunch of fire hoses, hit the flames. Aru glanced up to see Hanuman shooting water from his mouth. He must have slurped up a whole lake. The fire died, steam hissing in the air.

Once the smoke cleared, Aru expected to see an army of soggy zombies. But instead, all she saw was the wreckage of the Night Bazaar: Stalls overturned. Strips of night sky dangling down in the air. A couple of shopkeepers shouting about insurance. Aru ignored all that.

The zombies had disappeared completely. Not a single trace of them was left.

Mini coughed. "That was awful!"

"I know," said Aru. "All those zombies—"

"And the *smoke!*" Mini reached for her backpack and took out her inhaler. "It almost gave me an asthma attack."

"How?" asked Aru.

"Well, there're these small airways in your lungs called bronchioles, and if you have asthma, the airways become inflamed, which—"

"No! Not the asthma! The *zombies!* Where did they go? There were, like, hundreds! Can zombies disappear?"

Mini wheezed. "They can if they're being controlled by something else. Like that bow and arrow." She pointed her chin toward the now-weaponless Pandava girl. Mini walked over to her, still clutching her inhaler, and Aru followed.

Behind them, the Guardians alighted on the ground.

Aru crouched beside the new girl.

"Hey," she said gruffly. She shook the girl's shoulder.

Mini lifted the girl's wrist and looked at her own watch. "Her heart rate is seventy beats per minute and strong. That's good."

Sluggishly, the Pandava blinked up at them. Her hazel eyes grew wide.

"Sit up slowly," coaxed Mini in her best *one-day-I'm-going-to-be-a-doctor* voice. "That was a rough hit. How's your vision?"

Leave it to Mini to be super nice to the person who had wrecked their Saturday. Aru crossed her arms, scowling.

The girl blinked again and looked around. Then her gaze focused on Aru. She pushed herself off the ground, shoving Mini aside.

"I can see just fine," growled the girl. "I can see the *thief* right in front of me. Hand it over."

"*I'm* not the thief, *you* are!" said Aru, holding up her hands. "But that rakshasi—the one who looked like me—took the bow and arrow. Just so we're clear, I'm the *real* Aru." She gestured at her outfit. "Note the lack of denim on denim."

The girl smacked her hands down. The moment they touched, Aru felt a shock, as if a live wire had snaked between them.

Wind stirred the dirt. Then it rose up in a cyclone around the other girl, lifting her off the ground.

Honestly, if it had been Aru, she would've started screaming. But this girl just *smiled* and raised her arms. Aru really wanted her to say, *All shall love me and despair!* But she didn't. Maybe she hadn't seen the Lord of the Rings movies.

A pale blue light burst around the Pandava. A flag—the symbol of Vayu, the god of the wind—rotated above her head. It was, Aru had to admit, *epic.* And the girl didn't even seem surprised that she'd been claimed! She didn't blink once when she was lowered back to the ground and a glowing blue weapon that looked like a caveman's club thudded next to her. She just picked it up, swung it over her shoulder, and started marching toward Aru.

Whoa, thought Aru. *How come she automatically gets a celestial weapon?* Aru and Mini had been forced to trudge all the way through the Kingdom of Death before their weapons turned into more than a Ping-Pong ball and a compact mirror.

That was . . . that was completely unfair.

Only then did Aru notice they had an audience. On the outskirts of the Night Bazaar, shoppers and store owners pressed closer, eager to get in on the drama.

Mini raced in front of Aru and held up her hands. "Listen, sometimes people make mistakes, which you clearly did back there. . . . But we saved your life! You can't be mad at us!"

"I *am* mad," said the girl, not breaking her stride. "You stole the bow and arrow. Where are they?" Her stomach growled loudly. She paused, adding, "And I'm hungry."

"Maybe you've got hypoglycemia—very common, and probably makes you irritable," said Mini, talking fast. "Want a Snickers?" She pulled a full-size bar from her backpack and held it out in front of the Pandava.

Aru was really glad Lord Vayu had placed his soul daughter a good distance away from the two of them. Even so, when the girl swung her club like a baseball bat, wind exploded around Mini and Aru. They both dug in their heels, but the gust lifted Mini into the air. The Snickers bar fell on the ground as she was carried off, shouting, "But I offered you candyyyy!"

Aru waited until she saw Mini safely, though rather unceremoniously, plop onto the ground a few feet away.

"You could've hurt her!" said Aru angrily.

"So? What are *you* going to do about it?" demanded the daughter of Vayu.

Vajra turned into a lightning sword. Electricity crackled down the blade.

"Oh, so that's how you wanna play it, *thief*?"

"*You're* the thief!"

Hanuman and Urvashi raced toward them, shouting, "Okay, girls, there's no reason to fight!"

Someone off to the side shouted, "Catfight! Catfight!"

Someone else goaded, "Grab her by the horns!"

Another chimed, "She doesn't have horns!"

"STOP IT, BRYNNE!" shouted Hanuman. "Father will not be pleased."

"ARU, PUT THAT SWORD DOWN!" hollered Boo.

And then a blast of wind shot Aru straight up into the sky. Her arms started pinwheeling. She glanced down—that was a huge mistake. Everyone looked like really catty ants.

As she fell, the last thing she saw before blacking out was a pair of giant hands reaching to snatch her out of the sky.

THREE

Aru Shah: Demigod and Hamster Impersonator

Aru woke up floating among the clouds in a gigantic glass bubble. A hole opened up beneath her, and Aru's stomach lurched. Hundreds of feet below, she saw the colorful (though torn-up) tents of the Night Bazaar and the last wisps of smoke from the epic fire. She scuttled backward in her bubble before looking up. Nothing but clear sky. Hanuman had dropped her in there as if she were a misbehaving hamster.

Fine, thought Aru, *I'll be a hamster.*

She started running, trying to get the sphere to move. In the distance, a thunderstorm let loose a low growl. Aru couldn't help but think it was the tiniest bit of scolding from her divine dad.

"She started it!" protested Aru.

The thunder growled again. It sounded like it was saying *Oh, really?*

A dusky cloud unraveled in the wind, allowing Aru to catch sight of two other giant bubbles floating just a couple feet away from her. One of them carried Mini, who was sitting cross-legged and reading a book. When she saw Aru looking at her, she gave a small, sad wave. In the bubble next to her was Brynne.

"Let me out!" shouted Brynne, but it sounded muffled. She beat her fist against the glass, and spiderweb cracks bloomed on the surface.

Well, if she can do that, I definitely can, too, thought Aru. She slammed a fist against the bubble. Pain shot through her arm. "OW, OW, OW, OW!" she shrieked, clutching her hand.

In the other bubble, Mini raised her eyebrows.

Aru tapped into their telepathic Pandava link. Usually, she only felt a connection to Mini's brain. This time, though, she sensed the presence of a second pathway. If Mini's link felt like velvet, this other path was thorned. It had to belong to the other girl, and there was *no way* Aru would tap into that link.

Did you see that?

Did I see you almost break your hand? Yep.

HOW DID SHE DO THAT?

I think she's the reincarnation of Bhima the Strong? She could probably bite through a steel beam. But she shouldn't try. Might be dangerous without a tetanus shot....

Aru's mind went elsewhere. Bhima the Strong was the second-oldest Pandava and the son of Lord Vayu. That meant she was Hanuman's half sister. Which explained why Hanuman had said *Father will not be pleased.*

Aru recalled that Brynne hadn't been the least bit surprised when her soul dad swept her up into the air. She'd looked so... graceful. Like a real Pandava. And Aru hadn't forgotten how she'd fought. Like a fully trained hero.

A pang of jealousy shot through Aru, followed by a strange

memory. Just before she'd gone unconscious, she'd felt a cold, smooth hand against her forehead and the unsettling sensation of someone rifling through her memories like files in a desk drawer.

Who'd done that?

She plopped down in the middle of the hamster ball. It couldn't have been Mini. Though they shared a Pandava mind link, she could block her friend's entry if she wanted to. This person had rudely barged in and made themselves right at home, and Aru had been powerless against them. Maybe it was *Brynne*, Aru thought with a flash of fury.

Aru gazed over at Mini now and saw her urgently pointing and mouthing *Look down!*

About fifty feet below them, the Council of Guardians was gathered in its elaborate Court of the Sky, a flat plane of marbled clouds where a semicircle of golden thrones and a round table floated in eerie splendor. Aru hamster-jogged until her glass bubble drifted nearer to them—close enough so she could get the gist of what they were saying.

As usual, not all the Guardians were in attendance. There was the beautiful Urvashi. She took an angry swig from her water bottle, and Aru saw through the semitransparent plastic that it didn't contain water, but sunshine. Beside Urvashi, Boo was perched at the top of his throne, squawking loudly. Hanuman was there, too, dressed in an all-white tuxedo. A fourth seat was occupied by King Jambavan, the giant bear, whose crown, Aru could now see, looked like small constellations knitted around his forehead.

All of them were arguing with whoever was seated in the fifth throne. Aru couldn't see who it was, because a cloud was in the way. She pushed one end of the glass bubble, trying to steer it as best as she could, until the person came into view: the ancient *naga* woman.

Most Otherworld beings appeared eternally young or at least aged *super* slow. The nagini's bronze skin was shriveled. Her mouth had a hard set to it, as if she'd forgotten how to smile. The lower half of her was obscured by the table, but Aru knew that somewhere mid-torso, the woman's human body melded with that of a serpent. On her head, the naga woman wore a tiara of moonstones and aquamarines. It made sense that she had so many jewels. Nagas were treasure guardians, after all. But it was strange that she didn't have the customary jewel in the middle of her forehead.

"—a *seriousss* offense!" the nagini was saying. "They stole the bow and arrow from the naga treasury! None can do that save for someone with extraordinary power. Someone like a *Pandava*. No one else can get past Takshaka. Trust me. He does not need his sight to sense everything around him."

The naga woman gestured to a male naga who was standing at her side. He looked immortally youthful, but he had an ancient and powerful aura. Serious burn marks roped across his brown chest and face. His eyes were milky white with blindness. A dark blue jewel gleamed at the center of his forehead. Supposedly, each naga's jewel was tied to their heart or something. That made it all the weirder, thought Aru, that the nagini had no jewel on her forehead. All Aru saw there was a hollow dent, marked with a white scar.

"The girl was holding the bow and arrow of Kamadeva," the naga woman continued. "She must be held accountable."

Kamadeva. Aru knew the word *deva* meant god. So that meant the bow and arrow was a celestial weapon. No wonder Vajra and Dee Dee hadn't worked. Celestial weapons couldn't battle one another. Aru fought the urge to point at Brynne and go: *You are in serious trouble. HA!*

"Aru had nothing to do with it!" exclaimed Boo.

Wait, what? ME?

Aru glanced up at Brynne's bubble. The girl was taking a savage bite out of a candy bar. She grinned evilly at Aru, but it vanished with the Council's next words:

"Aru *is* to blame, and so is Brynne," said the naga woman. "Both of them were seen in the Otherworld with the bow and arrow."

"How much could one really see?" demanded Boo. "There was a fog of magic concealing the whole of the Night Bazaar. I bet a rakshasi was behind this. After all, the thief was a shape-shifter. Surely you noticed *that*, Queen Uloopi?"

Uloopi? Aru knew that name from the stories. In the *Mahabharata*, an ancient Sanskrit epic poem about the war between the Pandavas and their cousins, Uloopi was not only a famous naga queen, but also one of the wives of the Pandava Arjuna. Supposedly, she brought him back to life after he was killed on the battlefield. But Aru didn't know what happened to her after that.

You were his favorite queen! Trust me, I know. I've got his soul! Aru wanted to say. *Please don't kill me?*

Clearly Uloopi's devotion to Arjuna didn't transfer to his reincarnations.

"Oh, I know what I saw," said Uloopi darkly. "And I do not put my trust in anyone, particularly you, Subala. Your nickname was once the Great Deceiver, was it not? Perhaps now that the

Sleeper is awake and building his army, we need to question your allegiance to the devas...."

Boo squawked and ruffled his feathers indignantly. Aru and Mini stood up in their respective bubbles at the same time, wearing twin expressions of fury. Uloopi's accusation wasn't fair. Boo had changed since the days he was the devious Shakhuni, king of Subala. He'd proven it by being a loyal friend to Aru and Mini.

Hanuman leaned forward in his throne. His tail whipped behind him. "That comment was uncalled for, Queen Uloopi. Besides, when the Otherworld alarm first went off, *I* was training the young Pandavas. They couldn't have stolen the bow and arrow."

"The alarm went off when we discovered the breach in security," said the naga man beside the queen. "*Not* at the moment of theft. For all you know, their training session with you was designed to provide an alibi for their whereaboutsss."

Hanuman glowered and started to speak again, but Uloopi cut him off.

"Takshaka raises a worthy point," she said. "Things are shifting. None of us has been able to locate the Sleeper, though he is undoubtedly to blame for the recent spike in demonic activity. Perhaps the one who stole the bow and arrow of Kamadeva is *his* accomplice. For all we know, these Pandavas might not even be our true allies! As has been foretold, nothing will be as it seems when the inevitable war breaks out."

"We have always known that the Pandavas awaken only when danger is present," said Hanuman in his deep, booming voice. "But they are on our side."

"Are they?" mused Takshaka. His blind gaze turned to Aru, and guilt surged through her. For a moment, she thought he was going to say it was her fault the Sleeper was stirring up trouble. The problem was...it would be true. She was the one who had let him out of the lamp in the museum. She'd stumbled in their last confrontation and accidentally allowed him to escape. Now the demon was at large, who knew where, still hell-bent on his mission to bring down the gods.

She'd failed everyone.

Even so, how could the Council think she and Mini were their enemies? Their Saturday goals were simple: imitate potatoes on a couch. Instead, they ended up fighting dentist zombies, and this was the thanks they got? Rude.

Urvashi raised her hand and twirled her wrist. Aru lurched forward as her glass bubble was pulled downward.

"You have spoken long enough, Uloopi," Urvashi said. "You heard the testimony from all sides. You witnessed the girls' memories—"

"I *tried* to," cut in Uloopi. "But because they are Pandavas, their minds are harder to access. There are gaps! Enough to make it difficult for me to believe they are innocent."

A cold prickle traveled down Aru's spine. So it was Uloopi she had felt rummaging through her brain. Her face flamed. Did that mean Uloopi had seen Aru singing "Thriller" and doing the shoulder-dance move in the bathroom mirror?

"I have heard quite enough from everyone," said Uloopi.

Urvashi looked outraged, but even she deferred to the great naga queen.

"Including the other witness..." added Uloopi.

At this, the naga beside her—Takshaka—shifted. A scowl appeared on his face, but it disappeared so fast Aru wondered if she had imagined it. As her hamster bubble kept descending,

Aru looked around the court (half checking to make sure there wasn't some magical screenshot of her singing in the mirror), but she didn't see any other witness present.

Her glass bubble gently bounced on a carpet of mist before dissolving around her. Slippers magically appeared on her feet to protect her from falling through the patchy white clouds. Way up here, where the Court of the Sky hovered, the air was thin and cold, and it burned in Aru's lungs. The two other glass bubbles landed on either side of her and dissolved, too, leaving Mini on her right and Brynne on her left.

Brynne was no longer smug. Instead, she was looking at Aru as if she'd sprouted a second head that had just introduced itself as *Kathy with a* K.

"*You're* the other Pandavas?"

Aru made jazz hands. "Ta-daaaaa!"

Brynne frowned at her, then at Mini. "But I saw you steal…."

"And I saw *you* running through my neighborhood with a bow and arrow that I'm pretty sure weren't yours."

"Are you calling me a thief?" said Brynne.

"Well, I know for a fact *I* didn't steal it."

Brynne gave her a head-to-toe look and smirked. "Actually, I believe that. The thief *I* was fighting actually seemed like a Pandava. You, on the other hand, barely look trained."

Oh no she did not.

"We *are* trained!" said Mini.

"We are seriously deadly," added Aru.

"Yeah!" said Mini, taking a step toward Brynne.

At that moment, Mini stumbled. She would've fallen face-first into a cloud without her enchanted slippers, but instead she just vibrated in place like a plucked guitar string.

Brynne rolled her eyes and deadpanned, "I'm screaming."

"You know what?"

"Girls!" hissed Boo.

All three of them snapped to attention. The round table had disappeared, and the Council of Guardians' thrones were now fanning out around them. On the one hand, Aru was glad she wasn't wearing pajamas this time. On the other hand, she really wished her backpack weren't bright purple with HAKUNA MATATA! spelled out on it in huge letters.

"You have all been judged," said Uloopi.

"But wait a minute—" said Aru.

Takshaka's tail whipped out, stirring mist off the clouds as he hissed, "Keep *quiet* when your elders are ssspeaking!"

Even Boo shot her a disapproving look. Aru had a horrible feeling of acid spreading through her veins. Red-faced, she hunched her shoulders and looked at the naga queen. Up close, she was even more intimidating. Uloopi sat high on her throne, her emerald serpent tail coiled beneath her like a cushioned seat.

"The theft and *misuse* of Kamadeva's bow and arrow will have serious consequences in the mortal world," said the queen.

Duh, thought Aru angrily. People would start screaming *Zombie apocalypse!* and lose their minds, and the Internet would probably crash, and then it would *really* be an apocalypse.

"The thief is kidnapping human men at an alarming rate, turning them into those slack-jawed creatures you saw in the Otherworld."

That was *not* what Aru expected to hear. That meant all those zombies weren't zombies at all...but kidnapped victims. Her stomach churned.

"If the bow and arrow are not recovered soon, the effects

on those men will be permanent. They will be Heartless for all eternity."

Heartless? Aru gulped, remembering the weird scars on the zombies' chests. Had someone actually...?

Uloopi interrupted her thoughts with a declaration. "The Pandavas must prove their innocence." She leaned forward, her crown glittering so brightly that Aru couldn't look at it straight on. "You are hereby charged with retrieving the bow and arrow in ten mortal days' time. If you fail, there will be a cost. Your memories of the Otherworld will be wiped. You will not remember you were ever Pandavas, and your Pandava souls will go dormant. Furthermore, you will be banished from the Otherworld. Forever."

FOUR

We Literally *Just* Went on a Quest

Aru couldn't breathe.

Memories wiped . . .
Pandava no more . . .
Banished forever . . .

If they failed, all those men turned Heartless would stay zombies! It seemed like a fate worse than death. Plus, if this generation's Pandavas were exiled, who would stop the Sleeper?

She glanced over at Mini, who looked like Aru felt: *stricken.* And then she realized that, if they failed, she wouldn't even remember Mini. This whole life would be erased. This tiny claim to magic, this sense that, for the first time, she could breathe easy because she had found her home . . . It would all be taken from her. Simply because Queen Uloopi refused to believe the truth.

Aru couldn't let that happen.

Vajra, now shaped like a humble bracelet, crackled against her wrist. She could feel her temper seething inside her chest, a hot pressure on her lungs that made it difficult to breathe. From his throne—which had transformed into a single golden tree branch suspended in the air—Boo made tiny *don't-do-it!* gestures with his whole body. Aru ignored him. She opened her mouth to speak. . . .

But someone beat her to it.

"Are you *serious*?" demanded Brynne.

Aru looked over at her. There were tears in the other girl's eyes. All the color had drained from her face.

"Tasked as I am with maintaining law and order in the Otherworld, I find no reason to joke about these matters," said Uloopi coldly.

The rest of the Council looked grave and solemn. Even through her own fury, Aru could sense that Uloopi took no pleasure in this. But the person beside her—Takshaka—didn't seem to mind at all. The corner of his mouth twitched.

"Do the Pandavas find Queen Uloopi unmerciful?" he asked with a sneer. "Hersss was the deciding vote in allowing you to prove your innocence. The witness's photo didn't fool me." He flicked his tongue in Brynne's direction. "I know firsthand how manipulative anyone of *asura* lineage can be, even if she isss a Pandava."

Brynne's lower lip trembled for just an instant, but she quickly set her jaw and glared at the serpent king.

So Brynne was part asura. That would explain why she could shape-shift—only asuras and rakshasas had that ability. While being an asura or rakshasa didn't automatically make someone demonic, it did make them harder to trust. Aru had seen Otherworld people act suspicious—even cruel—toward them.

But if Brynne really *was* the thief, she wouldn't look so upset. And Aru had to admit that Fake Aru had been convincing. It was...possible...that Brynne really *had* been trying to catch the true culprit.

Aru quickly shared her thoughts with Mini, whose response was brief: *I don't think she's the thief.*

"Don't worry, Pandavas. If you fail, a new batch of warriors will come along," Takshaka said. "It doesn't matter."

It doesn't matter. Aru felt those words clang through her. She didn't matter.

"You're wrong," she said quietly.

Mini sniffled, nodding fiercely. "We'll prove it."

Uloopi looked at Aru, Brynne, and Mini as if she were seeing them for the first time. Finally she said, "What a strange vessel for such a soul," eyeing Aru. She sighed, sounding as if she had needed a nap for the past five thousand years. "I have a great-grandson your age."

Aru's eyebrows skated up her forehead. *What?*

That was *not* what she had expected Uloopi to say.

But maybe raising her eyebrows was the completely wrong thing to do, because Uloopi's face darkened.

"What?" she spat viciously. "Did you think that because my son with Arjuna died in battle I was supposed to mourn for the rest of my days? No! I had a kingdom to rule! People who looked up to me! I was not just someone's *wife.*"

Aru glanced between Brynne and Mini. Mini shook her head like *I have no idea what is happening.*

"Um, I never said that you—"

"*I* have had as many consorts"—it took Aru a second to remember that *consort* was just a fancy word for spouse—"as there are days in a year. And as many children as there are flowers in the world!"

"That's . . . a lot?" offered Aru.

"Can you lay eggs?" asked Mini. "I'm just thinking how, statistically, that would work. A wax scale insect can lay more than ten thousand eggs in one sitting! *Ow!* Aru, why are you elbowing me?"

Something about Uloopi's face told Aru that the naga queen did not appreciate being asked if she could lay eggs.

Boo flew in front of their faces, flapping wildly. "Your Majesty, the girls mean no disrespect. They are very, very, *very* young. Eons younger than you and—"

Uloopi raised her eyebrows. *"Eons?"*

Boo's feathers poufed in embarrassment. "Which is not to say that you're ancient, except you are, but not in a way that—"

"This wearies me," said Uloopi, rising up on her coils. "I have issued my proclamation. You have ten days, Pandavas. Return what was stolen to restore the Heartless to their former selves. Or be banished."

Beside her, Takshaka made a slit in the cloud floor, creating an opening that was probably a portal back to the naga realm. Without another word or glance, Uloopi slipped through and disappeared. Takshaka, though, took his time. He swung his head in their direction. And even though Aru knew he couldn't see her, she *felt* the weight of his attention. It made her shudder, and she instinctively called Vajra into her hand as a lightning bolt.

"Good luck," he said.

It didn't sound like he meant it.

And then both of them were gone, leaving Aru and Mini alone with a new quest . . . and a new sister.

The other Council members bent their heads, whispering together.

Brynne tossed her wind mace over her shoulder. "Right," she said, all businesslike. "I would be *honored* to clear our names. You two stay here—"

"No way!" said Aru. "Me and Mini have done this before." She summoned Vajra to her hand. "We're the professionals. *You* stay here."

"'Professionals' is kind of a stretch," Mini mumbled.

From her throne, Urvashi snapped her fingers and pointed at Brynne. "You are not going alone."

"Why? Just because I wasn't on some quest where these two got lucky?" demanded Brynne. "*I* could've gotten it done faster. *I've* been training in the Otherworld for years. Have you?"

Aru decided not to point out that she and Mini were in the middle of remedial classes.

"So what if you've had training?" shot back Aru. "As far as I remember, *you* weren't with us."

Brynne turned red. "I would have if . . ." She stopped herself, her hand turning to a fist at her side. "Whatever."

"Why don't we start over," said Mini, putting herself between Aru and Brynne. "Three heads are better than two! Unless it's like *craniopagus parasiticus*, which wouldn't be good, but that only happens in four cases out of ten million—"

Boo interrupted by fluttering down and alighting on Aru's shoulder. Aru reached up to pat his head, and the pigeon pecked her hand. "Not just the three of you," he said.

Aru smacked her forehead. "Oh, duh! And you, too, of course. What would we do without you, Boo?"

"I am afraid my presence will not be allowed," he said heavily. He looked back at the remaining Council of Guardians members. Urvashi had tears in her eyes. Hanuman looked stony. "It would seem that I am to be held in custody until such time as my allegiance against the Sleeper is proven."

Aru's ears burned. Fury shot through her veins.

"They can't do that," she said loudly. "You haven't done anything wrong!"

Boo sadly ruffled his feathers.

"Do not worry," he said. "I am permitted to send someone in my place. I have chosen the Council's witness, someone who has proven himself committed to the truth. It is thanks to him that some Council members doubted that you stole the bow and arrow."

"I mean, good job and all, witness dude, but we don't want him," said Aru. "We want you."

"We don't even know who he is," pointed out Mini.

Boo held up a wing. "I am getting to that. He is a brilliant student: exceptional with a sword, familiar with the Otherworld—thanks to his semidivine lineage—and quite knowledgeable. As a student of ours, it is his duty to fight on behalf of the devas alongside this generation's Pandavas. Therefore, he has been granted temporary Pandava security clearance."

Right on cue, a door opened in the sky, and the clouds parted. Sunrays illuminated the court.

Aru considered herself something of a "film buff" (a phrase she only recently learned did not mean that watching movies gave you muscles). She knew a lot about Bollywood movies in particular. There was a formula to them: Someone always got slapped. Someone always cried. The movies almost always ended with a wedding. And, oh right, everyone knows when the love interest shows up, because the wind starts magically blowing their hair.

At that moment, wind started blowing. But that was because Brynne had dropped her mace. Aru literally started choking on the rush of air. Then Mini panicked and started clapping her on the back, which didn't help. In the middle of a coughing spell, Aru lost hold of Vajra.

"Uh-oh," said Brynne.

Aru looked up in time for Vajra to bonk her on the head, knocking her to the ground. *"Ughhhhh,"* she said, rubbing her crown. "Today is not my day."

In the midst of all this chaos, a boy walked up to them. He was tall, with sandy brown skin. A shock of black hair fell over his forehead, and he wore a dark green long-sleeved hoodie, faded jeans, and bright red sneakers. Slung against his hip was a serious-looking camera.

"Girls," said Boo, "allow me to introduce your companion, Aiden Acharya."

Aiden? As in the dimpled, curly-haired new boy at school? The person she accidentally word-vomited to and told him she knew where he lived? He made eye contact with Aru for a split second before quickly looking away.

Aru pinched Vajra, and the lightning bolt sent a shock through her skin. Well, she was definitely awake. Aru could forget about today not being her day.

Nope, thought Aru. *Today is cancelled.*

FIVE

This Is Fine. Really

Aru did not have a crush. That was for certain. What she had was a desire not to look like someone who combed their hair with a fork and thought eggs grew on trees or something equally ridiculous. That was all. She especially didn't want to look like that to someone who smelled nice and had dark eyes and who had only been in school for, like, a second and was already more popular than Aru could ever dream of becoming, even if she brought an actual elephant to class and cookie cake to homeroom for the rest of the year.

"Called it!" shrieked Brynne happily, punching Aiden in the arm. "Knew you'd come through."

He winced before grinning back. "Always." He held up a picture on his phone. "Managed to get a shot of you and the thief who shape-shifted into Aru, and then the real Aru in the background."

In the picture, Brynne and Fake Aru looked like they were in the middle of an epic battle. In the background, Real Aru looked like she was in the middle of an epic sneeze. Great.

"I thought this would be enough to prove it, but the Council didn't believe me," he said unhappily. "Do I still get lasagna as a reward?"

Brynne laughed. "Depends on whether Gunky has any left over."

Aru and Mini glanced at each other and shrugged. It seemed Brynne and Aiden were friends. Good enough friends, apparently, to share lasagna and know someone named Gunky. *What?*

Brynne paused, looking between Aru and Aiden. "But . . . how'd you know her name?"

Aiden looked over at her. His expression got a little strange. "She, um, goes to school with me and lives across from my house."

"Wait," said Brynne. A slow smile spread across her face as she spun one of the dozens of gold bracelets on her wrist. "The girl *across* from you?" She turned to Aru, her eyes sparkling. "Are *you* the one who said 'I know where you live'? The creepy stalker girl?" Then she started to laugh.

Aru really wished her cloud slippers would fail so she could fall through the sky. Bright red spots appeared on Aiden's cheeks. But he didn't deny talking about her with Brynne. In that second, whatever scrap of *something* she might have almost felt for him died on the spot.

Aiden Acharya was officially cancelled. Along with today.

"I was tired," said Aru. "I said something weird. Get over it."

"Yeah!" added Mini. "That's nothing! Aru says *lots* of weird things. You get used to it."

"Awesome. Thanks, Mini."

Mini beamed.

Boo looked between Aru, Aiden, Brynne, and Mini and mumbled something that sounded like *Why is this my lot?*

"It is time," said Urvashi, appearing at Boo's side.

Hanuman popped up, too. "Say your good-byes."

"Now that we have survived introductions," Boo said to them, "I must go."

Aru's heart lurched. She *had* to get back that bow and arrow. She couldn't lose her Pandava life, and she wouldn't let Boo pay for a crime he didn't commit. Boo might have done bad things in his past, but that was then. . . . Now he was like family. When he was in a good mood, he sometimes told her bedtime stories—except he called them *evening lectures* and flat-out refused to say *once upon a time.*

Urvashi waved her hand and a dainty golden bar appeared in the air.

"What is that?" asked Mini warily.

Urvashi gently lifted Boo from Aru's shoulder. The golden bar floated over to him and settled across the back of his neck. He hung his head. Then each end of the bar folded down and clamped his wings.

"You can't do that to him!" said Aru and Mini at the same time.

Urvashi looked away. "We do not have a choice. It is the law that all possible accomplices are held in custody until they are proven innocent."

"What about 'innocent until proven guilty'?" asked Aru. "You didn't even read him his Miranda rights!"

Boo whispered to Mini, "Who's Miranda?"

Aru felt proud that her *Law & Order* marathons had finally come to good use, but Hanuman and Urvashi did not seem impressed.

"The four of you can change his fate," said Hanuman,

placing a large hand on Aru's shoulder. "Find the bow and arrow to reverse the state of the Heartless. Because you are suspects, there is little we can do to help. The law is the law."

Aru felt like someone had kicked her in the stomach.

"Wait—" said Mini, rummaging through her backpack. "One for the road." She held up a cookie.

"An Oreo!" said Boo, brightening. "Sweet girl. Thank you." Mini stuck it in his beak.

Urvashi murmured a few words, and Boo dissolved into the ether.

"Where did you send him?" Aru demanded.

"Don't worry. He will be comfortable," assured Hanuman.

Aru said nothing. Mini clutched her backpack tight to her chest. Beside them, Aiden fiddled with the strap of his camera. Aru rarely saw him without that camera in school. Even though Aiden was only one year above her, in eighth grade, apparently his photographs were so good that the high school newspaper, the *Vorpal Blade*, often used them. Aru scowled. If he was such an important witness, he should've taken better photos of the fight between Brynne and Fake Aru. Then Boo wouldn't be locked up, and she and Mini wouldn't be at risk of banishment from the Otherworld.

Hanuman let out a long exhale, his gaze falling on Brynne. The moment he looked at her, Brynne went from smug to serious. She slipped her mace off her shoulder and held it respectfully by her side.

"Brynne."

"Bhai," said Brynne in a small voice.

Bhai meant *brother.*

"You have a great task ahead of you," said Hanuman.

Brynne gripped her mace tighter. "I know."

Mini nodded. "We *all* know."

"Remember," Hanuman said in a tone that Aru had come to recognize as *trust-me-I'm-super-wise*, "nobody wins when the family feuds."

Aru frowned. "Did you just quote Jay-Z?"

Aiden started snickering, but he stopped short when Brynne glared at him.

Hanuman's tail switched, and he scowled. "What? *No.* Okay, maybe. Listen, I don't know where I hear everything. I've been around a while, kid. Now, my advice is to go home and pack what you need. Afterward, report immediately to Urvashi in the Warehouse of Quest Materials."

Warehouse? Aru had never heard of a place like that....

Urvashi waved her hand, and a portal appeared in the sky. "Aiden, I've already spoken with your mother. She sent some belongings ahead to Brynne's house. It'll be easier for you to travel from there."

"It's technically a penthouse," corrected Brynne.

Aru rolled her eyes.

"Thanks, *Masi*," Aiden said to Urvashi.

Okay, now Aru had *many* questions. First, it didn't seem like Aiden was shocked by the idea of going to Brynne's penthouse (chill, Brynne), so he must go there a lot. Second, Urvashi was his *aunt*? He'd called her *masi*, which is a way of addressing your mom's sister, but Aiden couldn't possibly be her nephew. Urvashi and her three sisters were ultra-elite apsaras, and as such weren't allowed to marry mortals. But Boo had said Aiden was only semidivine.

"C'mon," said Brynne excitedly. "If we pack fast enough,

there might be time for my uncles to feed us lasagna. I'm starving." Without a single word to Aru or Mini, she disappeared through the portal.

Aiden hesitated. Then he said to Urvashi, "Did my mom say anything else? I don't mind stopping by home first if she needs me...."

Urvashi's face softened. "I wouldn't do that, child. You know how hard things are for her right now. Just know she sends her love."

"Fine," said Aiden, but his jaw seemed tight. He barely looked at Aru and Mini. "See you soon."

Aru stepped out of the stone elephant's mouth and onto the floor of the Museum of Ancient Indian Art and Culture. It was 7:00 p.m., so all the visitors had left and Aru could take a moment to breathe deep, closing her eyes. She smelled the polished bronze of the statues, the ink that the museum's head of security, Sherrilyn, used to stamp guests' hands as they entered, and even the candied fennel seeds in brass bowls that her mom had left out for visitors. It smelled like home.

But lately it hadn't felt very homey.

When Aru opened her eyes to the lobby, she saw the memory of her battle against the Sleeper, her ... *dad*. It was still too weird to process. Sometimes when she slept, their epic fight replayed in her mind. And yet the worst nightmare of all wasn't how awful he was then ... but how kind he'd been long ago. In the Kingdom of Death, she'd seen a vision of him in the hospital when she was born, his T-shirt reading I'M A DAD! He must have held her when she was a baby. He must have once, even if only for a second, loved her.

"You okay?"

Aru shook herself. She'd almost forgotten that Mini had asked to come over.

"Yup!" she said with false cheer.

"Need help packing?"

"Not really?"

"Okay, but what about a first-aid kit? Or I could help your mom around the house? Or—"

Aru crossed her arms. "Why are you avoiding your own home?"

"Am not!"

"Are too!"

"D2—" Mini broke off with a grumble. "I hate when you do that."

"Just tell me," said Aru.

Mini sighed. "I love my parents, and I know they love me, but they're . . ."

"Putting a ton of pressure on you?" asked Aru.

"A bit, yeah."

She'd been over to Mini's house loads of times, and "a bit" of pressure was an understatement. Mini's parents had a full-blown Pandava regimen for her—*Run two miles a day! All the vitamins! No Internet after 8:00 p.m.!*—on top of a five-year schedule to get her into a top college and a top medical school.

"They're going to freak out once they hear that we could be banished," said Mini.

"That's not your fault."

"Might as well be," said Mini. "I know what they'll think. . . . If my *brother* was the Pandava, this wouldn't have happened."

Aru shook her head. "If they get mad, just tell them it's not like you gambled away your whole kingdom and got everyone exiled to the forest for a bajillion years."

Mini frowned. "What are you taking about?"

"That's something Yudhistira—aka *you* a bajillion years ago—did. He set the bar pretty high for mistake-making, so don't worry so much."

Aru's mom had told her the story a while ago. The eldest Pandava brother, who had a reputation for being morally upright, lost a game of dice, and his family was kicked out of the palace and into the forest as a result. Imagine having to explain that during a family meeting. *So . . . good news and bad news. First, who likes camping?*

If Mini's parents honestly thought a guy would've made a better Pandava, this story might raise some doubts. But instead of laughing, Mini's face paled and she walked back to the elephant statue.

"Hey!" said Aru. "Where're you going?"

"Home," huffed Mini. "I got the message, Aru. If *he* made a mistake like that, imagine all the things *I* might do wrong. I gotta go and get ready."

Now Aru felt ridiculously guilty. "Mini, that's not what I meant. . . ."

"I'll see you at the warehouse." And with that, Mini disappeared into the portal.

Aru was about to go after her when she heard her mom call down from the top of the stairs. "Let her cool off, Aru," she said. "She'll come around."

Aru glanced up. As always, Dr. K. P. Shah looked beautiful but exhausted from doing research long into the night. Ever since the Sleeper had reappeared, Aru's mom had been tireless in her search for a magical artifact that could stop him. Her travel schedule was still brutal, but she was making an effort to be "more present" when she was home. Recently, they'd had lots of great talks. Just not about Aru's dad.

Your mother needs more time before she can talk about him, Boo had tried to explain. *It's hard for her.*

That had just left Aru more frustrated. As if this wasn't hard for *her*? How much time did her mom need? What if they were running *out* of time and there was something she wasn't telling her?

As her mom walked down the stairs, Aru saw she was carrying the morning newspaper and Aru's "emergency quest" backpack, which was full of clothes and snacks so that she wouldn't be stuck wandering through the Otherworld in Spider-Man pajamas... again.

"I know you have to go soon," said her mom. "Urvashi sent me a message. And then there was the news this morning."

She held up the newspaper, where a bold headline screamed:

MASS KIDNAPPINGS THROUGHOUT THE WORLD!

THE SEARCH CONTINUES...

Aru shuddered, thinking of the crowds of Heartless she'd seen in the Otherworld. They only had ten days before those people would be stuck like that *forever*.

"Urvashi told me a lot of things, actually," said her mom.

Oh no.

"Anything you want to talk about?" asked her mom.

"No."

"What about the Acharyas' son across the street—?"

"*No.*"

"Because you know you can tell me anything."

Aru mumbled, "I'd rather walk in front of a bus."

"What was that?"

"I'd rather get going and not...make a fuss."

Aru liked talking with her mom about lots of things, like the newest acquisitions for the museum. Or movies that Aru loved or hated. Or student gossip, like how Russell Sheehan somehow smuggled in a herd of llamas and let them loose on the football field of Augustus Day School. What she did not like to discuss had, unfortunately, become her mother's new favorite topic....

Feelings.

Sometimes after dinner her mom would make them cocoa and they'd snuggle on the couch and watch movies (which was nice), but sometimes Aru's mom would launch into a discussion about the "tumultuous adolescent psyche" (which was not so nice) and start spouting things like *You're a young woman now.* Which made no sense, because what was Aru before? A young horse?

"What about your new Pandava sister?" pressed her mom. "I hear she's rather accomplished. She goes to one of the top private schools in the country."

"Ugh," said Aru. "Not you, too. I get it. Brynne is the best." She waved an imaginary tiny flag.

Her mom got that *I-am-feeling-wise-and-maternal* look. "Did I ever tell you the story about Ekalavya's thumb?"

"*Who?* Is this about that family friend's son who stapled his hand on a dare?"

Her mother sighed. "No, Aru. It's a story from the *Mahabharata.*"

"Oh."

"Arjuna was a great warrior—"

"Breaking news," grumbled Aru.

"—but he had flaws, too. He could be prideful and insecure."

That was unexpected. Whenever Boo told them stories about the legendary Pandavas, he pretty much stuck to all the happy *look-how-awesome-you-used-to-be* versions.

"When Arjuna was a student, he witnessed an incredible feat of archery," her mom began. "It made him very jealous, and he got scared that he would no longer be the best archer. His famous teacher, Drona, discovered that the impossible shot had been made by Ekalavya, the son of a tribal chief. Ekalavya asked Drona to train him in archery, but the teacher refused him because of his lower status. Ekalavya meditated on Drona anyway, and even went so far as to build a statue of him out of mud. This led Drona to demand *guru daksina*, a way of honoring a teacher. He asked for Ekalavya's right thumb, so no one would be better than Arjuna, and Ekalavya agreed."

Aru gagged. "One, that's gross. Two, that's awful. Why didn't Ekalavya just say 'no thank you'?"

"He was honorable, and he'd agreed to do anything his guru asked of him."

"Mom, what's the point of this story?" asked Aru, shuddering. "Don't be insecure or someone will get their thumb chopped off?"

Her mom sighed and put the backpack on Aru's shoulders. "All I'm saying is that no one can take your place if you make room for them. Trust yourself more than you distrust others. Does that make sense?"

"I'm still thinking about how that guy *gave up his thumb.*"

Her mom shook her head and hugged her, and Aru breathed in the smell of her jasmine perfume.

"You've got so much potential," said her mom.

Aru cringed. Potential could go either way. Even now, Aru couldn't forget what the Sleeper had said. *You were never meant to be a hero....* What if she was more like him than like her mom?

"What if it's the wrong kind of potential?" she asked quietly. "He said—"

Her mom pulled back immediately.

"I don't want to hear about *him*," she said sharply. "Forget what he said."

Aru's jaw clenched. *Every time.* Every time she brought him up, she got shut down.

"I love you," said her mom, pushing the hair back from Aru's forehead. "Think about what I said, okay? And just know that I believe in *you*, my Swedish Fish–eating, slightly bizarre child."

"Love you, too," said Aru, but she didn't raise her gaze from the floor.

She hoisted the backpack higher, stepped into the portal of the elephant mouth, and waved good-bye to her mom. Magic from the Otherworld prickled over her skin, waiting for the command for where to take her. Aru breathed deep and said:

"Take me to the Warehouse of Quest Materials."

SIX

The Warehouse of Quest Materials, aka "Do *Not* Touch That"

Aru looked out of the portal tunnel and saw the vast night sky salted with stars.

The portal had opened a foot above a thin cloud upon which sat a white marble mound with a little door and a sign that read WAREHOUSE OF QUEST MATERIALS. The structure was so small, Aru doubted even she—at her magnificently intimidating height of five foot nothing—could stand comfortably inside of it.

"What is this?" scoffed Aru. "A warehouse for ants?"

Out of habit, she looked to her right, where normally Mini would've been on the verge of laughter. But she wasn't there, and Aru remembered with a pang that her friend was angry at her.

She sighed and prepared to jump through the door. Before she did, a pair of slippers peeled off the cloud and covered her feet.

From behind the mound came a muffled squeak. "Aru?" Mini poked her head out.

Then they spoke at the exact same time: "I'm sorry."

"I overreacted—" started Mini.

"I didn't mean it like that—" said Aru.

They stood there, waited a moment, and then started laughing. It wasn't their first fight, and it wouldn't be their last. But fights between good friends are a bit like lightning: a flash of anger, and then it's fine.

"We should go in," said Aru.

"I know, but I was waiting for you," said Mini as she walked out from behind the mound.

Aru's eyes went wide. Mini was dressed in head-to-toe black, including black combat boots. Her shirt had a skull on it, and there were faint traces of eyeliner under her eyes.

Mini frowned. "What is it?"

"Nothing."

"Say it," said Mini.

"Nothing. You're just leaning into the whole daughter-of-the-god-of-death thing pretty hard. I dig it."

"Is it too much?" asked Mini, glancing at her own outfit as if she'd just seen it. "I only wore black because dirt doesn't show up on it that easily."

"What about your goth shirt?"

"Oh, that?" Mini smoothed down the front. "I like being reminded of my own mortality, you know? It makes stuff meaningful."

"You do you, Mini."

The warehouse was a whole lot bigger on the inside than it looked on the outside. When the doors opened, Aru saw rows upon rows of shelves disappearing into the distance. Once she stepped onto the polished marble floor, her cloud slippers vanished.

Aiden, Brynne, and Urvashi were waiting for them. Brynne muttered, "Way to show up on time."

Aru ignored her, choosing instead to skim the small labels affixed to the bottom of each shelf. They had strange names, like OMINOUS DREAM SEQUENCE and A SHARP KICK IN THE REAR.

"This is our Warehouse of Quest Materials," said Urvashi. "Each of you is allowed to take one item. The item will vanish on the tenth day, so use it wisely."

"But how do we know what to pick?" asked Mini, looking overwhelmed.

"Choose what speaks to you," said the apsara. "I cannot tell you any more than that. Remember, you are considered suspects until the bow and arrow of Kamadeva are found."

"But you know we didn't steal them!" said Aru. "It isn't fair."

Urvashi smiled sadly. "What is *fair* and what is *just* do not always look the same. I know only that I believe in you, but I cannot help you beyond offering this piece of advice: as with any lost item, the best way to find it is to speak with the owner first."

"You mean Kamadeva?" asked Aiden.

"That's *all* you want us to know?" asked Mini.

Urvashi sighed. "Though it doesn't help you, know that I do not agree with the naga queen's decision."

"What's Uloopi's problem, anyway?" asked Brynne.

Urvashi's eyes looked far away, and even though she was eternally young, she seemed *old* in that moment. "She is very powerful, and she suffered a great tragedy. I believe it hardened her. Besides, she bears an incredible burden." The apsara raised her hand in blessing. "Be well, children. I eagerly await your return."

With that, she dissolved into the moonlight.

Aru looked around at her questmates: Mini, trying to pretend she wasn't feeling anxious. Aiden, seemingly preoccupied with his camera. Brynne, who clearly wished she and Aiden could go off on their own. Not exactly primed for success.

"Well," said Aru, "I guess it's time to go shopping."

Brynne was immediately drawn to a shelf marked SHARP THINGS. Mini ran a finger along the one that read MISCELLANEOUS SIDEKICKS. It held bottles marked with things like TALKING DEMON-HORSE, WITTY GHOST, and UNREMARKABLE DRAGON.

Aru saw apples with golden skin, and those silver pistachio cakes from Indian weddings that always look better than they taste. Aiden had walked over to a shelf marked KITS OF NECESSITY that had small satchels filled with different materials such as SUNSHINE ON YOUR SKIN, A GULP OF AIR, A FIVE-SECOND PAUSE, TWO NAPS SQUEEZED INTO TWO SECONDS, and even A CLIF BAR.

Aru couldn't decide what to get. There were too many options, and she had no clue where they were going after this. She walked over to a shelf marked BRIGHT IDEAS. It was covered with slender glass vials, each filled with a cloudy, colorless liquid. Something about them drew Aru closer. She moved to pluck one off the shelf when she felt a tap on her shoulder.

"No, Mini, I don't think it's poison," said Aru tiredly. "And yes, if it was, it would probably kill me."

"It's not Mini?"

Aru whirled around to see Aiden. He had his hands shoved in the pocket of his dark green hoodie.

"What do you want?" asked Aru, not very nicely. She didn't feel very nice after Brynne had ridiculed her in front of him.

Aiden flushed. "Listen, I know we got off to a bad start. I was thinking we should all just start over. Is that cool?"

Aru glared at him. What did he want, a friendship bracelet? She crossed her arms and then, after a moment, let them fall to her side. Borrowed Jay-Z lyrics or not, Hanuman was right. Fighting would get them nowhere. She wasn't going to hold on to a grudge if that meant Boo would stay imprisoned and she'd be exiled. Aru took a deep breath. From here on out, she resolved to be the best, heroine-est version of herself. She was ARU SHAH. Devourer of Twizzlers and Swedish Fish. Bearer of a Ridiculously Powerful Lightning Bolt. Daughter of the God of Thunder and Lightning. Vessel of Movie Quotes.

She was not going to let herself feel embarrassed in front of anyone. Especially not Brynne and Aiden.

Aru smiled at him, then looked over at Mini, whom she hoped would say something like *Good diplomatic Pandava move.*

Instead, Mini sent over a mind message: *You've got something in your teeth.*

Aru stopped smiling.

"Fine," she said. She held out her hand.

"Really?" asked Aiden, smirking.

Aru said nothing, mostly because she was still trying to work out whatever was stuck in her teeth.

Aiden sighed, then shook her hand. "Still can't believe you're a Pandava."

Aru glared, and sparks of electricity shot off her lightning bolt bracelet.

Aiden quickly stepped back. "Not in a bad way! It was just weird to look across the street and realize—"

"Hold up," said Aru, raising her hand. "So you *knew* I was a Pandava before the gods told you?"

Aiden went wide-eyed.

"How?" demanded Aru.

At this, Aiden looked a little shifty. "Uh, well, earlier today, I saw something kinda weird through my window. You had a lightning bolt."

"How did you know it was a lightning bolt?"

Aiden ducked his chin and mumbled something. Aru only caught one of the words: *zoom.*

She glanced at his camera. "*Zoom lens?* You took a picture of my lightning bolt?!"

"I didn't mean to! You were leaning out the window!"

"And *I'm* the creepy stalker?"

"Okay, I'm sorry!"

"Say you're a creep."

"Can't I—?"

"Say it."

"I'm a creep. And I'm sorry. But it was a lightning bolt...in your hand...and that threw me."

Vajra beamed, clearly flattered. Aru ignored it.

"Don't spy on me ever again," said Aru, "or I will lightning-bolt you." Aru was not sure *lightning-bolt* was a verb, but she also didn't care.

Aiden squared his shoulders. "Fine, then don't spy on me, either."

"I didn't—"

"I saw you, Shah."

"Okay, fine. Sorry."

"Me too," said Aiden. He shuffled in place for a bit before adding, "Also, I know Brynne can be a . . . a lot? But she means well. She just—"

At that second, Brynne strolled over wearing shiny metal sneakers that she must have picked up from the shelf marked SHARP THINGS.

"Check it out." She grinned, showing them off. She pointed her chin at Aiden. "These kicks enhance the wearer's fighting ability. They can only be used in one battle, though, so you gotta make it count. What'd you get?"

Aiden held up a kit of UNIDENTIFIED NECESSITIES.

"Classic Aiden," said Brynne. "You're such an *ammamma*."

Aiden tucked the kit into his camera satchel. "I'm not a grandma."

"Do you or do you not have snacks in your purse-slash-camera-bag?"

"Let me live, Bee," he said, but he was smiling.

Bee? Ammamma? They were, Aru realized with a strange pang, close enough to have nicknames for each other. Aru turned to Mini, who had just walked over with a little bar labeled POWER NAP.

"What'd you get, WebMD?"

Everyone stared at Aru blankly.

Mini pointed at herself. "Are you talking to me?"

Aru laughed, and desperately wished she'd chosen a different fake nickname. "Oh, Mini, you kill me. Duh, I'm talking to you. You're WebMD."

Mini frowned. "Since when—?"

But Brynne cut her off. She glanced at the vial in Aru's hand. "In need of a lot of bright ideas, Shah?"

"You never know," Aru said defensively.

"I know that something sharp works better than a bottle full of nothing," said Brynne. Her mace had taken the form of a blue choker around her throat. It glowed ever so slightly.

"A bottle full of nothing works better than a head full of nothing," Aru shot back. Despite her pledge to not hold a grudge, she blurted out, "I can't believe you got us involved in all this! If you didn't steal the bow and arrow, then how did you end up with them, anyway?"

Brynne sniffed. "You wouldn't believe me."

"Try me," said Aru.

"I found them on the sidewalk outside my house," she said.

"Oh, sure. A celestial weapon just happened to—"

"See? I knew you wouldn't believe me! You think just because I've got asura blood that I'm a liar—"

"Trust me, it's got nothing to do with your blood," said Aru.

That seemed to confuse Brynne, but before she could say anything more, Mini stepped between them, her arms extended to keep them a safe distance apart. "*I* believe you," she said to Brynne, then she shot a glare at Aru.

"Maybe the bow and arrow were planted there," said Aiden. "I mean, that's a pretty obvious place for someone to leave them...."

"Yeah," said Mini. "You could've been framed?"

"Exactly!" Brynne said. "Someone knew I would bring them to the Otherworld to find the rightful owner and—"

"And somehow that released an army of Heartless..." Aru added, somewhat reluctantly. Her mind was spinning. Who was Fake Aru? And what did she want with the bow and arrow?

Aiden tapped his fingers against his camera. "It's like this massive conspiracy," he said excitedly. "Imagine breaking that story on the news. It'd be epic."

"Look!" said Mini happily. "We're all on the same side!"

Aru and Brynne just glowered at each other.

"So...since we're going to be working together," said Aiden, "I think we should put everything behind us....For the sake of the mission?"

Aru was beginning to see why Brynne called him Ammamma.

"I'm ready to move on," Aru said. "But it would be nice if *some people* at least *pretended* to be grateful that we're trying to clear her name."

"Grateful?" scoffed Brynne. "What, you want another fan just because you went on a big Pandava quest?"

"What fans?" said Aru. She gestured at the empty space around them. "There's no one here but us and a bunch of weapons. What's your problem? And in case you haven't noticed, *you're a Pandava, too.*"

At this, Brynne turned her head away. "Not really."

Aru ticked off two points on her fingers. "You got claimed by your soul father. And you got a cool weapon. Bam! Pandava."

"Is that all this means to you?" When Brynne looked back at Aru, her eyes were glossy.

Aru looked down. Of course that wasn't all this meant. For the first time, she felt like she belonged. That wasn't something she would give up for anything. When she thought about never being able to come back to the Night Bazaar, never again holding magic in her hands, her stomach dropped. But it wasn't like she was going to tell all that to this girl.

Mini cleared her throat. "We have just as much to lose as you do," she said quietly to Brynne.

Brynne stayed silent, her jaw clenched.

"How about a group elbow bump?" suggested Mini. "Hand-shakes are really unhygienic."

"No," said Brynne and Aru at the same time.

A flash of light went off.

"Ugh!" said Aru, holding up a hand to shield her face. "No paparazzi!"

Aiden lowered his camera, frowning. "*Not* paparazzi."

"He hates that word," said Brynne, teasingly. "He prefers to be known as a 'photojournalist.' He takes pictures of everything."

"Including whatever dish Brynne experiments with in the kitchen," said Aiden.

We get it. You're BFFLs, Aru thought grumpily. But at least they'd broken the tension.

Brynne pointed at her shoes. "Okay, we've got the quest stuff. Where do we go from here?"

"Urvashi said we should speak to the owner—Kamadeva," said Aiden. "But where do we find him?"

"Er, quick question," said Aru. "Who *is* Kamadeva?"

"'*Who is Kamadeva?*'" repeated Brynne. "Don't you know *anything*?"

Faint sparks shot out of Vajra, but once again Mini steered Aru away from a fight.

"Kamadeva is the god of love," said Mini. "The bow and arrow belong to him—he uses them to shoot gods and mortals to make them feel passion for someone. Although the weapon didn't look anything like how I imagined...The legends say that the bow he uses is made out of sugarcane, and the string is made out of honeybees." Mini shuddered. "Not that I'm disappointed. I'm allergic to bees."

"Er, that's all great information, Mini," said Aiden. "But where does he live?"

"Somewhere in the Midwest, I think? That's what Boo said in class."

"Okay, so we'll take a portal to Kamadeva," said Aru.

"I've got a better—and *faster*—idea," said Brynne. She brought two fingers to her lips and whistled.

The domed ceiling of the warehouse slid open, and down came a rush of wind. The sound of bleating filled the air. Aru had to remember to close her mouth when four gigantic gazelles the size of elephants burst through the clouds.

Whenever Aru thought of a gazelle, she pictured one of those nature documentaries where a British dude calmly announces, *And now the gazelle is in the jaws of death as the mighty lioness drags its carcass through the Sahara. Nature is cruel, but magnificent.*

These gazelles, on the other hand, looked like they snacked on lions for fun.

SEVEN

Who Doesn't Like Vegan Granola?

"Thanks, Vayu!" hollered Brynne. She blew a kiss to the air, then looked coolly at Mini and Aru. "Gifts from my dad. Clearly, he sends his regards."

"He...he talks to you?" Mini asked.

Brynne just lifted her shoulder and smiled smugly.

Aru couldn't help herself. She was jealous again. Far above, she could see the glimmering outline of the celestial city of Amaravati, ruled over by none other than her father, Lord Indra. Amaravati was where the apsaras danced. Supposedly, the whole place was covered in sacred groves and magical wonders, including a tree that granted wishes.

Aru lifted her hand to wave at Indra, and then thought better of it. It wasn't as though he would have seen her. And anyway, he hadn't come to her defense when she was wrongly accused of stealing Kamadeva's weapon. Aru tried not to feel disappointed, but it was like he was saying *Cool! Bye!* at the prospect of Aru no longer being part of the Otherworld. Was she so bad at being a Pandava that her own soul dad couldn't stick up for her?

"I think any god would acknowledge their offspring, as long as that offspring was worthy," said Brynne.

Mini's lips tugged down, and she held Dee Dee a little closer to her chest. Vajra, on the other hand, looked as if it were ready to unfold and strike Brynne upside the head.

Before them, the four gazelles each shrank down to a more manageable size, about as big as a horse. They looked slightly familiar to Aru. . . . Then it came back to her—they'd been there during the battle in the museum, to help fight the Sleeper. But she doubted they remembered her.

Brynne strode in front of the gazelles and waved her arm like a game show host. "These are the four winds that my father controls. He lent them to me," she said loftily. "North." A gazelle the color of blue ice swung its head. Icicles dangled from its slender black horns. "South." A gazelle the color of a blazing fire sank to its forelegs. Flames danced atop its horns. "East." A gazelle the color of a pale pink rose lifted its chin. Flowers wound around its horns. "And West." A gazelle the color of bright green grass, with horns that looked like twists of moss, bowed its head.

"As daughter of the god of the wind, *I'll* choose first," said Brynne.

But when she moved to the gazelles, they took a step away from her and toward Aru and Mini instead.

"We remember you, daughter of Indra," said the Gazelle of the West, bowing again. It turned to Mini. "And you, too, daughter of the Dharma Raja. It was an honor to fight by your side, and it would be an honor to carry you now."

Aru smiled widely. Her grin had nothing to do with Brynne's shocked and furious face. (Fine, maybe it did, a little.)

She reached for the Gazelle of the West and swung onto its back. Mini chose the Gazelle of the North. Aiden chose the Gazelle of the East, and Brynne leaped savagely onto the back of the Gazelle of the South. She gripped its horns, and flames danced around her fists.

"To the abode of Kamadeva!" she shouted.

The gazelles took off, galloping past the shelves in the Warehouse of Quest Materials before they leaped into the sky. Clouds broke over Aru's head and cold air burned in her lungs as they headed back toward the mortal realm.

Flying in the open air at night was unlike anything Aru had ever imagined. It was beautiful. Hundreds of feet below them, the city lights shone like fallen stars. Silvery clouds scudded across a black velvet sky. She could hear Aiden snapping pictures beside her. When he saw her looking, he said, "What? This is so cool!"

"How are you taking pictures in the dark? They won't come out."

Aiden raised his camera. "I bought some enchantments for it, like night vision and emergency accessory transformation."

On Aru's other side, Mini was holding tight to her gazelle's horns. "Did you know you can get hypothermia from air this cold? We could—"

"Die?" asked Aru wearily.

"Or your limbs could freeze and turn black and someone would have to cut them off," said Aiden cheerily.

"Yes!" said Mini, her voice brightening. "How'd you know?"

"I have a big book of diseases," he said. "My mom gave it to me. She's a microbiologist."

Aru waited for someone to say *Did we just become best friends?*

But no one did. For the next twenty minutes, Aiden and Mini talked over Aru's head about weird medical conditions while she tried to close her ears. Aiden's comment made her curious, though. How could his mom be a biologist if Urvashi was his aunt? That would make her an apsara. Was it his other parent who had blood ties to Urvashi?

"What about your dad?" she asked. "What does he do?"

Aiden's tone instantly flattened. "He's a lawyer. He's going to practice in New York after he and Annette get married."

Annette? Suddenly, it was clear why Aru never saw his parents together, even though they lived in the same house. They were getting a divorce.

"Oh," said Mini softly.

Aiden shrugged, mumbled something about checking on Brynne, and pushed his gazelle past them. Mini drifted toward Aru.

"Should we say sorry?"

Aru shook her head. "I think if we make a big deal out of it, it'll only be worse."

Mini nodded. "Did you know his parents were splitting up?"

"I didn't put it together until now," said Aru.

But she had noticed there was something off about the Acharya household. It seemed like every time his dad's car pulled into the driveway, Aiden would leave the house, his camera slung over his shoulder. His mom, Malini, rarely smiled at anyone.

Wow, Shah, you really are *a stalker,* she told herself.

I am observant, Aru thought. *Huge difference.*

And you talk to yourself.

Aru grumbled.

"It must suck for your family to break up," said Mini sadly.

Aru didn't know what to say to that. She partially agreed with Mini. The divorce had to be hard for Aiden. But she didn't agree that it meant his family was broken. Lots of kids at school had divorced parents, and not all families needed a dad and a mom to be whole. Some had two dads, or two moms, or just one parent, or no parent at all. It wasn't like her family, with just her and her mom living in a museum with a bunch of statues, was exactly "standard." And anyway, families weren't like a box of standardized-test-taking number two pencils. Families were like a box of assorted-color Sharpie markers: different, kinda stinky (but not in a bad way), and permanent whether you liked it or not.

They passed through the border between the Otherworld and the human world, which looked like a thick, rolling fog. Time had moved forward in the mortal realm. Weak morning sunlight streamed across their skin. They were still surrounded by a barrier of magic, but to Aru it seemed as flimsy as frost on a windowpane and just as easy to see through. As the gazelles loped down highways and pranced across the tops of billboards, their delicate hooves sometimes bounced off the barrier with a sharp bell-like chime.

When they were barely ten feet away from a minivan with a bored kid inside, Aru asked, "Can they see us?"

"Nah," said Aiden. "Watch."

The kid was more or less looking in their direction. Aiden waved his hands wildly and pulled his face into strange expressions. No reaction.

Aru laughed, then did the same...and maybe the light caught her, because the kid started pointing and screaming.

"Uh-oh," said Aru. She tugged up the reins, pulling the gazelle higher. Oh well. Maybe she'd livened up someone's game of I Spy at least.

Soon they arrived at a little park. Below, the trees were bare and ice sleeved the branches. The gazelles gently lowered themselves to the ground, and Aru and her three companions found themselves in a clearing in front of a gleaming green sign that said LOVES PARK, ILLINOIS.

"We're a *long* way from *A-T-L*," said Aiden. He rolled up his sleeves, and for the first time Aru noticed twin leather bands around his wrists. Before she could ask about them, the trees started changing right in front of their eyes. Blossoms burst from the branches. The pale sky transformed into a sheet of vivid blue. Puffy white clouds rolled above them and sparkling sunshine drenched the world. *Now* it looked like the home of the god of love.

The three of them slid off the gazelles, gaping in astonishment. It was as if they'd skipped winter and gone straight to spring in a matter of seconds. After bowing, the gazelles opened their mouths at the same time and said, "The temperature is sixty-three degrees Fahrenheit, seventeen degrees Celsius. The southeast winds are blowing at six miles per hour, and the humidity is forty-three percent. All in all, favorable conditions in Loves Park. Fair winds, Pandavas!"

"I'm not a Pandava! I just got special clearance or whatever!" Aiden called, but the gazelles had already disappeared.

"Why is it spring here?" asked Aru, looking around.

Aiden snapped a photo of the scenery. "Probably because we're close to Kamadeva. He's the god of love, and love is supposed to feel like eternal spring."

Aru and Mini exchanged a look. Mini smothered a laugh, and Brynne glowered.

"Aiden, are all your Instagram captions Ed Sheeran lyrics?" asked Aru.

Aiden rolled his eyes. "It's just something my mom told me."

"Aiden's an *artist*," said Brynne, but she said it like *ar-teest*. "That's just how he thinks."

Aru mimicked *ar-teest* in her head for a good five seconds. Love like eternal spring? No thanks. Her favorite season was autumn, but she didn't want love to feel like that. It would be crunchy and orange. Or worse...pumpkin-spice-flavored.

Mini rubbed her eyes. "Ugh, spring. My allergies are acting up. I can already feel my eyes getting watery and I don't have tissues—"

Aiden reached into his camera bag and pulled out a tiny packet of Kleenex. Mini squealed with delight.

At the same time, Brynne's stomach let out a massive grumble. She clutched it, moaning, "God, I'm so hungry....I didn't have anything this morning except two Belgian waffles, four poached eggs, granola, homemade yogurt, six peaches, and a piece of toast."

Aru stared at her. "Yeah...who *wouldn't* be hungry?"

Aiden wordlessly handed Brynne a candy bar.

"You da best, Ammamma," she said happily.

Mini shuddered. "My mom would *kill* me if I was eating candy first thing in the morning, wouldn't yours?"

At the word *mom*, Brynne's face shuttered. Angrily, she shoved the candy bar into her pants pocket. "Let's go," she said gruffly, charging down a path through the spring woods.

Guess you hit a sore spot, Aru thought to Mini.

The rest of them followed. At the end of the path, the trees opened into a new clearing with a large pond. Just beyond it, hovering in the air above the pond rushes, was a blue door. Two signs hung from the tree beneath it. One said:

ALL PERSONNEL MUST SUBMIT

IDENTIFICATION PRIOR TO ENTRY

The second sign read:

VISITORS MAY GAIN ACCESS WITH GUEST PASS

"Personnel?" asked Mini. "I thought we're seeing the god of love, not a CEO?"

Brynne parted the pond rushes with her mace. "I don't see a guest pass anywhere." She looked at the door. "We could always just smash it open...."

"Wait," said Aru. "I think I see something."

A glint of gold appeared on the shore of the pond. Aru stepped through the weeds and stopped short when she came across a large pile of sticks and dirt.

"A nest!" said Brynne, pushing past her.

In the middle of the nest was a golden key. Beside it napped a miniature white swan, no bigger than someone's palm. It looked like it could fit inside a teacup.

"Aww!" said Mini. "So cute!"

"That key must be the guest pass," said Aiden. He lifted his camera, snapped a picture, and then examined the digital file. "Hmm... The lighting is off...."

"Leave it, Aiden!" Brynne said. "Let's grab it and go." She started to reach for the key.

"Do you think we can pet the swan?" asked Mini. "Or maybe not? Can swans give you bird flu?"

"Wait, Brynne," Aru said.

"What's wrong, Shah? Frightened by a tiny bird?" Brynne eyed the swan. "You know, swan used to be a delicacy."

"Gross! I don't want to eat it! I want to *avoid* it. Have you ever seen a swan in action?" asked Aru. "They're vicious."

"Shah, that swan is the size of a toy," said Brynne. "We'll live."

Brynne plucked the key from the nest. All four of them watched the swan. Nothing happened.

"See? Told ya!" Brynne started walking toward the hovering door.

Aru hesitated for a moment before following. Now she felt dumb. Maybe she had been overreacting....

They were halfway to the door when the warm spring air turned cold. Aru couldn't see her shadow on the ground anymore.

"It got cloudy quickly," said Mini, rubbing her arms.

Aiden looked up. His eyes widened. "It's not a cloud."

Slowly, Aru raised her head. That teeny-tiny, itty-bitty, *so-cute-I-just-wanna-squeeze-you* swan was no longer itty-bitty. In fact, it had grown to the size of a three-story house. Its long white wings fanned out to either side, obscuring the sun. With a heavy *whoosh*, it landed right in front of them, blocking the door to Kamadeva's abode. It cocked its head sharply to one side. The feathers on its long white neck bristled.

"No sudden movements," Brynne said to them, holding up her mace.

Mini ignored her. She dug into her backpack and pulled out a half-eaten granola bar. She broke it in two and tossed it to the swan. The swan looked at the granola, looked at Mini, then looked back at the granola.

"It's vegan?" offered Mini.

The swan raised one webbed black foot. And it crushed the granola into the dirt.

"But it's an excellent source of fiber!"

Apparently the giant swan did not agree. With a loud, honking *squawwwwk!* it charged.

EIGHT

Swans Are the Worst

Aru sized up the monster swan as it came at them. And herself, too. She knew she was small. She wasn't that strong, either.

But she didn't have to be.

The battle was a game in her head—dodge and jab, use the enemy's own momentum against them, and let *them* do all the work.

"Mini!" shouted Aru.

Her sister knew immediately what to do. Dee Dee flashed and grew, sprouting from Mini's sleeve. Purple light exploded in a burst in front of them. The swan squawked and stomped back, its webbed foot crushing the pond reeds that had surrounded its lake.

Beside them, Aiden tapped his leather bands and two shining scimitars shot out from the magical arm braces. He pushed a golden button on the top of his camera and it, along with his camera bag, folded up until it became a watch on his wrist.

Aru's eyes widened. So that's what *emergency accessory transformation* meant. *Whoa.*

A moment later, the swan found its balance and stalked toward them. Aru mentally ran through some strategies, but before she could say anything, Brynne leaped into the air and shouted, "Aiden, I'll distract it! Take the key, but don't go in without me!"

"Wait up!" said Aru. "We haven't—"

"Stay out of the way, Shah!" shouted Brynne. "I've got this!"

She threw the key to Aiden, who caught it in his fist.

Then Brynne morphed. Blue light blazed around her. Where she had once stood, there was now a blue elephant almost as large as the swan. Elephant-Brynne swung her head. Tusks out, trunk raised, she charged at the bird. Aru had just enough time to roll away before she got trampled.

As it turned out, elephant trumpeting and swan honking sounded a lot like how Aru imagined fighting dinosaurs would. Elephant-Brynne tried to dig her tusks into the swan. It honked loudly, thrashing. Feathers exploded in the air. The swan pumped its wings. They unfurled to the length of an airplane. And when they were flapped vigorously, the effect was like that of a jet turbine. Even the puffy white clouds overhead were blown back by the wind. The tops of the trees swayed. Aru grabbed hold of a branch just to keep from flying away while Elephant-Brynne tumbled head over heels and smacked into a tree trunk.

The wind died down. With a loud *TAKE-THAT-WEIRD-BLUE-ELEPHANT!* honk, the swan toddled forward. Its target was clear:

Aiden.

He had only just recovered his balance. Staggering forward, Aiden brandished his scimitars. The swan started pecking at him like he was a particularly yummy breadcrumb. Aiden dodged, parrying the swan's stabbing beak as if it were a sword. But the swan was faster.

Elephant-Brynne came charging back into the scene. "DO SOMETHING, SHAH!" she bellowed, which, firstly, was supercool, because she could be a talking animal, but secondly, was *not* helpful, because Aru *was* doing something. At first, she'd tried to throw her lightning bolt, but Vajra missed. Near Aiden, Mini's force fields kept flickering, weakened by her fear.

Aru needed to think....

If Hanuman had taught her anything, it was to assess a fight not just from her point of view, but also from the eyes of the enemy. What did the swan want?

Elephant-Brynne trumpeted again, but the swan didn't turn around to face her. Its entire attention was focused on Aiden— who had the key. The key that had been lying in the middle of the swan's nest ... like an egg. Which meant the swan considered the key its baby!

"I have an idea!" shouted Aru.

Brynne's bellowing drowned out her voice. That left Aru only one option—the Pandava mind link. The last place she wanted to be was inside Brynne's head, but she didn't have a choice.

She closed her eyes, reaching for Brynne's mind the way she reached for Mini's....

Brynne?

Elephant-Brynne jumped up and let out a startled cry. *WHO THE—?*

I need you to turn into a bird.

What?! Why? GET OUT OF MY HEAD! And no, I got this—

Dude, you just got thrown into the trees.

Aiden was tiring quickly. His scimitar jabs were slowing even as he ducked and danced through the swan's legs. Finally, Mini cast a shield just in time to block a peck from the swan's wickedly sharp beak. Aiden dove into a thicket of springtime hedges.

Brynne tapped into her thoughts: *What kind of bird?*

Aru grinned as she answered her. Then she sent a message to both Brynne and Mini. *New plan. We have to work together. Mini, do you remember what the key looked like? We need a duplicate.*

On it! came Mini's reply.

The swan pecked at Mini's violet force field. The bird made one, then two cracks in it, and finally the shield splintered. The swan was waddling past Mini toward Aiden's hiding place when Aru ran forward and shouted:

"Did you know some people *eat* swans as a delicacy?"

The swan lifted its webbed foot. Aru stepped back. The swan drew closer as she retreated, matching her step for step. All the while, the bird's narrow head swayed back and forth. *Foe or food?* it seemed to be asking.

"Would you rather be a swan burger or a swan panini?"

The swan hissed.

"Oh, sorry. Swan pasta, maybe?" Aru taunted. Then she telepathically asked Mini, *How's the decoy coming along?*

Nearly ready.

Just as the swan let out an outraged squawk, Mini shouted, "Look what I've got!" She waved a perfect replica of the key in the air.

The swan paused. It looked at the hedges, then at Mini. Then it squawked something that sounded a lot like *WHAT FRESH BETRAYAL IS THIS?*

Now, Brynne! Aru ordered.

In a flash of blue, Brynne changed from an elephant to a regular-size swan. She swooped down low and snatched the fake key from Mini's outstretched hand. Then, with two powerful pumps of her wings, she shot off into the sky.

The swan let out a strangled cry—meaning *MY BABY!*—and took off after Brynne.

When Aru was sure the swan was gone, she and Mini ran over to the hedges. Aiden clambered out of his hiding spot, his face pale.

"That was a total Slytherin move," Aiden said to Aru, dusting himself off. Sparks of electricity shot off Vajra and Aiden quickly added, "Not that that's bad."

"Is that your House?" Mini asked Aru.

Yes.

Aru shrugged. "Maybe? I dunno. I'd totally pretend to be Hufflepuff just to stay closest to the kitchens, though."

Aiden stared at her. "You're bizarre, Shah."

It didn't sound like an insult. For a split second, Aru felt that same tug of . . . something.

Aiden touched the watch at his wrist. His camera bag and camera returned to his hip. He lifted the camera to his eye, toggling one of the switches.

"I see Brynne," he said.

Aru squinted up at the sky, but all she saw were two birdish specks.

"Where'd you get an enchanted camera?" asked Mini, awed. "Is that legal? Because according to the Otherworld Transportation Security Guidelines—"

"Not this again," groaned Aru.

"—you're not allowed to bring a purchased enchanted object back into the mortal realm unless you're over the age of eighteen."

"How do you even know that?" asked Aiden.

"I like rules," said Mini primly.

Aiden lowered the camera. He rubbed his thumbs along its sides. It wasn't sleek or modern, but that wasn't a bad thing in Aru's opinion. She could tell that for Aiden, the camera was like a blanket or teddy bear (or, in Aru's case, a pillow in the shape of a fried egg named Eggy). Kinda dumpy-looking, but obviously loved.

"It's a Hasselblad that belonged to my dad," said Aiden. "It's from 1998, back when he wanted to be a photographer. A mechanic in the Night Bazaar modified the internal mechanism of the SLR and converted it into your modern digital SLR *and* added a Bluetooth chip. That way, the photos don't have to be developed but automatically get sent to my phone, to check out, and to my laptop, for editing."

Aru and Mini just blinked at him. Aru had *no idea* what he'd just said.

"That's...good?" offered Mini. "Especially that he gave it to you?"

"Yeah," said Aiden, but then the corners of his mouth tugged down. "He said it was a present, but I think he just didn't want it anymore. He doesn't want a lot of things anymore."

A loud squawking made the three of them look up.

Aiden looked through the camera. "Uh-oh."

Suddenly, ringing so loudly in their minds that both Aru and Mini clapped their hands over their ears (as if that would make a difference), came Brynne's voice: *GET TO THE DOOR!*

No longer was Brynne a distant speck in the sky. Now she was zooming back toward them, and she wasn't alone. The monster swan was hot on her heels, squawking loudly.

"*RUN!*" Aiden shouted.

They raced to the hanging door.

"Vajra!" called Aru.

The lightning bolt had been lying on the ground, waiting for her command. Now it transformed into a glittering hoverboard, long enough to hold the three of them.

"Woo-hoo!" Aru said.

Getting Vajra to transform was no easy feat. But at least Aru was getting better at it. All she had to do was keep her focus. They jumped on, and Vajra zoomed toward the bright blue door. Aiden held out the key.

Behind them, they heard loud squawking from the other bird. Aru risked a glance over her shoulder and saw Swan-Brynne flying as fast as she could toward the door.

"Faster, Aiden!" yelled Mini, as he tried to jam the key into the lock.

"I'm going as fast as I can!"

Finally, the key turned. The door swung open. The three of them tumbled onto the floor. Vajra swung backward, and the force of the lightning bolt slammed the door shut.

"Oh no! Brynne's still out there!" said Mini.

Aru, her chest heaving, jumped to her feet and threw open the door. "I'm sure she—"

Swan-Brynne flew straight into Aru. Both girls were

knocked down. Aru hit her head, *hard*, against the floor. It hurt like anything. There was another flash of blue light as Brynne transformed back into a girl. She was breathing heavily. Her eyes were red and...teary?

Aru's sarcastic *Thanks a lot!* died on her lips. "Brynne?"

"Did you try to leave me behind?" she asked. Brynne was gripping her mace so hard that Aru felt bad for the weapon.

Mini was the first to recover. "No? That's why Aru opened the door...."

Brynne lowered the mace. She took a deep breath. "I knew that." Then she raised her chin and crossed her arms. "Well, go on. Say it."

"It was *my* idea, too. I'm not saying thank you—"

Brynne looked shocked. "*Thank you?* That's what you thought I meant?"

Now it was Aru's turn to be confused. "What'd you think I was going to say?"

"No jokes about turning into a bird?"

"Birds are nothing to joke about," said Mini, shuddering.

Brynne looked embarrassed and instead turned around to gaze at their new surroundings.

The building they were in reminded Aru of pictures she'd seen of the New York Stock Exchange. The floor was polished marble, and it seemed like they were inside a lobby. Large windows revealed different views: sleepy neighborhoods, bright cities, coastal towns, and sunlit meadows. A shimmering veil of soundproofing magic—the same kind Urvashi used in her dance studio—separated them from the clusters of giant circular hubs that dotted the entire floor and hundreds of Otherworld people in sharp suits who were screaming into their headsets. Aru was used to sky ceilings, and the god of love had chosen the night heavens for his. It was beautiful. The cosmos seemed closer than usual, as if Aru could reach out, pluck a planet, and put it in her pocket. On one wall, enchanted screens that looked like panes of moonlight buzzed with numbers. They were similar to the stock screens her teacher had showed them in their Civics and Economics class. Aru didn't remember much from that class, but she had learned green arrow = good; red arrow = bad. And right now, she was looking at a ton of red arrows.

UNIVERSAL HEART SKIPS	▼ –1000.23
INTENTIONAL EYELASH FLUTTERING	▼ –800.21
FAKING INTEREST IN YOUTUBE CAT VIDEOS	▼ –900.41
PEOPLE MAKING ED SHEERAN PLAYLISTS	▼ –3000.18

At that moment, an extremely handsome young man walked toward them. His hair was a shock of black curls. He wore a dark Nehru jacket, and a bright blue parrot rode on his shoulder. He would have looked like the executive of a global corporation and also like a Bollywood movie star if it weren't for one strange detail: his skin. It was bright green. This man could only be one person. Or god, to be exact.

He was Kamadeva, the god of love and desire . . . and the owner of the bow and arrow that had been stolen.

The four kids respectfully bowed and touched the ground before the god, but Kamadeva seemed unmoved.

"Lord Kamadeva—" started Aru, trying to take a step forward before she found that she couldn't. Her feet were frozen in place.

"Teens are usually my favorite consumers," said Kamadeva. "But thieves? Not so much."

Four gleaming swords appeared in the air. They hovered for a second before the blades turned and pointed at the kids' throats.

NINE

That One Time I Got Incinerated

"We're not thieves!" said Brynne.

"*I* will be the judge of that."

Kamadeva smiled. Aru had never seen a more beautiful—or crueler—smile in all her life.

"Ah, one of you thinks I am weak..." he said, his gaze turning to Brynne. "Is it because you do not see me wielding a mace? Or a sword?"

"I—" started Brynne, but she couldn't lunge at him, not with a sword pointing at her throat.

"You think desire is nothing, do you? Empirical evidence points to quite the opposite. I can start a war, you know."

Kamadeva waved a hand and the four of them stared down as a scene unfurled across the marble floor:

In the woods, Surpanakha—an ugly tusked demoness with red eyes and sagging gray skin—confronted two handsome men and a beautiful woman. When Surpanakha saw the handsome Rama—who was an incarnation of the god

Vishnu—and his younger brother Laxmana, she transformed into a beautiful woman, and tried to make one of them marry her. But Rama pointed to his wife, Sita, an incarnation of the goddess of good fortune. And Laxmana refused Surpanakha with a vehement *Heck no!* (At least that's what Aru imagined he said.) Furious, Surpanakha rushed at Sita, and Laxmana cut off the demoness's nose, revealing her true nature.

Humiliated, Surpanakha ran to her brother, the great demon king Ravana. She told him about her dishonor and blamed the beautiful Sita.

Ravana's ten heads turned to Surpanakha. "What does this Sita look like?"

Aru knew what happened next, because it was the story told in the epic poem the *Ramayana*. Ravana stole Sita, and Rama launched a war to get her back.

Kamadeva waved his hand, and the image changed. "Or I can end a war."

The land had been ravaged by a terrible demon. A council of the gods declared that only the son of Lord Shiva, the god of destruction, and Parvati, the Mother Goddess, could do away with the culprit. There was only one problem, though... Parvati had been reborn on Earth and had never met Shiva. So there was no kid.

"Allow me to assist," Kamadeva said to the concerned council of gods.

He found Lord Shiva meditating in a clearing in the

middle of a lush forest. The beautiful Parvati was approaching. Kamadeva ran around the glade rearranging leaves and flowers. "Look alive, people!" he shouted. "This is it! First impressions are *everything!*"

Just as Parvati was about to enter, Kamadeva reached for his bow and arrow.

"And one...two...three..." said Kamadeva. "Spring breeze."

A light wind rolled through the forest clearing.

"Perfume!"

Flower blossoms opened.

"Music!"

Soft drumming and a flute echoed in the clearing.

"Lights!"

The afternoon sun's rays dimmed to a golden glow.

"And now...a touch of je ne sais quoi."

Kamadeva gently blew some glittery dust from his palm and the air looked star-touched.

"Perfection!" he said, stringing his bow—

"Wait..." said Aiden. At the sound of his voice, the image on the floor froze with a sharp sound like a record scratch. "Isn't this the part where you get incinerated?"

Kamadeva dusted the shoulders of his suit. "Oh, so you've heard this story before."

Brynne frowned. "You got incinerated?"

"A little."

Aiden shook his head, which was hard to do with a blade at his throat. "That's not what *I* heard."

Kamadeva scowled. "Let's just call it a beta test that went wrong, okay? As it turns out, immortal beings don't like their hearts being tampered with. You cannot *rush* love. And I wasn't! I'm simply one aspect of attraction. Like a prickling awareness, you know? In this form, I'm just here to open your eyes and open your heart, you understand?"

The four of them wore matching expressions of *nope*.

"What about the bow and arrow?" asked Brynne. "The ones we *didn't* steal," she emphasized.

Kamadeva's expression turned sly. "Oh, I believe you," he said. "While you were watching my stories, I had a peek inside each of your hearts. Very interesting things there. Lots of sorrow. Lots of yearning. So very, very ripe." His gaze lingered on Aiden. "You, especially. Look at that handsome face! All the makings of a tortured, brooding hero. I could make you a star!"

Aiden looked horrified. "Please don't?"

Aru was tired of people looking inside her without her knowledge or permission, but she let it go for now. "If you've seen our hearts," she asked, "then can you tell Uloopi we're innocent?"

Surely the god of love could convince the naga queen, Aru thought. Then they wouldn't have to be banished from the Otherworld. And Boo—poor Boo—he'd be free.

"She'd never listen to me, I'm afraid. She blames me for making her fall in love with Arjuna, which led to her present condition..." said Kamadeva. His face turned rather solemn. "But that is not my story to tell. What I can tell you is that the only way you'll convince Uloopi of your innocence is by bringing her my bow and arrow."

Mini raised a timid hand. "But...it's *your* weapon."

"True, but I had to put it away. You see, after I was blasted to smithereens, my beloved wife, Rati, carried the bow and arrow for me while I awaited reincarnation. But she felt the pain of my loss so keenly that the song in her soul—"

"What song?" cut in Brynne.

Aru gently tapped her collarbone (is that where souls hide?), wondering if a song might burst out someday. What if her song was really dumb? What if, when she was about to die, every cell in her body started singing *The hills are aliiiiiiive with the sound of musiiiic*—?

"It's not a song you can perceive," said Kamadeva, with a sharp look at Aru. She dropped her hand back to her side. "It's the humming of harmony, the subtle dance of pulses, the rhythm that two hearts beat together in blissful accord."

Aiden looked like his eyes were going to roll back in his head out of pure boredom.

"My Rati's soul song fled...and it granted my bow and arrow a dark power. Anyone struck by grief and armed with the knowledge of enchantment could carve out their own soul song. The sheer desperation of that act would give them the power to wield the bow and arrow for a terrible purpose, allowing them not to join hearts together, but to *rip them out* instead. That's why, after Rati's soul song returned and we were reunited, I gave the weapon to Uloopi. The queen has kept it safely stored in the great vaults of the naga realm for thousands of years... until now."

"Does that mean you don't use the arrow anymore to make people fall in love?" asked Aru.

"Correct," said Kamadeva. "But trust me, I don't miss it. These days I'd have to lie in wait at coffee shops, or youth group lunches, or take intro to philosophy classes at eight thirty a.m., or scroll through Reddit *Fortnite* threads. No thanks."

"You said that the bow and arrow could rip out people's hearts..." said Mini. "Is that what that wound was on the Heartless?"

Kamadeva nodded, and Aru shuddered, remembering the strange scars in their chests where frost spiderwebbed out onto their skin.

"Why would someone want an army of Heartless?" asked Aiden.

That was the same question Aru was going to ask. She glared at him.

"As you've seen, they're nearly invincible," said Kamadeva.

"Nearly?" asked Brynne.

"Their strength is tied to the one who made them Heartless. If that person's soul song is returned, then the negative effects of the bow and arrow would be reversed, thus changing them back into human form."

"Do you know who the thief is? Could you help us?" asked Mini excitedly.

"Or...you know...go after your *own* bow and arrow?" pointed out Aru.

For a moment she thought the god of love would curse her and turn her into an unfeeling toad or something, but instead he shook his head sadly.

"The task was given to *you*, Pandavas," said Kamadeva. "I am not allowed to interfere. Besides, the Soul Exchange is in dire straits—just look at the stocks! There's far too much chaos going on in the mortal realm right now, and the investors are up in arms. But I can tell you this. Whoever corrupted my bow and arrow had to leave their soul song in the place where the weapon was stolen."

"The naga realm," said Brynne.

"Specifically, the treasury," said Mini.

Aru recalled the blind naga king who guarded the treasury: Takshaka. He hadn't seemed to like them at all, though she didn't know why.

"What's a soul song look like?" asked Aru. "Sheet music or something?"

She really hoped it wasn't that. She couldn't remember anything about reading piano notes except some weird acronym.... *Each good bear delivers frogs?* That couldn't be right.

"The song might take a variety of forms," said Kamadeva. "It'll be representative of the thief's soul, but it won't look like any ordinary object."

Well, that was helpful. *Not.*

"Once you have found the song," said Kamadeva, "you must speak the name of the thief over it. Then the song will reveal the location of the stolen weapon. When you retrieve it, you must plunge the arrow through the heart of the thief. Only then will the Heartless be restored to their human selves, and the arrow cleansed of its dark power."

Plunge the arrow through the heart? Aru thought that sounded kind of violent. Then again, getting your heart torn out and basically becoming a robot wasn't great, either.

"How are we going to get to the naga realm?" asked Aiden.

"It's not like Uloopi and Takshaka are exactly fans of ours. They might have guards waiting for us at the portals."

"There's a way around that," said Kamadeva. "But you'll have to watch out."

"For what?"

"Sharks, obviously."

TEN

That Went Well ... Not

Accarding to Kamadeva, the best way for them to get into the naga realm would be via the aquatic airport. "You can blend in with the other tourists that way," he told them.

"Why would an underwater transportation system be called an *air*port?" Mini asked. "Isn't that an oxymoron?"

The god of love dismissed her questions with a wave. "The Otherworld authorities sometimes pick names just because they like how they sound, like Abattoir Spa. It's very French. It also means *slaughterhouse*. Anyway, come with me to my office!"

The four of them followed him from the lobby to the vast floor of the Soul Exchange. All around them hovered giant monitors filled with long lists of names and zodiac signs. Overhead, swans swooped across the night-sky ceiling, honking and trumpeting. After their encounter with the swan outside the Soul Exchange, Aru had to fight the urge to yell *Back, beast! Begone!*

"The six o'clock news headlines are here!" shouted one of the swans. "'Are the Pandavas on the verge of exile?'"

Aru groaned and pulled her hoodie tighter over her head. They'd gone from being legends to losers in the space of a day.

"'Naga queen demands justice for stolen treasure—'"

"'Mortal realm full of panic as the number of missing persons triples every hour!'"

Aru's stomach dipped. *More* people missing meant *more* people who might never be human again...and all of it depended on whether they found the thief before time was up.

And finally: "'Which Hollywood Chris are you? Chris Pratt, Chris Evans, or Chris Pine? Take the quiz and find out!'"

Brynne's mace glowed as she grumbled, "Someone should put a stop to the gossip about us. It's not helping our case."

"Ignore it," said Mini mildly. "People enjoy seeing other people feel bad. It makes them feel better about themselves. Don't feed the trolls."

Aru had to hand it to Mini. She could be totally weird, but with her weirdness came wisdom. Brynne lowered her mace and it returned to choker form around her neck. Aiden, on the other hand, looked completely unconcerned with the rumors. He kept trying to take pictures of the Soul Exchange, but every time he came close, Kamadeva raised his hand, and light beamed off the camera lens.

"Can't have my competitors learning my secrets!" said Kamadeva.

The tips of Aiden's ears turned red, but Aru saw him try to sneak photos anyway.

As they approached the end of the atrium, the atmosphere of the Soul Exchange shifted. It became darker somehow. Brynne started anxiously spinning her many bracelets.

Aru was close enough to see that they were all engraved...
BRYNNE RAO, FIRST PLACE! BRYNNE RAO, CHAMPION!

Brynne caught her peeking and shrugged. "I had my trophies melted down to make bracelets," she said, raising her hand proudly.

Aru's mouth fell open. "Who *does* that?"

"Winners," said Brynne smugly.

Aru shot Mini a *can-you-believe-this?* look, but her best friend was blissfully unaware, and too intent on following Kamadeva's instructions.

At the far side of the Soul Exchange, the desks were pitch-black, and the space was divided into two large cubicles, one labeled SPITE and the other INDIFFERENCE. Here, patches of fog hid the sky ceiling from view. In a few places, moonlight broke through, revealing delicate silver staircases that spiraled up to those gaps. The same pair of words appeared in the filigree of each step: LISTEN and LAUGH, LISTEN and LAUGH, LISTEN and LAUGH.

A grand staircase made of polished silver and twined with jasmine vines suddenly appeared between the two desolate cubicles.

"Ascension!" called Kamadeva. "Finally."

They climbed the grand staircase and entered an executive's gigantic corner office. Rosy light filled the room. A hanging garden formed the ceiling, and lush flowering vines crawled down the walls. A pair of smoked glass doors appeared on the right wall, dark shapes shifting eerily behind them.

"All aquariums in the United States have access points to the underwater realms of the Otherworld," explained Kamadeva. "The larger aquariums lead to major destinations."

"Like local airports versus international ones?" asked Mini.

"Precisely," said Kamadeva. "The one you'll be taking has portals to many different underwater realms. Just *be sure to take the door on the left*. Do you understand?"

"Door on the left," repeated Aru.

"Right," said Brynne.

Aiden groaned. "No, *left!*"

"Right, I know that!" said Aru.

"Stop saying *right!*" said Aiden.

"Stay focused. The Heartless may be after you as we speak," said Kamadeva. "If you truly need help, there is one person whose assistance you should seek. But I warn you now . . . you'll have to be *very* polite to him."

Kamadeva handed Aru a business card. It read:

S. DURVASA

DO NOT BOTHER ME WITH INFANTILE CONCERNS

I WILL CURSE YOU FOR WASTING MY TIME

He sounds like my guidance counselor, thought Aru. She wanted to ask who, exactly, S. Durvasa was, but Kamadeva beckoned them to the glass doors.

"You must hurry," said Kamadeva. "You only have nine mortal days left. Find my bow and arrow, and I will grant you each a boon. Something fitted to *each* of your needs." As he said this, his gaze moved to Brynne, Mini, and, last, Aru again. She could hear his voice in her thoughts: *I've seen your terrors, Aru Shah. I've seen your guilt, your battle with your very soul. . . . I can help.* Aru thought of the unending nightmares of the Sleeper and shame coiled inside her.

Next, Kamadeva turned to Aiden and said aloud:

"As for you, Aiden Acharya. I will give you that which you desire most. Though I no longer use my arrow, I do have plenty of its milder brethren in supply, and I shall gift you a single one to use at your discretion."

Brynne reached out and squeezed Aiden's shoulder. Aru wasn't sure what to make of that. Aiden wanted a love arrow? It's not like he needed the help. . . . At school, tons of girls had crushes on him. Aru rolled her eyes, even as she remembered that the first time he'd smiled at her, she'd felt like she'd been hit by a truck.

Kamadeva opened the doors on the right wall. A burst of cold, wintry air blew through Aru's hoodie and she shivered. So long, pretty springtime. Hello, cold and misery and despaiiiir. She stepped over the threshold and into the blinding light. Kamadeva hadn't said which aquarium airport he'd chosen, but it sure didn't feel like the Maui Ocean Center. Rats.

Kamadeva waved. "Farewell, Pandavas!"

"I'm not a Pandava!" called Aiden as he stepped through.

But Kamadeva only smiled. "I know what I said."

Once they crossed, they found themselves on a sidewalk, facing an empty road. Aru blinked against the cold sunlight and pulled her hoodie tighter. Across from them was an aquarium where a fish tail attached to a giant *G* glowed bright blue. The Georgia Aquarium on Baker Street! She'd come here just last month on a school field trip. For half an hour she'd tried speaking whale to the resident beluga, and she could've *sworn* she'd heard a voice say *My God, that's an appalling accent!* But it was probably just her imagination.

Today the aquarium was entirely empty, which was bizarre.

It was almost always bustling with tourists. A cold wind swept a sheaf of white papers across the ground.

Mini picked up one of the flyers and read it. Her face paled. "There're more people missing...."

"More people turning Heartless, you mean," said Brynne. "That's what the headlines in the Soul Exchange said, too."

Aru grabbed a flyer. In bold black letters it said:

HAVE YOU SEEN THIS PERSON?

There were offers of rewards, and also some weird details that Aru honestly did not need to know. One description read, *Charles is easily recognizable, because he only wears boxers that have rubber duckies on them.* Another said, *Thomas looks a bit like an organic egg. Bald. Brown. Speckled.*

"Poor Thomas," said Aru.

Aiden pulled out his phone. "Check it out," he said, holding up the screen. "It's the first time in a while I've had any bars."

The girls leaned in and saw a text-message warning:

ALL CITIZENS ARE ADVISED TO STAY INDOORS.
ANY SUSPICIOUS ACTIVITY CAN BE REPORTED
TO THE FOLLOWING NUMBER...

"We should move inside as fast as we can," said Aiden.

Across from him, Mini—and even Brynne—looked thoroughly creeped out.

"It's okay," said Aru, even though that was far from how she felt. "There's no one here."

On her wrist, there was a surge of heat from Vajra.

"I think you spoke too soon, Shah," said Brynne.

When Aru looked up from the flyer, she nearly stopped

breathing. What had been an empty street before was now filled with Heartless. There were at least fifteen stalking toward them, each with a blank, slack-jawed expression.

Aru heard a *click* as Aiden snapped a photo.

"This is *so* not the time for that!" she said.

But Aiden ignored her. He seemed to be focusing on something she couldn't see.

"We're blocked off!" said Mini, pointing at the entrance to the aquarium.

Kamadeva's instructions had been clear: *Take the door on the left.* But they couldn't get to it. A line of Heartless stood there, as if they knew that was where the Pandavas and Aiden were headed.

One Heartless stalked closer. He was wearing an Apple store shirt that said HI! I'M A GENIUS. HOW CAN I HELP? In one sharp move, Aiden hit the pavement with his scimitar. The Heartless hissed and reared back.

"What happened to your aim?" demanded Brynne.

"I did it on purpose," said Aiden. "If I hit one with a sword and he doesn't get hurt, they'll all just attack."

"Oh right. We can't use our weapons against them," said Brynne grimly. She raised her fists in a fighter's stance. "So be it."

"Hold up, Rocky," said Aru. "We have to get to the door on the left. But we can't let them see where we're going...."

Mini brandished Dee Dee and a shield flickered around them, but the Heartless didn't stop. They groaned and shuffled closer.

"We can't fight them," said Aru. "We have to do something different."

"Like hide?" asked Mini.

"Don't be such a baby," Brynne scoffed.

That made Mini stand up straighter. In her daughter of the god of death outfit, she *looked* scary in that second.

"I'm the oldest Pandava, remember? And I meant what I said," asserted Mini. "We can still use our weapons, just not to fight. We can use them to *hide*. What if I turned my shield into a mirror?"

Aru snapped her fingers. "YES! That'll trick them!"

"Good idea," said Aiden.

Guilt flickered on Brynne's face. Aiden gave her a gentle nudge.

Brynne looked at the ground, fidgeting with one of her trophy bracelets. "Um, I can add to that?"

Mini nodded. "Good."

Mini's purple shield ballooned over the four of them. It was her best casting yet. Brynne turned her choker back into a mace and swung it over her head. A cold wind picked up. All at once, the sheets of paper covering the sidewalk lifted into the air. Brynne twirled the mace as if she were going to lasso the papers, and they spiraled like a cyclone toward the charging zombies. At the same time, Mini made a quicksilver substance pour over her shield. It made a one-way mirror they could see through but the zombies couldn't.

The Heartless stopped short.

"HNGHHHHHH?!" the Apple-Genius-Heartless zombie shouted in confusion.

It sounded a lot like *Whoa! Where'd they go?!*

Aiden snapped another photo.

"Seriously?" demanded Aru.

"The lighting is perfect!"

Slowly, the four of them shuffled across the street under the dome, the mirror illusion hiding them completely until they got to the left-side door of the Georgia Aquarium. This one looked older than the polished glass entrance on the right. It was made out of driftwood and a sea smell rolled off it. Light leaked out around the edges—a light Aru was sure no human would be able to recognize.

Brynne opened the door first, and Mini finally let down her shield.

"You saved us back there," Aiden said to Mini, grinning.

Aru elbow-bumped her, and Brynne—bright red in the face—mumbled something.

Aru wasn't sure, but it sounded like *sorry.*

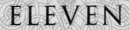

ELEVEN

Terminal C. Get It? LOL

The four of them walked quickly down a long tunnel—well, everyone except Aru.

"*Why* are you moving so slowly?" demanded Brynne. "Stop gawking!"

"Can't help it!" said Aru, awed. "We're *underwater*."

Aru gestured around her. They were walking through an invisible tube that kept them completely dry. Outside, jellyfish bobbed peacefully. A shark darted overhead. Mini, however, was not convinced by the magic. She was huddled beneath a spotted umbrella, which made her look like a traveling mushroom.

"We're also on a deadline," said Brynne. "You heard Kamadeva. *Nine* mortal days left—"

"And time moves faster in the Otherworld," Aiden pointed out in a worried tone. "We're obviously not in Atlanta anymore."

"This is as fast as I can walk, honest," said Aru. "So unless you want to carry me, then— Wait, Brynne. Why are you looking at me like that? Hey!"

Brynne lifted Aru and threw her over her shoulder like a sack of potatoes.

"Shouldn't you at least take a vote?" asked Aru.

"All in favor?" asked Brynne.

"Aye," said Aiden.

"Aye," said Mini sheepishly.

"Betrayal!" shouted Aru.

Actually, Aru found it pretty comfortable. The walk to the aquatic airport was long, and her legs were tired from all the walking through Kamadeva's endless Soul Exchange and the running from the Heartless. It wasn't *so* bad being carried. In fact, it was kinda nice....

A few minutes later, she was unceremoniously dumped on the floor.

"Hey!"

Brynne had her hands on her hips. "You fell asleep."

"Did not!"

"You started snoring."

"Oh…"

"I can't have you drooling down my back," said Brynne.

"Look!" said Mini, lifting her umbrella and pointing up ahead. "We're almost at the entrance to the aquatic airport!"

Something zoomed past them on the right: a giant eel with a transparent bubble on its back crammed with members of the Otherworld. Beyond the eel, Aru could see what looked like a runway in the distance. Large glowing fish swam in straight lines, guiding orcas and humongous sea turtles that were carrying their own passenger pods. As for the arrivals, a huge octopus detached the pods from the aquaticrafts—handling several at once—and then slotted them into hatches in the "airport." Aru wondered if the octopus ever got things mixed up.

Through the water, she could hear the dim crackle of

someone announcing, "Leviathan, you're cleared for Runway One with service to Avalon." Aru looked around, trying to choose which of the sea creatures she'd want to take them to the naga realm.

"Hopefully they're not boarding immediately," said Brynne, patting her stomach. "I'm hungry again. Aiden, got anything?"

"You ate it all," said Aiden distractedly. He was staring at his phone screen. Though there was no cell service or Wi-Fi in the Otherworld, Aiden's enchanted camera was somehow still able to transmit his digital photos to the phone.

Brynne's stomach grumbled louder.

Frowning, Aiden lifted his phone to show them a picture of a zombie. "You know what's weird?"

"The fact that you don't have any snacks?" asked Brynne grumpily.

"No. . . . All the Heartless we've seen so far are all guys," said Aiden. "Why would the arrow thief only choose men?"

"Because the thief hates the patriarchy?" suggested Aru.

Brynne raised a fist in solidarity, and Mini snorted back a laugh.

"I'm serious!" said Aiden. "It's weird."

It *was* weird, but they didn't have long to sit with Aiden's realization, because they'd pushed through the bright coral doors of the aquatic airport. Being inside was like standing inside a large, blown-glass jellyfish that protected them from the water outside. Slender, translucent tentacles disappeared into different transportation docks with the names of places that Aru had always thought were out of myth: LEMURIA, AVALON, ATLANTIS . . . NAGA REALM.

There were businesswomen typing away on glowing laptops. Men pushing strollers across the hard-packed sand floor. Naga kids dragging suitcases shaped like tiny BB-8s. Jellyfish floated in the air overhead, carrying digital readouts announcing the departures and arrivals of various transports. A sea turtle flapped lazily through the jellyfish, trailing an ad banner that said: TIRED OF WAITING IN LINE? SIGN UP FOR EXPRESS PRECHECK SERVICE! COST = JUST ONE YEAR OF YOUR LIFE!

"'Terminal C for Naga Realm,'" Mini read aloud from an information screen inside a giant open clamshell. She folded her umbrella, stuffed it in her backpack, and scanned more lines before groaning. "Oh great, there are no more departures to the naga realm after dusk."

"What do they mean, *after dusk*? That's so imprecise!" said Brynne. "The time for sunrise and sunset isn't always the same. How are we going to know when—?"

Aiden coughed and pointed up.

In the ceiling above them, a large sand dollar slowly rotated. Words were written on it in different colors. A faint line of light shot out from its middle, looking like one hand on a clock. It was close to hitting a word in purple ink: DUSK.

"Oh no, oh no, oh no!" said Mini. "We gotta run!"

Aru was staring up at the inky water beyond the ceiling, where she was 99 percent sure she'd just seen a mermaid, when Mini's words registered.

"Right, I'm ready!" she said quickly.

Aiden raised an eyebrow and Mini shook her head.

"Why are you guys looking at me like that?" Aru asked.

Brynne took a step closer.

"Not again—"

Once more, Aru found herself dangling over Brynne's shoulder. To be fair, Brynne *was* fast. Unlike Aru, she didn't stop to look around at all the airport's marvels. In a matter of seconds, they found themselves in the security line, which looked almost exactly like the one at the entrance to the Night Bazaar. All passengers had to step through a glittering archway. To the right was a crystal conveyer belt. And at the end stood a very bored-looking naga flipping the pages of the latest Dan Brown book.

"Please take out all laptops, cellular devices, cursed items, and weapons of mild devastation. Bottled constellations or enchanted bodies of water must be kept in a three-ounce container. Please note that Samsung Galaxies are now banned, as per the Otherworld Transportation Security Guidelines," droned the naga.

Aiden went first, placing his camera and satchel onto the conveyer belt. He moved through the arch without incident.

The naga man pawed through Aiden's bag and examined his wallet, pulling out a photo that had been tucked inside. "Is that...? No, it can't be!" said the security guard. "Is that *Malini*? The apsara celebrity? She hasn't been seen for ages! How do you know her?"

Aiden snatched back the photo. "That's my mom."

The guard blushed. Since he was mostly green, he didn't turn red, but bright yellow. Aru quickly looked away. *Now* she knew why Aiden had called Urvashi his aunt. Malini was a famous apsara dancer and singer, one of the elite sisters of Urvashi. Aru vaguely remembered a signed poster of her in Boo's classroom.

Next was Mini, whose purple backpack passed through easily. After her went Brynne. Aru lagged behind.... She'd never had much luck with Otherworld Transportation Security. Something *always* went wrong.

The naga picked through Brynne's stuff. "Why did you pack *salt*? You are aware that this could be construed by some species of the underwater worlds as an act of aggression?"

A family of sea slugs on the other side of the conveyer belt huddled closer together.

Brynne crossed her arms. "I always carry salt with me. I hate when food doesn't have enough salt."

When Aru looked up again, the family of sea slugs was nowhere to be seen.

Probably for the best.

"Tell the truth, asura girl," said the naga man.

Brynne turned red, and Aru remembered how Takshaka had treated her in the Council of Guardians. As if her lineage made her dangerous. Anger spiked through her, but Brynne defended herself:

"Just because I've got asura blood doesn't mean I'm lying."

"I have reason to doubt you, and that's all I require," he said with a sneer. He confiscated the salt. Next, he picked up what looked like a photo album. "And this?"

Brynne clenched her jaw. "That's personal."

The naga man leafed through it. From what Aru could see, it was just a bunch of pictures of Brynne. Brynne with her #1 medals and trophies before they'd been turned into bracelets. Aru rolled her eyes. Self-confidence was great and all, but what kind of person needed to carry around proof of their successes? It was just weird.

The security officer carelessly tossed the album back to Brynne. Then he turned to Aru. "Your turn."

Okay, you got this, Shah.

She felt a zing of reassuring warmth from Vajra, which was now in Ping-Pong-ball form in her pocket. Aru placed her backpack onto the conveyer belt and put Vajra into a separate bin. She walked through the scanner only to meet the naga man's upheld palm.

"Miss, please wait."

"'Kay," said Aru.

One minute passed...then two....

She could spot the others well ahead of her. Mini was purchasing tickets near a vast glowing pod. Passengers were lined up to enter. First they had to give a sea-glass ticket to a naga lady in a green uniform. She would scan the chips over a coral tube and then, one by one, the travelers would walk in and find their seats.

Brynne had finished repacking her stuff and was now at a kiosk ordering food. Aiden was talking to the owner of a stall marked MESSAGE DELIVERY SERVICE, and pointing to a bouquet of flowers. Wow, he was really going through a lot of trouble for someone, thought Aru. First he secretly wanted a love arrow from Kamadeva, and now he was sending *flowers?*

Aru felt the slightest twinge of envy. It wasn't that she wanted to be the girl on the receiving end of Aiden's flowers—or, heaven forbid, the god of love's arrow.... She just wished she could inspire that kind of attention.

Her mom certainly did. Over the years, Aru had had to sign for lots of deliveries of elaborate bouquets from different men who were smitten with her beautiful, brilliant archaeologist mom. Usually her mother tossed the flowers straight in the trash, and that's where they stayed...except on Valentine's Day. Every February fourteenth, Aru would fish a bouquet out of the trash and bring it to school (never mind if the blooms were slightly crushed and had a bit of eggshell on them) and tell everyone that they'd been delivered to her house (which, technically, was not a lie).

Oh well, thought Aru. *At least I have Vajra.*

The naga security guard coughed. "Your lightning bolt keeps transforming and I cannot properly scan it."

Aru sighed. Sometimes Vajra got skittish. It would change from Ping-Pong ball to sword to rope and whatever else, refusing to settle down.

"Sorry…"

The scanner whirred impatiently. Aru started to panic. The last thing she wanted was to have to demonstrate Vajra's full capacity, which was something a security rakshasa had required on her last quest. It had taken *literally* a thousand years.

Or at least twenty minutes.

Whatever.

They didn't have twenty minutes to spare. Already, the ray of light on the sand-dollar clock was about to hit DUSK, and the pod to the naga realm was losing its glow. The green-uniformed passenger-service agent tapped her serpent tail impatiently. From the ticket kiosk, Mini mouthed to Aru, *HURRY UP!*

Time to turn on the charm, Shah.

"I keep thinking I'll see Luca Brasi here," she joked to the security guard.

"Who?"

"You know, from *The Godfather*? 'Luca Brasi sleeps with the fishes'? It's, like, a famous quote about this guy who—"

"Miss, if you know of any Luca Brasi who is trying to find lodging with fishes and has been reported missing, it is your civic duty to notify the authorities per Otherworld Transportation Security Guidelines—"

"Oh my god, it's a *joke*!"

"Jokes are prohibited in the security area," said the naga man. "Also, sleeping among fishes is no laughing matter. They *never* blink! Do you know how disturbing that is?"

At that moment, the crystal scanner beeped. Vajra popped out on the other side looking, Aru imagined, rather grumpy for a ball of light. When Aru reached for it, it zinged her with a tiny bolt of electricity.

"You may go," said the naga man sourly.

"Thank you. Bye!"

Aru raced over to Mini, who was waiting for them at the gate. Aiden strolled over with a bag full of candy he had bought.

"For emergencies only," he said, catching Aru's greedy eyes. "Sorry that took a while. Had to send something to my mom in case she got worried."

Oh... thought Aru, feeling a bit silly. So that's who the flowers were for.

"Where's Brynne?" Mini asked. "The pod is going to leave soon!"

"I thought she was getting something to eat?" said Aiden.

Over at the food kiosk, they saw a bull-headed rakshasa nervously pacing and wiping his hands on his apron, but they didn't spot Brynne at first. The three of them crept closer. Behind the counter, wearing an apron and laboring over a fire, was Brynne. She held out a spoon to the rakshasa, who took it gingerly, and sipped.

"THAT," Brynne yelled, "IS FOOD! Notice how it satisfies the five basic tastes? Sweet! Sour! Bitter! Salty! Umami!"

Aru's eyebrows soared up. *Whose mommy? What?*

"I *will* come back," said Brynne menacingly. She tore off her apron and threw it on the floor. "And I *hope* you've learned to cook by then."

"Yes, m-ma'am. Sorry, m-ma'am," stammered the rakshasa, clutching the spoon for dear life.

Brynne stomped toward them, still glaring and mumbling, "If I want something good, I always have to make it my*self*...."

Mini and Aru tried to meet her halfway, but Aiden held them back.

"Some advice for the future," he whispered. "Do *not* get in the way of Brynne and food."

The four of them just barely reached the pod before its door closed. They were the only non-naga passengers aboard, which made Aru feel self-conscious. She took a seat on a plushy pink anemone and pretended to read a *Divine People* magazine while she snuck peeks out the window.

The pod was spat out of the dock and into the ocean, only to be snagged by an octopus tentacle that attached the bubble to the top of a humpback whale. Aru—though thrilled—was half-terrified that she'd go catapulting out the pod from all the turbulence. Mini examined the translucent walls like she feared they were going to spring a leak any minute. Aiden snapped pictures—though they were going so fast, Aru thought they'd all come out blurry. Brynne concentrated on eating.

After a short flight (swim?), they docked and de-whaled in a vast but dark indoor terminal that reminded Aru of an art deco train station. The walls were covered with overlapping jewels that looked like serpent scales. Living, hissing cobras with tongues of flame cast the only light. At the end of the hall, their glimmers turned wavy, like moonlight hitting the sides of a sea cave.

There were two exit tunnels. Above the one on the right, a sign read BAGGAGE AND SCALES CLAIM. The sign above the left tunnel said: CUSTOMS FOR NON-NAGA RESIDENTS.

"That's us," said Aiden, heading to the CUSTOMS sign.

"Kamadeva didn't say anything about having to go through customs," said Mini. "Do you think that's safe?"

"Too late to worry about that now," said Brynne. "The last whale just departed."

Aru had been to the Otherworld plenty of times by now. She was used to the sensation of being surrounded by magic. But the feeling here...this was different. Her skin prickled. Sea mist surrounded her and left her thoughts sticky with fear. Even Aiden, who was always documenting the world around him, hadn't raised his camera.

Aru glanced down and quickly wished she hadn't. Flat black tiles cut into the shapes of snakes formed the floor. In the dim, flickering light, they kinda looked...*alive.*

At the customs checkpoint a tired-looking nagini official sat inside a glass booth.

"Identify yourselves," she intoned, bored.

Mini blanched.

"I'm sure it'll be fine," Aiden said, nodding encouragingly to her. "Just go with the flow."

The four of them held up their celestial weapons.

"We are the Pandavas," said Brynne, lifting her chin.

"But not me," said Aiden quickly.

The customs officer scowled at them. "No Pandavas,

including their associates, are welcome in Naga-Loka, the illustrious"—the naga said it like *illustriousss*—"capital of the naga kingdom, by the order of Queen Uloopi."

"But we're trying to *help* Queen Uloopi," protested Aru. "She's the one who sent us on this trip to find the bow and arrow, and—"

"Ah. *You* must be the daughter of the Lord of the Heavens," said the officer. "Lord Takshaka, guardian of the treasure room, left special instructions for you."

Aru remembered the scornful naga man who had sat next to Queen Uloopi high above the clouds. What was that guy's *problem*?

Just then, the floor opened beneath Aru, plunging her into frigid pitch-black water. Vajra immediately changed from a bolt to a bracelet, leaving her hands free. Her head came back up to the surface quickly, but as she tried to keep herself afloat, she accidentally swallowed a mouthful of the seawater and started coughing.

"ARU!" screamed Mini and Brynne.

Aiden scrambled forward, trying to grab her hand, but the nagini officer's tail whipped out and sent her friend flying backward. As Mini bonked the guard with Dee Dee, Brynne extended her mace to Aru. She tried to grasp it, but her fingers kept slipping. Finally, she got a hold....

But apparently she wasn't alone in the water.

A cold tendril wrapped around her ankle and dragged her under.

TWELVE

Aru Shah Is a Piece of Sushi

Cold, dark water closed over Aru's head, pulling her deep into the ocean until she lost all sense of direction. She started to panic. Were there sharks in this water? Because they terrified her. Aru kicked out, shaking off the tendril that had grabbed her, and swam forward.

Light, she commanded.

Vajra, in bracelet form, sent out a beam. Aru had that painful, tight feeling in her chest that only comes from holding one's breath for far too long. Any second now, she'd run out of air. She looked up, but even with Vajra's light, she could no longer see the surface. She was far beneath the waves. She'd probably drown here....

Something zipped past her—something that felt pointy and sharp. Aru gasped.

And then...she gasped again. Which, technically, she shouldn't be able to do unless...

Cautiously, Aru inhaled. No cold water rushed into her nose and mouth. Air filled her lungs. She could *breathe*. She could breathe underwater! COOL! Wait, since when had she been able to do that?

By now, her eyes had adjusted to her surroundings. As she swam over the seabed, phosphorescent seashells lit it up like a motion-activated sidewalk. Shadows carved out a sunken, ruined city. Aru dove down to investigate, and when she reached the bottom, she discovered that she could stand and walk upright. She could even hear everything around her as if she were on land. Being under the ocean sounded like there was a never-ending thunderstorm in the distance. Seaweed-choked statues of nagas stuck up out of the sandy bottom. Fish darted in and out among them, flashing iridescently.

Aru looked up at the surface again, but it was far out of sight. If Brynne, Aiden, or Mini had fallen in here, too, she couldn't see them. She also didn't know if they could breathe underwater, like her.

Aru took a moment to process this. She could *breathe underwater*. Think of all the pranks she could pull! She could strap on a dorsal fin, pretend to be a shark, and clear the beach to have it all to herself.

But that depended, of course, on her getting out of here.

Takshaka didn't like her—that was made obvious when Aru was dropped through a trapdoor. *Rude.* But that wasn't going to stop her from getting to the treasury and finding the thief's soul song.

How was she going to get there, though? It wasn't like she could ask someone for directions. She might as well find a coconut, name him Wilson, and grow a beard.

A blue fish swam past her.

"Got any coconuts?" she asked wearily.

The usual answer from a fish would have been: *bubble* *gape* *bubble* *disappear*

But this fish said, "I believe there's some Indonesian kopyor dwarf coconuts being sold in the upstream naga market. Or, if you're interested in the Philippine variety, a ship has just sunk southeast of here."

Aru screamed.

The fish looked highly affronted. "If you don't want the answer, then don't ask! *You're* the one asking about coconuts in the off-season!" it huffed. "Foolish girl!"

Aru glared. "Well, *you* swim in your own toilet!"

The fish did not have an eyebrow to raise villainously. But its tone managed the effect well enough. "And you'll never know *when* I use the ocean as a toilet. Enjoy the mystery."

It flapped its tail and swam off.

Why was everything so rude?

And why did the fish have a British accent?

One thing at a time, Shah. So far, she had discovered that she could breathe underwater, walk underwater, talk underwater, and also argue with a fish. She wondered if anything else could understand her down here.

Aru tapped into the mind link she shared with Mini, but only static ran through her thoughts. She hoped her friends were okay. Maybe they were still stuck in customs.

She turned Vajra full-size and held it tightly. *Dad?*

The lightning bolt glowed.

Encouraged, Aru asked, *Could I get some help? I'm not popular with snakes—surprise. Also, I can talk to fish? Is that normal?*

Up ahead, something emerged from the sand. Naga statues

fell left and right as a huge, speckled eel lifted off the ground. The words SEA LINE were written across its dorsal fin. The eel opened its mouth, and passengers—fish, people, fish-people, and... Was that Tilda Swinton?— streamed out of its jaws. The human passengers wore clear bubble helmets. Most of the nagas were wearing headphones and had canvas bags slung over their shoulders. Only now did Aru notice that there were little trails stretching across the ocean floor. In the distance, she could see the colorful lights of what might have been a naga market.

So this was an underwater subway stop?

Was this a subtle sign from Takshaka to get the heck outta here, or had he hoped she'd just drown? Aru didn't want to think too deeply about that....

The eel coughed up some sand and then said in a monotonous voice, "Next stop, the Will of the Sea. All who enter waive their right to submit a complaint, per Otherworld Transportation Security Guidelines. You hereby acknowledge that if you end up in the mouth of a larger sea creature, or if I get hungry, or if you are lost to the Bermuda Triangle, you brought it upon yourself and that's that."

Vajra glowed brighter.

"You're kidding," said Aru. "Dad, you really want me to board *that*?"

While riding on a whale had been fun, riding *inside* a sea monster didn't seem that great. That thing had *teeth*, and lots of 'em!

Vajra continued to glow.

Aru crossed her arms. "*N. O.* I am *not* going in there. I'm not interested in becoming monster snack."

Vajra turned back into a bracelet.

Aru relaxed. "See? You agree with—"

A long, thin tail stretched out from the bracelet.

"Uh, what're you doing?"

The tail stretched out farther, growing thicker, winding its way to the eel.

"Vajra, why do you look like a rope?"

Vajra *yanked*, and Aru zoomed through the water like a piece of bait on a fishing line.

"BETRAYAL!" she hollered.

Vajra whipped Aru into the eel's mouth and then changed back into a Ping-Pong ball, retracting its tail and sliding into Aru's pocket. She felt like she was on an invisible Slide of Death. Down, down, down she went into the belly of the beast. It was empty except for benches on either side covered with moldy upholstery. A rank subway scent wafted from them as she took a seat, and Aru wrinkled her nose. Elevator music boomed from the eel's sharp teeth, still visible even from far away:

Tall and tan and young and lovelyyyyy, the girl from Ipanema goes walking and—

A belt of seaweed wound across her lap. Aru tried to wrestle herself out of it, but the belt just got tighter.

"All passengers must wear some manner of protection, per Otherworld Transportation Security Guidelines," said the eel. "The presence of a seat belt may not, however, prevent some passengers on the Will of the Sea route from being digested."

Hysterical laughter bubbled through Aru. She plucked at the seaweed belt. "I'm sushi."

The eel snapped its jaws shut, plunging her into darkness. It surged forward, causing a *whoosh* to hit Aru's stomach. She took the Vajra ball back out for some light, but all it did was make the eel's pointy teeth glow at the front of the train.

"Where's it going?" muttered Aru under her breath.

Once more she attempted to reach Mini and Brynne telepathically, but only static filled her head.

She tried to ignore the panicked racing of her heart, but it was impossible. Where were they? Did they think she had drowned? Had they just accepted her death as Uloopi's judgment and continued on the quest? Or maybe they were planning to retrieve the bow and arrow before trying to rescue her. And then what? If the others returned the weapon without her, would she be the only Pandava cast out of the Otherworld?

The eel stopped. The seaweed seat belt retracted. Aru held her breath. This was it—either digestion or destination.

THIRTEEN

I Mean, Technically,
We're Family....

Thankfully, the jaws opened.

"Arrival," said the eel. "The Palace of Varuna.
Please exit to your left and mind the gap in my teeth."

Varuna?

Varuna was the god of the waters, and he was known for
being as fickle as the sea itself. In all the paintings of him Aru
had seen, he rode a gigantic *makara*, a creature that looked like a
crocodile-lion. The last time she'd met a makara, it had asked
if she was a rodent. At least it hadn't taken a bite to find out
for itself....

Aru stepped carefully along the slippery ridges of the eel's
gums, trying to avoid getting impaled on its rows of needle-
sharp teeth. A couple of moments later, she jumped out of the
creature's jaws and onto a rocky pedestal. Just when she was
beginning to wonder where she was supposed to go next, a
current caught her and pulled her through the ocean until she
was dropped onto a pathway made of polished mother-of-pearl.

"Whoa," breathed Aru, when she looked up.

The word *palace* didn't even begin to cover it. It was the most beautiful (in a slightly bizarre way) place Aru had ever seen. On the one hand, it looked a bit traditional. The path wound through a sea garden of blooming anemone, stately coral columns, and topiaries of kelp in neat, organized plots. But there was other stuff tucked in among the domed spirals. One section of Varuna's palace was hauled-together parts of shipwrecks. A neon Jimmy Buffett MARGARITAVILLE sign beamed above a spire. The front steps were patterned with spare change that had fallen to the bottom of the sea. At the open entrance stood a huge blue lotus flower, its petals waving gently in the water. Each petal bore the name of a different ocean: ATLANTIC, PACIFIC, INDIAN, and ARCTIC, and also one Aru hadn't expected to see: THE OCEAN OF MILK.

Its Sanskrit name appeared beneath it: KṢĪRA SĀGARA.

When Aru first heard about the Ocean of Milk, her initial thought had been: *That must have taken a lot of cows.* Her mother had told her the story all the time when she was little. After being cursed by an angry sage, the gods began to grow weak. The only thing that would cure them was *amrita*, the elixir of immortality, which was hidden somewhere deep in the cosmic Ocean of Milk. In order to find it, the gods would have to stir up the entire ocean. They couldn't accomplish this task alone, so they turned to the asuras—semidivine beings who were sometimes good and sometimes straight-up demonic—for help. The gods promised the asuras that they would be rewarded with some of the nectar. In the end, though, the gods tricked the asuras and drank all the amrita themselves.

Some asuras had been waging war with them ever since.

Unfortunately, those resentful asuras cast a shadow on all the others, which Aru thought was ridiculous. You can't look at a part and judge the whole. No wonder Brynne acted so defensive all the time.

Aru's favorite detail about the Ocean of Milk story was all the stuff that came out of the waters when it got churned. Like the moon! And a tree that granted wishes! The ocean even unleashed goddesses.

Goddesses like the one who suddenly materialized in the middle of the entrance and glared ferociously at Aru.

Aru almost squeaked. "Uh...hi?"

The goddess towered over Aru. At first, her skin was a deep garnet color. But when she took another step toward Aru, it changed. Now it was...*sparkling.* And golden. It reminded Aru of champagne. Which was disgusting. The one time she'd sneaked a sip from her mom's New Year's Eve glass, it had tasted like rotten soda. However, it *was* pretty.

The goddess's black hair swept the floor and looked like the ocean at night—the waves rippled, and every now and then Aru saw miniature glittering fish dart through her dark ringlets. Aru thought back to the paintings she had seen in her mother's collection.... If she was in the Palace of Varuna, the god of the sea, then that meant this goddess was his wife, Varuni. The goddess of wine.

Varuni crossed two of her arms, but she had two others. Her third hand held a blue lotus flower. In her fourth hand, she gently swirled a glass of red wine.

Must be enchanted red wine, thought Aru, because it completely defied physics that the liquid should stay in its glass underwater.

"Mortals are not allowed here," said Varuni.

"I—"

At that second, Vajra began to glow brightly in Aru's hand.

Varuni's eyes zipped straight to it, lingering for just a moment before her gaze snapped back to Aru's face. "Oh, I see. Very well then," the goddess said. "Come with me."

Pretty much every instinct in Aru was screaming *Don't do it!* But when a goddess gives a direct command, there's no way to say no. They walked (well, Aru walked, Varuni glided) past the open entrance and into the glittering caverns of the Palace of Varuna. The whole time Varuni didn't say a word.

"You have a beautiful home?" Aru attempted, padding after her. It was weird not swimming underwater, but whenever she tried to paddle instead of walk, she tripped. Magic could be very annoying.

"I know," said Varuni, with a flick of her wrist.

The wine goblet in her hand changed to a tall glass of iced liquid with a sprig of mint sticking out of the top.

Varuni led her into a vast atrium. Chandeliers of jellyfish and moonstone floated above. A giant crocodile was curled up in a corner on a rug inscribed with the words DADDY'S LITTLE GIRL. When it saw Varuni, its tail thumped happily. In the middle of the room was a large velveteen lotus flower that looked a lot like an armchair. Aru couldn't see anyone in it, but from the other side came a loud yell.

Aru went still. Vajra lengthened into a sword, but Varuni continued on, unfazed. She stopped at the large lotus, two of her hands on her hips.

"*Jaani*, we have company."

Jaani was like saying *dear* or *honey*. Mini's parents called each other that all the time…which meant that Varuni was talking to her husband, the god of the sea. Humbly, Vajra folded back into a demure Ping-Pong ball. Varuna yelled something incomprehensible again, and Aru braced herself. He *had* to be yelling about her. Was he furious that a mortal was inside their palace? And she hadn't even brought a host gift! She should've grabbed a coconut, at least....

"THE MATCH REFEREE IS NOT DOING HIS JOB!" shouted Varuna.

"It can wait!" said Varuni. "Our guest is far more important!"

"But the *game* is on, jaani," wheedled the man. "I'm watching Virat Kohli...."

Kohli? The cricket player? Aru only knew that name because Boo was a huge fan of the game.

With an irritated sigh, Varuni spun the lotus chair around, and Aru got her first glance at the god of the waters. He looked just as shocked as Aru felt. Varuna's skin was the color of cut sapphires. His four hands waved around him. In one hand he held an iPad, where a cricket match was playing on the screen. In another he had a conch shell. A noose dangled from his third hand. And in his fourth hand was a bottle of Thums Up, a soda from India. Her mom loved it, but Aru thought it was too sweet. Besides, it always struck Aru as deeply weird, because the logo was a bright red thumb and yet the name wasn't spelled right.

Varuna dropped his iPad and gestured toward Aru. "Are you seeing what I'm seeing?" he asked his wife.

"Obviously," she said, rolling her eyes.

"Well, sometimes I'm not sure," said Varuna, with a pointed glance at her drink.

"I'm Aru Shah?" said Aru, hating that her voice went up at the end. It wasn't like she didn't know who she was, but she felt cowed by the presence of the ancient gods.

"A Pandava, to be exact," said Varuni.

"But why is she here?"

Aru was getting a little tired of being referred to as if she wasn't in the room. "Honestly, it's a bit of a misunderstanding," she said. "I was trying to get to the naga treasury with my friends, the other Pandavas. Well, except Aiden isn't one—that's another story. Anyway, I'm looking for the bow and arrow of Kamadeva and—"

Varuni interrupted her by taking a loud slurp from a large wide-brimmed goblet that had a tiny umbrella in it.

Varuna groaned, his chin dropping in his palm. "Must you make that *sound*?"

"Yes, I must," said his wife primly. When she looked up at Aru, her eyes were glowing. In a very different, more solemn voice she said, "I *see*."

Just then, Aru remembered that Varuni wasn't just the goddess of wine.... She was also the goddess of transcendent wisdom.

"What is it? What do you see?" demanded Varuna. He sat up straight, dropping everything else he was holding. "I want to know, too! Wives shouldn't keep secrets from their husbands."

"Husbands shouldn't keep conch shells on the floor where wives can trip on them."

"And maybe wives shouldn't drink and walk at the same time!"

"Ha! *You* try being around you for a couple millennia and see if *you* don't do the same!"

"What's that supposed to mean—?"

"Uh, is this a bad time?" asked Aru.

"Time has no inclination toward evil or good," Varuni announced.

"Here she goes..." muttered Varuna, massaging his temples with all four hands.

"I see what you don't see," said Varuni. Her speech slurred just a tad as she waved her glass and pronounced:

"The girl with eyes like a fish and a heart snapped in two
will be met in battle by a girl named Aru.
But take care what you do with a heart so broken,
for uglier truths will soon be spoken.
You, daughter of Indra, have a tongue like a whip,
but be wary of those to whom you serve lip,
for there is a tale beyond that soon you shall see—"

"But all that depends on your surviving the sea," Varuna finished with a grin.

Varuni blinked, and then frowned. "You rhymed *sea* with *see?*"

"What's wrong with that?" demanded Varuna.

"It's lazy," said his wife.

"Homonyms are not lazy. They are *subtle.*"

"Subtly lazy."

"*You*—"

"Excuse me," said Aru, "but I *have* to get to the naga treasury. I need to find someone's soul song. And, um, my dad sent me here, so I was thinking, you know, because we're like family and all—"

The Lord of the Waters laughed. "Do you think I care? No offense, of course. But not even the great king Rama—"

"'—who was Lord Vishnu himself and had been reborn in the form of a mortal man, could control me, for I am the great and tempestuous sea, and none can rein in my power,'" recited Varuni in a bored voice. "We know, dear."

Varuna sulked for a minute, and then shook it off. "It is curious, Pandava, that you do not even know what it is you seek. It is the soul song of the thief, yes? And then you must speak the thief's name to discover the location of the stolen bow and arrow.... But how will you find out the name?"

Aru's spine tingled. She hated that the god was right. Part of her had hoped the thief's name would be written on the back of the soul song, like a tag, but something told her that wasn't going to be the case.

"If you know that much," Aru said, "then do you also know who took the bow and arrow? Could you tell me?"

Varuni inspected the nails of three of her hands. Her drinking vessel had changed to an iced copper mug. "The sea gives—"

"And takes," chimed in Varuna.

"It is generous—"

"But not prone to charity."

Which was fancy godspeak for *NOPE. YOU'RE ON YOUR OWN.*

"But we can grant you straight passage to the treasury," said Varuna. "It is a secret route, and none shall discover you. All you have to do is satisfy the whims of my guard pet."

Aru snuck a glance at the crocodile now napping in the corner. It had flipped onto its back, its stumpy legs twitching like a dog having a dream.

"It's very hungry," said Varuni. "So you only have to fill its belly."

Aru did not trust the gods. She lifted her chin. "You *can* get me to the naga treasury, or you *will*?"

Varuni laughed. "I like you, daughter of Indra," she said.

"I *will* help you, child," said the Lord of the Waters. He

clapped his hands and a small blue crab scuttled into the hall. "The illustrious Pandava girl has agreed to fill the beast's belly," Varuna said. "Show her the way."

The crab bowed to the gods and waved one pincer to Aru, motioning her to follow.

Aru waited for a moment. Varuna and Varuni hadn't exactly been kind, and she might not like them very much...

But that didn't mean she didn't respect them.

If Boo were here, he would've pecked her ears for not showing respect sooner.

At least I eventually remembered, she thought, as she walked forward.

Aru bowed her head and performed *pranama* by touching the feet of the two gods. She felt Varuna's and Varuni's hands at her shoulders, drawing her up. Varuni's glass had changed to a flute of sparkling champagne.

"See well, daughter of the heavens," said Varuni.

For his part, Varuna said nothing, as he was once again absorbed in the cricket game.

FOURTEEN

Heeeere, Monstrous Kitty!

The blue crab shuffled down a hallway lit by massive anglerfish that swam alongside them. Aru tried not to stare at their gaping jaws and long rows of sharp teeth. From their scaly brown foreheads swung tiny pendulums of light. Aru realized she had *zero* idea about what she had just agreed to do. Was she supposed to find something for the gods' makara to eat?

Maybe Varuna had been talking about a different pet. Aru crossed her fingers and hoped it was a dolphin. Or maybe a non-stinging jellyfish. Or, better yet, a seahorse.

Aru was so busy thinking about what kind of pets Varuna might keep that she nearly stepped on the blue crab.

"HEY!" it shouted. "WATCH IT!"

"You can talk?" she asked, startled.

"No," said the crab bitterly. "This is all in your head. Of *course* I can talk."

"Sorry," she mumbled. "Still getting used to this whole talking-to-underwater-animals thing."

"Hmpf."

"So . . . can you sing, too?"

The crab went utterly still. "Why. Does. Everyone. Ask. Me. That?" It turned around and snapped its pincers sharply. "Did you also expect me to be bright red and have a Jamaican accent? Because if so, I am *not* sorry to disappoint! Just because my brother went Hollywood doesn't mean that *I* sing and dance, too!" The crab scuttled ahead, muttering something that sounded a lot like *Mother wouldn't understand.*

Talk about crabby, thought Aru. Her second thought was *Ha! No pun intended.* Her third thought was *I am talking to myself again. I should stop.*

"You should never seek help from the Lord of the Waters," said the crab darkly. "He is fickle and unpredictable, just like the ocean. The sea has a temper. Also, it keeps things it likes. Bright baubles that catch its eye. Pretty girls and boys who look at their reflection in the water for too long . . . never realizing that the water is looking back."

Aru shivered.

"The sea is hungry today." The crab's voice sounded intentionally dramatic, and Aru imagined it holding a flashlight up to its face, like one of her classmates at a sleepover.

Too bad the sea isn't hungry for blue crab bisque, thought Aru.

The crab seemed to glare at her, its two stemlike eyes narrowing, and she wondered whether it could read thoughts, too.

"So, what exactly is this pet, and what am I supposed to feed it?"

"You'll see."

Aru followed the crab down a darker, narrower passageway. There were no fish lanterns here. The only light came from naturally phosphorescent shells that had been set into the walls.

They passed several wooden doors locked with menacing iron bolts until they stopped at the last one. The crab tapped it with a pincer, and it swung open. Inside, the room was massive. It was hard to see much in the dark space, but it looked like an arena of sorts. Smooth black sand covered the floor and a net stretched along the sides of the room, as if to keep back spectators. It took her a moment to realize that she was no longer walking underwater. The room was some kind of magical air pocket.

But she didn't see any pet. Was she supposed to call it? How *did* one summon a celestial pet? *Heeeere, monstrous kitty!* Aru stepped in, peering into the darkness . . . and a cold shadow fell over her thoughts. If she was supposed to be feeding this thing, then where was the food? Because there was no big bag of Otherworld pet kibble lying around here.

What Aru did see was a cage dangling over the middle of the arena.

And trapped inside were Mini, Brynne, and Aiden.

Brynne was the first to see her. "Aru!"

Aru's heart nearly burst with relief. "You're here! Did you come to save me?"

"What'd you say?" shouted Aiden. "Do I like gravy?"

"No!" said Mini. "She said, 'Do you guys blame me?'"

"She said 'Did you come to save me?'" grumbled Brynne, loud enough that Aru could hear.

"Oh! Well, we were *about* to," said Mini. "But a naga guard threw us all into a pod and transported us here."

"In other words, we got trapped," said Brynne, crossing her arms.

Aru turned to the little blue crab, which had been oddly silent the whole time. A horrible feeling snuck through her.

"Why are my friends in a trap?" she asked. "And where, exactly, is the food I'm supposed to feed the pet creature?"

The crab didn't smile, probably because it couldn't. But it did do a weird happy scuttle, like it was saying *Gotcha!* "You already know the answer to that, Pandava girl."

Aru began to slowly spin around the chamber. "What about the creature?"

A shadow grew over her then, and a louder *click, click* sound filled the air. The hairs on the back of her neck prickled all at once, and Aru turned to look behind her. The blue crab was beginning to grow bigger and bigger.... Now it was three times the size of Aru. It crouched and said:

"That would be me."

FIFTEEN

No, I Can't Sing. Leave Me Alone

The crab stepped forward. "There's no one to rescue you, little Pandava."

From out of the corner of her eye, Aru saw Aiden picking the lock on the cage with one of his scimitars. Mini was using Dee Dee as a flashlight to help him. The cage door swung open silently, the sound redirected with a wave of Brynne's mace.

As silent as shadows, Brynne, Aiden, and Mini dropped to the ground.

Aru grinned. "I wouldn't be too sure of that."

With a great roar, Brynne rushed at the gigantic crab. The crab reared up, swinging one of its pincers, and Brynne went flying against the wall. She slid down, shook her head, and then got back to her feet. She twirled her mace, probably trying to make her trademark wind cyclone . . . but instead of air, a force of bubbles surged forward, popping on the crab's shell.

The crab tittered. "That tickles!"

Brynne examined the end of her mace in confusion.

Aiden tried to flash his scimitars, but his movements

were strangely slowed, as if he were fighting a strong wind. The crab caught him around the leg, and he tripped backward. The crab stabbed the ground with a pincer, but at the last second Aiden rolled across the sand.

"Bubble power it is!" hollered Brynne, pointing her mace so that a stream of bubbles momentarily blinded the crab.

The crab stumbled, its legs nearly crushing all of them until Mini let loose a force field.

A crackling sphere surrounded the four of them. The crab batted away the last of the bubbles and then tapped at the sphere with one claw.

"Come now," it coaxed. "I'll be very quick about it. I'll eat you in one bite if you come out now. Two bites if you make this difficult."

"That's super enticing," muttered Aru.

Quickly, she told the others what had happened with Varuna and Varuni.

"You promised to 'fill its belly' without asking what you're supposed to fill it *with*?" demanded Aiden. "Nice going, Shah."

The crab had grown to the size of a submarine. All of them barely came up to the first joint in its spindly blue leg.

"Can't we just blast it with something?" whispered Brynne.

"With *what*? Everything works weird in here!" Aiden said in an equally low tone. "It's almost like we're underwater without the water."

"Besides"—Mini grunted, straining to keep up the shield— "the Otherworld will not like it if you break your promise to Varuna, Aru."

Aru eyed the crab. "So let's keep my promise. Let's fill its belly. Just not for long."

"What, like make it eat something and then spit it out?" asked Brynne. "What would even fit inside it?"

Aiden caught on to Aru's idea first. Then Mini. The three of them looked at Brynne.

"You've *got* to be joking."

The crab loomed above them. It slammed its pincer into the shield, and a crack spiderwebbed through it. Mini winced.

"Why do people always stare at me like that?" the crab roared.

For their plan to work, they needed the crab's mouth open *wide*. Wide enough that something could fly straight down its throat without it noticing. Which meant that they needed it to be talking...or shrieking.

"Ask him to sing," whispered Aru.

"What, like the crab in *Moana*?" asked Aiden loudly.

"WHO SAID *MOANA*?" thundered the crab.

The shield broke. Down came the pincer. The four of them rolled in different directions. The crab rotated, trying to catch them all at the same time. Brynne conjured another bubble storm around her. Aru threw out her lightning bolt, intending it to be a distraction. After all, her lightning bolt was a weapon of the sky, so it probably wouldn't work well in here either. But, to her surprise, a net crackling with electricity covered the crab's eyes.

"What the—?" breathed Aru.

Vajra, sensing her confusion, weakened. The crab tore the net from its eyes.

"My *brother* can sing," said the crab furiously. "But me? Oh no! I HAD TO PLAY THE CLARINET!"

It stabbed the ground angrily. As Aru dodged out of the way, she sent messages through the Pandava mind link:

Brynne, turn into a fly! Mini, we're going to need a distraction. Tell Aiden.
I don't want to go in there!

Just do it, Brynne! Mini, you've heard the crab. You know what it doesn't like. Count down. . . .

"Three!" shouted Aru.

Mini popped out of her shield and screamed, "Why don't you have a Jamaican accent?"

The crab whirled on her, pincers raised. It roared.

"I mean, you *are* under the sea, you might as well sing it!" shouted Aiden.

"Two!" called Aru.

The crab paused. And then it let out a long shriek. It sounded like someone had dropped a death metal band into a thunderstorm and thrown in a braying donkey just for the heck of it. "Is this what you wanted, Mother? Me to be taunted and tortured? Are you happy now? Yes, Jayesh is talented, but I bet he's never eaten a Pandava!"

"One!" Out of the corner of her eye, Aru saw a flash of blue light. Brynne had disappeared.

Aiden held out his scimitars and said hurriedly, "Aru, touch these with your lightning bolt—"

"You'll get electrocuted!" she said.

"Trust me," said Aiden. "Light 'em up, Shah."

Something in Aiden's voice made her believe him. She tapped both of his weapons with Vajra and electricity crackled around the metal.

"Whoa!"

"Told ya," said Aiden, running forward. He must have adjusted his pressure to account for the strange air resistance, because this time his scimitars connected with the crab.

"Hot! Ow! Too hot! Stop that!" shouted the crab. Its weird stem-like eyes waved wildly. With each stab Aiden made, the crab let out a shriek, its blue jaws gaping wide. It lifted its legs, trying to get them out of the way, but Aiden was faster.

Aru cast Vajra. Her lightning bolt soared to the right. Mini threw Dee Dee to the left. Each of the crab's eyes went a different way, which left a blind spot in the center, where a small blue bug sailed through, right into its mouth.

Aru heard Brynne in her head:

I hate you guys.

You're a heroic parasite! sent Mini.

Brynne went silent.

Brynne? called Mini. *Did I say something wrong?*

Now all that was left was a waiting game. The three of them dodged the crab, but within moments, the electricity had faded from Aiden's scimitars. It was taking Mini longer and longer to bring up new shields. Aru was getting tired.

"Enough!" shouted the crab. "Daughter of Indra, you have failed to keep your word! I—" The crab stopped and its eyes bulged out. "I—"

"What's wrong?" asked Mini. "Upset stomach?"

"Do you feel a song coming on?" asked Aiden.

The crab swayed. Aru, Mini, and Aiden braced themselves. This was supposed to be the easier part, the part when the weakened crab, with Brynne stomping around in its stomach, started to lose focus. But if anything, the opposite happened. It rushed at them with terrible force.

"WHAT DID YOU DO, PANDAVAS?"

Aru had always assumed that if something was beginning to feel pain, then that something would keel over and squirm on the ground. That's what *she* would do, anyway. But this crab was not living up to expectations.

Its claws started spinning like manic drills, and it thrust them far into the ground. Black sand flew everywhere. Mini tried to create a shield, but she wasn't fast enough. Aiden dropped his scimitars, his hands going straight to his eyes. Sandy grit sprayed Aru's face. She fumbled for the lightning bolt, but without being able to see it, she couldn't channel it properly. She might hit Mini or Aiden by accident.

Vibrations rattled through the sand, then they stopped.

"Coming to get youuuuu," sang the crab, coming closer.

The crab was right. It could not carry a tune worth its life.

"Jeez, that's awful," Aru muttered.

Aru *felt* the crab looming over her. Blearily, she saw Vajra's light pulsing. The crab stabbed its pincers into the ground again. Aru braced herself, ready to thrust up the lightning bolt....

Then the crab's stomach gurgled loudly.

"Mother?" The crab groaned. "I don't feel so good...."

Aru's vision finally cleared. She opened her eyes to see the crab's mouth widening, a blue light filling its jaws.

It took Aru less than a second to realize that she needed to get out of the way.

Unfortunately, that was still too late.

Brynne had taken the form of an elephant. She trumpeted victoriously, standing at the lip of the crab's mouth. The crab swayed and started gagging, and then something spewed out of it. That spewed-out something started to yell.

"CANNONBALL!" Brynne trumpeted.

"Wait! NO! Brynne—" Aru started.

Just before Brynne landed on Aru, she transformed back

into her human girl self. That said, her human girl self wasn't exactly light.

Aru got flattened.

And doused with crab puke.

"That can't be hygienic," said Mini.

The crab pulled its legs into its shell and moaned in pain.

Brynne got off Aru and summoned a bubble bath with her mace to clean them up. Her face shone with triumph. "How'd I do?"

Aiden and Mini rushed over, grinning.

Aru continued to lie on her back, Vajra glowing weakly beside her. "Can I borrow your spine?" she croaked. "I think I broke mine."

The others hauled her up, and the four of them faced the monstrous crab. It looked less like a monster now. The only thing that stuck out of its shell were its two eyes, slanted in fury.

"That," it said, "was *tricksy*. As soon as I have the energy, I will eat you—"

"I don't think so," said Aru. "I held up my part of the bargain."

"You did no such thing!" said the crab. "You were supposed to feed me. Am I fed? No. Am I thoroughly disgusted? Yes. Notice how those are two entirely different things."

Aru *hated* it when people spoke in rhetorical questions. Her computer science teacher did that all the time. *Is teaching you kids how to use Microsoft Excel the highlight of my day? No, it is not. And am I excited about today's "funky mushroom" lunch special? No, I am not.*

"Actually, the command from Lord Varuna and Lady Varuni was to fill your belly."

Brynne took a bow. "Consider your belly filled."

"But it didn't *stay* full . . ." protested the crab.

"The gods never specified how long your stomach was supposed to stay full. You should always read the tiny print," said Aiden. "That's what my dad says. He's a lawyer."

"Go easy on your stomach for a while," suggested Mini. "You shouldn't eat anything after you vomit up an elephant."

"Mother *will* hear about this," said the crab darkly.

It dug a hole in the sand, and disappeared into it.

An exit light blinked into existence at the other end of the arena.

"That was *sick*," said Aiden, grinning. "Literally."

Brynne strode over and raised her hand in a high five. "We did it!"

Mini squeaked out, "Gross! Elbows only!"

Her elbow-bumps with Mini and Aiden were fine, but Aru was pretty sure Brynne's damaged her funny bone.

"Ow," said Aru, rubbing her arm even as she smiled. "Easy, Brynne. We get it, you're a beast."

Brynne dropped her arm, her face stricken. "I'm a what?"

Aru looked from Mini to Aiden. Had she said something wrong? Mini looked just as confused, but Aiden's face crumpled with sympathy. Maybe *beast* meant something totally different to Brynne than it did to Aru. Too late, Aru remembered how Brynne had expected them to make fun of her after she'd turned into a swan near Kamadeva's abode.

"A *beast*," said Aru, trying for lightness. "You know, like superstrong! It's a good thing. Honest."

Brynne looked to Aiden, and he nodded in confirmation.

"Okay," said Brynne uncertainly. "Sometimes people don't say that like it's a good thing. Especially when you're part asura."

Aru made a *pish* sound. "They're just jealous."

"Of me?"

"Duh."

Brynne's smile was shy and quick but then turned into a smug grin. "I mean, *obviously*. Now let's go, I'll lead the way."

And with that, she strode to the exit with her shoulders thrown back and her head held high.

"Wait," said Mini. "Where do you think that exit leads?"

"I don't know," said Aru. "It could open into the ocean...."

"Maybe there's a transportation pod waiting for us outside?" Mini asked hopefully.

Brynne stopped and turned around. "Well, I'm not staying in here any longer. Aiden?"

"Just a sec," said Aiden. He pulled the kit of "unidentified necessities" from his camera bag. "I've got us covered. With these inflatable air-bubble helmets, we'll be able to breathe underwater. Just in case."

He handed one to each of them, but Aru waved hers away. "Don't need it," she said.

The others looked at her in a combination of shock and disbelief.

"Honest," said Aru. "How do you think I got here? Somehow I can walk, breathe, and even talk to fish underwater." She tried to say it like it was no big deal, but Brynne still scowled at her.

"What?" said Aru. "I guess we *both* have friends in high places." She remembered how Vajra had been stronger than the other celestial weapons in the crab's arena. *Why is that?* she wondered.

Brynne shrugged, still frowning. She inflated her air bubble and put it on over her head. The helmet automatically tightened around her neck in a perfect fit. Mini followed suit, and they started toward the door.

Before putting on his own helmet, Aiden fell into step beside Aru. "I can tell that Brynne does like you guys. Honest."

Aru almost snorted. "How do you know?"

He shrugged. "I just know."

"How'd you two even become friends?" asked Aru.

Aiden got quiet. "Brynne has always been bullied because she's part asura. One time, when some of the Otherworldly kids were trying to make her change shape by accident, I kinda, um, cursed them."

"*What?* You can do that?"

"My mom *is* an apsara," he said haughtily. "I've got *some* abilities."

"I thought your mom is a biologist?"

"She is now," said Aiden, his face turning red. "She was an elite apsara once, but to marry my dad, she had to give up her place in the heavens."

Give up her place? Considering how famous she once was, Aru thought, she must have given up a lot....

"So what other kinds of abilities do you have?"

"Not important," said Aiden quickly. "Long story short: I had Brynne's back, and she's had mine ever since."

Oh, thought Aru, feeling somewhat...lopsided. It made sense that he and Brynne would be so close. What didn't make sense was the stab of jealousy she felt. It wasn't like she'd known Aiden very long.

"Good for you," she said stiffly.

Aiden gave her a weird look but she ignored it, jogging

ahead to Brynne and Mini and shouting, "What's Aiden's secret apsara power?"

Brynne started laughing. "It's actually kinda great, Aiden can—"

"Nope!" hollered Aiden. "I am invoking the best-friend rule, Brynne! Don't!"

Brynne sighed. "Fine."

Okay, now Aru *had* to find out.

"Why don't *we* have best-friend rules?" Mini asked Aru.

"Because we defy rules, dude."

Mini hung her head. "But I don't *like* defying rules."

Even with their helmets (or Pandava power, in Aru's case) on, they each took a deep breath before Brynne pulled the door open. But it wasn't necessary. The corridor on the other side was dry.

Varuna and Varuni stood there arguing.

"I told you so!" said Varuni primly. She sipped on something that looked like tomato juice and had a piece of celery sticking out of it.

"Well, you have divine knowledge!" huffed Varuna. "You already knew they'd be fine!"

"I knew no such thing," she insisted. "You lost the bet, my love, which means..."

Varuna sighed. "No iPad for a month."

"Think of all the *quality* time we can spend together!"

Varuna grumbled something that sounded a lot like *I hate quality time.*

Aiden, Mini, and Brynne removed their helmets and paid their respects to the water gods.

"I kept up my end of the deal," said Aru. "Please grant us passage to the naga treasury."

"Okay, fine," said Varuna. "The tunnel on the right will lead you there. We'll remove the water so you can traverse it. But keep in mind, I said nothing about this tunnel being *safe*. It hasn't been accessed in thousands of years. Who knows what surprises might lie in your path."

"And remember to keep my words close, daughter of Indra," said Varuni, tapping her drink. *"A tongue like a whip..."*

"Oh, and one more thing, Pandavas," said the Lord of the Waters, ignoring Aiden's usual protest about being lumped in with them. "The sea gives. But it also takes."

SIXTEEN

Mini Gets a (Spooky) New Power

"Go into ancient tunnel. Check."

Aru held out Vajra as a lantern, which revealed a ceiling of dark kelp waving above them like the tangles of a sea giant's beard.

Mini squeaked. "This is creepy."

"Says the girl in the goth outfit," teased Aru.

"I'm going to get eaten!"

"They'd probably use you as a toothpick," said Brynne. "*I*, on the other hand, would be an entrée."

Aru rubbed her temples. "I can't believe you're bragging about being eaten first. Who *does* that?"

"Brynne does," said Aiden. He clutched his camera protectively to his chest.

"I'm just pointing out that I make a better meal," said Brynne, twirling one of her dozens of trophy bracelets. "Than anyone."

They walked down the damp passage slowly. Mini had charmed Dee Dee into a spherical mirror that cast light and illuminated corners, but it still wasn't enough to remove the undeniable essence of *creepy* that lurked there.

"At least it's mostly dry," Aiden said cheerily. "I thought we were going to have to swim."

"Piece of cake for Aru. The rest of us? Not so much," said Brynne. "How come you can do so much underwater? It makes no sense. Indra is the sky god, not the sea god."

Aru shrugged. "I dunno."

"Maybe your mom's part nagini?" suggested Aiden.

"Nope," said Aru.

"What about your real dad—?" Brynne tried, but Mini cut her off with a swift shake of her head.

Aru pretended she hadn't seen Mini's gesture, but she couldn't pretend she hadn't heard the question. Her *real dad*. It sounded simple, but it wasn't. The Sleeper might be her biological father, but he was also their enemy . . . the reason behind the demonic mischief, the shadow of fear that had fallen over the Otherworld, even their quest to find the thief of the god of love's bow and arrow. When Aru thought of him, she didn't picture the person who had cradled her as a baby. . . . She saw a puppet master pulling strings behind a dark curtain.

"Well, that's the only explanation I can think of," said Aiden awkwardly. "Otherworld kids always inherit their parents' traits."

"Does that mean you dance really well, Aiden?" asked Mini. "Like an apsara?"

"I. Don't. Dance."

"Um, yeah you do!" said Brynne, laughing. "One time, Aiden didn't know I was there, and—"

He clapped his hands over his ears. *"La-la-la-la-la-la-la-la—"*

"I'd ask my soul dad where I got the underwater skills, but it's not like he talks to me," said Aru, mostly to herself, before adding, "*ever.*"

Vajra glowed, and the light seemed sorrowful to her. Mini touched her shoulder briefly.

After a time, Brynne said, "No Pandava's soul dad is allowed to speak to them directly."

"*Yours* does," Aru pointed out.

Brynne's shoulders fell. "Not...exactly. He keeps to the rules and doesn't interfere, but he did sometimes send messages before I was officially claimed, through my half brother Hanuman. Not often, though. When I got my first Otherworld trophy, Vayu sent a tiny whirlwind of daisies to my room. And there's other ways I know he cares....Like, I never have to wait for my baking to cool. I just ask the air to blow on the food, and *voilà!* Room temperature. Pretty useful for cooking."

"Not to pry," said Aru, totally prying, "but how long have you known you're a Pandava?"

Brynne shoved her hands deep into her pockets. "Since last autumn."

Autumn...Right around when Aru and Mini had gone on their first quest and into the Kingdom of Death.

"I've always been really strong and stuff, but one day a car was heading straight for my uncle and I pushed it out of the way. The second I did it, I felt wind rushing through my blood. I know that sounds weird, but that's what it felt like." Brynne shrugged. "My uncles told me the soul of Bhima had awoken in me. They thought I was going to be summoned to go on the quest to stop the Sleeper. It made sense—Bhima *was* the second-oldest Pandava brother. But then"—she paused, swallowing hard—"but then no one came to get me. I figured the gods didn't want an asura Pandava. I dunno."

Aru could picture it. . . . Brynne and her two uncles excited, waiting for her to go with Aru and Mini, because why wouldn't she? Brynne was the kind of heroine people expected. Aru wasn't. Brynne must have waited and waited . . . for nothing. Aru knew that feeling. It was the sinking sensation she got every time she was chosen last for a team during PE. Or when she wasn't invited to a party. It sucked. And she was beginning to see why Brynne was so . . . well, Brynne. Part of her even felt guilty that she and Mini had been summoned first, and not her.

"The gods just had you in reserve," Aru said firmly. "They were saving you until they needed your specific skills, and that's right now."

"I bet your uncles and parents are really happy you're on this quest?" tried Mini.

"My uncles are," said Brynne, pulling at one of her bracelets. "I dunno about my parents. Never met my dad. My mom said he was a musician. As for Mom . . . she doesn't really visit me. But I know she worries about me. I know she cares."

Aiden moved closer to Brynne, suddenly protective. Aru knew why. The last two things Brynne had said sounded jumbled together and flimsy, like unpracticed lies. Aru could detect those on the spot. She even recognized how Brynne held herself, shoulders up around her ears, gaze shifty. Like she was waiting for someone to call her bluff.

"I'm sure she does," agreed Aru.

Brynne lowered her shoulders. When she looked at Aru, it wasn't with snootiness or nastiness like before. . . . Instead, she looked relieved.

The tunnel opened up into a courtyard.

Perhaps, long ago, it had been part of a sea kingdom. But it was mostly dry now, with just a few tidal pools scattered around the ruins—serpentine pillars and crumbled walls studded with sapphires and emeralds. The courtyard might have once been the site of glamorous parties. Fish spines crunched underfoot as they made their way across it, toward a massive black rock in the distance. The whole place felt...sad. Shriveled, somehow, like all the life had been sucked out of it.

"I bet this was a grand naga palace once," said Mini. She crouched down, plucking a piece of kelp off a broken coral-and-pearl chandelier.

"It's...it's *Uloopi's* old palace," said Aiden. He had brushed aside some seaweed to read the writing on a collapsed wall. "It says her name.... 'This palace was built in honor of Queen Uloopi and...and her consort, Prince Arjuna.'"

That felt *deeply* weird to Aru, who carried his soul.

"Um...say what now?" she asked.

The others were looking at her as if she was supposed to know something about this place, but it was from—literally—*lifetimes* ago. It's like when your parents show you a baby picture and say *Remember when...* and it's physically impossible to remember that because you had like five brain cells at the time.

"How'd Uloopi and Arjuna meet?" asked Aiden.

"According to the stories, she saw him by the riverbank, thought he was cute, and took him into the ocean," said Mini.

Brynne nodded. "Aggressive. I like it."

"Nothing says romance like casually stalking someone and then dragging them underwater," said Aru.

"Well, when you say it like *that*..." said Brynne.

Mini continued. "And then they got married, but he had to go back and fight in the great war against his cousins, the Kauravas, so he left. And then...I can't remember, honestly. I think at one point she saved his life? With a magic jewel?"

"But then what?" asked Aiden.

Mini shrugged. "She lived with his wives in the palace after the great war, I guess."

"How many wives did you have?" Aiden asked Aru.

She rolled her eyes. In the stories, it seemed like Arjuna collected wives as if it were a hobby. *Get other hobbies!* Aru always thought. Why couldn't he have taken up stamp-collecting? Or fly-fishing?

"Can we not use the word *you?*" said Aru. "Arjuna and I are completely different people. That's like expecting Brynne to have the power of ten thousand elephants just because she's Bhima reincarnated! Or asking Mini to rule a country now just because she's got Yudhistira's soul! I'm *not* Arjuna!"

The others stared at her. Only then did Aru realize she'd raised her voice. Her face flushed. The truth was, Aru didn't recognize even a sliver of herself in the tales of Arjuna. Sometimes she thought that was a good thing. It meant that she was her own person. But other times, it felt horrible. Maybe, in a different person, Arjuna's soul could make someone a legendary hero. But in her? In her, it seemed just average.

"Dude, don't worry. We've seen you in action," said Aiden. "We know you're not Arjuna."

Aru didn't know if she wanted to thank him or strangle him. Maybe both.

"Let's just get through this place," she said. "It literally looks like a horror-movie set."

And then Mini shrieked.

They turned to see her scuttling backward.

"It—it—it talked!" she said, pointing at something on the ground.

The rest of them walked closer to investigate. It was a human skull.

Mini shuddered. "This place is cursed."

Brynne toed it with her the edge of her sneaker. "Hello?"

The skull did nothing.

"I think you're hearing things, Mini," said Brynne.

Mini tiptoed over, bent down, and tapped the skull gently. "Hi?"

As soon as Mini touched the skull, its jaws snapped open. A faint purple glow, like the light that Dee Dee gave off, bristled along the edges of the bone and lit up the entire courtyard.

Ah . . . We can strike a bargain, Daughter of Death.

Nearby another skull—or, honestly, little more than a jawbone—laughed and whispered, *You seek to undo a great wrong, but you do not know the name of the thief. . . . What good is capturing the soul song without a name to unlock its secrets?*

The first skull spoke again. Even though it didn't have eyeballs left (gross), something about its hollow sockets seemed fixated on Mini. *Daughter of Death, you must merely take our burden and we will give you what you seek. . . . It is the just thing to do. Are you not as just and wise as the Pandava prince who once held your soul?*

The ruins trembled as if in a small earthquake.

"Mini, stop!" called Aiden.

But she ignored him. It looked as if she'd fallen under some kind of enchantment.

"They know the thief's name. . . . All those Heartless could be saved…" she muttered as she moved in an eerie daze, touching every bone she could find. A multitude of voices rippled into the air.

"Hear our tale, Pandavas—"

"Arjuna was cursed—"

"Ah, how Queen Uloopi wished to free him—"

"But there was only one way."

"What?" asked Mini, her voice distant. "What was the way?"

Laughter filled the courtyard.

At first, Aru thought that a lot of skulls had started talking at once. Her immediate reaction was NOPE. But it wasn't the skulls.

She saw a flicker of movement inside one of the three caves in the black rock. Was that a tail?

"Brynne, hold Mini!" ordered Aru. She extended her lightning bolt into sword form. Energy crackled through her bones. Aiden moved closer to Aru, and they stood back-to-back, weapons raised. A tail whipped out from the middle cave, about ten feet away. The tail nearly wrapped around Aru's ankles, but at the last second it recoiled, as if it wasn't supposed to touch her. Brynne spun her mace. It brought forth a vortex that spun up the debris and skulls in a sandy hurricane.

"Foolish girl. Do you think you can intimidate us? We, who are the guardians of terrible secrets…" came a voice from the first cave.

"And knowledge…" said a voice from the second cave.

"And treasures untold," a voice from the third cave continued.

Aru's heart pounded. Out of the corner of her eye, she saw the edge of a purple backpack. *Mini.* She was walking toward the caves, still in a daze.

"BRYNNE, GET MINI!" Aru called out.

"Welcome, daughter of the Dharma Raja," the voices said in unison. "Pay the price of knowledge."

Three powerful tails whipped toward Mini, one from each cavern. Aru rushed at them, trying to protect her sister as an inky pool of darkness emerged from the caves and enveloped her.

Right then, Mini turned toward Aru. It looked as though she had snapped out of the trance. "I know the thief's name!" she said triumphantly. "It's—"

But Mini never got the chance to finish. A serpent tail as thick as a redwood trunk curled around her body and yanked her toward the cave.

"No!" shouted Aru. She threw Vajra at the tail, but fear frayed her thoughts and ruined her concentration. The lightning bolt missed. "MINI!"

Just as she ran after Mini, another tail slashed toward Aru. Someone hauled her back—Brynne. Beside her, Aiden sliced at the tail with his scimitars. The tail recoiled and a low hiss filled the courtyard as it retracted into its cave. The third tail followed suit.

When Aru looked up, Mini was nowhere to be seen. She had disappeared deep into the first serpent's cave.

Aru fell to her knees, tears streaming down her face and a scream caught in her throat. The Lord of the Waters' voice drifted through her head: *The sea gives. But it also takes.*

In that second, Aru hated herself. What was *wrong* with her? The Sleeper was right. She wasn't meant to be a hero.

Her words echoed back to her: *I'm not Arjuna.* That much was obvious. Arjuna would never have lost his family. He was a brave warrior, and he'd also had Krishna by his side, whispering advice in his ear, helping him every step of the way.

But no god spoke to Aru. No help came. And in the end, Aru was left with the terrible consequence of how different she was from Arjuna....

She had lost her sister.

SEVENTEEN

Uloopi's Secret

ini was gone.

Mini? MINI? MINI! Aru called through the Pandava mind link. Nothing. It was like Aru's thoughts were being thrown against an invisible wall.

She had to do something—now! Aru struggled against Aiden, who had helped her get back to her feet.

"Don't panic, Aru," he soothed. "We'll figure this out. We'll get Mini back."

Aru whirled around to face Brynne. "I told you to hold her!"

"The snakes were coming for all of us!" shouted Brynne. "I had to handle that first!"

"You should've listened to me!"

"Why?" demanded Brynne. "Who says you get to call the shots?"

Aiden moved in between them, his arms held out. "Stop fighting!" he said, his voice raw. "Just...take a deep breath! Let's think for a minute...."

But Aru was too wound up, and so was Brynne.

"You're not better than me, Shah. So stop acting like it."

Aru was so furious in that second. Furious that Brynne wouldn't admit she was wrong. Furious that Aiden wasn't standing up for her when she was in the right. Furious that none of them had gotten to Mini in time.

"You want to know why you weren't chosen for that first quest? It's because of this," said Aru coldly. "You only want to *act* like a hero. Not actually *be* one."

Brynne recoiled as if Aru had slapped her.

Aiden dropped his arms. Disappointment was plain on his face. "That went too far, Shah," he said quietly. "And you know it."

There was a moment when Aru could have—*should have*—admitted that it wasn't just Brynne's fault. Yes, Brynne should have held on to Mini. But then again, Mini shouldn't have walked straight toward the serpents' caves. And Aru should have kept a closer eye on her. They were all to blame.

"Brynne—" started Aru, guilt flooding her, but the hissing sound returned and all thought of talking left her head.

The three of them turned to face the caverns where Mini had disappeared. A naga woman streamed out of each one. Their skin was the dark shiny gray of hematite stones. Ragged white bandages covered their eyes. Their tails were powerful silver coils.

Brynne held up her mace. "What did you do to our friend?" she demanded. "Give her back, or—"

"Ssshe…" said the first.

"…isss…" said the second.

"…ressssting…" said the third.

The three naginis laughed.

Resting? Aru's stomach dropped. What did that mean? There was a reason why people wrote RIP when someone died. It stood for *rest in peace. Rest* was another word for death. Did that mean that Mini was . . . dead? One of the naginis' tails whipped the sand, and Mini's purple backpack sailed through the air. Aru grabbed it, clutching it tight. Her whole body felt cold with panic.

"Is she . . . ?" asked Aru, unable to finish the question.

The first serpent woman gave a sly smile and shook her head. "She is sssafe . . ."

"And ssstuck," whispered the second naga woman.

"Her knowledge came at the price of energy. She is a Pandava and has much energy to offer . . ." said the third. She rolled her head from side to side like she was waking up from a long nap. "*Ahhh* . . . for the first time in centuries I can taste sssecrets again." She flicked out a forked tongue. "I taste abandonment," said the nagini, her sightless gaze pivoting toward Brynne. "A heart broken from being left behind all her life."

The second nagini turned her head to Aiden. "In you, I taste a vengeful heart. A heart that aches."

And then the first faced Aru. "Your heart is full of doubts. And want. I taste a heart that has everything to lossse. . . . But we are not here to gulp down your secrets like candied jewels. . . . Oh no, we need this energy to impart to you a treasure."

"We don't want your treasure!" said Aru. "We want Mini! Give her back to us!"

"Ooh, such a lovely fire to your words!" said the second. "You think your sister is the key to your success. But if you abandon your quest in order to rescue her, you may miss your only chance to locate the thief's precious song. And without it you would be—"

"Ruined!" sang the third.

"Ruined!" sang the first.

"Ruined," echoed the second with a cruel sneer. "Oh yes, we know what you seek. You seek to undo the pronouncement of Uloopi and prevent your own exile. Such a sssmall thread you tug in a greater tapestry."

"You should thank us for what we are about to offer you," they said in unison. "But our gift will mean nothing if first you do not learn the truth of this place."

The three naginis shot up in the air, their tails waving powerfully behind them and swirling the sand. Aru, Brynne, and Aiden gasped as the scenery changed. The broken spires regrew, the toppled walls righted themselves, the skeletons faded away, and the ruin became a picture of its former grandeur. And at the center of it was…Uloopi.

Well, a vision of Uloopi, as her younger, more beautiful self.

Her hair was strewn with gemstones, but nothing shone brighter than the huge emerald in her forehead. It glowed with an unearthly light. Uloopi's serpent tail was wrapped tightly around her torso and…she was weeping. Pleading. Before her was an enormous black cobra. At the center of its forehead sparkled a ruby the size of a football.

"He will die, Father," Uloopi said. "You know the curse! The gods foretold that Arjuna will be killed by his own son's hand. I can save him from his fate."

The cobra's deep voice echoed through the courtyard. "And

what concern is his life to me? Men die. That is what they do best. You have already given him many gifts, my dear. You made him invincible underwater. You gave him the gift of communication with all sea creatures. Let that be enough."

"I cannot watch him die," said Uloopi fiercely. "He is my own, my husband."

The great serpent laughed. "You had his attention for one night, and he has your heart for the rest of his days? Think of what you are saying, for you will never die and he was always meant to."

"He would do the same for me," she insisted.

"Would he?" asked the serpent gently.

"Please," begged Uloopi. "Give me the jewel that will restore his life. Then, if the curse comes true, I will be able to snatch him back from the Kingdom of Death."

The cobra bowed. Uloopi reached for the jewel glimmering on his scaly forehead, but before she could grasp it, the serpent pulled back.

"That is not the jewel you seek, my child," he said.

Uloopi gasped in pain, her hand flying to her face. When she removed her hand, a sparkling green emerald—the one that had been in her forehead—now lay in her palm. She clutched it tightly.

"Now do you understand the price?" pressed the serpent. "Without your heart jewel, you will age . . . and you will be vulnerable among the immortals of our kind. You will no longer be able to tell when someone is lying to you. A shadow will fall across your reign."

"Prince Arjuna will return it to me," said Uloopi. "You'll see."

＊　＊　＊

Aru and the others did see, in a different vision....

Uloopi, in her human form, glided out onto a battlefield. A mortal woman was already there, weeping and crouched beside a fallen soldier. Aru knew, even without seeing the man's face, that it was Arjuna. And from the way the mortal woman clutched him, Aru could tell that she was one of his wives. Aru thought she'd feel something looking at this former bearer of her soul, but he was a stranger to her.

Uloopi approached them. She set the emerald—her heart— on top of Arjuna's chest. A few moments passed, and then he stirred...his chest rising as he drew breath once more. But when he finally opened his eyes, he did not look at Uloopi. He gazed at the woman beyond her. And it was with the other woman that he shared the first smile of his renewed life.

The vision changed again to show Uloopi returning to the sea.

Another naga greeted her, and Aru recognized him instantly. Takshaka, the blind guardian king of the naga treasury. He looked just as he had when Aru had first seen him in the Court of the Sky—young, and covered with burn scars.

"The Pandavas have all left this earth, my queen. And as I suspected, your beloved husband never returned your heart to you, did he?"

Uloopi remained tight-lipped and stone-faced.

"I do not mean to gloat," Takshaka went on. "I only meant to say that I was among those who tried to warn you. Just because he is a hero does not mean he cannot also be a monster. The Pandavas burned down my home, after all. I have not forgotten."

Uloopi seemed distant. "I refuse to believe Arjuna would leave this earth without returning it, when he knew how precious it was. Will you tell me if it is found?"

"Of course," he said. "You have my word, Queen Uloopi."

"Thank you, Takshaka. You are a true friend."

Aru blinked and the vision disappeared. So this was why Uloopi was old compared to the other naginis. Her heart had never been returned. Something else struck Aru, though. *You will no longer be able to tell when someone is lying to you. A shadow will fall across your reign.* Uloopi had trusted the word of Takshaka...but what if Takshaka had *lied*?

"The sssea may take," said the first nagini.

"But it also givesss," said the third.

"We are cursssed for withholding the truth from the queen, and it is a sssecret we no longer wish to bear." Something shiny fell before them, thudding softly into the sand. "Return this to the queen, and our souls shall be free. Perhaps it shall aid you, too."

As one, the three naginis laughed. Their laughter shook the courtyard, which was once again in ruins. The whole place had taken on a different hue during the naginis' story about Uloopi, and it was back to feeling desolate.

Now Aru understood why the naga queen despised her. Now she knew where her own special underwater abilities had come from.... They were gifts not from her soul father, but from Uloopi to her love. Aru had inherited them from Arjuna.

"Our energy borrowed from your sssister fades now," said the first nagini.

"We have done our duty," said the second.

"But Mini—" started Aru.

"Is in the land of sssleeeeep," said the third nagini. "Far from the reach of mortals...."

"You are welcome, Pandavas, for thanks to us, she holds the thief's name," said the first.

And with that, the naginis crumpled into shadows and seaweed. Aru, Aiden, and Brynne stood in silence for a moment. Then Brynne cleared her throat:

"One thing at a time, Rao," Brynne murmured right before she started talking. "Mini is in the land of *sleep*?"

Aiden frowned, tugging at his hair. "I know where it is.... It's near the Court of the Heavens and is ruled over by the goddess Ratri. But the naginis are right. You can't just *go* there on a wind antelope—"

"*Gazelle,*" corrected Brynne.

"It's dangerous," continued Aiden, "even if you have Otherworldly blood. That place is soaked in celestial power—you'd need protection from a sage just to walk through it. Mini should be safe while she's in the land of sleep, but there's no way she can get herself out safely."

Aru's mouth turned dry with panic. "You mean she's stuck there? Forever?"

Brynne pounded her hand with her fist. "So let's go right now! We'll find a sage and get her!"

"And risk not being able to get back into the naga realm? Or find the song in time?" pointed out Aiden. "We only have six mortal days left according to my watch...."

"Are you honestly suggesting we leave her there?" asked Brynne.

Aiden crossed his arms. "Not *leave* her there. But get her *after* we find the song."

Brynne scowled, then turned to Aru. "Aren't you going to say anything, Shah?"

Aru remained quiet. Hurt and worry and confusion tore through her thoughts. Mini's backpack was still in her arms, the zipper halfway undone. She tried to shut it, just to buy her some extra time before she had to answer them, but something blocked the zipper. It was the corner of the Post-it notepad Mini wrote on sometimes. Aru frowned.

"Can I get some light, Vajra?"

The lightning bolt glowed softly, revealing the last list Mini had written before she'd disappeared:

THINGS TO REMEMBER WHEN I'M SCARED
1. *Water kills 99% of germs*
2. *I am the daughter of ~~death~~ ~*~dEaTh~*~*
3. *If I freeze up: <u>W</u>hat <u>W</u>ould <u>A</u>ru <u>D</u>o?*

Aru's whole heart ached with guilt. Mini was wrong. *Aru* couldn't do anything. Instead, she thought about what *Mini* would do.... Mini wouldn't want to jeopardize the lives of all those human Heartless.... Mini would put others before herself. Like she always did.

Aru shoved the notepad into the backpack and slung it across one shoulder, next to her own pack.

"We're so close. We can't leave now, not without the thief's song," she said.

"But Mini—" Brynne started.

"Is *strong*," said Aru firmly. "She's also the key to this. We need the soul song *and* the thief's name. So let's get the song out of the treasury, *then* get to Mini. Immediately."

"I agree," said Aiden.

Brynne looked between them and threw up her hands. "Fine! Let's go. And don't forget to pick up that stupid jewel the naginis gave us."

In her concern over Mini, Aru had almost forgotten about the heart of Uloopi.

"I wish we could just go to the Council and throw it in their face," said Brynne, "but I bet they'd accuse us of stealing it or something."

With that, Brynne stomped off, and Aiden followed her.

The jewel was half-buried in the sand near where the first nagini had stood. Aru pulled out the emerald and rubbed it on her hoodie until it glittered. As much as Aru hated to admit it, Brynne was right. The Council of Guardians might not believe them if they showed up without the bow and arrow and the name of the thief. Takshaka would just lie about the heart of Uloopi.

Right now, Aru didn't *trust* the Council of Guardians. And that frightened her. Because if she couldn't trust the people who were supposed to be looking out for them, who was left?

EIGHTEEN

A Chocolaty Truce

Dream logic is weird.

In a dream, Aru could show up to school wearing a gown made out of paper clips only to be supremely embarrassed that she'd forgotten her homework. And no one would care about the gown. Which was why it didn't seem odd to Aru that she was strolling through Home Depot dressed up as a stuffed olive. Mini walked beside her in the dream, wearing her all-black getup.

Earlier, Aru, Brynne, and Aiden had camped outside what they figured was the secret entrance to the naga treasury. According to the symbols on the door, it wouldn't open until dawn.

"There goes another day," Aiden had said. "Only *five* left. I'm setting a timer on my phone so we'll be up and ready to go first thing."

Brynne had only nodded in agreement.

Aiden threw his satchel on the ground, laid his head on one half, and closed his eyes. Brynne flopped down, taking the other half of the satchel pillow. No one offered Aru anything. Not that she blamed them. She'd had plenty of time to apologize for blaming Brynne earlier, but she hadn't. Too many other things had been darting through her head, like Mini's face as the naginis stole her away into the cave.

So Aru had curled up alone and fallen into a miserable sleep. And when she saw Mini in her dream, it was like none of the bad stuff had happened.

At first, Aru didn't even notice that they were strolling through the massive hardware store. Which made no sense, because the last time she was there, she'd gotten into trouble for accidentally turning on a radial saw and was kindly "asked" not to come back.

Ever.

In fact, she was pretty sure there was a picture of her face at every cash register, asking the employees to be on the lookout.

"Whaddup," Aru said, nodding at Mini.

"Why are we in Home Depot?" asked Mini.

"Why would we *not* be in Home Depot?" asked Aru. "This place is awesome. They literally have an aisle that's just door-frames. It's fun to stumble out of them. And then if you run up to people asking 'What year is it?' they get all confused. It's great."

"You're a menace to society, Shah."

"I try."

Mini laughed, but then her face turned serious. "I don't wanna be trapped here forever."

"In Home Depot?"

"No! In the land of sleep. That's where the naginis put me to steal some of my waking energy, and now I'm stuck here!"

"In Home Depot?"

"Aru," said Mini, grabbing her by the shoulders, "remember the card that Kamadeva gave us? For when things get really bad?"

Vaguely, Aru recalled a business card being placed in her hand. The name S. Durvasa...and a warning not to waste his time. "Yeah?"

"Use it! We need the sage's protection to get me out of here. I have the true name of the bow and arrow thief, but the naginis enchanted it so it can only be heard in person," said Mini. "Go to Durvasa. He can get me out of—"

"Home Depot," said Aru.

Mini rolled her eyes. "Yes, Aru. *Home Depot*."

"Got it. Let's go look at the doors now!"

"Aru, one more thing," said Mini. There were tears in her eyes. "I miss you guys a lot. But don't be mad at anyone, okay? There's something else I need to tell you, but I'm running out of time....Just *use music*. Okay?"

"Okay, okay! Let's go find a saw!"

"Aru. Say 'music.'"

"*Mooooooo-zique.*"

Mini took a deep breath. "I don't know how much of this you're going to remember, and I'm going to try my best to tell the others too, but just try, try, *try* to remember what I've told you. Music and Durvasa."

Someone was shaking Aru's shoulder.

"What year is it?" she asked muzzily. Then she laughed. "Gotcha."

"Shah, wake up!" the voice said. "It's almost dawn! We should be able to get into the naga treasury soon. Let's get moving."

ROSHANI CHOKSHI

Aru opened her eyes. Aiden was crouched beside her.

Behind Aiden, Brynne was still waking up. She yawned and said groggily, "I had the *weirdest* dream."

Aru blinked. In bits and snatches, her own dream came back to her. *Mini.* Mini talking about using something? Cows...? She distinctly remembered someone saying *Mooooooo.*

"Mini was in it," said Brynne. "Warning me about dancing? No, that's not right—she was telling me *to* dance. But I was mad that the grocery was out of salt and basil leaves, and I didn't want to make pesto without them."

That made Aru sit up straight. "Wait, really?"

"I mean, you *can* make pesto sauce with cilantro, too, but basil adds—"

"No, about Mini! I dreamed about her, too."

"Same here!" said Aiden.

"Were you in Home Depot?" asked Aru.

The others looked at her funny.

"No? Okay, never mind."

"If we all had the same dream, maybe Mini was trying to reach all of us," said Aiden. "She *is* in the land of sleep. Maybe she had special access to our dreams?"

"Yeah, maybe," said Aru.

Aiden looked between Aru and Brynne. "Mini is okay... for now, at least. She wants us to keep going, so we can find the song and save her. But we're not going to get far if you two can't get along."

"Ugh," groaned Brynne. "Don't say it...."

Aiden crossed his arms. "I think you guys should talk."

His words hung in the air. Brynne and Aru caught each

other's eyes and then looked away quickly. Aru remembered Mini telling her not to be mad at anyone. It was hard, when she was missing Mini so much...but fighting with Brynne seemed pointless.

While Brynne had her back to them, Aiden wordlessly handed something to Aru—a brown paper bag labeled FOR EMERGENCIES ONLY. Inside was a slightly smushed 100 Grand candy bar. Aru bit back a scowl. She hated 100 Grands. They tasted great, but she would never forget when a neighbor offered to pay her "a hundred grand" to clean out the garage. Aru had spent hours battling spiders (death) and cobwebs (more death) in mid-July in *Georgia* (such death that she'd been reincarnated twice in the space of an hour) only to get a melted chocolate bar as payment.

"Betrayal..." said Aru, glaring at the candy.

"I'm going to check the door," Aiden said, leaving them.

Aru knew what he wanted her to do. He and Mini were right. She took a deep breath.

"Brynne?"

"No."

"I'll give you a hundred grand."

"What?" Brynne turned, then saw the chocolate bar. "Very funny, Shah. Are you trying to bribe me with candy?"

"Will it work?"

Brynne was silent for a moment, and then she sighed. "Yeah. Give it."

Aru tossed her the 100 Grand. "I'm sorry about what I said."

Brynne caught it, ripped open the wrapper, and took a bite. "No one expects me to be a hero. Not with asura blood."

Aru felt her throat tighten. "Yeah? Well, try being the daughter of the Sleeper, the guy who started all this and is off building an army to take over the world or some other villain cliché," she said. She tried to laugh, but it came out as a grunt.

Brynne looked at her sharply, as if seeing her for the first time. "You're better than that. We both are."

Aru nodded. She wanted to believe that, but sometimes she wasn't sure. Sometimes, when things went wrong, it was easier to blame what was in her blood than to take responsibility.

"Aiden is right..." she said, sighing. "We have to work together."

"Yeah," Brynne said, the corners of her mouth pulled down. "I guess I'm just used to doing stuff alone."

Aru fell quiet. She remembered how scared Brynne had looked when she'd assumed they were going to leave her behind. Aru thought of the trophy bracelets on her wrist and the photo album she carried around in her backpack, as if she was hoping to show them to someone.

"Well, you're not alone anymore."

Brynne rubbed at her eyes, still frowning. Then she stood up and helped Aru to her feet, too. Next, Brynne did something Aru had never imagined possible. She broke off half the candy bar and held it out to Aru.

"Eat up, Shah," she said gruffly. "You'll need the energy. I don't care if you're family—I'm not carrying you anymore."

Aru took a bite, and even though she'd had 100 Grands before, this one tasted extra special, like the beginning of something new.

The two of them started walking over to the secret door.

"Did Aiden give you that candy bar?" asked Brynne.

"No?" And then a few seconds later, "Yeah, he did."

Brynne just smiled. "Classic Ammamma."

"You guys ready?" asked Aiden.

"Yeah," said Brynne and Aru.

"Good," said Aiden. Aru thought his smile looked a bit smug.

"Weapons out," said Brynne, touching her blue choker. With a flash of azure light, it turned into her celestial mace.

Aiden put his wrist cuffs together, and scimitars flashed into his hands.

When Aru reached into her pocket for Vajra, her fingers brushed the business card Kamadeva had given them. She pulled it out and showed it to Aiden and Brynne.

S. DURVASA

DO NOT BOTHER ME WITH INFANTILE CONCERNS

I WILL CURSE YOU FOR WASTING MY TIME

Flashes of her dream came back to her.

"*This* is who Mini wants us to contact!"

Though she wasn't sure why. Mini had said something else, too.... What was it?

Aiden let out a whoop of joy. "The *S* probably stands for *sage*! We'll go straight to Durvasa after we find the song. Now, how do you think this door works...?"

Brynne took one look at it and kicked it open.

"Wait...that's *it*?" said Aru. "I thought there'd be more to it! Like in *Lord of the Rings*, where there's a riddle door with the message 'speak friend and enter.' Except I can't remember what *friend* is in Elvish."

Brynne rolled her eyes, but her smile was warm. She stepped through first.

Aiden held open the door for Aru. As she walked past him, he said, "It's *mellon*, by the way."

"Nerd."

Varuna had said that the route to the naga treasury was secret.

The good news was that he had told the truth.

The bad news was that they were picking their way through sewers.

They were beneath the naga city, which—based on what Aru could see from the sewer grates—was nestled in a giant air bubble in the middle of an ocean. It was like living in a snow globe! But she could barely concentrate on how cool that was, because the *worst* stench rolled toward them. Aru thought the smell alone had burned away all her nose hairs.

They three of them stood in a sprawling underground network of tunnels. Slime oozed down the walls. Under Aru's shoes, snake skin crumpled like soggy paper.

"Ooh," said Brynne, cheerily toeing a pile of rotten vegetables. "This would make great mulch. Great mulch means great dirt, and great dirt means great vegetables, and great vegetables make great food!"

Aiden gagged. "Stop saying 'great.'"

"How can you even *think* about food?" demanded Aru. Because her sleeve was covering the lower half of her face, it sounded like *Hah can yoo eben hink abou foo?*

Brynne rapped her knuckles on her stomach. "Ironclad gut."

"I need an ironclad nose," said Aiden woozily.

Brynne raised her wind mace to her lips. She blew on it,

and a continuous breeze wafted around them, carrying away the stink.

Brynne immediately took the lead. As the daughter of the Lord of the Winds, she had a perfect sense of direction. She always knew whether they were going north, south, east, or west. Aru cast out Vajra like a torch, and the three of them stomped down one of the less nasty passages. Occasionally, Aiden had to hack through strings of black gunk with his scimitars to clear an opening for them to step through.

When they came to the occasional grate in the tunnel, Aru caught glimpses of the sprawling naga city above them. They had to be careful to stay in the shadows in case there were guards on the lookout, but they saw enough to get a sense of the enchanted kingdom that Uloopi ruled. It reminded Aru of New York City. Wide boulevards. Fashionable nagas and naginis slithering down the streets, shopping bags in hand. Sometimes Aru caught the names of storefronts: FANGS "R" US and OPHIDIAN EMPORIUM: YOUR ONE-STOP SHOP FOR ALL THINGS SCALY.

There was even an Apple store.

But what she loved most were the seascrapers—huge, twisting spires that looked like they were hewn out of the bones of some long-forgotten sea creature and were so tall they almost touched the top of the air bubble. The sea might not have stars, but the water surrounding the naga realm was lit up with its own magical lights. Anemone the color of moonlight bloomed in the alleys.

At one of the grates, Aru was lucky enough to get a glimpse that lasted more than five seconds. Sadly, that was just when someone decided to drop their coffee cup. A red holiday cup from Slitherbucks, with a green-and-white logo of a crowned naga on it, fell through the grate...

...and splashed all over Aru's shirt.

"This is just awesome," Aru muttered. "How could it get any worse—?"

Brynne held up a hand. "We're here," she whispered.

Aiden looked around, and his confused expression matched Aru's feeling. How could *this* be the legendary treasury of the nagas? They were in the middle of the sewage system, below-ground, and there was no door or anything else marking an entry to another place.

"Are you sure?"

"Yes, I'm *sure*," said Brynne. "I *am* the daughter of Lord Vayu. I never lose my sense of direction."

Aiden peered at the ground. With his right foot, he scraped aside some of the goop. There was a small bronze insignia there, along with a couple of raised bumps that looked like buttons. He bent down, shining his phone's flashlight app to get a better look—which was a good thing, because Vajra refused to get anywhere near this ground, thwacking Aru in the head when she tried a couple times to lower it. She finally just changed it to a bracelet.

Aiden's scimitar hovered over one of the bronze buttons. "Huh," he said, "I wonder if—"

He didn't have to wonder long. The second his blade touched the button, a circular plate beneath their feet suddenly *whooshed* downward. The three of them screamed as the surface fell away and they were plunged into darkness.

The plate stopped nearly three hundred feet down from the sewers, straight in the belly of the naga treasury. Wall torches in the shape of snakes with tongues of flame dimly illuminated a wide circular space about the size of a football field. Hundreds of shelves that ran from floor to ceiling surrounded them. Piled onto their surfaces were untold wonders that Aru recognized from stories: a crystal goblet full of bright jewels, which was labeled PROPHETIC DREAMS; bottled constellations; and the jawbone of some deep-sea creature, which opened and closed as if it remembered chewing a former enemy.

"Whoa," said Brynne, slowly rotating.

Aiden reached for his camera, but Brynne batted it down. "Someone might see the flash!" she scolded.

"There's no one here, Bee," said Aiden, snapping a couple of pictures. "That was the whole point of the secret passage. And no way am I going to miss documenting this."

"You're not a journalist in a war zone!"

"*Yet,*" said Aiden.

Aru didn't see any sign of the thief's soul song, but they'd only just started looking.

Then, from high above, Aru heard a faint hissing sound. The three of them moved into a tight circle. They looked up . . . and there, hanging from a shelf, was a huge scaly tail. Aru traced it to the prone torso of a man. A little farther and she found his familiar face, with ropy scars and milky eyes.

"Aru Shah. You and I have unfinished businesss," he hissed.

NINETEEN

Dehhhh-Spah-CITO

Takshaka slithered down the shelves of treasure. As he moved, jewels clattered to the floor. He swung his head, tasting the air with his forked tongue. The end of his jet-black tail quivered, as if the sound of the falling treasure had disoriented him.

Something dug at Aru's thoughts. Something she was supposed to know. Like a name dangling at the tip of her tongue.

"Don't think that because I cannot see that you are invissssible," he said softly. His face rippled as he transformed from his half-snake to full-snake form. He lifted his now scaled head. Ancient scars striped his diamond-shaped forehead. "There are three Pandavasss...."

Aiden opened his mouth to say something, then closed it. It's best not to correct a gigantic, venomous serpent king.

Quietly, the three of them spread out across the treasure room. Aiden stood by the wall behind Aru. Brynne was off to her right, out of whispering distance. But then she saw Brynne mouthing a word.

The good thing was that Takshaka couldn't read lips.

The bad thing was that neither could Aru.

It looked like Brynne was saying . . . *Stalin?* What? Like the dictator from history? Then Aru heard Brynne screaming through her mind link: *STALL HIM!*

Aru didn't have to try to get Takshaka's attention, because he was headed straight for her.

"You laid wassste to my lands, Pandava. You killed every living creature that tried to escape the fire. You killed my *wife*. I thought I had ended your line," said Takshaka. "But you came back. Like a pestilence."

Aru's head was still ringing from Brynne's command. Very slowly, she started to back away from the king. "That's a bit harsh, don't you think?" she asked him. "I mean, that was like a millennium ago. And I'm not Arjuna. We just have the same soul. It's like getting someone's hand-me-down socks, honest. Why don't we just start over? Like this: Hi, I'm Aru. I like Swedish Fish. Now it's your turn."

Takshaka tested the air with his forked tongue, getting a bead on her. "I didn't believe it at first. The great Arjuna's soul harbored in the feeble body of a small girl."

Vajra pulsed on her wrist, but Aru didn't reach for her lightning bolt. *Not yet.*

"Surprise?" Aru said with false cheer.

"The gods are cruel," said Takshaka. "Of course they would summon a uselessss girl. Of course they have no interest in protecting this world. Despite their immortality, despite their powersss, the gods never keep their word. Just like your father didn't."

Aru froze. *The Sleeper?* Her throat felt tight. She wondered whether Takshaka was going to tell her that she was just like him. Destined not to keep her promises, either.

But then Takshaka spat, "Indra failed me."

Oh. *Indra.* Her soul dad. Not the Sleeper.

Takshaka's tail whipped, agitated. He slithered farther down the shelves until he was barely twenty feet away. "Once, I lived in the great Khandava Forest with my family. Back then, Indra was my friend. But one day, Agni, the god of fire, grew hungry, and he decided that nothing would sate him except my forest. My *home.* And you helped him. You helped him burn it all down."

Aru's mouth went dry. Now she knew how he had gotten the scars on his face and chest. That was *awful.* And even though it had been Arjuna and not her, her heart ached with guilt.

"Your father was supposed to protect me," hissed Takshaka. "He sent his favorite rain clouds to put out the fire. But it wasn't enough to defeat you, O Arjuna the Great. You had Lord Krishna by your side, and it became too much *work* for Indra to fight against you."

Aru faltered. She had never heard that story about Arjuna. Surely, it couldn't be true.... Arjuna was supposed to be virtuous. He wouldn't have burned down someone's home ... would he? Aru knew so little about him. Out the corner of her eye, she saw Aiden and Brynne circling their hands as if to say *Keep stalling!*

But, for the first time in a while, Aru didn't know what to say.

"Now you have no gods whissspering in your ear," continued the serpent king. "You are nothing. And you are alone."

"Listen," said Aru, gentling her voice. "I'm really sorry that happened to you. Honest. But maybe, uh, you can talk to Indra about it? Meet up for coffee? Work things out? You guys were friends once...."

"I have new friendsss now," said Takshaka. He smiled then, slow and vicious. "I believe you know one of them *very* well."

Aru felt nauseated. *Now* he was talking about the Sleeper. Of course he was behind this.

Takshaka reared back.

And then he struck.

Takshaka moved so fast that Aru almost didn't see him coming. *Almost.* His jaws missed her face by an inch. As she pivoted out of the way, Vajra jumped into her hand, fully expanded. Aru threw the lightning bolt like a spear. Takshaka neatly dodged it. Vajra spun back to her, and this time Aru concentrated with all her effort, focusing on the serpent's writhing tail, wanting to pin him in place like a butterfly in a display. Vajra shot forward like an arrow. But Takshaka was faster. His powerful tail whipped out and knocked the lightning bolt aside like it was a toy.

Aru looked to her friends for help. Brynne was snorting and stomping her feet like an angry bull, but Aiden was holding her back. *Why?*

"Hoverboard!" Aru shouted.

Vajra flattened, but Aru jumped on a second too late. Takshaka's tail lashed through the air and caught her in the stomach. She crashed into the wall and slid down, shaking her head.

Takshaka started laughing. "It's too easssy."

Aru felt woozy, but she forced herself to stand. On the opposite wall Aiden was leaning casually and—Aru wanted to scream at him—*checking his phone.*

Brynne's voice tapped into her thoughts:

We know something Takshaka doesn't like.

Us? thought Aru.

Close your eyes. It's going to get windy in here.

"Reveal yoursssself, Pandava," said Takshaka. "I shall make this quick."

Aru was so tired of that line! Why were monsters always offering to make death go quickly? Why not offer *no* death at all?

As Takshaka edged closer, Aru shut her eyes and flattened herself against the wall. Wind blew against her face. She could hear the treasures rattling off their shelves and crashing to the ground with loud, indignant howls.

"You will pay for thisss," said Takshaka.

A snippet of Aru's dream floated back to her. Mini standing in Home Depot, shaking Aru by the shoulders and . . . imitating a cow? No. Aru did that. *Mooooooo-zique.*

Music.

Music!

Just then, Takshaka hissed. Even with her eyes closed, Aru could sense him rearing up. Dirt and grit whipped her skin. *I'm totally going to die here*, thought Aru.

Then a new sound joined in . . . a sound that suddenly explained why Aiden had been on his phone. Aru cracked open one eye. Aiden stood in the center of the room, holding his phone over his head like a gigantic beacon. Rising above the din, like one of those ancient warriors blowing a horn . . .

Dehhhhh-spaaaaa-cito!
Quiero respirar tu cuello despacito!

Takshaka roared, "NOOOOOOOO!" He writhed. "NOT
THAT SONG! I'm *sick* of it! MAKE IT STOP! MAKE IT
STOP!"

Aiden kept blasting the music. Now he was salsaing. Apsara
kids always have an artistic talent. Dancing was not Aiden's.

Brynne pointed her mace at Aiden's phone and picked it up
in a swirl of dust. Takshaka snapped, lunging for it, but every
time he got close, the wind danced farther away. Takshaka quivered, now moving across the floor and shelves, oblivious to the
screaming treasure.

Brynne sent Aru an urgent message: *Any sign of the thief's
soul song?*

I'm on it! Aru sent back.

Nothing on the bottom shelf. Nothing on the next row up,
either. But when Aru scanned higher, a flash of red caught her
eye. She zeroed in on a scarlet orb the size of a large pendant. It
was huddled against the wall as if it were frightened. As Aru's
gaze lingered on it, a feeling of terrible loss surged through her.
Kamadeva had said that the song wouldn't be like actual music,
but a representation of the thief's soul... and now that made
sense. The soul song seemed to Aru like a piece of someone, a
piece that had been abandoned.

I found it! Aru told Brynne through the mind link.

All Aru had to do was turn Vajra into a hoverboard, zoom
over Takshaka's weaving head, and grab the song from the shelf.

Vajra had just flattened when Aru heard it....

Deafening silence.

The music on Aiden's phone had paused for a commercial. *"Unsatisfied with your car insurance?"*

Takshaka grew still. His hooded face tilted, and the corners of his jaw turned up in a smile.

C'mon, c'mon, c'mon! Aiden mouthed as he shook his phone.

Brynne kept summoning tiny cyclones, trying to distract Takshaka, but the naga's forked tongue tasted the air and caught the scent of blood. He darted toward Aiden. Aru had to bite her lip to keep from screaming.

Brynne whirled around, panic clear on her face, and as the mace turned with her, it sent Aiden's phone soaring high into the air on a blast of wind.

"No!" he yelled.

Takshaka's cobra hood flared. "Found you," he hissed.

Aiden pulled out his scimitars. Wrong move. The sound echoed around the room. Takshaka's mouth curved into a smug fanged grin. He reared to strike.

Aru didn't think—she just reacted. Hopping onto Vajra, she leaned back on her lightning-bolt hoverboard and shot up toward the phone, which was spinning on top of a mini tornado. She stretched out her fingers, straining to reach it. *Just . . . a little . . . farther.* If the phone fell and broke, if they had no way to fill the chamber with music, they'd all die.

She thrust her hand into the column of wind and grabbed. Aru felt the cold weight of the phone in her palm just as a new song started. It was hard to hear it over the howling storm.

She glanced behind her.

Aiden had shoved one of his scimitars into Takshaka's

mouth, propping open his powerful cobra jaws. The serpent thrashed his head, dislodging the blade, and brought down his tail like a merciless whip. Aiden went sprawling, his remaining scimitar skidding across the treasury floor.

Aru cranked up the volume.

"TAYLOR SWIFT?" roared the naga king.

"What's the matter? You a Katy Perry fan?" Brynne taunted, but her face was pure panic until Aiden rose blearily to his feet. She blasted some air in his direction so that his two scimitars were within grabbing distance.

Aru and the hoverboard rocketed higher.

Takshaka whirled around, slamming his tail onto the ground. More treasures rained down from their shelves, and this time he reacted to every sound.

Aru spotted the red orb. It was rolling toward the edge of a shelf. She grabbed it just before it fell off and found that it was on a neck chain. Instantly, a cold tingle went through her arm and she heard a piercing note in her thoughts: the sound of someone stifling a cry. It took Aru by surprise and a gasp slipped from her lips.

Takshaka heard it.

Down below, Brynne yelled and jumped, trying to distract him. But the serpent king paid her no mind. His tail slashed through the air, knocking Aru off her hoverboard. Brynne's wind caught her just in time, and the hoverboard flew back under her feet. Aru wobbled, trying to get her balance. While her grip tightened on the soul song, the phone slipped out of her hand. Below, Aiden and Brynne ran to try to catch it. The phone seemed to fall slowly as it blasted music all the way down:

I'm sorry, the old Taylor can't come to the phone right now.
Why?

Takshaka raised himself up to his full size, so large it seemed he could have blotted out the sun. The phone hit the treasure-littered floor with a *crash*. Its screen shattered. Takshaka slammed it with his tail again and again until the music cut off.

"Oh," said Takshaka mockingly, "'cause she's dead."

TWENTY

I Don't Trust Nobody and Nobody Trusts Me

"Give it to me," said Takshaka.

Aru stiffened. Her grip on the soul song tightened even more. "Give you what?"

"I know what you have," he said.

"Oh, and what might that be?" she asked. "There's all kinds of treasure in this room." She wondered if he knew that she had Uloopi's heart jewel, too.

"Hand over the thief's soul song."

"So you let it happen! You let the bow and arrow be stolen!" said Aru.

Takshaka laughed. "Who do you think let her in here in the first place?"

Let her *in* . . .

The arrow thief was a woman. Was she a nagini? A rakshasi?

Aru didn't exactly like Uloopi—she *had* threatened to exile them, after all—but now she felt bad for the naga queen. Clearly, she trusted Takshaka. Maybe she even thought of him as family. And he'd betrayed her. He'd kept her heart from being returned. He made her weak. Aru's jaw clenched.

"How could you do that to Queen Uloopi?"

Takshaka reared back as if struck. "This is beyond you, little Pandava. Give me the song. You cannot protect that which we seek. After all, your very heartbeat will betray you."

Your very heartbeat.

What did that *mean*?

But there was no time to think about it. The serpent king lunged and Aru barely had a moment to react. She zoomed away on Vajra, narrowly escaping his fangs. Seconds later, she dropped down on the opposite side of the room from Brynne and Aiden. Quickly, Aru looped the soul-song necklace around Vajra and shot it over to Aiden and Brynne. Aiden leaped up, catching it in his fist.

"Missed me!" Takshaka gloated.

He didn't need to know that Aru hadn't been aiming for him. To keep Aiden and Brynne safe, she needed Takshaka to be focused on her and to believe that she still had the song.

The great serpent snapped forward. His fangs sank into the shelves above Aru's head. She swerved out of the way, narrowly missing a blow from a heavy book as it toppled down.

Vajra returned to Aru's hands in the shape of a discus. Aru hadn't had much practice using it in this form. The few times she'd tried it, she had thrown it like a celestial Frisbee, which she wasn't great at. Merely flinging it at Takshaka would be point-less. He was ridiculously fast. She had to aim not where he was moving *now*, but where he was moving *next*.

Aru tapped into the Pandava mind link. *Get his attention, Brynne.*

You got it, she messaged back.

Brynne motioned to Aiden, who began banging his scimitars

against the shelves. Takshaka twitched and whirled toward Aiden and Brynne. As he started to move forward, Aru aimed her lightning-bolt discus just ahead of him.

Bang!

The discus hit Takshaka right in the forehead. A net of electricity fell down on the snake. He thrashed his way out of it and said with a cackle, "No weapon of Indra can harm me, Pandava! Your father was my friend once, after all. And a boon is a boon, no matter how long ago it was given. I am immune."

He zigged and zagged, his great coils winding way up the shelves and blocking the entrance in the ceiling above.

"Aru!" shouted Brynne.

She turned just in time to see Vajra's lightning net coming at her. Usually Vajra just spun back into her hand. But making contact with Takshaka had weakened it. It did not change form, and it did not aim for her hand. Aru tried to leap out of the way, but the net caught her around the foot and tripped her.

"This is the end," said Takshaka when he heard Aru hit the floor. He looped back over himself and down toward her. "I hope to bring you as much pain as you caused me. You are no hero. You are a pawn in a game beyond your understanding. You are *nothing*."

Takshaka's fangs lengthened. They were stained yellow, and one was chipped. Venom dripped onto the ground, hitting the floor with a steaming *hiss*. Aru squeezed her eyes shut. Aiden and Brynne were too far away to help her. And even if they'd wanted to, if they rushed over, it would only lead to all three of them getting killed. *This is it*, thought Aru.

A rush of air hit Aru just as Takshaka lunged.

Brynne.

With her wind mace, Brynne had lifted a shelving unit into the air. She tilted it until it formed a barricade between Takshaka's jaws and Aru's body. Her face shone with sweat.

Where the shelves used to be, Aiden was scaling the wall, using his scimitars as grappling hooks. He climbed quickly, but he didn't reach the exit fast enough. Brynne created a gust so strong that Takshaka was blown backward. He slammed into the wall Aiden was climbing, and the vibration sent the boy tumbling. He hit the floor with a nasty *thud* and didn't move.

"Aiden!" shouted Aru, scrambling out of the lightning net.

He didn't answer.

Aru and Brynne huddled close. Aru shut her eyes as wind lashed around them. Vajra, now back in bolt form, flickered weakly. Aru felt helpless. There was no way they could get out of here, which meant Boo and Mini and the Heartless would be imprisoned forever. And forget about being exiled from the Otherworld—she'd just die here instead.

And then . . .

Thump-a thump-thump. Thump-a thump-thump.

Rhythm shook the floor. More treasures quivered and fell off the shelves. Takshaka hissed, pulling back as the sound of drums filled the air.

Brynne lifted her head, frowning. "Is that . . . is that *bhangra*?"

Bhangra is a kind of upbeat music that is often played at Indian weddings. Aru had no idea how to dance to it, but then again, neither did any of the brown uncles at parties. Their favorite bhangra dance technique was to pretend to screw in a lightbulb and pet a dog at the same time. And then start jumping.

Brynne's shoulders began to move up and down to the beat. "Now is not the time!" said Aru.

Then again, it was almost impossible *not* to dance when it came to bhangra. Even Takshaka, who had recovered, started swaying. His tail thumped to the rhythm as Panjabi MC and Jay-Z started rapping. The Panjabi lyrics filled the room:

> *Mundiya to bach ke rahi*
> *Nahi tu hun hun hui mutiyarrr*

But then, over the music, came a new sound: "RUN!"

Aru's gaze flew to the other side of the room. A section of shelves opened like a door, allowing a naga boy about her age to enter before it swung closed behind him. He had come from some kind of secret passageway. From the waist up, he wore a bright orange hoodie, but from the waist down he had a crimson snake tail banded with yellow stripes. He also wore sunglasses, which was absurd, considering how dark the chamber of treasures already was. His ears were covered by a pair of heavy DJ-style headphones. He held up two speakers, pointing them at Takshaka. The serpent writhed as if someone had doused him with spiders.

"RUN!" the boy said again.

Brynne was the first to act. She hoisted Aru to her feet and the two of them rushed over to Aiden. Aru tried to lift him by the arm and stumbled.

"I got this," said Brynne. She gathered him up like he was a bundle of blankets and threw him over her shoulder.

They ran to where the naga boy stood by the door. His

head turned toward them when they approached, but his focus seemed like it was elsewhere, as if he was looking at something just to the left of them.

Now that she was close to the door, Aru could see that it was a portal. It was slightly ajar, and through the crack Aru could glimpse street signs and a cement sidewalk, cars disappearing around corners, even people in winter coats walking their dogs.

But just as Brynne reached to pull it open all the way, a low hiss startled them, and the door slammed *shut*. At first, Takshaka had been enthralled by the bhangra rhythm, swaying back and forth, even happily rapping along. But now he was stiff and alert, his blind eyes fixed on the boy.

"You!" he snarled. "You are not fit to call yourself my dessscendant."

The boy with the headphones flinched, but he didn't drop the speakers. "What you're doing is wrong, Dada-ji."

Dada-ji. That's what you called a grandfather. Who was this boy?

"Do you fancy yourself some kind of hero?" hissed Takshaka. "Ssstep aside and I may forget how your very existence is a disss-grace to my lineage."

"Hero?" repeated the boy. "I mean, yeah, I guess, if you call stopping murder on a Saturday heroic. Be mad at me all you want—you probably won't even remember this later."

And with that, he put the speakers down on the floor, pulled a phone out of his hoodie pocket, and punched in some numbers. The music grew louder and Takshaka fell into a deep trance.

The boy held open the door for Brynne and Aru. "Ladies and unconscious dude."

Aru and Brynne just stared at him.

"Who *are* you?" demanded Aru.

"You're supposed to say thank you."

"I'm not thanking anyone!" said Aru. "How am I supposed to know what's behind that door? And you're his grandson! Why should we trust you?"

Brynne stepped on her foot. *"Thank you."*

"I can tell you what's *not* behind the door," said the boy in sunglasses. "Definitely not an ancient serpent king that wants you dead. But lots of traffic. And maybe even some help."

"You—"

"Saved your life, and I'm offering you a way out," said the boy. But now he was standing with his back against the door. That didn't seem like a way out. He crossed his arms. "Your move."

Maybe some people would be willing to help for no reason other than to be kind. People like Mini, for example. But this kid clearly wasn't one of those.... There was something too sly about him. And even though she was an inch away from a total meltdown, Aru wasn't so gone that she hadn't noticed how Takshaka had spoken to his grandson. This boy was, to put it lightly, not a family favorite.

There was something else, too. She'd seen him before somewhere....

"You're that boy from the Night Bazaar," she said.

It was during their last quest. This boy had smiled at Mini, which had led her to walk straight into a telephone pole.

"Hard to forget a face like this," he said, cupping his chin and grinning.

"Why are you helping us?" demanded Aru. "What do you want?"

"Aru!" said Brynne, sinking a little under Aiden's weight. "Why are you arguing?"

"Because he wants something." She knew it in her gut.

"You're right," said the boy. "I want your number."

"You *what*?"

First, Aru *never* gave out her number to boys (then again, it's not like any boy had ever asked for it, but that was neither here nor there), and second, Mini had walked into a telephone pole after seeing him.... On principle, that just wasn't right.

"Your. Number," he repeated slowly. "Unless you want me to send you a message by carrier pigeon or something. C'mon, it's important. Trust me."

"*Aru*," said Brynne. "Just do it, and let's get out of here."

It was now or never.

"Fine," she said. She gave him her number.

"I'll text you," he said, finally stepping out of the way. "I'm going to need your help, Aru Shah."

"How do you know my—?"

But he was already closing the door. The last thing Aru saw was a smug grin.

TWENTY-ONE

The Dangerous Samosa

Aru blinked and found herself staring at a brick wall covered in flyers for lost pets, more missing men, household help wanted, and remedies for baldness (*Hair transplants! Now you don't have to be bald and creepy! You can just be creepy!*). A hard crust of frost clung to the cement, and strings of Christmas lights wound around the potted trees near the storefronts. The cold air smelled like winter...and curry. A few pedestrians bustled past. A brown woman wearing a parka over her *salwar kameez* disappeared into a grocery store. On the other side of the street, a young white couple pushed their baby in a stroller and took turns eating out of a paper bag filled with crispy samosas, an Indian snack of fried pastry filled with potatoes and spices.

"Where *are* we?" asked Aru. She was freezing. They definitely weren't in Atlanta, that was for sure.

Brynne gently lowered Aiden onto the sidewalk. He groaned, shook his head, and looked around groggily.

"Snake?" he asked.

"He's off dancing bhangra."

Aiden blinked. "'Kay," he said fuzzily and slumped against the brick wall.

Brynne licked her finger and raised it to the air.

"Does that actually work—?" Aru asked.

"We are 40.5187 degrees north and 74.4121 degrees west."

"In English!" said Aru through chattering teeth.

"Edison, New Jersey."

Aru blinked. Now the stop signs, smells, and even the different storefronts made sense. "So, we're in Little India."

"Yep."

It was no secret that there were lots of South Asian families in this pocket of the United States. Aru was pretty sure she'd even read a newspaper article about it once.

Now that she knew where they were, Aru returned Vajra to ball form in her pocket and looked at everything a little more closely. Snake boy had said they'd find some traffic, and maybe even some help, but nothing looked helpful here.... This city too had contributed to the growing number of Heartless. In the display window of an appliance store, TV screens showed news anchors frowning above tickers that pronounced:

SEARCH FOR THE MISSING CONTINUES

EXPERTS SUSPECT BIOCHEMICAL FOUL PLAY

IS THERE SOMETHING IN YOUR WATER?

"Is the thief's song safe?" asked Aru.

Brynne nodded, tilting her head to one side, so Aru could see the hint of the necklace's chain. "Now all we need to do is rescue Mini. Once we get her and she gives us the thief's name, it's all over. And we know we have to go to Durvasa. How hard could it be?"

It *did* sound easy. Then why was Aru so nervous?

"How far away is the land of sleep, anyway?" asked Aru. "And what about Aiden? Are we going to drag him behind us the whole time?"

"I've got him," said Brynne, scooping him up like a sack of rice.

Aiden groaned. "This is humiliating. Put me down."

"You're about to pass out."

Aiden raised his eyebrows. "Fair," he said groggily, and slumped back to sleep.

Brynne shivered and shrugged. "C'mon, we can sort everything out over some chaat."

Chaat didn't mean a talk, but savory Indian fast food—a combination of things like crispy potato pieces, spiced chickpeas, and yogurt sauces bursting with flavor. Just thinking about it made Aru's stomach rumble hungrily. Pulling her sweatshirt tighter around her, she followed Brynne—who was half-cradling Aiden—into a nearby chaat shop. The three of them squished into a booth. The table surface was kinda sticky, which made Aru miss Mini even more. If she were here, she would've brought out a one-gallon bottle of hand sanitizer. Brynne ordered them a ton of food, and within minutes, the table was covered with steaming samosas, paper-thin dosas next to bowls of bright green chutney, sweet gulab jamun sitting in a dish of syrup, and iced mango lassis.

"First things first," said Brynne, picking up Aiden's water glass. He didn't notice, because his head was on the table and he had started to snore. "Aru, can you take Aiden's camera?"

"Why?" she asked.

"Just do it."

Aru gently pulled the strap off Aiden's shoulder—careful not to disturb him—and laid the camera on the chair next to her.

"We don't want it to get wet," said Brynne.

"Dude, we're indoors. It's not going to rain—"

Brynne dumped the glass of water on Aiden's head.

"HEY!" he shouted, startling awake.

"You'll be fine," Brynne said breezily. "Have some food."

He scowled at them, still somewhat out of it. Then he touched his shoulder, and his eyes widened. Panicking, he bolted to his feet and looked right and left. Droplets flew from his wet hair. "Where's Shadowfax?!"

Aru, drinking her water, almost did a spit take. Shadowfax was the name of Gandalf's horse in *The Lord of the Rings*. And she would have *definitely* noticed if Aiden had been hauling around a horse.

"Shadowfax is fine," said Brynne, pointing at the camera. "Aru has it."

Aiden exhaled in relief as Aru handed back the camera.

"You named your camera Shadowfax?"

Aiden patted his camera like it was a puppy.

"Is it hungry?" asked Aru. "Want me to feed it?"

"Go away, Shah."

"How about a belly rub?"

Aiden flicked a piece of samosa at her face. Aru caught it in her mouth, but she was so surprised she'd managed it, she started choking. *Death by samosa! No! What a dumb way to go!* Brynne had to thump her back a couple times until she hacked it up.

"Did I dream it, or did some guy save us back in the naga treasury?" asked Aiden.

"Takshaka's grandson," Aru said after catching her breath. She was still hungry but now distrustful of samosas, so she stabbed one a little too violently with her fork to make sure it knew who was boss. *Don't get any ideas, food.* "He said he's going to need our help later, but he didn't say with what."

Brynne tore into her dosa and said through a mouthful, "And he asked for Aru's number."

Aiden raised his eyebrows. "Why?"

"Wow, thanks."

He flushed. "I didn't mean—"

"Never mind," said Aru, ignoring the slight sting. "We have the thief's song. That's all that matters."

Brynne took off the necklace with the scarlet orb and laid it on the table. All three of them winced at the same time, and Aru knew the others were picking up the terrible sensation that the soul song evoked, of being utterly *lost.*

Aiden shook himself. "That's definitely what we were looking for."

He poked it experimentally with a fork.

"Stop it! That's someone's soul!" said Aru.

"It gives off bad vibes," said Brynne. "Why couldn't it just play a sad song instead?"

The three of them leaned forward. Smoke whirled in the orb. For a moment, Aru thought she saw a flash of sharp red fingernails, but the image disappeared instantly. No music whatsoever. By now, that sinking feeling of abandonment had vanished.

"The important thing is we have it," said Brynne. "Now we need Mini."

"And a sage to help us get her," said Aiden. "Where's that business card?"

Aru pulled it from her back pocket and slid it across the table. The three of them stared at it.

S. DURVASA

DO NOT BOTHER ME WITH INFANTILE CONCERNS

I WILL CURSE YOU FOR WASTING MY TIME

"He sounds like Brynne when she's hungry," whispered Aiden.

"Or just Brynne in general."

Brynne scowled. "I'm right here, you know."

"Is there anything on the back of the card?" asked Aiden. "Like an address or something?" He flipped it over. In very tiny font it read:

DMV (DEPARTMENT OF MANY VOICES)

LOCATION REVEALED WHEN INQUIRER
STATES NAME AND PURPOSE

INQUIRIES ANSWERED IN THE ORDER IN
WHICH THEY ARE RECEIVED

"Department of Many Voices?" repeated Brynne. "Is that like a call center?"

"Or the Department of Motor Vehicles," Aiden said with a groan. "I had to go there with my mom once. It's the most boring place in the world."

"Well, if we want to find out, I guess we should try talking to the card," said Aru. "Ready?"

"It's all up to you, Shah," said Brynne, slurping down the rest of her mango lassi.

Aru held the card out in front of her and cleared her throat. "Um, hi?"

The card continued to act like a piece of paper.

"My name is Aru, and—"

"Use your full name," cut in Brynne. "Way more official-sounding."

Aru hesitated. She felt weird saying it in front of the others. "My name is Arundhati Shah. I'm with..."

"Brynne Rao."

"That's not your full name," said Aiden.

Brynne groaned. "Okay, fine, it's technically Brynne Tvarika Lakshmi Balamuralikrishna Rao."

Aru's eyebrows skyrocketed up her head, but she continued. "Um, we need to find our sister. Her name is Mini... Yamini Kapoor-Mercado-Lopez. She told us to find S. Durvasa."

At first nothing happened, and they all felt stupid for talking to a card. Aru put it back down on the table. While they waited, Aru eyed Brynne.

"So..."

"Yeah, I know, I've got a thousand names...I'm a Telugoose—" She paused at Aru's confusion, then said, "You know, Telugu from South India? I never met my dad, though. I think Anila said he was Irish."

"Telugoose," clucked Aiden, making chicken arms. Brynne flicked his ear and he laughed.

"It's a pretty name," said Aru. "But imagine if you were a

spy! You could never say something like 'Bond…James Bond,' because then the villain would be there all night—"

Brynne threw a piece of samosa at her forehead.

Then, right in front of them, the corners of the business card folded down all on their own. The card twisted and creased and tore itself until it resembled an origami clock with an actual moving hand. The clock ticked down.

Aru frowned. "Now what?"

"Now," said Brynne, "we wait for an answer."

For the next few minutes, Brynne went Full Brynne. She sent back three dishes. One because the coconut wasn't toasted enough. The second because it was too salty. The third because it wasn't salty enough.

Aru was glad she'd had enough to eat by then. There was *no way* she was going to chance ordering anything else from this kitchen. Half the staff would probably spit into it, thanks to Brynne.

"That's it," said Brynne, starting to get up. "I'm going back there—"

"No," said Aiden calmly as he pulled her into her seat. "When you're angry, say the numbers one through ten."

"One through ten. Now can I go?"

"You should be on a cooking show where you just yell at people. Like Gordon Ramsay," said Aru, trying to distract her. The last thing they needed was to get thrown out of the restaurant before they had their answer from S. Durvasa.

Brynne emitted a happy sigh. "That's my dream."

"Where'd you learn all this stuff about cooking, anyway?" asked Aru.

Brynne flicked the paper timer around the table, not looking up at them.

"My uncles taught me," she said. "I moved in with them when I was four, after Anila left."

"Anila?"

Brynne's jaw looked tight. "My mom."

"Oh," said Aru, embarrassed.

"My uncles said that she had me too young and wasn't ready to be a mom," said Brynne. She started tearing her dosa into smaller and smaller pieces. "She still isn't. But, I dunno, maybe she'll change her mind someday."

Aru thought about the photo album that Brynne kept in her backpack, and all those trophy bracelets on her wrist. Now Aru got it. Brynne carried them not as proof to herself that she was awesome, but as proof for someone else . . . someone like a mom who didn't stay.

"I like cooking, because you know what's going to happen," said Brynne quietly. "You have a good idea of how things will react and taste, and if you don't like how it comes out, you can start over."

"Brynne makes really good lasagna," added Aiden.

"The *best* lasagna," she corrected him with a smile.

In the middle of the table, the little origami clock began to spin. A thin trail of smoke curled out of it and snaked through the restaurant and out the door. Aru looked around, but none of the other customers seemed to have noticed. In her pocket, Vajra hummed.

A little voice whispered from the folded paper, "Sage Durvasa has accepted your request for an appointment."

"Sage!" said Aiden. "I knew it!"

A sage is a very wise person. Aru's mom had told her that some have special powers, because of their religious focus. Once there was a sage so formidable he put a curse on the gods themselves—he caused them to lose their immortality. Aru did *not* want to run into someone like that.

Before their eyes, the trail of smoke began to glow. The card spoke again.

"Please proceed to the highlighted route. Then your route guidance will begin."

TWENTY-TWO

Aiden Brings the Smolder

Aru, Aiden, and Brynne followed the bright smoke out the door.

The second they crossed the threshold of the chaat shop, Aru felt a pull of magic right behind her belly button. It was the same feeling she got every time she used a portal. She blinked, and when she opened her eyes, they were no longer on a street in Edison, New Jersey. Instead, they were standing on a stretch of lawn facing a massive building. The trail of bright smoke led right to the front door.

It was, Aru thought, the most *unmagical* structure she had ever seen. Squat, long, screaming *nine-to-five adult job*, and painted a shade of depressed supermarket egg. And yet, she knew they were somewhere in the Otherworld, because no matter which direction she faced, she found herself staring at the same building. It didn't feel like winter here. It didn't feel like *anything*. Aru couldn't even see the sun.

"Freaky," said Aiden, spinning in a circle.

"*That* is the Department of Many Voices?" asked Brynne.

"Definitely looks like a DMV," said Aiden.

"Not only the DMV," said Aru, looking at the plain white sign on the lawn. In small letters, it read ASHRAM. Whenever Aru thought of an ashram, she imagined a posh spa where rich people paid someone to identify the color of their aura. But she knew that the word *ashram* had originated in India. It was like a monastery, a place where hermits went. The austere outside of the DMV definitely fit that definition.

The three of them walked up the sidewalk and through the pair of glass entrance doors. In the lobby—which had both hand sanitizer and hoof sanitizer dispensers on a stand—there was a wide reception desk with a calendar and a box of paperclips, and a box of what looked like Kleenex but read: CURSE WIPES. A girl their age poked her head up behind the desk. She was a fair-skinned nature spirit, a yakshini, with tendrils of frost for hair. A badge on her black shirt read:

WINTER INTERN

MY NAME IS IRIS. HOW CAN I HELP?

"What," said the yakshini girl, clearly bored, when they approached the desk.

Brynne stepped forward and slid the S. Durvasa business card across the table. "We were referred by Lord Kamadeva, the god of love—"

"Identification," the yakshini said in the same exact tone.

"I'm getting to that," said Brynne, bristling. "You see, we're actually Pandavas—"

"Right, and I'm Kim Kardashian," said the girl. "The wait

time will be"—she paused to consult a stack of papers on her desk—"three centuries. You can take your place in—"

"*THREE CENTURIES?!*" exploded Brynne.

"If you'd like to lodge a complaint about the wait time, please fill out this form in standard blood-of-my-enemies ink," said the girl. A piece of paper popped up in front of each of their faces—except, in Brynne's case, the piece of paper smacked her in the nose. "Please take your number and have a seat."

"You can't speed it up? Please, Iris?" asked Aru, flashing her most charming smile.

Iris reared back as if Aru had a super-contagious gum disease.

"Um, *no*," said the girl. "If you *want* to be first in line, you've got to have one of *these*"—she paused to wave a glowing green ticket sitting on her desk—"and you don't. So *sit down* or get out!"

Aru was going to try again, but Brynne yanked on her sleeve. Aru followed her and Aiden to the entrance, which was out of the yakshini's range of hearing.

"What?" asked Aru.

"We gotta get that green ticket," said Brynne.

"How are we going to do that?" Aru laughed. "Just pluck it out of her hands and run?"

"Yeah, pretty much. You know what that means, Aiden."

His eyes widened. "Oh, c'mon. Don't make me do it—"

"It's the only way!"

"*What's* the only way?"

"So, as the kid of an elite apsara, Aiden can—"

He groaned loudly.

"Aiden can *what*?" asked Aru excitedly. "Ooh! Can he

summon a flash mob? Will we all start dancing in perfect choreography? Like everyone does 'Thriller' at the same time, and then we take the ticket and run?"

"Aiden can *smolder*," explained Brynne. "It's temporary, obviously, but the effects should last for at least an hour, which is long enough for S. Durvasa to see us."

Aru was very confused. First, because *smoldering* sounded like a talent only the Rock could pull off. Second, did that mean Aiden was going to burst into flames? Because, sure, that'd be a pretty decent distraction while she and Brynne took the ticket.

"You know how apsaras were always sent to distract sages?" said Brynne.

Aru nodded. In stories, apsaras were the ultimate temptation, because they were unnaturally beautiful and magical. Between spending time with a celestial Miss Universe or meditating in a forest, there's clearly a winning choice.

"Well, apsaras have a kind of hypnotic power. They can render themselves impossible to look away from, and even make people follow them," said Aiden. Then, without looking at either of them, he added, *"AndIcandothattooandthatwayyoucanstealtheticket."*

Aru bit back a cackle. "So . . . when you do this whole smolder thing, does it look like a Bollywood movie? Will someone burst into song? Invisible wind and all that?"

Brynne elbowed her, but a smile pulled at the corners of her mouth.

"I'm only doing this for Mini," he said, and stomped off.

That sobered Aru immediately. She and Brynne watched as Aiden approached the yakshini at the desk.

"Be careful not to look at Aiden's face, okay?" whispered

Brynne. "It sounds like a dumb power, but it's dangerous. Even more dangerous if you're into him."

Aru snorted. "Good thing I'm not."

Brynne looked like she was about to say something, but instead she nodded and gestured Aru forward. "Okay, let's go."

When Aru looked up, Aiden was still standing there. Enchantment radiated off him, pulling the light differently so that he appeared as if in a beam of sunshine. The yakshini girl was standing too, staring at him as if he'd told her she'd a) won the lottery b) gotten her letter from Hogwarts and c) soon be receiving a lifetime supply of Oreos. *That's some smolder,* thought Aru, as she and Brynne crept to the desk.

"Watch the entrance," said Brynne.

Aru did. But even though she avoided looking at Aiden, she could still hear him. His voice changed, and not in that sudden broken way of the guys in her grade. He sounded the same, but it was like someone had lined his voice with velvet.

"Hey! *Aru!*" Brynne waved the green ticket in her face. "Let's go! Aiden!"

"I'm here," said Aiden.

Aru was very glad his voice had returned to normal.

"I wish *I* had smolder power," she said.

"I don't," said Aiden, shuddering as if he felt bugs crawling on his skin. "I only use it in case of emergencies."

"Why?"

He turned his camera in his hands before pressing a button that once more concealed it, and his bag, inside a magical watch. "I've seen my aunts and uncles take it too far.... It doesn't seem right to do that to someone when they didn't agree to it."

By now, the three of them had turned the corner from the yakshini's desk and come to a great spiral staircase. At the bottom of the steps stretched a wide room filled with a hundred or so rickety wooden seats facing a row of empty glass-framed booths. It reminded Aru of the lobby of a dentist's office. Some of the Otherworld members were slumped over, fast asleep. Others were wide-awake, yelling at their laptops while they waited. The lights overhead were white moths, fluttering around aimlessly and spreading a strange luminescence that reminded Aru of cafeteria lighting. In the corner sat a dark-skinned *gandharva*, a celestial musician with bright golden wings. At first he didn't see them, because he was listening to an ancient-looking stereo with huge headphones. He took them off when the group got closer.

"Good luck to you, dudes," said the gandharva. "They've all been on the longest lunch break."

"Who has?" asked Aru.

"The sages...*duh*."

Above the booths were little neon signs bearing the names of various sages: BHRIGU, KINDAMA, NARADA—and DURVASA!

"They're probably meditating or something," said the gandharva, irritated. "We've no choice but to wait for them to be done. A few minutes ago, Sage Narada stopped by, but I couldn't talk to him, because I was in the middle of listening to this *sick* solo. So he cursed me to keep waiting, and to lose all sense of time." The musician laughed. "But don't worry—that's just talk. It's still 1972!"

"Actually—" started Aiden.

"PANDAVAS," boomed a voice coming from the Durvasa booth.

Aru's heart rate kicked up a bit. They needed Durvasa to

help them bring back Mini. Surely he would, right? Mini had mentioned his name for a reason.

In a corner, a light-skinned girl with antlers rocked back and forth, muttering, "*Nextinlinenextinlinenextinline . . .*"

Aru, Aiden, and Brynne walked over to the booth. A little metal box marked TICKETS hopped up and down until Brynne dropped the green ticket into the slot. There was a shimmer in the air and an old man appeared behind the glass. He had a generous belly, nut-brown skin, and black hair piled into a matted bun on top of his head. He was wearing a white polo shirt with a small badge that read:

S. DURVASA

THE ANSWER IS NO

This was the great sage?

"I didn't like him, he had a horrible haircut," the sage was muttering. He started scribbling something in his book. "And did he offer me a place to sit? Inquire about my health? No! *And* he breathed through his mouth. *Disgusting.* Hmm . . . What to do, what to do? Ha!"

He licked his pen and wrote in the air. Sparkling letters appeared:

> *May all the chocolate chip cookies you reach for*
> *turn out to be cleverly disguised oatmeal raisin.*

"Yes, yes." He cackled to himself. "FEAR ME, MORTAL!"

The sage steepled his fingers together. He riffled through someone's file and scoffed. "Ugh. This person asks for a mantra for better sleep? *This* is what people choose to waste my time with? Abominable. Oh yes, I have a *blessing* for you—"

Once more, he wrote in the air:

When you go to bed, may both sides of your pillow be slightly too warm, and may your door keep opening a crack as soon as you get sleepy.

Aiden inhaled sharply, whispering, "Harsh."

But the sage wasn't done. His list of curses continued:

May your spoon always fall in your cereal.

May you always fumble with your credit card in Starbucks when there's a huge line behind you.

May your towel after a shower always be a smidge too far to reach, so you have to step out.

"Hey—" started Brynne, but Aru yanked her arm.

The sage paused. It seemed as if he was giving them a moment to decide whether or not to disturb him. They were hardly a foot away. There was no way the sage couldn't see them, but Aru felt a prickle of foreboding. This was a test.

She remembered Kamadeva's warning: *BE VERY POLITE.*

Something itched at the back of Aru's skull. There was a reason why Durvasa's name had stuck with her...a reason why she'd been a little wary. Goose bumps pebbled her skin. She suddenly felt about the size of an ant.

Aru tapped into the Pandava mind link.

Brynne's response was immediate: *What is it?*

Remember the sage who cursed all the gods to lose their immortality? sent Aru. *And that's why they churned the Ocean of Milk for the nectar of immortality and everyone lost their minds and the universe descended into chaos?*

Yeah?

Well, sent Aru, *I just figured out who Durvasa is. HE'S THE SAGE WHO CURSED THEM.*

TWENTY-THREE

Leave the Rock Outta This

Sage Durvasa fixed them with an angry stare.

"Pandavas," he said, sneering.

"And—" Aiden started.

The sage cut him off. "I know what I said. And I know why you're here. You want to retrieve that *obnoxious* girl who has a fixation on physical illness."

That definitely sounded like Mini.

"The one with the allergy card?" asked Aru.

"Hand sanitizer?" asked Brynne.

"Glasses?" asked Aiden.

Durvasa made an irritated grunt. He shuffled through some things on his desk before standing up. "Yes."

"So, will you help us get her back?" asked Aiden.

"It's critical, sir," Aru said, trying her best to sound kind. "You see, Mini knows the name of the thief who stole Kamadeva's bow and arrow. And we have the thief's soul song." Brynne pulled out the necklace chain, revealing the soul-song pendant. "If we can just put everything together, we can fix the Heartless. Please?"

Aru was going to say more, but then Brynne shouted into her brain: *DON'T SOUND WEAK!*

Aru was quiet after that. She had left out parts of the story.... Like the fact that their entire connection to the Otherworld would be severed if they failed, and the fact that Boo was being held captive for crimes he didn't commit. But maybe Brynne was right. Maybe it was better to sound heroic versus hurting.

For a moment, it seemed as if Durvasa were considering her request. His gaze went somewhere beyond them. Then he shook himself, and his brows flattened over his black eyes.

"No." And with that, he exited the booth.

Aru stood there for a moment, shocked. Mini had said Durvasa would help them.... What were they supposed to do now?

The sage began walking down the row of glass booths. Aru, Brynne, and Aiden followed him until they got to a locked golden gate with scrollwork that looked like a fanned peacock's tail. Durvasa opened it with a fancy key and stepped through, shutting it behind him.

"Can we change your mind?" called Aru. "Do you like Oreos?"

"How about lasagna?" asked Brynne. "I make *great* lasagna!"

Durvasa scowled. "Oreos make my teeth look atrocious, and I *despise* lasagna."

He turned on his heel and pushed open a door beyond the golden gate. The red sign above it said DIVINITY ONLY. Durvasa slipped inside without even waving good-bye.

"Who doesn't like Oreos?" demanded Aru. "That's inhuman!"

Meanwhile, Brynne looked as if someone had punched her in the heart. "But I make *great* lasagna...."

Out of nowhere, Aiden let out a hoot. Aru frowned, ready to yell at him. What was there to be happy about? Their last line of help had straight-up refused, Mini was still imprisoned, and the thief was still out there somewhere.

But Aiden was grinning. He sat cross-legged on the floor, the kit of "unidentified necessities" on his lap. He'd chosen well in the Warehouse of Quest Materials. Aru wondered if she'd ever get a chance to use her vial containing a single "bright idea."

"Look," said Aiden, holding up a large golden key. "This can change to fit any lock."

He got up and held the key against the lock. It transformed in his hand, assuming the same shape as the peacock design on the gate. He stuck it into the keyhole, and light burst around it. The gate swung creakily open.

"Nice work!" said Brynne, high-fiving him.

Out of solidarity with Mini, Aru offered only her elbow.

"Durvasa couldn't have gotten far," said Aru quietly.

The three of them snuck through the gate and then, with some trepidation, the divinity-only door. But maybe they counted, because they were *part* divine and Aiden had a special Pandava dispensation for this quest.

Unlike the building's dull exterior, the interior of the DMV was huge, like a cosmic gallery. Beneath them, the floor glittered, as if someone had paved it with crushed stars. The ceiling looked like that of the Night Bazaar, an open sky that was half in daylight and half in darkness. The longer Aru stared at the ceiling, the more details she noticed. Like how there seemed to be a slender silver bridge that connected day and night, and how, if she waited for the clouds to move, she could make out two grand palaces, one in each realm. The palace in the daytime half of the sky looked like it was studded with carved rubies and garnets. The palace in the nighttime half looked like it was chiseled out of sapphire and moonstone.

But as uncanny as everything seemed, that was nothing compared to the sight on the wall opposite them. Inside a row of glass display cases, there were statues...that appeared to be alive. They twisted and morphed in place, sometimes looking human, other times resembling asuras and apsaras.

"What *is* this place?" asked Brynne. "It gives me the creeps."

Aru walked up to a statue of a beautiful woman sitting on the ground and weeping. A metal plaque at the bottom of the case read SHAKUNTULA.

"I know that story," said Aiden, walking up beside her. "Shakuntula was so distracted by thoughts of her husband that she ignored the sage who came to visit her. He put a curse on her that whoever she was thinking about would forget her."

"That's...hostile," said Aru.

"At least her husband remembered her again. I forgot how. Something to do with a fish..."

Yeah, right, thought Aru. *Because nothing says true love like a fish.*

The statue in the case beside Shakuntula was just a rock. Curious, Aru moved toward it, but Brynne grabbed her by the wrist.

"Stop looking at statues!" she said. "We've got to find Durvasa! He could be anywhere."

"*He* is right behind you."

All three of them jumped, spinning around to face the sage. He loomed over them, his arms crossed.

"Get *out*, Pandavas! The sign said 'divinity only'!"

"We're divine!" countered Brynne. "Sorta?"

"Yeah, check it out!" said Aru, brandishing Vajra.

But at the sight of the powerful sage, her lightning bolt wilted into a meek noodle.

"Vajra!" hissed Aru.

The lightning bolt turned into a Ping-Pong ball and zoomed back into her pocket.

"Coward," whispered Aru.

Vajra stung her spitefully.

Durvasa smirked. "It seems your father has not forgotten my might. It was I, after all, who punished the gods. I took away their immortality for spiting me."

"What did Lord Indra do to make you mad?" asked Aru.

"I gave him a beautiful garland. And what did he do? He put it on that cloud-spinning elephant's head! The elephant decided the flowers tickled too much, and the creature threw it on the ground! So, just as my gift had been cast down, I decreed that the gods should be cast down, too."

Aiden frowned. "But it was the elephant, not Indra, that—"

"*Pah!* Why have you followed me here? I told you to leave."

"We were just…admiring your rock?" tried Aiden. "It's, um, a great rock."

Durvasa scoffed. "That's not just *a* rock. It's *the* rock."

"*The Rock?*" echoed Brynne, looking horrified. "How could you *do* that to Dwayne Johnson?"

"No, not the wrestler-actor-man!"

"Oh."

"That rock was once the famously beautiful apsara Rambha. Someone sent her to disturb the meditations of a *rishi*, to prevent him from becoming too powerful. Obviously she was not successful, for she was cursed to assume the form of a rock for ten thousand years."

Ten *thousand* years as a rock? Just because you followed orders?

Aru scowled. "That's not fair."

Durvasa shrugged. "Fairness is but an idea conceived by someone who has the power to make such pronouncements. As for curses themselves, well, they are finicky, spiteful things."

"But she was just doing her job," said Aiden.

"As am I," said Durvasa. "According to the legal ordinances of the Otherworld, I am forbidden from assisting or blessing anyone who is suspected of committing a crime. And you two"—he nodded at Brynne, then Aru—"have been accused of thievery. And I might believe it, too. Don't think I don't know *how* you got to be first in line." He raised an eyebrow.

"It's not like we had a choice!" protested Aru. "That girl told us we had to wait three centuries, and according to her office calendar, we barely have three *days* left before the Heartless stay that way forever."

"I hate Otherworld time," grumbled Brynne.

"If you are innocent, let someone else concern themselves with the matter," said Durvasa. "Unless there is some other reason you care?"

When a few seconds passed without anyone speaking, Durvasa did an about-face.

"Wait!" Brynne called out. "Please! Okay, fine.... If we don't manage to return Kamadeva's bow and arrow to Uloopi, she will ban us from the Otherworld. We won't be part of... part of anything anymore."

Aru felt like her heart was being squeezed. Like Brynne, she didn't want to be cast out of the one place where she felt like she mattered. At the same time, she couldn't stop wondering if she didn't really deserve a place in the Otherworld, because her dad was the Sleeper.

You were never meant to be a hero.

Aru banished the thought.

"And we won't be able to fix something that went terribly wrong," added Aiden, rubbing his thumb along the top of his camera, which had reemerged from the magical watch.

Aru wondered what he meant by that. Was he talking about Mini's abduction? She didn't think so. But clearly Aiden wasn't on this quest merely to earn one of Kamadeva's arrows. She thought at first that Aiden had wanted a love arrow for some girl in middle school...but now she was beginning to suspect she'd gotten it all wrong.

"People are going missing," said Aru, thinking not only of the men who were becoming Heartless, but Mini, too. "And also...because it's the right thing to do." *For Boo...and even Uloopi,* she told herself. Uloopi deserved to get her heart jewel back after spending so much of her immortal life wasting away because of Takshaka's deception.

Durvasa stood before them, impassive as ever. "I cannot help you," he said haughtily.

Brynne wiped her eyes and sniffed loudly before glowering. Aru knew how she felt. There was nothing worse than being honest with someone and then having them throw it back in your face. It was like salt in a wound.

"Come on, guys," said Brynne, turning to leave.

Aru clenched her jaw. "Haven't you ever wanted a different

ending? Or thought about what would happen if you didn't follow the rules? All the things that could change?"

Durvasa hesitated for just a second. His shoulders fell a fraction of an inch.

"I still cannot help you," he said stonily.

Aru turned to leave, but Durvasa kept talking. "I cannot tell you, for instance, that your friend lies fast asleep at the Bridge of Dawn and Dusk."

The three of them froze.

"I certainly cannot inform you that you will have to do battle with your very nightmares." Durvasa examined his fingernails. "There is absolutely no way I will tell you that all you must do to reach her is walk through there, or that the mere fact I'm speaking to you has granted you adequate protection in the celestial realms," he went on, pointing across the room to a wooden door marked THE BRIDGE OF DAWN AND DUSK. "Or that you must be back before sunrise or my protection will vanish."

Aru smiled. "Thank you."

"Don't thank me," Durvasa said, scowling. He waved his hand, and a plushy armchair sprouted up in the middle of the room. "I will be watching exactly one *Planet Earth* documentary on Netflix. After that, I will *not* be here."

Brynne was already racing to the door.

"Do you hear me?" Durvasa shouted after her. "I am only watching *one* documentary and then I'm gone! *Gone!*"

Aiden grinned, patting Shadowfax. "No one has ever documented the inside of the celestial realms. It's going to be *awesome!*" When Aru scowled at him, he added, "And we're getting Mini!"

"What about the part where we battle our nightmares?" pointed out Aru.

"It's the celestial realms, Aru, not nightmare land. I'm sure he's exaggerating."

Aiden followed after Brynne, but Aru lingered.

"What made you decide to, um, not help us?" she asked Durvasa.

The sage studied her, and in that second he looked very tired and very old.

"Let us just say that there are some endings that I, too, wish could be avoided. Now go. See well."

See well. That was what Varuni and Varuna had told her in their palace. But Aru didn't have long to think about it. Brynne and Aiden had already gone through the door.

Aru opened it to discover that the other side was an empty white expanse. The idea of stepping into nothingness was intimidating, to say the least. *Do it for Mini*, she told herself.

She took a deep breath and jumped in with her eyes closed, assuming she'd fall through the air. Instead, Aru floated upright, as if on an invisible hoverboard. She opened her eyes and found herself next to Brynne and Aiden in a beautiful moonlit stand of trees. A small sign had been staked into the ground in front of it:

THE DREAMING GROVE OF RATRI

Ratri was the goddess of night. Aru didn't know much about her except that her sister was Ushas, the goddess of dawn, who brought forth a new day in a chariot pulled by red cows.

A path of pure darkness cut through the grove, winding toward a bridge in the distance. It was the same silver bridge

Aru had seen from below, when they were in the cosmic gallery. A tingle of nervousness shot through her. They weren't *technically* in the clouds, so she didn't need cloud slippers, but they were standing on a narrow strip of solid black—like one of those glass sky bridges—and it felt as if it would give way at any second.

Now that they were getting closer to Mini, Aru cast out her Pandava senses, trying to reach her telepathically...but it was like a call that kept going straight to voice mail. She just wasn't getting through.

"Wow," breathed Aiden, snapping a couple pictures of the beautiful scene.

Aru really wanted to walk over and examine the trees up close, but she didn't dare move from the path. There was no sign that said DON'T DEFILE THE NIGHT GODDESS'S GARDEN, but for Aru, there didn't need to be. Growing up in a museum, she had learned not to disturb rare and unusual objects. In fact, she considered herself the museum's designated *NO TOUCHIE!* hollerer, a job she took very seriously.

Brynne, however, went straight for the strange night trees. Their trunks looked like spirals of dark smoke, and their branches were like black lace against the starry sky. Hanging from their branches were oval fruits with glittering silver rinds.

"I bet I could make a really yummy pachadi with this..." mused Brynne. She reached out to touch one of them.

"Brynne, don't!" called Aru.

The moment Brynne's fingers met the fruit, it fell from the branch, hitting the ground and chiming like a struck bell. Aru ran forward and snatched up the silvery fruit before it could make any more noise.

All three of them held very still.

Then Aiden let out his breath. "That was close. For a second there, I thought—"

The rest of his words were cut off by a low growl.

Slowly, Aru turned to see three huge night-black hounds prowling toward them. Saliva dripped from their jaws. Their eyes looked like round mirrors, but instead of reflections, they revealed moving images. Aru's blood ran cold as she saw the Sleeper taunting her . . . then a scene of four Pandava sisters turning against her. She saw Boo still imprisoned, his feathers falling out, because she had failed him. As the hounds stalked closer, she saw her mom shutting the apartment door behind her and never coming back. Aru squeezed her eyes shut, trying to keep the nightmares out.

"Don't look at their eyes!" she warned the others.

She bent down and fumbled for something on the ground. She found a stick and threw it far away from her. Then she cracked open one eye. "Go fetch?"

Instead, the nightmare hounds started barking and snarling at her.

"Never mind!" she shouted to the others. "RUN!"

TWENTY-FOUR

Mistakes Have Been Made....

Aru, Brynne, and Aiden fled down the night path toward the silver bridge.

Behind them they heard growls and the thumping of galloping paws. Brynne aimed her wind mace at the hellhounds, but the powerful gust didn't even slow them down.

"Keep running!" yelled Brynne. "I've got this!"

A second later, she transformed into a blue jaguar as big as one of the hellhounds. Aru looked back to see Jaguar-Brynne hissing and clawing at the hounds, but they leaped straight *through* her. Brynne changed into an eagle and flew straight for Aru and Aiden.

"Never mind!" cawed Bird-Brynne. "I do *not* got this!"

Aru cast out Vajra like a net, but the net slipped off them, bouncing back into her palms.

"They're nightmares!" said Aiden, out of breath. "They're not real!"

Aru shuddered at the thought of the hounds' long teeth

and the terrible visions in their eyes. "Yeah, I'm not testing out that theory."

Time slowed, and Aru felt that they really *were* stuck in a nightmare. No matter how hard they tried to reach the silvery Bridge of Dawn and Dusk, it kept getting farther away from them. The only part of the landscape that changed was the grove of night trees. They grew thicker, crowding the path before them, until it was a forest ripe with shadows.

Brynne jumped behind one of the biggest trunks, pulling Aru and Aiden with her. The hounds slowed down...and started sniffing the ground.

"We can't even get to the bridge!" Brynne whispered. "And what are they going to do when they find us?"

Aiden shushed her. The three of them huddled together. The sound of snuffling got louder and louder...and then it stopped. Brynne changed into a blue snake, slithering up the tree to get a better look.

"They're gone!" she reported when she changed back into her human self.

"Have you ever tried doing that in a zoo?" Aru asked her. "Like, just pop up behind the glass and scare the kids?"

Brynne crossed her arms. "No, because I'm not a troll."

"I'm not a troll, either. It's called *genius.*"

Aiden stuck his head around the trunk. "So where did those dogs go?"

Brynne shrugged. "Who knows? But I *never* want to see them—or those eyes—again."

"Me neither," said Aru. "It was like they knew everything."

Now that they'd stopped running, Aru realized she was still

holding the silver fruit. It was cold in her hands. Curious, she raised it to her face and inhaled deeply. Aru had never smelled a fruit like this.... It didn't give off a scent as much as a feeling. It felt like a moment on the verge of passing. Hot cocoa on the brink of turning cold. The end of a good book. The prickling sense of waking up that always cuts a good nap short. It made her happy and sad all at once. She lost herself in it.

"Guys, did you—?" Aru broke off.

When did it get so quiet?

"Guys...?"

Aru turned around, and staggered backward. Brynne and Aiden were both curled up on the ground. A nightmare hound loomed over each of them, staring at them with eyes now as big as television screens.

The fruit dropped from Aru's hand as she ran over to Brynne and pulled on her arm. "Brynne! Get up!" she screamed.

Aru tried to push the hounds away, but her arms went right through them. Brynne had her eyes squeezed shut, but in the closest creature's eyes, Aru saw an image of a beautiful college-aged girl and an angry middle-aged woman.

The girl—Aru now recognized her as an older version of Brynne—held up her photo album.

"What is this?" asked the woman.

"Mom..." started Brynne.

Her mother groaned, rubbing her temples. "Don't call me that!"

"Sorry, Anila," said Brynne, her eyes shining. "I just thought you'd want to see—"

"If I wanted to see how you're doing, I would have stayed."

In the vision, Brynne's chin lowered. Her shoulders caved in.

Aru shook the real Brynne. "It's a nightmare, Brynne!"

But it was as if Brynne were sound asleep and couldn't hear her. Aru let go of her arm and ran to Aiden. He pressed his hands tightly to his face, and he rolled back and forth.

"Hey! Snap out of it!" she said, waving her hand in front of him.

But he too remained in a trance.

Aiden's nightmare blasted like a horror film in his hound's eyes.

Mrs. Acharya was weeping. "Maybe if I'd never had you, he would still love me. You ruined everything."

"Don't cry, Mom. Please don't cry. I can fix it," said Aiden, reaching out for her. "I'll get an arrow from Kamadeva. Then everything will go back to normal, I promise. Mom?"

She started to fade.

"Aiden?" asked Aru.

But he didn't answer. He just closed his eyes tighter as the next nightmare began to play.

A cold shadow fell across Aru. She froze. Behind her, the growl of the third hound made her shiver, but she held still, refusing to look at it. Vajra glowed bright in her pocket, but there was nothing her lightning bolt could do. She couldn't strike down a nightmare. It would be like telling someone to go punch fear. It was impossible.

The hound moved closer. With every step, Aru sensed her nightmares scratching at the base of her skull, like a monster reaching out from under the bed.

The Sleeper's voice taunted her: *You were never meant to be a hero.*

When she blinked, she saw the image that always haunted

her nightmares—her Pandava sisters all lined up to fight her, hate twisting their features. It felt like a prophecy in that moment, that no matter how hard she tried to be a hero, something inside would always cause her to fail. That was why she hadn't been able to defeat the Sleeper. That was why Boo was locked up, his hope for her slowly dwindling.

The Sleeper's voice kept whispering, dark and terrible....

You are a deceiver, Aru Shah.

Just like your father.

Aru wanted to disappear. Her heart felt like an open wound. She knew better than to look at the hellhound, but it was so hard to resist. Something about that nightmarish voice promised that if she only turned around, she'd see whether or not its visions were true.

But Aru didn't want to end up like Brynne and Aiden. She stared at the ground instead, where a bright glint caught her eye. The silver fruit had rolled close to her feet. Unfortunately, it had a reflective surface, and in it she saw...

Not the nightmare hound.

No, only a big, fluffy white dog, like the Great Pyrenees she had always wanted. It panted heavily before lying down next to her with a grunt.

The Sleeper's voice at the back of her head faded to an echo, something she was used to ignoring....

"Dog?" she asked.

In the reflection, the dog lumbered to its feet and wagged its tail. When she risked a peek behind her, she still saw a hulking, snarling form. How come it looked different in the reflection? She looked back at the fruit, and an idea came to her....

She couldn't punch a nightmare. But she could end it by

waking up. Right before he'd fallen into his bizarre nightmare coma, Aiden had said they weren't real. He was right.

Aru couldn't fight fear by ignoring it. She had to look it straight in the eye.

Slowly, she turned around. The hound's snarling grew louder. Aru dragged her gaze up from the fruit on the ground, where four dark paws impatiently scratched at the dirt. In the back of her head, the din of her nightmares grew louder and louder. They screamed that she wasn't enough, would *never* be enough. . . .

But she pushed hard against the painful thoughts clamoring around her.

Sage Durvasa's words rang out in her mind: *See well.* . . .

"Fine," she said, raising her head to look at the hound straight on. "I see you."

The nightmare hound started to whine.

"I see you for what you really are," said Aru.

It lay down, putting its head on its paws, and blinked at her.

"You're not a nightmare," said Aru, raising her voice.

The hound rolled onto its back, tail wagging.

"You're a floof."

A second later, that's exactly what it became. In the place of the nightmarish hound was a large, fluffy, somewhat dopey-looking white dog. It had badger markings around its eyes and a tail that looked like a feather duster.

"Wake them up," said Aru sternly. She crossed her arms, even though what she really wanted to do was hug the dog and take it home.

Dutifully, the dream dog trotted over to Brynne and Aiden. It licked their faces, and the other nightmare hounds dissolved. Aiden and Brynne shook themselves, then stared at the pooch.

"Did we have a dog this whole time?" asked Brynne.

Aru felt a burst of relief when she heard Brynne's voice. The sound of it almost banished the Nightmare-Sleeper's voice still echoing in her head.

"Nope!" Aru scratched its ears, cooing, "Hello, former monster! You are the *fluffiest* monster!"

The dog's tail went in a circle. Brynne reached out to scratch under its chin, and the big canine let out a contented sigh.

"Aru, you know you can't keep it, right?" said Aiden. "It might switch back...."

"You're not my mom!" said Aru, fluffing the dream dog's ears. "You can't tell me what to do."

"But *I* can," said a melodic voice.

The air shimmered, and the goddess Ratri appeared before them. She wore a black-and-purple salwar kameez that looked like evening fading to night. Her sable skin was star-spangled. Her hair ended in smoky black wisps and around her forehead shone a bright constellation crown.

Immediately, Brynne, Aiden, and Aru pressed their palms together and bowed low. The dog stretched its front legs out and bowed, too.

"It requires no small amount of skill to free oneself from one's own demons," said Ratri.

Brynne turned red. "Sorry I plucked the silver apple thing."

Ratri laughed softly, then picked the fruit up off the ground. "It's not an apple at all. This is a Dream Fruit."

"So you eat it and have good dreams?" asked Aiden, staring at it longingly.

"Not quite," said Ratri slowly. She knelt on the ground and dug a small hole in the earth, which inspired the white dog to do the same. With hands that were somehow still clean, Ratri placed the fruit in the cavity and covered it with dirt. "It shows you what you cannot normally see. That is one of the purposes of dreams: to help you see things in a different way. Sometimes a more truthful way."

When she said this, her eyes went to Aru. "Dreams connect people," said Ratri, getting to her feet.

"Wait.... Was it you who brought Mini to us in our dreams?" asked Brynne.

Ratri smiled and pushed a lock of hair behind one ear. "Perhaps," she said gently. "I try to be subtle in the ways I provide assistance . . . unlike my dear sister, who is a bit more obvious."

She gestured over the bridge to the shining Palace of Day. From here, the distance to it seemed like the length of a supermarket aisle, but when it came to the Otherworld, things that looked far could be near and things that looked near could be far.

The dream dog woofed.

"Why are you helping us?" asked Aru.

Ratri bowed her head. "I do it not for you, but out of memory for a friend who has lost their way.... It is my hope, Pandavas, that you always see well. Remember, in one light something may seem monstrous, and in another it is perhaps not so terrible after all."

A friend who has lost their way? Was she talking about Boo? But he had tried to make up for his past by being their teacher.

"Go," said Ratri, pointing to the bridge. "My sister will wake soon, and the protections of your sage will fade."

Brynne and Aiden bowed again before heading to the bridge. Aru lingered a little longer.... The dream dog had cocked his head to one side, as if wondering why she hadn't invited him to join her.

"I have seen your nightmares, Aru Shah," said Ratri.

Aru startled. "What?"

"They grow in my land, after all," said Ratri, pointing at the dark expanse of her realm. "They are seeded with moments of doubt, watered with the pain of tears not shed, and pruned by the ghosts of paths not taken. But that does not make them true."

Aru felt as if a great weight had been lifted from her heart. She didn't think she'd ever feel *okay* with everything that had happened with the Sleeper, but at least her fears weren't necessarily realities.

Ratri stroked the white dog's head. "I think he has taken a bit of a shine to you. Perhaps he will help guard your dreams from nightmares, daughter of the gods."

For years, Aru's mom had told her she could get a dog "in her dreams." Now that didn't seem like such a bad thing.

"Bye, buddy," she said, then she jogged off after Brynne and Aiden.

"One more thing, Pandavas!" called Ratri. "Beware the red cows, for once they cross the Bridge of Dawn and Dusk, you will be stuck here forever."

TWENTY-FIVE

And Then Came the Fiery Cows

Things that scared Aru Shah included the following:

1. Packets of only yellow Starbursts.
2. Butterflies. (Mini told her they've got really weird curly tongues.... That is not right.)
3. Mannequins. (Because obviously.)

At the top of the list of things that did *not* scare Aru were cows. First, cows were adorable. Second, cows were about as terrifying as a loaf of bread. Third, any animal that makes ice cream wins at being an animal.

But that was before Aru saw the red cows of Ushas.

The three of them had finally made it to the Bridge of Dawn and Dusk. From a distance, it had looked like a thin silver band because of how the light hit it. But now that they were close, they saw that the bridge was made of enchanted sky marble: clouds reinforced with thunderstorms. Aru willed her stomach not to lurch. She wondered if she would ever get used to the queasy feeling of walking thousands of feet above the earth on what was really just a thin puff of water vapor.

Far below them sprawled the twinkling Night Bazaar. Even from where they stood, Aru could see the great blue lotus where Urvashi taught them dance. She spotted the forest of chakora birds where Hanuman taught them strategy. Hovering above the forest floated the glass bubble in which Boo held his lectures. It was empty now. *We're going to free you*, promised Aru silently. *I swear it.*

Across the center of the bridge fell a sparkling veil. And just on the other side, a familiar shadow caught Aru's eye.

"MINI!" she shouted excitedly.

Mini didn't respond.

They ran faster. Aru braced herself as they approached the veil. She'd learned to be more cautious about seemingly ordinary objects. She was half expecting the veil to go *Surprise! I am actually a brick wall!* But luckily, it remained quiet. Aru pulled it back gently.

"Woo-hoo!" yelled Brynne.

Mini was suspended in the air, hovering at eye level. Aru felt like sunshine had burst through her. Her best friend was safe! Mini was curled on her side, fast asleep. But the best part? Mini—daughter of the god of death, who could not only wield the fearsome Death Danda but also talk to bones—was sucking her thumb.

Aiden immediately snapped a picture.

"Aiden!" yelled Brynne. "How could you?!"

"Yeah!" said Aru. "What about us?"

"My bad."

Aru jumped in front of the camera and made bunny ears

with two fingers behind Mini's head. Brynne crouched down and pretended she was carrying Mini. Aiden snapped another picture.

"She's totally going to kill us," said Aiden.

"No selfie of all three?" asked Aru.

Brynne laughed and Aiden visibly recoiled.

"I don't *do* selfies."

"Snob," said Aru.

"Troll," said Aiden.

Now that they had ducked under the veil, they could more clearly see the Palace of Day on the other side of the bridge. Ushas, the goddess of the dawn and sister to Ratri, lived there. It was Ushas's duty to drag the sun from her realm to the rest of the world, and her palace was so bright, it was difficult to make out details. Here and there Aru could discern the shapes of golden spires. And was that an enormous gate lifting? What were those moving red things?

Sharp light—the kind of morning glare that hurts your eyes—poured onto the bridge. But soon enough Aru could see dozens of red mounds as big as houses, with wicked sharp horns of molten gold, start to lumber in their direction.

"If Mini wants to kill us," said Brynne, "she's going to have competition from those cows."

"Those are *not* cows!" squeaked Aru. "They're ginormous!"

"Well, duh, they have to be that big if their whole job is to pull the sun into the sky," said Brynne. "It's not even out yet...."

"Do you think she keeps the sun in a garage?" asked Aiden thoughtfully.

"Okay, the cows of Ushas are officially cancelled," said Aru.

"Mini, WAKE UP! We gotta go! I am *not* becoming bovine roadkill."

Brynne yanked on Mini's arm, but the sleeping girl didn't budge.

"It's like she's stuck," said Brynne.

"She's in the land of sleep—it's not going to be easy to wake her up," said Aiden.

"Shouldn't Durvasa have told us what to do? What happened to the *sage* advice?"

"Hey, he got us here, didn't he?" said Aiden as he walked all around Mini, examining the situation. "Hmm. I don't think we can just pull her down from there, either."

"Got any water?" asked Aru.

"Nope," said Brynne. She lifted her wind mace. "Let's try a gentle breeze."

Brynne aimed the mace and said, "*Gali.*" It let out a sound like a blow-dryer being turned on right next to someone's ear. Even Aiden jumped.

Mini's hair went streaming behind her, but she simply batted at it, muttering, "No, I don't want to be a fairy...." She sighed. "Don't like heights."

"Okay, new technique," said Aru, bringing out Vajra. She gently touched Mini's hand with the tip of the lightning bolt.

"I'm gonna tell her you tried to electrocute her," said Aiden.

"Shh!"

Vajra pinged Mini, who just giggled and resumed sucking her thumb.

The cows began to moo. In the past, Aru had considered this a rather gentle and soothing sound. But when the cows were

T. rex–size, every *moo* became supersonic, even when they were still fifty feet away. Aru wobbled and nearly lost her balance on the bridge. She glanced over her shoulder. One of the cows had begun to paw the ground like it was planning to charge.

Then there came an even more disturbing sound: a high-pitched giggle.

"GOOD MORNING, WORLD!"

The herd parted to allow the goddess Ushas through. As she passed her cows, she stroked each one on the forehead. Ushas wore a golden robe and fuzzy golden slippers. Bright orange flames danced through her black hair, creating dramatic high-lights. To Aru, the red-skinned goddess looked like a rich teenage girl with an epic sunburn.

Ushas snapped her fingers and two attendants rolled out a chariot of pure gold. They began to harness the cows, adjusting each strap and checking each hoof.

"Hey!" shouted Aiden, frantically waving his arms. "Give us a minute here, will you?"

But Ushas didn't hear him. Loud music started blasting from somewhere in the clouds—a remix of the Beatles' "Here Comes the Sun." Ushas started singing along. The cows mooed louder. Mini's foot tapped to the beat.

"Okay, okay. Focus, Shah!" said Aru, jumping up and down. "Mini can obviously hear."

"Maybe she isn't waking up because she doesn't think all this is real," offered Brynne. "What if we made her *want* to wake up? We could shout her favorite things."

"That might work!"

"Does she have a celebrity crush?" asked Brynne. "Look, Mini! Dominique Crenn is right behind you!"

"Who—?" asked Aru.

"She's a chef!" said Brynne.

Mini just frowned harder.

"I can't think of anyone!" said Aru. The cows were all lined up now, ready to go. Ushas climbed into the cab of the chariot.

Aiden tugged on a lock of his hair. "Could we scare Mini awake?"

Now *there* was a thought....

The bridge beneath them shuddered and quaked. A sphere of white-hot light rolled through the gate, and flames appeared on the tips of the cows' horns. It was so hot that Aru had to turn her face away.

"It's the sun!" said Brynne, her eyes wide. "Mini, wake up. Monsters are coming!"

Mini just snorted and murmured, "I'm the daughter of the god of death, and I want cake."

"Monsters don't scare Mini," said Aru.

"Then what does?" demanded Brynne.

Aiden snapped his fingers. He walked up to Mini and said, "Okay, Mini, you're stuck in a public bathroom."

Mini started to wail.

"They're out of soap!"

Aru flashed Aiden a thumbs-up sign, then said, "Oh no, what's happened to all the hand sanitizer in the world? It's been...destroyed! In a huge fire. No more antibacterial anything. Ever."

Mini tossed and turned. Aru could see her eyelids fluttering. It was working!

"Someone has just sneezed into their hand and now you have to shake it," said Brynne.

ROSHANI CHOKSHI

"Nooooo!" moaned Mini.

The bridge trembled even more furiously as the cows stamped their feet impatiently. Ushas put on sunglasses and a huge pair of headphones, then pretended to play the drums with her reins.

It's now or never, thought Aru. She cupped her hand around Mini's ear and whispered her soul sister's most despised phrase:

"Five-second rule," said Aru.

Mini jerked awake, shouting, "NO!" She immediately dropped to the ground, where she landed on her butt.

"Hooray!" said Aru. "You're back!"

"W-what?" Mini asked with a yawn. And then her eyes lit up. "You did it! You rescued me!"

She tried to get to her feet, but she slipped. Mini rubbed her temples.

"I feel so...drained." She groaned. "The naga women. They took my energy while I was sleeping."

"I've got you," said Brynne gently.

She picked up Mini as if she weighed as little as a feather. Mini thanked her with a weak smile, but then her eyes widened.

"Um...guys? Did you know there are cows charging toward us?"

"Unfortunately, yes," said Aiden.

"Yeah, about that..." said Brynne. "We gotta go. Like, yesterday. Durvasa said we had to be back before daybreak."

Aru didn't even bother looking over her shoulder. She already knew what she'd see, because she could feel the oncoming heat. Beneath her feet, the slender bridge had begun to fade, melting beneath the sun's rays.

"I'll fly ahead to get the door to the DMV open," said Brynne, setting down Mini and leaning her against Aiden. "Aru, can you take these guys?"

"Yup."

In a flash of blue light, Brynne transformed into a hawk. She cawed once, then bent her head and lifted off. Aru threw Vajra to the ground and it transformed into a wide hoverboard.

"All aboard!" she hollered.

Aiden helped Mini sit on the hoverboard. Aru risked a glance back and saw that the red cows were gaining ground. Now they were barely twenty yards away. Their golden hooves pounded onto the bridge. In her chariot, Ushas was still pretending to play the drums, this time to "Good Day Sunshine." Aru suspected that, behind her sunglasses, her eyes were closed.

Mini clutched the sides of the board, but she looked pale and sickly just from the effort.

"I feel like I haven't slept in years," she said miserably. "And I might possibly have hypoglycemia, too. I'm still so tired...."

"Don't worry. You just need some food in you," said Aiden, patting her back. "We'll get you fixed up at the DMV."

"Ready?" asked Aru from the front. "Everyone hold on tight."

The lightning bolt lifted and flew over the bridge, back the way they had come. Behind them, Ushas let out a loud "Hi-ya!" and the red cows galloped, pulling the chariot and the sun. Wind blew against Aru's face. Tendrils of electricity laced over the tops of her shoes and around her ankles, holding her in place as they zoomed toward the Grove of Ratri.

"Woo-hoo!" she yelped.

But then she felt a heavy hand clap her shoulder. Aru nearly stumbled as she turned her head. Aiden had one arm around Mini; his other hand was on Aru.

"Take it easy!" he shouted. "She's too weak!"

Sure enough, Mini looked airsick. She was listing to one side even though Aiden was holding her.

Aru had one of those moments when she saw something before it happened. One second, Mini was upright. The next second…

She flopped over.

Aiden lost hold of her. He dove forward and Aru only just managed to grab Mini before she fell. Immediately, Vajra secured Mini with electrical strands around her ankles, but Aru's lunge had been too sudden, and the hoverboard tipped…

…sending Aiden sprawling into the herd of fiery cows.

TWENTY-SIX

Cows Are Officially Cancelled

Aru and Mini both screamed.

"I don't see him anywhere!" yelled Mini.

Aru had brought Vajra above the red cows. But the herd was moving so fast, it looked like nothing more than a blur of crimson. On top of that, the heat of the oncoming sun was becoming intolerable. The sage's protection spell was waning.

"You don't think he's—" Mini started.

"No!" Aru said abruptly, cutting her off.

Maybe it was silly, but Aru thought she would've *felt* if Aiden had . . . died.

They couldn't linger here. Ahead of them, the bridge was beginning to fade. The cold silver moonlight of the dusk end was dissipating as the sun came closer. If they didn't leave now, they'd be stuck between dawn and dusk.

"Brynne can find him," said Aru, thinking fast. "She's got hawk vision."

But Brynne had flown ahead—she didn't even know that Aiden was in trouble. They had to let her know right away.

Aru forced all her concentration into propelling Vajra forward. The hoverboard careened into the Grove of Ratri and skidded to a stop in the dense thicket of night trees. Aru and Mini tumbled headfirst into the grass.

"Ha!" said a voice above them. "It's official. I'm *faster* than a lightning bolt."

Brynne, still in hawk form, stared down at them from her branch.

"Bam!" she said. "Add that to my trophies."

Electricity twitched across Vajra, as if the hoverboard were highly affronted by such a statement. And then it stung Aru for good measure, because it was clearly her fault for making it look bad.

There was no time to argue.

"Aiden fell into the cows back there!" Aru said, gesturing over her shoulder.

"He was trying to save me," added Mini. "You have to go after him! But we don't know where he is...."

Brynne just pointed her wing. "You mean *that* Aiden?"

Aru whipped around. As it turned out, Aiden was not dead. He was fine. In fact, he was more than fine. He was seated on a giant red cow and wearing a pair of sunglasses. Behind him was Ushas, her smile so dazzling that Aru couldn't even look at her. Aiden waved at them, then held up a bright gold phone that could only belong to the goddess of dawn.

"Is he...?" started Mini.

"He is," confirmed Brynne.

Aiden *I'm-an-Artiste* Acharya was taking a selfie.

A couple of seconds later, Aiden leaped off the red cow and rolled into the grove. Ushas paused long enough to scream:

"I am *such* a fan of your mom! I used to try to practice her dances when I was working, but then I almost incinerated the world. Whatever." The goddess tossed her hair back. "Can't wait to post our photo!"

And with that, she waved good-bye and let out a loud "Yee-haw!" The red cows zoomed over them, dragging the flaming sun in their wake.

Aiden swaggered over, grinning.

Aru frowned. "What happened to 'I don't take selfies because I'm an artist' or whatever?" she asked.

"I made an exception, considering I pretty much delivered daylight to the world today," he said and took a bow.

Aru raised an eyebrow. "You fell on a cow."

"I *rode* a cow—"

"But first you fell. I saw it happen and was just about to retrieve you when Ushas snatched you up," said Brynne. "Remember? You were curled into a ball—"

Aiden stuck his fingers in his ears. "Can't hear you! The sun's rays have burned away your negativity!"

"Let him have this one," Mini whispered to Aru and Brynne.

Aru might have grumbled out loud, but on the inside, she wasn't grumbling at all. Because even though her hair was singed from being too close to the red cows of Ushas, and even though her brain was being tugged in a hundred different directions, *this* was all she wanted. This bunch, together again. Mini forcing sunblock on everyone. Brynne wondering when they were going to eat. Aiden herding them to the exit and helping Mini—who was still weak—walk to the door. Sure, they were an odd assortment, but whoever thought cookies would go so well with milk? Or macaroni with cheese? Some things just fit together. This group was one of them.

The moment they left the Grove of Ratri behind, reality dropped on their heads again. They had the thief's song, and they had Mini back, but there was still so much to do and barely three days left. . . . Already, the sun was beginning its trek across the world.

Sage Durvasa was waiting for them in the cosmic gallery, levitating above the ground as he scribbled in the air.

"We did it!" said Aru triumphantly, propping up Mini as proof.

Mini weakly pressed her palms together in greeting.

Durvasa didn't even look their way. "What do you want? Congratulations?"

Aru's shoulders dropped. "No. But we could use more of your help?"

"I didn't help. That would be against the rules."

"Fine, how about more of your not-help?" asked Brynne. "And some food."

"Or a nap," said Mini tiredly, but then she brightened. "Wait! I think I've got one in my backpack! From the warehouse!"

Aru, who had been carrying Mini's backpack, dropped it and opened the zipper. Sure enough, a small bar labeled POWER NAP shone at the bottom of her bag. It looked like a Hershey bar. Aru unwrapped it and handed it to Mini, who chomped it down in two bites. Instantly, the pallor of her skin improved and her eyes were more alert.

"Much better," she said, patting her stomach.

Brynne's stomach grumbled noticeably and she stared longingly at Mini's bag.

"So..." started Aiden, "about that *not*-help?"

But the sage didn't answer. Instead, he continued to write out petty curses, pondering aloud. "This fiendish girl cut up someone's dress.... How to repay her, I wonder?"

Aru cleared her throat, trying to get the sage's attention, but he was deep in thought. The only way to make Durvasa pay heed was, it seemed, to talk about what *he* wanted to talk about.

"What if you cursed her to have really itchy tags that she can't take off without ruining her clothes?"

Durvasa paused for a second, then nodded. "Amateurish... but serviceable. And how about a person who put worms in someone else's spaghetti as a prank?"

Brynne looked appalled. "How would *they* like it if all their food was always too hot or too cold? I hate that."

Durvasa grinned. "I suspect they would not like it at all.... And what curse would be appropriate for a person who tied someone else's shoes together and laughed when they tripped?"

Aru had nothing to suggest, but Mini did. Her cheeks turned red, and Aru suspected that the exact same scenario had happened to her once.

"Maybe one shoe should always feel more tied than the other? They can never fix it."

"Ah, how delightfully inconvenient!" said Durvasa, clapping merrily.

Only then did Aru notice that Aiden was looking at all three girls as if they'd sprouted horns.

"You guys are..."

"Clever?" suggested Aru.

"Just?" asked Mini.

"Powerful?" tried Brynne.

Aiden crossed his arms. "I was going to say diabolical."

"Meh," said Aru. "Close enough."

"You were of no help to me," said Durvasa, putting down his curse pen. "And so now I will be of no help to you. Though it seems that you are in need of plenty of not-help. You claim to have the song of the thief—"

"I do!" Brynne blurted out, pointing at the necklace, but Durvasa held up his hand.

"Not now," he said.

"And I know the thief's name! The naginis told me in exchange for my energy. That's why I was so tired!" Mini said rapidly.

Aru eyed the remains of the power-nap chocolate bar. Must have been pretty potent.

"It's—" started Mini.

"Not here," Durvasa said tightly.

It seemed to Aru as if all the air had been sucked out of the room. Durvasa—the all-powerful sage who had caused the gods to lose their immortality—was *scared* of someone overhearing. Who? A spy working for the Sleeper? Aru cursed herself—yet again—for letting her dad get away.

"What are we waiting for?" Brynne demanded.

"Be patient," Aiden told her through a clenched-teeth smile. "I'm sure the wise sage knows what he's doing."

Durvasa led them past the display case of cursed-people statues and down a hallway lined with what looked like offices. Durvasa opened one of the doors and gestured them inside.

Usually, whenever Aru entered an office, it looked a certain way. Always the same faded carpet the color of dead dreams. A brown desk with a framed picture of a family on it. A poster of a sunset with a slogan like *Live. Laugh. Love.* And, of course, a plant that she could never be sure was real or fake (Aru could never resist tearing a leaf to find out; she always felt a bit guilty or strangely victorious).

This was not that kind of office.

It was a chamber in space, which was disorienting at first. There were no ugly carpets or posters. Instead, there was a fathomless black atmosphere, studded with stars, above, below, and all around them, sculpting the illusion of a room. But they didn't fall through it—their feet walked on an invisible floor. A strange luminescence surrounded them. The room felt at once impossibly huge and cozy.

"Welcome to the astral plane," said Durvasa, his voice echoing.

Aru, who had only been on a plane once, was convinced that this was not a plane, but she chose not to point that out to Durvasa.

"You mean, where people go when they die?" asked Brynne, her eyes wide.

"No, that's the Kingdom of Death," said Mini. "We went there last time."

Aru could tell that Durvasa was struggling to control his temper. After a deep, cleansing breath, he continued. "At the DMV," he said, "the astral plane is a sanctuary. What you discover here is considered sacred. It will not be revealed to anyone else." Then he stepped back.

Mini gestured for Brynne to give her the soul song. Gingerly, Brynne took the red orb off her neck and placed it on the floor.

Before she stood, she dragged her finger across the stars speckling the floor, like they were sugar crystals on a plate.

"The name, child," said Durvasa.

In the astral plane, the song orb had taken on a strange pulsing glow, reminding Aru that this was actually a part of someone's *soul*. Someone had wanted the god of love's arrow so dearly that they'd been willing to part with their very essence. When Aru leaned close, she thought she heard the orb make a sound...like a soft sigh.

Mini knelt on the floor and in a clear, loud voice said, "The name of the thief is Surpanakha."

TWENTY-SEVEN

Sage Durvasa Curses

The moment Mini uttered the thief's name, the soul song flared. Saying the name was supposed to unlock the thief's location, but the image forming within the orb was still too hazy to make out.

"It will take a while," said Durvasa.

Aru sat on the floor and sighed, resting her chin on her hand. Magic was supposed to be fast! Actually, it was a lot like the Internet—sometimes speedy, other times taking forever just to buffer one measly cat video.

"Sur-pa-na-kha," said Aiden, drawing out every syllable. *Soor-pah-nah-kuh.*

It was really hard for Aru to say the name aloud without bursting into the "Supercalifragilisticexpialidocious!" song, but she restrained herself. Where had she heard that name before?

"I know what you're thinking," said Mini, looking at Aru. "You're wondering where you've heard that name before."

"Can you read minds, too?!"

"No, you were humming that *Mary Poppins* song, so I just guessed."

"Oh."

"Surpanakha is the sister of the demon king Ravana, remember?" asked Mini. "Boo taught us."

At the mention of Boo, Aru felt a wave of sadness. Poor Boo. . . . Wherever he was, she really hoped someone had managed to smuggle him some Oreos.

"Yeah, I remember," said Aru. "She's the one who got her nose cut off, right?"

"Yup," said Mini.

"Why?" asked Brynne, reflexively protecting her own nose with her hand.

"In the stories from the *Ramayana*," said Mini, "Surpanakha attacked Sita, Lord Rama's wife. Rama and his brother Laxmana fought her off. In the process, Laxmana hacked off Surpanakha's nose."

"Yeah, but why the nose?" wondered Aiden.

"Was hers superspecial?" asked Aru. "Like an elephant trunk that could pick up a sword and stab people?"

The others laughed softly, but Durvasa's deep voice cut through their smiles. "It was an act of humiliation."

The great sage had chosen not to sit anywhere near Surpanakha's soul song. Instead, he stood off to the side, as if the object intimidated him.

"According to the stories," he went on, "Surpanakha was so dazzled by the beauty of Lord Rama and Lord Laxmana that she offered herself to them in marriage. They refused her. One might say they were not as kind as they could have been."

"Yeah . . . but wasn't she hideous and demonic-looking . . . gray skin, red eyes, fangs the size of your arm?" asked Aru.

"Not everyone with rakshasa or asura blood looks demonic," said Brynne grumpily. "That's a stereotype."

Aiden nodded. "Plus, I just don't think people should be mean to someone because they don't like the way they look."

Aru felt a little chastened. "You're right. I'm sorry," she mumbled.

"S'okay," said Brynne, thumping her back. Except, because Brynne was ridiculously strong, Aru almost went sprawling.

"So what happened to her after that?" Mini asked.

"She ran back to her brother, the ten-headed demon king," said Aiden.

Dimly, Aru recalled the images she had seen on Kamadeva's floor. The rakshasi fleeing through the forest, then complaining to her brother about the injustice that she had suffered… and describing Rama's beautiful wife. In the tales, her brother became obsessed with Sita and kidnapped her from Rama.

Surpanakha's humiliation…her pain…had started a great war.

"That story is thousands of years old," said Mini. "Why would she be stirring up trouble now?"

Aiden turned his camera over in his hands. It was a habit of his, Aru had noticed. He always reached for Shadowfax when he was thinking through something or trying to remember a fact. When he caught her looking, Aru quickly found the spot of black nothingness beside him intensely interesting.

"Yeah," echoed Aiden. "Why steal Kamadeva's bow and arrow?"

In the background, Durvasa said nothing, but his posture seemed rigid.

"Maybe she wants vengeance?" suggested Aru. "Aiden, you were the one who noticed that the thief was only choosing men as her victims."

"It's ancient history!" said Brynne. "Even *I* don't stay mad that long."

"Takshaka has stayed mad at Arjuna all these years, though," said Aru, shivering as she remembered the intense hatred in his milky cobra eyes.

"What'd you—" Aiden started, before catching himself. "I mean, what did Arjuna do?"

Aru fiddled with her sleeve. She didn't like the answer, because it was cruel. It flew in the face of everything she'd been taught about the great hero.

"He burned down Takshaka's forest," she finally admitted. "Lots of creatures died, including Takshaka's wife."

"That's awful…" said Mini. "Why'd he do it?"

Aru looked to Durvasa, but the sage had closed his eyes. Perhaps he was meditating.

"I don't know," said Aru. She wished she weren't telling the truth.

Aru glanced down at the song between them. The smoke inside the orb had changed to what now resembled liquid silver, but it was still swirling around.

"Maybe Surpanakha is just waiting for the right time to strike," said Brynne. "It definitely fits her name."

"What's her name mean?"

"Oh! I know!" said Mini, raising her hand.

Aru laughed. "This isn't school. You don't need to raise your hand."

"Right," said Mini, flushing. "Um, it's Sanskrit. It translates to *she whose fingernails are like slicing blades.*"

"Yikes." Aru shuddered. "Who gives a kid a name like that?"

A couple of years ago, there was a French girl in her class named Hermengarde, but everyone just called her Ehrmagawd! But at least Hermengarde had been funny and nice. By all accounts, Surpanakha was *not*.

By now, the soul song had finished its activation sequence. The orb shivered a little before it melted into a silver pool. A scene rippled across it, and the four of them leaned forward to watch.

Surpanakha was moving past what looked like a row of men. Aru saw a variety of crisp suits and rumpled sweatshirts, boots and bare feet. The view was low, making Aru think Surpanakha must be short—until she realized they were seeing things not through the demoness's eyes, but from the perspective of where her soul had lived in her body: *heart level.* Aru kind of wished Surpanakha would lean way back. Looking out at chest level basically meant just seeing a bunch of buttons.

The image in the mirror went still, as if Surpanakha had stopped walking. She reached up toward one of the men— perhaps to stroke his cheek, it was hard to tell. Aru thought Surpanakha's skin would be gray and mottled, her nails long and ragged. But her hand was a warm brown, with trimmed nails painted a shade of red.

"Soon," said Surpanakha. "You are nearly enough in number...."

Aru didn't know what surprised her more—the fact that the vision had audio, or that this was the voice of the hideous fanged demoness. Aru had assumed that someone named after terrible nails would have a screeching voice, but Surpanakha's tone was sweet and melodious.

She must have been talking to some Heartless, Aru realized. But where *were* they? The soul song was supposed to reveal the thief's location, but she didn't see anything recognizable. Peering between the row of men for any clues, Aru glimpsed a shimmering white landscape. Snow? It almost looked like mother-of-pearl. Was it…moving?

"Princess!" called a voice behind Surpanakha.

She whirled around, and the view showed a naga man slithering toward her. Aru recognized him immediately—Takshaka! He was in his half-snake/half-man form.

"What is it?" asked Surpanakha sharply. She didn't sound so sweet and melodious now.

"I merely came to celebrate with you," said Takshaka smoothly. "We've almost gained access to the labyrinth. Once we have that, the amrita will be ours, and we can leave this miserable place."

With that, the soul song's vision ended and the mirror rolled back up into a pendant-size orb.

"It is a dangerous thing to cast off a part of one's soul," said Durvasa. "She's exchanged it for power, and there is another bargain in the making." Warily, he picked up the orb and stowed it in a small bag at his side.

"They're after amrita?" asked Mini, shocked.

Honestly, Aru had forgotten what amrita was. The only Amrita she knew was a girl in the grade below her, who stuck a marble up her nose on a dare and had to be taken to the emergency room. Aru was pretty sure she was *not* what Surpanakha and Takshaka were after.

"Isn't that...a drink of some kind?" asked Aiden. "I can't remember."

"It's impossible," the sage muttered to himself.

"What is?"

"They can't be after amrita. It cannot be done."

"But what *is* it?" pressed Aru.

Durvasa waved his hand. In the middle of the astral plane floor, a new image appeared: a large golden cauldron tipped forward ever so slightly to reveal a glowing liquid.

"The nectar of immortality," said Durvasa. "Once, long ago, someone caused the gods to lose their immortality—"

"*Someone?* Don't you mean...*you?*" asked Aru.

Durvasa glared at her. "Let me tell the story! Ahem. Anyway, the gods needed amrita to restore their immortality. They would have to churn the Ocean of Milk in order to find it. The gods convinced the asuras to help by promising them a sip of the amrita."

"But then the gods reneged on their promise," said Brynne.

"It had to be done," said Durvasa. "Asuras, though semidivine and gifted with magic, were never meant to be immortal."

"Well, no wonder they're after it now," said Brynne. "It's kinda unfair...."

Aru understood why Brynne felt that way. After all, she *was* of asura descent, but Aru was surprised to find that she sided with her. The gods hadn't kept their promise. The fact that a god could be a villain made Aru's head spin. As a Pandava, she was expected to fight on their side...but how could she do that when she wasn't sure she could trust them?

"Just because something is not fair does not mean it is without reason or even compassion," said Durvasa serenely. He closed his eyes and pronounced: "Fairness is like a multifaceted gem. Its appearance can vary, depending on the angle of the beholder."

He cracked one eye open. "WRITE THAT DOWN!" he scolded. "That was free wisdom I just dispensed!"

"Whoops! Sorry!" said Mini, grabbing her Post-it pad and pen from her backpack.

"Sage Durvasa, you said it was impossible for someone to get the amrita," said Aiden. "Why?"

"What an inane question," huffed Durvasa. "The amrita is hidden deep beneath the Ocean of Milk, inside a golden dome that can only be opened with a magic spell. The dome covers a labyrinth that is not only impossible to navigate but also is guarded by fire serpents that will incinerate anything with a heartbeat. It's foolproof."

Mini frowned. "But it's not." She started jotting something on her notepad.

"*Pish!*" scoffed the sage. "You might as well wait for Surpanakha to fail, then just return the bow and arrow to Uloopi. Done. Quest finished." He wiped his hands together. "Now it's time for you all to get out of here. I detest this much socialization."

"You said the fire serpents will 'incinerate anything with a heartbeat,'" Mini pressed. She held up a sketch that looked like: →♥. "By using Kamadeva's arrow, that's exactly what you get rid of—a heartbeat."

Aru caught on immediately. "The Heartless! They can get through the labyrinth and grab the nectar of immortality."

"She's building an army!" said Brynne.

"And she's hiding them in the Ocean of Milk," added Aiden.

For a moment, Durvasa said nothing. And then the sage did what he did best.

He cursed.

TWENTY-EIGHT

We'll Even Throw in Starvation for Free!

Once Sage Durvasa had finished cursing, he led them out of the office and locked the door behind him.

"Happy thoughts, happy thoughts," muttered Aru to herself. "Fire-breathing serpents? Cool, cool. That's fine. This is fine. Everything is fine—"

"Chill, Shah," said Aiden. "You really need a better pep talk."

"*I* am excellent at pep talks. Witness," said Durvasa. He cleared his throat. "You have approximately two days left before Queen Uloopi exiles you from the Otherworld. That which you seek will be well guarded, and the path to the shore of the Ocean of Milk is already treacherous. Not to mention the fact that Surpanakha is an accomplished warrior, and so is Takshaka. You are all woefully outmatched. There. How was that?"

Aiden lunged forward to catch Mini before she fainted. Even Brynne, the most confident out of all of them, let out a whimper.

Aru's jaw fell open. "*That* was your pep talk?"

"Yes. *P. E. P.* Preparing for Evil People. Surely that is what you meant."

"It was not."

"What's the quickest route to the Ocean of Milk?" asked Brynne. She was standing up straighter now, her jaw clenched in determination.

Durvasa glanced down both sides of the hall, wary of being overheard. "I would not go to the Mall of Meditation Groves," he said, fixing them with a strict glare. "And I certainly would not ask for transport to the Great Swamp of New Jersey.... There is no illegal portal to the Ocean of Milk that is closed to the public."

"*Illegal?*" echoed Mini. "Breaking *another* Otherworld law? How many laws have we broken by now?"

"Lost count," Aiden said with a shrug.

"Where's this mall?" asked Aru.

"It is not down the hall...and it is not to your left," said Durvasa.

He crossed his arms, his face imperious and grumpy once more. It was clearly a sign of *That's it. Not-help is over!* The four of them bowed and paid their respects. For the briefest moment, Durvasa's face softened.

"Now, seriously. Go away."

They hurried down the hall, which was lined with all sorts of plaques like:

BEST CURSE-DISPENSER OF THE MONTH: SAGE NARADA!

Or:

AWARD FOR BEST ENLIGHTENMENT MOMENT:
SAGE BHRIGU!

"Do you think the Ocean of Milk is filled with actual milk?" asked Mini, pushing her glasses farther up on her nose. "Because I'm lactose intolerant."

In the past, it had always been Aru's job to calm down Mini and distract her somehow—usually by asking about an obscure disease. But this time, Aiden beat her to it.

"It's probably magical and harmless," he said. "It may even have medicinal properties."

That piqued Mini's interest. "Really?"

"Maybe?" He looked over Mini's head and mouthed, *I have no idea.*

Aru laughed.

"We have to be ready to take on Surpanakha," said Brynne solemnly. "Kamadeva said we have to plunge the stolen arrow through her heart. Only when we do that will the Heartless be human again."

"I wish we didn't have to *stab* anyone," Mini said. "That's so violent."

"We're at war!" said Brynne, irritated. "Of course it's violent! Besides, she's a thief!"

Aru knew that . . . and yet she couldn't shake the sound of Surpanakha's voice. Sweet and sorrowful. It made Aru wonder if maybe they didn't know the whole story.

The Mall of Meditation Groves sounded to Aru like it would be the chillest place ever. The sages and rishis in her mother's stories had always acquired their powers through intense meditation, and Aru figured that could only take place in a beautiful natural spot where one could be alone and at peace, free from distractions and stress. The Mall of Meditation Groves was probably like a spa. A few leafy green trees surrounding a luxuriant circle of grass. Flute music playing softly in the air. Or maybe it was like the outdoor section of Home Depot, with all the plants and stuff.

But when they stepped through the door on the left, Aru saw she was completely wrong.

Stretched out before them was a vast convention hall with rows of fenced-in areas representing different kinds of meditation environments. Each area looked no bigger than a mall kiosk, and yet, as was always the case with magic, it seemed like a slice of something infinite. Aru scanned the different displays. There was a marshy patch of land where a lazy alligator basked in an errant sunbeam. Beside it was a Saharan plain, where a calm wind stirred the long tawny grass. Off to the left was a dark jungle draped in shiny green vines. And looming behind it was an outcropping of rock covered with fresh snow.

Taken on their own, the settings were breathtaking.

But taken in with the crowds of rishis and sages who were examining them, and the yakshas and yakshinis who were trying to outsell one another, the mall was *chaos*. It reminded Aru of a department store makeup section, where the clerks spray perfume on scraps of paper and shove them in your face.

A yakshini with living vines in her hair and lime-green wings on her back alighted before them. "Interested in spending days of meditation in the wilds of India?" she asked.

"Uh, no thanks," said Aiden.

But the nature spirit ignored his refusal. "If you select the Naga Manipuri Chin Hills, we automatically include one free

guard leopard, access to an array of nearly three hundred species
of medicinal plants, and complimentary bottled morning dew!"

"I—"

"Our hills are lush and beautiful!" continued the yakshini.
"Free of almost all demonic involvement! That said, *ifyouare
beheadedorsufferfromsevereburnsasaresultofdemonincineration,thiscompanyis
notliable!*"

Aru noticed that the yakshini's smile never moved, even
when she talked. It looked like someone had nailed it to her
face. Now Aru's own face hurt. *FROWN, WOMAN! I KNOW
YOU CAN DO IT!*

"It offers perfect photo opportunities, too!" said the yakshini, noting Aiden's camera.

That got his attention. "Really?"

"Okay, that's enough," said Brynne, shoving Aiden behind
her. "Thanks, but no thanks."

This time the yakshini's smile twitched slightly. "Of course!
Have a wonderful century. You know where to find us if you
change your mind!"

At the far end of the floor, Aru could see less traditional
meditation environments clustered together. The options
included skyscrapers and industrial ships, swamplands, and
even, though it grossed the heck out of Aru, the insides of
insect hives.

"I bet the swamp Durvasa mentioned is down there," said
Aiden.

"How are we going to get *through* all this?" asked Aru.

There were hundreds of rishis and yogis walking through
the mall, and the yakshas and yakshinis descended on unat-
tended shoppers like sharks.

"I'll handle them," said Brynne.

Aru half hoped that meant Brynne was planning to release a huge gust of wind to sweep everyone away. Instead, Brynne muscled Aru, Mini, and Aiden past a half dozen stalls, yelling and haggling and scoffing the whole way.

Which is to say, Brynne was having the time of her life.

"This place makes me feel *alive!*" she said fiercely.

"It's just like a shopping mall," said Mini, huddling closer to Aru. "I hate malls. Anyone can sneeze on you."

Aru agreed, though not because of the sneezing. Aru hated malls because there was always the chance she could run into someone she knew, and then what? She could never afford to buy anything. Once, when she'd spotted a bunch of her classmates coming her way, Aru had gone into every nearby high-end store and asked for an empty bag. That way she was able to flash an *oh-I'm-carrying-so-much-I-can't-really-wave* smile before hiding out in the parking garage and waiting for her mom.

"I can't take this place," said Aiden, pulling his hood over his face.

"Because of the germs?" asked Mini.

"No, it's all the loud haggling. Just a bunch of people screaming at each other," he said, hunching his shoulders. "It sounds just like home." The moment he said that, his face paled and his mouth set in a tight line.

Aru recognized that expression. It was the face someone made when they'd revealed too much. Aru remembered Aiden's nightmares from the Grove of Ratri: his mother's despair, and Aiden's guilt. There wasn't anything Aru could say that would make him feel better, but that didn't mean it wasn't worth trying.

"Sometimes it's good not to get used to something," she

said. "When you do, maybe it means you don't care enough to notice."

"I agree with Aru," said Mini. "It's usually a good thing! Unless you're practicing mithridatism."

"What's that?" asked Aiden.

Mini brightened. "It's named after this Persian emperor who was so scared of getting poisoned that he ate some every day to make himself immune."

"And it worked?" asked Aiden.

"Yep!" Mini said cheerfully. "He didn't die by poison. He got stabbed instead."

"Hooray?" tried Aru.

Aiden, on the other hand, looked shocked.

Up ahead, Brynne continued to bulldoze her way through the kiosks of meditation groves. By now, yakshas and yakshinis were diving in opposite directions when they saw her approaching.

"You're terrifying!" called Aru happily.

Brynne bowed. "Thank you."

The kiosk marked GREAT SWAMP OF NEW JERSEY was curiously empty. No beaming yakshini or crowd of eager ascetics here—just one sour-looking yaksha. He had whorled ears, a mop of icy hair that seemed all the more stark against his almond skin, and he wore a faded blue Giants sweatshirt. He quickly shut the *New Jersey Monthly* magazine he was reading when he saw them and flashed an oily smile.

"Customers!" he said.

But with his thick Jersey accent, it sounded like *cus-tah-maz*.

"You looking for a portal to the Morris County, I presume?

Step right up. We are *still* meeting the baseline requirements to qualify as an Otherworld sanctuary, despite increased rates of rakshasa attacks," he said.

No sooner had he finished speaking than the *N* fell off his sign. Now it read GREAT SWAMP OF EW JERSEY. What joy.

"Ain't it a place of beauty?" He swept his hand toward the portal and grinned.

This portal looked nothing like the pristine pools they had seen elsewhere. Instead, its lip was ragged and brownish liquid sloshed out. A roach skittered around the edge, then backed away as if saying *You know what? Never mind. I'm good.*

"Increased rates of rakshasa attacks?" asked Brynne.

"Oh yeah. A little dismemberment here and there," said the yaksha, waving his hand. "I think it adds a certain, uh, *character* to the place. You know?"

Mini was horrified.

"Whaddaya say, how 'bout we strike a deal?" asked the yaksha. He grinned and then eyed Aiden's camera. "You give me that chunk of metal, and I'll give you complimentary, VIP, executive, first-class transportation to the one...the only... *GREAT SWAMP!*"

Aiden clutched his camera tightly.

"No deal," said Brynne. "In fact, *you* should be giving us passage for *free*. Do you know who we are? We're Pandavas."

Aru tensed. It was the same tactic she'd used at the Court of the Seasons not too long ago, but it didn't feel right here. Maybe people *shouldn't* know where they were going...because if Takshaka, Queen Uloopi's right-hand man, could betray her, who was to say what side *any* person was on?

"Heavens!" said the yaksha, falling to his knees.

A little too dramatic, thought Aru.

The yaksha thanked them profusely, then bowed and stepped aside, allowing them access to the portal.

Brynne was triumphant. "Nailed it!" she whispered, beaming.

Aiden bumped her fist and Mini bumped her elbow, but Aru hesitated. The yaksha had reached under the desk of his kiosk. Aru had seen Sherrilyn, the head of security at the museum, do the same thing in emergencies. He was pressing a secret alarm button.

"Hey, wait a sec—" started Aru, but Brynne yanked on her wrist.

They plunged through the portal. Fortunately, its muddy water slicked right off them and they stayed dry. At least they did until Aru landed on her butt on a soggy piece of ground. They were surrounded by swampland: tall brown reeds, bare gray trees, patches of ice, and an empty wooden boardwalk, all under a leaden sky. It hardly looked like a secret entrance to the Ocean of Milk would be anywhere around here.

Brynne helped her up. "You okay, Shah? You looked a little nervous about the yaksha back there."

"Yeah," said Aru uncertainly. "He just seemed kinda shady, is all."

"I didn't like him, either," said Aiden, still protectively holding on to his camera.

"Well, duh," said Brynne. "He tried to take Shadowfax. At least it's safe here. Now come on—I think I see the entrance to the Ocean of Milk between those trees." She pointed to a copse up ahead.

"How do you know that?" asked Mini.

Brynne tapped her nose. "'Cause I'm the daughter of the god of the wind. I have a pretty good instinct for where we are in relation to stuff."

"But how are we supposed to get there?" asked Mini. "The trail is way over there."

Brynne transformed into a hawk and said, "I can give you a lift. Aru, you take Aiden. Not so sure he's going to trust that hoverboard again, though...."

"I know what to do," said Aru. "Vajra, make a car-seat thing—"

"I don't *want* a car-seat thing! I'll be fine," said Aiden defensively. "My dad always said to get back up on the horse after a fall."

"Sure, but what about a cow?" teased Aru.

Aiden glared at her as they climbed onto the hoverboard.

Brynne took Mini's shoulders in her talons and they launched into the sky with a "Whooaaa!" (That was Mini.)

Soon they could see what looked like an archway straight ahead, beneath a cluster of trees. The entrance! They dove for it, but right before they got there, they heard branches snapping, and the very air seemed to change, becoming heavier. The four of them landed on a pathway in front of the arch, and Brynne morphed back into a girl. Aru kicked the hoverboard up and caught it in her hand in Ping-Pong-ball form. Together, they formed a tight circle.

From the left, five figures in dark hoodies emerged from behind trees that were much too thin for anyone to hide behind. Where had they come from?

One of the strangers broke off—Aru assumed he was the

leader. His hoodie was drawn low over his face, and there were two holes cut out at the top. Sharp horns protruded from them, slick and black. So he was an asura.

"Heading to the Ocean of Milk?" he said with a grunt. "Fuhgeddaboudit."

TWENTY-NINE

Did Your Parents Really Name You Sparky?

The asura snapped his fingers.

Now, standing right in front of them, at the threshold of the Ocean of Milk, was another, taller figure wearing a black sweatshirt. Aru couldn't tell if he was an asura or not. He wore obnoxious sunglasses with white stripes across the lenses, and a red T-shirt with a ram on it that said LIT. Aru rolled her eyes so hard she thought they'd fall out of her head.

Someone in the asura's posse laughed, and their leader growled at them. Then, to Aru and her friends, he said menacingly, "Meet Sparky. *No one gets past Sparky.*"

"Your parents named you Sparky?" Brynne said.

Sparky lifted one corner of his mouth. He seemed... amused. Not angry like the leader.

"Move out of our way," said Brynne. "We have business to attend to."

"You're not going anywhere," said the leader.

Aru frowned. Where was this guy getting his lines from? Very slowly, she pulled Vajra from her pocket. Out the corner of her eye, she saw the others doing the same—Mini holding Dee Dee in its mirror compact form, Brynne tapping her choker, Aiden rubbing his thumb along his enchanted leather bracelets.

The leader braced his legs wider apart, like he was some kind of club bouncer. "No one is allowed into the Ocean of Milk, because—"

"YEAH! WE'VE GOT ORDERS FROM LADY M!" shouted a member of the group behind him.

Aru's ears pricked. *Lady M?* Was that the alias Surpanakha was working under?

"Dude, I was getting to that!" the leader said, his voice no longer sounding deep and raspy, but younger, and a little whiny.

Aru looked closer at the leader. At first glance, she'd thought he was way older than Aiden. But she saw now that his sweatshirt hung loosely, like he'd borrowed it from someone bigger and taller. And his sneakers were platformed to give him a couple extra inches.

"Look," said Aru, stepping forward. "I don't know what Lady M has told you, but we've been sent by the Council of Guardians to retrieve something that was stolen. You don't want to find yourself on the wrong side of the gods, do you?"

The leader grinned smugly. "That's exactly what she said you'd say."

"Did she tell you that you'd be stopping the Pandavas?" asked Brynne, crossing her arms.

One of the hooded figures in the back gasped, and his neighbor elbowed him sharply in the ribs.

"You're *Pandavas?*" repeated the leader. "Oh snap!" But then he started laughing. "Dude, who *cares?*" he asked. "Look at you.

You're all freaking pathetic. She told us why you got kicked out of the Otherworld—"

Aiden spoke up. "They weren't kicked out. You've been lied to."

"Awww, and you've got a lackey," said the leader. "That's cute."

Brynne growled, nearly lurching forward, but Aiden caught her by the wrist.

"It's not worth it," he told her.

"Aiden's right," said Mini loudly. "How could you even trust someone like Lady M? She's a *monster*."

"You got that all wrong," the leader said. He gestured to a member of the posse behind him. "Yo, Hira. Show 'em what she looks like."

A guy was pushed forward and his hood yanked back to reveal that he wasn't a guy at all, but a young girl with bright hazel eyes and light brown skin. There was something shy and skittish about her, as if her own shadow could take her by surprise.

"I don't want to—" she started.

"Do it or I'll get you thrown out, Hira," said the leader. "Then what are you going to do? Go back to your family? Oh wait, you don't *have* one."

When Aru saw Hira's lips trembling, she wanted to punch that dude. But then the girl transformed.

The moment Hira took a deep breath, light rippled down her body. She turned into a beautiful adult woman with shining black hair, long red nails polished to a high gloss, and golden skin that practically shimmered.

Aru was stunned. *That* was Surpanakha? She didn't look at

all like how the poems had described her. Where were the fangs? The dragging limbs and gray skin?

One of the boys let out a loud wolf whistle.

"Don't whistle at the image of my future wifey!" snarled the leader.

Mini whispered, "I wonder if Surpanakha used the love arrow on the two of them."

That was a possibility. Surpanakha could have also bewitched this whole group of asuras to see her as a beautiful woman and not a hideous demoness.

Hira changed back and rejoined the posse.

"Please don't make me do that again," Hira mumbled.

One of her cohorts laughed.

Another one said, "I dunno why you keep looking like that when you can change into a hot girl whenever you want to."

Aru glowered, but before she could act, Brynne pointed her wind mace at them. The two obnoxious asuras were blown into the reeds, landing with a satisfying splash and a wail of outrage.

"Enjoy the mud, pigs," said Brynne.

Three others—including the leader—were hurled against the trees by another blast of Brynne's wind mace.

Hira remained standing, thanks to a sphere that had shielded her. She stood there openmouthed and incredulous. Mini, on the other hand, had a sly smile on her face.

To her right, Aru heard a soft chuckle, and she realized that not all the thugs had been defeated. Sparky had also not moved from his place in front of the archway. He looked... taller than before, she thought. Even from behind his bizarre sunglasses, Aru could feel his intense gaze.

"Whoa! No way!"

Aiden's exclamation made Aru turn away from Sparky the Silent.

"Is that…?" asked Aiden. "Wait, I think it is!"

Thanks to Brynne's wind mace, all the asuras' hoods had been blown back. This whole time, Aru had thought they were in their late teens or twenties. But no. They were seventh and eighth graders. One of them had a bad case of acne. The other wore black eyeliner and a shirt that said 4.0 GPA. WITNESS ME. Two of them were wearing thin gold necklaces that had been looped around twice to look more like intimidating chains.

The leader lurched out of the trees, groaning and rubbing his back.

Aiden started laughing. "Dude. Navdeep, is that you?"

Aru squinted at the asura leader. She definitely had seen that guy at Augustus Day.

The leader went wide-eyed, then shook his head frantically.

"Um, we have homeroom together in Atlanta?" tried Aru.

"Nah, girl. I don't know you. You don't know me. And you def don't know how I live."

"We were lab partners in Mr. Dietz's honors bio class?" said Aiden.

"Bruh—" said the boy in guyliner.

Aru didn't know that. Then again, she was not in Mr. Dietz's honors science class. She had, however, been a frequent guest of Mr. Dietz's after-school detention.

The others had recovered by now and were advancing cautiously. Except Hira. She must have run off at the first chance.

"I'm getting tired of this," said Brynne. "You're going to get out of our way. Now."

She brandished her wind mace again. Aru, holding her

lightning bolt, fell into place next to her. Aiden and Mini flanked them with scimitars and Dee Dee.

Both sides rushed each other at the same time.

It was, Aru thought, like playing dodgeball. Except instead of a rubber ball, everyone had, you know, harmless stuff like swords and dangerous magic!

Fighting wasn't something Aru enjoyed. But fighting alongside her friends? That felt like music. Mini twirled Dee Dee in front of her, then tossed the danda high into the air as she whispered a single word:

"Adrishya."

Vanish.

Mini had been practicing invisibility defenses for a while now, but this was the first time it worked. A veil fell over the four of them. Dee Dee hovered, utterly still in the air, like the handle of a gigantic umbrella. The asuras startled backward, shouting: "Where'd they go?!"

Aru tapped into their mind link: *You finally got it!*

Mini responded: *Yup. Cracked it while I was sleeping.*

Jeez, thought Aru, *maybe I should nap more.*

Now invisible, Brynne summoned the wind, which stirred the dirt and forced the goons back farther.

"Aim!" shouted one.

"But I can't see them!"

One of the asuras uttered a magical word, and a jet of water broke through the dirt, splattering against Mini's invisible shield.

"Found you," said Navdeep viciously.

They ran forward, swords out.

"Shah!" hollered Aiden. He held out his scimitars and Aru touched each of them with Vajra so they crackled with energy.

"We've got defenses," said Mini. "I'm letting down the shield."

Aru and Brynne instantly stood back-to-back.

"Do it," said Brynne.

Mini reduced the shield, keeping it wrapped only around herself and Aiden. They herded the attackers with invisible jabs, forcing them into a tight circle. Brynne blasted them with wind, and Aru added the finishing touch: a golden electrical net to catch and pin them in place.

"You're trapped now," Brynne growled at them. "If you want us to free you, then promise to leave."

"Fine, fine!" said Navdeep. "Just let us go!"

Aru retracted the net. The four boys scampered away down a nature path.

Mini waited until they had become nothing more than specks in the distance before yelling, "IT WAS NOT NICE TO MEET YOU!"

Brynne laughed. "*That's* what you shout at the backs of your enemies? Not 'Don't mess with my squad'?"

Aiden shuddered. "Can we not say 'squad'?"

"Why? Does it annoy you? Does 'hashtag squad goals' make you mad?" asked Aru.

"Yes."

"Then we're a squad."

"'Squad' sounds like it should be a vegetable," said Mini.

Brynne rubbed her stomach. "Mmm... sautéed squad."

"Please stop," said Aiden.

The four of them, remembering what they had come for, turned back to the archway. And stopped short.

It would seem that not all the boys had run. Sparky had stayed behind, his arms still crossed, his face still inscrutable behind his weird sunglasses.

"Didn't you just see what happened to your friends?" asked Brynne.

Aru rubbed her eyes, blinked a couple times, and resumed staring at Sparky. That guy *had* to be getting taller by the second. Around his head, she could see a faint shining corona, like how saints in old paintings sometimes looked like they were wearing gold astronaut helmets. But it wasn't just saints who were depicted like that....

It was gods, too.

"I'm warning you," said Brynne. "These are *powerful* weapons."

Sparky clapped once. Aru felt a sharp tug in her chest, like someone had grabbed her heart and pulled. Mini made a pained sound, and even Brynne doubled over as if she'd been kicked in the gut. Aiden yelled, "Hey!"

Furious, Aru reached for Vajra and—

Her fingers closed around air.

Vajra!

Her lightning bolt was gone! How could her lightning bolt *not* be with her? It felt like she had lost a limb. But when she looked up, she saw it, shining in its Ping-Pong form, in Sparky's hand. In his other hand was Brynne's wind mace, Mini's Dee Dee, and even Aiden's enchanted scimitars.

"That's not how I like to fight," said Sparky.

It was the first time Aru had heard him talk. His voice was warm and crackly, like a fire.

Aru had no clue as to how Sparky *did* like to fight. But it didn't matter. She had no other weapons or defensive items left. In her backpack was a half-empty bottle of water, a package of Oreos that she'd shoved into its very depths so Brynne couldn't sniff it out, and a useless vial from the Warehouse of Quest Materials: a single "bright idea."

"Who...who are you?" asked Aiden.

Sparky shrugged. "Just someone who doesn't like fighting.... You want to go into the Ocean of Milk, and I have a theory as to why. But you'll have to earn your passage. If you want me to move out of the way, beat me in a contest."

"What kind of contest?" asked Brynne suspiciously.

Sparky grinned. "An *eating* contest."

"Eating?" Brynne echoed happily. "Sign me up! I've *never* lost an eating contest."

THIRTY

Brynne Loses an Eating Contest

Eating contests were for fairs or carnivals. They were not meant to be part of a quest to prevent a demoness from gaining immortality, so this was just rude.

There was nothing any of them could do about it, not that Brynne was complaining. Aru kept opening and closing her hands, willing Vajra back to her, but her lightning bolt was now tightly wedged under Sparky's foot, along with the scimitars and mace. At least he wasn't tossing Vajra up in the air and catching it, as he was doing with Mini's danda stick.

Mini sniffed. "Dee Dee doesn't like being treated like that. It's a very sensitive instrument!"

Sparky, who had his back to them as he muttered some enchantments, ignored her.

Beside Aru, Brynne started pacing back and forth and massaging her jaw.

"Please don't say you've got some kind of magical jaw that unhinges," said Aru. "If that's the case, I'm out."

Brynne said something like *Mah djaw dush not unhish!*

"In Hungry Brynne, that means 'It doesn't unhinge,'"

translated Aiden. Then he whispered, "Although it kinda looks like it."

"Almost ready!" announced Sparky, turning to face them. He stepped aside and swept his arm in a *voilà!* gesture.

Right in front of the entrance to the Ocean of Milk stretched a long picnic table with a red-checked tablecloth. Its entire surface was covered with bowls and plates of different foods. They stepped closer to examine it more closely, and the aromas made Aru's mouth water. There was steaming lentil soup, thick pieces of naan studded with fennel seeds and garlic, coconut and quince chutney, pickled mango, and hundreds of different kinds of vegetable stew. Aru saw one of her favorite snacks lying on the far side of the table: idli, savory disk-shaped rice cakes that she thought looked like UFOs.

But even Brynne looked a little wary of the mountains of food. Where had it all come from?

Mini, who hadn't had anything but a power-nap chocolate bar since being captured, started to reach for a piece of naan....

"Ah-ah-ah!" Sparky said, suddenly appearing beside her to slap her hand away. "Only for the contestant. Now, where did I put those utensils and napkins?" He rushed over to a picnic basket that had magically appeared on the ground.

Sparky moved ridiculously fast. One minute he was standing in one place, the next minute he was somewhere else. It was as sudden as a flame erupting at the end of a matchstick.

Aru sniffed the air. "Do you smell that?"

"I didn't do it," said Brynne, turning red.

"It smells like something is burning," said Mini. "But I don't see a fire.... Oh no. What if there *is* a fire? Do you know that in most fires people get asphyxiated by smoke, and then they—"

"Die?" asked Aiden and Aru at the same time.

"Yes!" said Mini.

"So, are you forfeiting or what?" yelled Sparky from the other side of the picnic table. He was seated at the far end, holding a fork in one hand and a spoon in the other, with a napkin tied around his neck. Aru wondered where he had stashed their weapons.

"No way," said Brynne.

She sat down opposite him. On her left was the naan and a couple of wet paper towels for her hands. On the other side was a tall glass of water. From Aru's short-lived stint in cotillion etiquette classes, she knew that water always went on the right and bread on the left, because if she pinched her index finger and thumb together while holding up the rest of her fingers, it looked like a *d* on her right hand (for drink) and a *b* on her left hand (for bread). It was the only thing she had taken away from class. (Oh, and half of some girl's braid, but that was completely by accident. Honest.)

"So, let's begin," said Sparky. "I've always had a big appetite. Sometimes it gets me into trouble."

Brynne cracked her neck from side to side. "Me too."

"One time, I ate only ghee nonstop for twelve years," said Sparky. He lifted a bowl to his mouth and started slurping.

Sparky *had* to be joking about the ghee. Aru thought ghee was disgusting on its own. It was just clarified butter!

Brynne must have thought he was joking, too, because she said, "One time, I ate everything in a bakery. In one day." Then she started inhaling food like she was a vacuum cleaner.

Whoa, Aiden was *not* kidding. Aru's jaw hurt just watching Brynne.

"Told ya," he said.

"How can she *breathe*?" asked Mini.

Sparky had one up on Brynne, though. Not only did he keep up the pace of his eating, but he could talk through it, too.

"No one devours as much as me. One time, I ate fifteen hundred dosas in less than five minutes."

Brynne ignored him and kept gobbling things down. Aru, Aiden, and Mini ran back and forth down the picnic table, replacing her empty dishes with full ones, tossing the dirty plates on the ground, wiping her mouth (and occasionally her nose if there was something really spicy), and holding the glass of water for her to sip. Sparky had to do everything by himself, but it didn't seem to be slowing him down any.

At one point, Brynne let out a particularly epic burp. Aiden was so impressed, he high-fived her.

Mini shook her head. "That can't be good for your esophagus."

Then Sparky followed suit. Only when *he* burped, he let out a belch of . . . fire. Flames scorched the middle of the picnic table.

They all froze for a few seconds, costing Brynne some valuable time.

"Is that normal asura behavior?" asked Mini nervously.

"Now, on to the desserts!" announced Sparky. The table magically filled with all-new dishes, and he surveyed them with delight, his eyes gleaming as hungrily as ever.

Aru wasn't sure, but she thought she heard Brynne groan softly.

"Ready to give up?" Sparky asked her. He dug his spoon into a bowl of creamy rasmalai. It was one of Aru's favorite desserts, nice and cold and with the perfect texture of a sponge cake. *Nommmm.*

"No?" said Brynne, but she was starting to sway.

"Are you sure about that?" asked Sparky, laughing. He drained the entire bowl of rasmalai, then popped the metal dish itself into his mouth and crunched down. "Once, I had such a bad stomachache that no one in the world could cure it. Not even sages. I had to go straight to the gods."

Brynne forced down a mouthful of carrot halwa.

"Once, I—" she began to brag. Then she stopped, too full to speak. She shook her head, then made a *go-ahead* gesture to Sparky.

Sparky looked very smug as he inhaled the rest of the desserts, talking all the while. "I had to eat ghee for *years*, all because some king wanted to conduct a great ritual.... *Twelve years of clarified butter!* Even Paula Deen would have run in the opposite direction."

Aru eyed Sparky. Over the course of the contest, he had grown even taller. His skin, which had always been a bit ruddy, now reminded her of embers. Even his hair, once a rust color, like a bad dye job, had changed. Now it looked multicolored— blue at the roots, orange in the middle, and yellow at the tips. Like a flame.

"One time I ate a forest. Nothing can sate my hunger," moaned Sparky. "Nothing at all!"

By now, he had snarfed down all the desserts. Instead of getting up from the table, he set upon it. The red-checked cloth disappeared into his mouth and when he burped, cinders fell on the tabletop.

Brynne groaned and rolled over onto her side on the bench. "I can't believe I'm saying this, but...I'm full."

Sparky didn't answer—he just stared into space, as if all concern about the competition had disappeared and he was thinking deeply about something else.

Behind him stood the archway, now clear of any obstacle. All they had to do was make a run for it . . . but Brynne couldn't move. And they didn't have their weapons, either. They couldn't go in to the Ocean of Milk without their armaments.

"The world became bleak when I started losing my luster," said Sparky. His voice got louder as his body grew bigger. No longer able to fit on the picnic bench, he stood up, as tall as the archway. "After all, I am the spark inside all living beings. I make things bright. I make things burn. It is my nature."

The sunglasses fell from Sparky's eyes, which didn't look human or even demonic. They glowed like twin fiery rubies.

"He's . . . definitely not . . . an asura . . ." said Aiden slowly.

"YA THINK?" demanded Aru.

"But the problem is," continued Sparky, "once I start, it's very hard to stop. . . ."

His LIT shirt ripped in half down the middle, revealing a bright red suit edged in flames. Sparky wasn't done eating. He was devouring everything within reach by setting it alight. Soon, the whole picnic table would be reduced to ash. The reeds around them burst into flame.

"We're going to be trapped!" cried Mini.

From behind Aru came a weak chuckle. Brynne, who still had not recovered from the competition, clutched her stomach and said, "I don't feel so bad about losing now." She pointed at Sparky. "At least I lost to a god."

A god?

It clicked then. The fire. The insatiable appetite that could devour a forest whole...

Sparky wasn't some kid with ugly sunglasses and an appetite that could destroy a city. He was *Agni*, the god of fire. And he was on the verge of consuming them.

THIRTY-ONE

Aru Shah Is on Fire. No, but Seriously. Like, *Fire* Fire. This Is Not a Drill

Agni had grown to the size of an elephant.

The picnic table was nothing more than a smoldering pile of embers. Now the trees around them began to crackle. Smoke churned through the air. Aru, Mini, and Aiden dragged Brynne's picnic-bench sickbed away from Agni and drew into a tight group, but what else could they do? They had no weapons—nothing but their wits and their backpacks. And their best fighter was down for the count.

"Oh, the pain!" moaned Agni. "I'm still so hungry!"

"Maybe you have indigestion?" suggested Mini. "I...I have something for that? For when food is too spicy? Maybe that's why you're burping flames...."

"I love spice," cut in Brynne. She was curled up in the fetal position and breaking out into a cold sweat. "I could eat, like, a whole bottle of cayenne pepper. Watch me."

And then she promptly threw up.

Aiden went over to offer her a sip of water from his canteen and wipe off her face.

Mini tossed a bottle of antacid pills at the god of fire. Agni caught it in one hand, where it immediately melted.

"Nooooooooooo!" he cried.

More trees began to catch fire. Mini covered her nose and mouth with a wet napkin to avoid breathing in the smoke.

"Help me, Pandavas!" shouted Agni, clutching his belly.

"How 'bout we fill some of these empty bowls with swamp water?" suggested Aiden. "Then we can throw it on him."

"It won't be enough. The water will just turn to steam," said Mini, "and then we'll choke and die."

"What about wet rocks?" asked Aru, looking around. "If we piled them up, would they put out the fire?"

"Not river rocks!" said Mini. "The water molecules inside will expand as they heat up, and they'll explode, and then we'll die!"

"What's an option where we *don't* die?" asked Aiden.

Agni groaned. "I'm starving...."

He was a raging inferno now. His scarlet suit gleamed. His arms ended in fireballs.

Aru never thought she'd say this, but: "I miss Sparky."

"You helped cure my appetite once before," pleaded Agni, "in the Khandava Forest. Do it again!"

Before...in the Khandava Forest? That was where Takshaka's wife had perished in the flames. The place where Arjuna had shot down any living creature that had tried to escape the fire. Every time Aru thought about it, she felt more grossed-out and guilty, even though she wasn't the one who had fired the arrows. But she hadn't known before now that the fire was caused by Agni....

"Aru!" screamed Mini. "Watch out!"

A huge burning branch overhead was about to fall on Aru's head.

Aiden yanked her back.

The flames had grown into a towering wall that blocked the entrance to the Ocean of Milk completely. Agni was back there somewhere, but Aru couldn't see him behind the fire.

"We have to move away from here," said Mini, as the flames danced toward them. "C'mon!"

Together, the three of them lifted Brynne's bench and hauled it farther down the walkway.

"We still need to get through there somehow," said Aiden, looking back at the archway. "If only we could bulldoze swamp mud onto the fire..."

"But we don't have the equipment," said Mini.

And then, from the bench, Brynne croaked, "We can ask?"

Aru and Mini looked at each other. Even without the Pandava mind link, they knew what Brynne was talking about. Asking their soul fathers for help.

"Do what you have to do," said Aiden. "I'm going to try to lead Agni away from the entrance."

He ran back toward the flames.

Aru took a deep breath. "Okay, time to make a few calls."

Mini closed her eyes, clasping her hands together. Brynne whispered to the air. Aru looked to the sky.

"Hi, Dad..." she said. "So...hope you're well. Um, if you can see me, you'll notice the flames that are about to consume... us? I know you don't like to interfere, but we're really desperate. Could we get some help? Please?"

She closed her eyes tight, trying to ignore the heat coming from the trees burning nearby. Then Aru felt the slightest tug on her backpack. She turned around, expecting to see Mini. But Mini was still standing next to her, silently praying. Brynne was still on the bench. Aru closed her eyes again and once more felt a tug on her backpack.

She dropped it on the ground, then rifled through it.

"Did you get a sign?" asked Mini excitedly.

"Is your backpack enchanted?" asked Brynne, sitting up.

"I just felt a tug, but there's got to be some mistake. There's nothing here."

The fire continued to move closer. Aiden raced back toward them. There were soot marks on his face and he was out of breath.

"I"—he coughed—"couldn't…make him move…."

Mini ran over to Aiden. She searched her bag and found him a bottle of water.

In a panic, Aru dumped out the contents of her backpack.

Nothing but socks, a package of Oreos—which prompted Brynne to say, "HEY! When I asked if you had any snacks, you said no!"—and the little vial from the Warehouse of Quest Materials labeled BRIGHT IDEA. The glowing blue jar was no bigger than one of her mom's perfume bottles.

"Open it!" said Aiden.

Aru tried to pull out the cork in the top, but it wouldn't budge. Everyone else also gave it a go, with no success. If they couldn't open it, how were they going to get to the idea inside?

"We're *doomed*," said Mini, tugging at her hair.

But Aru wasn't ready to give up yet. What if the answer was the bottle itself? A person could use up material things, like trees and shrubs, food and cloth…but it was harder to exhaust an idea. And the moment an idea was used, it changed shape.

An idea was impossible to burn.

"I think . . . I think I've got an idea," said Aru.

Under any other circumstances, she would have laughed at the unintentional joke. But Aru was out of laughs. She gripped the bottle tightly, then turned to face her friends. This might be their last chance to reach the Ocean of Milk.

"I'm going to try to distract Agni with this," she said. "When he turns, I want you all to run into the portal without—"

"No way, Shah," said Aiden.

"We're not going anywhere without you," added Mini.

Aru would have argued with them, but then Brynne spoke up.

"I'm not abandoning family."

That jolted Aru. Mini had been her soul sister for a while now, but Brynne and Aiden had only recently been shoved into her life without her consent. Since then, they'd made fun of one another and fought with one another and shared candy and battles and even awful road trips (with red cows). So, yeah, it was safe to say they were family.

She wasn't going to leave them, either.

A burning hand reached out through the wall of flames.

"I AM HANGRY!" Agni thundered.

When his head emerged, Aru couldn't make out the parts of his face anymore—except he had swirling red pits for eyes. It was as if being hungry for so long had made him pure element.

"I've got something for you!" she shouted, holding up the vial.

The head loomed forward.

"I'm going to need some height," Aru told the others.

"You got it," said Brynne, rolling onto her hands and knees. "Pile on!"

Although she was apparently too stuffed with food to change shape, Brynne was still superstrong. Aiden climbed onto her back, then Mini climbed onto his. Aru clambered up her friends. In theory, it should have been like going up stairs. But it did not go as smoothly as planned.

At one point, Aiden grumbled, "Shah! Your foot is on my face!"

And he did not take kindly to Aru's suggestion: "Then get your face off my foot!"

They teetered back and forth as Agni rolled their way. Waves of fire skirted around them, nearly blistering their skin and blackening the wooden planks beneath their feet. Agni opened his jaws, getting ready to swallow them whole. All Aru could see were searing flames, the air in front of her heat-warped and furious.

"Now, Shah!" screamed Brynne.

Aru pitched the "bright idea" forward. The blue light of the bottle looked like an iceberg in a sea of flame. Agni lurched forward to grab it between his molten teeth. The moment he bit down on it, a wave of energy coursed through the national park, blowing them off the boardwalk and sending them into the shallow, reed-filled swamp.

The cold water stunned Aru. Quickly, they stood up and waded over to the pathway, shivering. In front of them, Agni was struggling, contorting himself and chewing furiously.

"WHY…" he grumbled.

"CAN'T…" He choked.

"I…" He gasped.

"EAT…" He chewed.

"YOU?" he roared.

Agni spun around, trying to find Aru and the others. The flames on his body flickered and hissed. Slowly, he shrank from the size of a raging forest fire to that of a big, glowing man. His clothes smoldered and burned, smoke unraveling in the air above him. The fires he had ignited rolled backward, instantly restoring everything that had once been consumed. No—not restoring. *Changing.* The trees, once reduced to cinders, grew tall again, but their trunks and branches were now made out of gold. The dirt, previously dull and covered in brambles, was now the rich brown of hot cocoa, and studded with small jewels instead of rocks. Bright red flowers carpeted the areas that had been full of reeds.

"What-t-t d-d-did you d-d-do to that v-v-vial?" Aiden asked Aru, his teeth chattering in the cold.

She shrugged. "N-n-nothing. I just had an idea and p-p-passed it on to him."

"What idea?" Brynne didn't even seem cold, maybe because she'd just eaten more than her own weight in spicy Indian dishes.

"I wondered what would happen if n-n-nothing around here was edible," said Aru.

"Look at the t-t-treasure!" Mini said, pointing.

The picnic table was back, but now, instead of being piled with food, it was piled with jewels of all kinds.

"Man," grumbled Brynne. "He couldn't even leave us some naan?"

But the biggest change was in Agni himself. Now that his fire had receded, he'd turned into Sparky 2.0. He was tall, but no longer monstrously so. His ugly shirt had been upgraded to a scarlet *sherwani* jacket edged in flame designs, and his cheap plastic sunglasses were now a pair of Ray-Bans. A scarf of molten lava hung around his neck, and his hair looked like banked embers—which was definitely an improvement over the weird dye job. At his side trotted a bright red ram, which Aru recognized as his *vahana*, or celestial mount.

Agni stretched his arms above his head, yawned, and patted his stomach. "Oof…That was a lot of calories I just ate. I feel a food coma coming on."

He belched, scorching a patch of grass next to the path. The god was still chewing on the bright idea, Aru noticed, like it was a piece of gum.

"Smart thinking," he said, pointing at his idea-filled cheek.

"Can't take all the credit," said Aru, glancing up at the sky.

She didn't see any sign of Indra there. No thunderclaps or flashes of lightning. But she and her friends were no longer dripping wet, and the air seemed warmer, as if the world were pleased.

The four of them still huddled close. Agni might have pulled back on his terrible splendor, but it was hard to trust someone who had tried to consume you in flames.

Agni noticed and waved them closer. "Technically, we're family!" he said happily.

The four of them were too horrified to move.

"Oh, I can see you're still not over the whole set-you-on-fire thing," said Agni.

DUH! Aru wanted to say, but she knew better.

"I'm not evil. Destructive, sure. But destruction isn't necessarily a bad thing," said Agni, gesturing at the golden trees and jeweled picnic table. "At my most elemental stage, I'm a force of change, even purification."

"But we're not the bad guys here," said Aru. "Why would you want to stop us?"

"I was doing my duty, as we all must," Agni said. "My duty is to burn, and long ago, the gods tasked me to fulfill it against anyone who tried entering the Ocean of Milk."

"That's just great," said Brynne. "So we're still trapped here?"

"Not at all," said Agni, moving aside to clear a path to the archway. He nodded to Aru. "You found a way to extinguish the fire, so you may pass with my blessings."

THIRTY-TWO

Presents from Uncle Agni

"Well?" Agni asked. "Go on, then! Go forth and kill and what have you."

Agni snapped his fingers and their weapons appeared out of thin air and zoomed back into their hands.

"Vajra!" said Aru joyously.

She never thought she'd want to hug a lightning bolt, but today was one of those days. Her lightning bolt thrummed in her hands, then dove into her pocket as if relieved to be home. Mini was fussing over Dee Dee, inspecting it for any kind of fire damage, while Brynne's mace blew her hair around her face like a happy blow-dryer. Aiden slid on his scimitar cuffs without saying anything, but Aru saw him double-check that Shadowfax hadn't gotten singed by Agni's flames.

"Let's go!" said Brynne, pointing in the direction of the archway. "How many days do we have left, anyway?"

Aiden checked his watch, his face paling. "One."

One day left? Aru thought she'd hurl. Through the archway lay the entrance to the Ocean of Milk. They were so close; they had their weapons back...they even had the blessing of the god of fire...and they were running out of time...but Aru couldn't make herself take a step forward.

She knew who she would have to face in the Ocean of Milk.

She was ready for Surpanakha. But there was someone else, too... Takshaka, the naga king.

He had lost his wife in the Khandava Forest fire because of Arjuna and also, apparently, Agni. Arjuna hadn't acted alone, of course. In the stories, the god Krishna always fought beside him. But Aru didn't understand why Takshaka's friends and community had had to die in those flames. Why hadn't the gods spared them if they hadn't done anything wrong? It was unfair, and even though she was mad at the serpent king, she also understood why Takshaka would want to take everyone down.

"What's up, kid?" asked Agni, raising a knowing eyebrow. "You look confused. You've only got one opportunity, so you might as well ask me your question."

Aru checked her friends. Brynne seemed mildly irritated, but she bowed her head as if to say *Go ahead, if you must.* Beside her, Aiden and Mini nodded encouragingly.

Aru turned back to Agni, who showed no traces of his former raging self. Now the heat radiating from him was as comforting as a roaring hearth in winter. His expression was warm and lively, exuding a coziness that draws families and friends together, and his eyes flickered with the kind of light that inspires stories.

Aru took a deep breath before asking, "Why did Arjuna kill Takshaka's family?"

Agni leaned against one of the golden trees that only minutes ago had been a pile of ash.

"That's not the real question you're asking, kid, but I get it. Here's the truth. A long time ago, I got really sick. When *I* get sick, *everything* gets sick."

"You don't say," Brynne said drily.

Agni ignored her. "I'm a sacred part of every prayer! You know at weddings, there's a holy fire that the bride and groom walk around? That's me! So it's not good when I'm not well. And when nothing could cure me, I went straight to Brahma himself. He told me that I had to eat the Khandava Forest. Only by doing so would the universe be in balance again."

The universe being out of balance definitely didn't sound good.... "But what about—?" started Aru.

"Let me tell you another tale. Ever heard of Jaya and Vijaya?"

"No?"

"They're, like, attendants to the god Vishnu, aren't they?" asked Aiden.

"How do you know that?" asked Aru.

"My mom used to tell me their knock-knock jokes. They're *really* bad. Trust me."

"Ah, yes, your mother," said Agni, stroking his chin. "It's hard to forget the famous apsara dancer Malini. Tell her I finally mastered the salsa. She taught me, you know."

"You could tell her yourself?" tried Aiden hopefully.

"Against the rules," said Agni, shaking his head. "Malini gave up her connection to the Otherworld when she married a mortal man. They made an exception for you, though." Agni shrugged. "Hope it was worth it for her. Anyway—"

Aru snuck a glance at Aiden. He was standing there, stricken, and Aru wasn't sure what to do. Brynne reached out to hold his hand, and Aru looked away, feeling as if she'd been caught spying.

"Jaya and Vijaya are the doorkeepers to Vishnu," Agni continued. "One day a group of four sages shows up. Only problem is, they look like kids. Jaya and Vijaya don't know they're sages, so they tell them to get going, because Lord Vishnu is sleeping. Well, the kid-sages don't like that, and they curse them to live human lives—"

"How come living like *us* is always the curse?" asked Aru.

"Yeah! What's so bad about being human, minus the allergies, politics, death, illness, reality TV shows—" Mini stopped. "Never mind."

"Ahem. *Anyway*," Agni went on, "Jaya and Vijaya are horrified by their fate, naturally, so Vishnu offers them two choices. Either they take seven births on Earth as good, pious devotees of Vishnu, or they take four births on Earth as Vishnu's sworn enemies. Which do they go with?"

"Seven births," said Mini. "Who'd want to be the enemy of Vishnu?"

"I agree," said Aiden.

"Four births," said Brynne. "I'd just want to get it over with."

Aru pointed at her. "Yup. Same."

"Jaya and Vijaya agreed with you," said Agni, nodding at Brynne. "One of the most famous lives they lived was as Ravana and his demon brother."

Aru knew that name. "*Ravana?* Like, the demon king who stole Rama's wife?"

"The very one."

Ravana was an enemy and a villain, but, as Aru's mom had

always told her, sometimes villains can do heroic things and heroes can do villainous things, so what did it mean to be one or the other? And now Ravana's sister, Surpanakha, had stolen the bow and arrow. Aru's head was beginning to hurt.

"But I don't understand how this story answers my first question," said Aru.

"Oh, but it does," said Agni. "You think what happened in the Khandava Forest was unfair, and maybe it was. It goes to show that, as with Jaya and Vijaya, bad things happen to good people, and good things happen to bad people. Sometimes life isn't fair—but that doesn't mean things happen without a reason. We just don't always know what the reason is. The world is inscrutable. It doesn't owe you answers. You should only concern yourself with doing your duty. Understand?"

Aru would have found it more understandable if she had cut open an apple and found orange pulp inside.

"Not even a little."

"Good!" said Agni. "If you understood, you'd be omniscient, and trust me, that's a real headache."

Aru stood there, her confusion wanting to give way to peace. Maybe, by retrieving Kamadeva's bow and arrow, she was doing exactly what she was supposed to be doing. She didn't have the god Krishna by her side the way Arjuna did, but she had her family and her instincts, and if at the end of the day she could say she was doing her best, that had to count for something...right?

"I'm ready," said Aru, even as doubt coiled low in her stomach.

Agni smiled. "I'm glad to hear it. You're going to need to be ready for the fight that's ahead," said the god of fire. "You know, the last time Arjuna and I hung out, I bestowed him with gifts. For tradition's sake, I think I should do the same now."

Aru, Brynne, and Mini made identical sounds that meant *OhmygodpresentsIhopeitsshiny.*

Aiden rolled his eyes.

Agni cupped his palms together and held them out to Mini. When he opened his hands, there appeared a beautiful burning rose with black petals.

"To the daughter of the god of death, I give a Night Flame," he said. "You will never be lost in the dark."

Mini paid her respects to Agni by touching his feet. When she took the Night Flame, it turned into a black hair barrette that she immediately used to keep her bangs out of her face.

"Much better," said Mini. "Thank you."

"To the daughter of the god of the wind, I grant your mace the power of flame," said Agni, waving his red hand over Brynne's weapon.

The blue mace now had a red stripe. Brynne grinned, then swung the mace to try it out. Fire flashed in the air.

"To the daughter of the god of thunder, I grant you this...."

Aru could barely keep it together. *Please be a flaming sword!* Not that she would really know what to do with one ... She was a lot better with spears and other thrown weapons whenever Hanuman led their battle training sessions, but *still.* How cool would that be? Also, toasting marshmallows would be a cinch.

But Agni didn't hand her a flaming sword, or a flaming any-thing. Instead, he gave her a gold coin that read IO(F)U.

Um, RUDE? thought Aru. *Also, not very subtle....*

"Incendiary Offers for Future Use," clarified Agni.

"Oh."

"I have an arsenal of weapons that you will have need of, daughter of Indra," said Agni. His voice sounded rather distant, as if he had glimpsed something of the future. "When that time comes, call on me."

Aru pocketed the coin, feeling the slightest dig of disappointment. "Okay, well, thanks," she said.

"I'm not quite done," said Agni, pointing at Aiden.

Aiden's eyes widened. "*Me?* I'm not a Pandava—"

"Yes, yes, we know," said Agni. He pointed at Aiden's camera. "May I?"

"But Shadow—I mean, my camera—is really old and—"

"I merely want to enhance it," said Agni.

Reluctantly, Aiden held out the camera. From Agni's fingertips erupted a ribbon of fire that encircled the camera and made it glow. When Agni handed it back, it was free of the scuffmarks and fingerprints that it had accumulated on their trip.

"I added a fire battery. The power will never run out, and the camera will always have enough memory."

Aiden's face shone. "Wow...thank you!"

"Be careful out there. The golden dome over the labyrinth is known to deactivate all celestial weapons." Agni inclined his head. "See well, Pandavas."

Aiden automatically said, "I'm not a—"

But the god of fire had disappeared, leaving only a burning ember on the spot where he'd once stood.

THIRTY-THREE

But Real Talk, *Where* Are the Cookies?

Aru worried that passing under the arch would mean falling headfirst into a huge glass of milk and some giant confusing her with an Oreo. But the portal didn't work that way. The moment the four of them stepped through, they found themselves standing on pale sand. Suspended above them, stretched out like a creamy sky, was a rolling sea. The Ocean of Milk.

On the one hand, being so close to it was overwhelming. All around them were the scattered remains of the huge cosmic event when the Ocean had been churned for the nectar of immortality. The stories said that hundreds of precious treasures had leaped out of the waves when the gods and asuras churned the sea, and Aru could see the proof. Jutting from the smooth white sand were thick, sparkling branches the size of towering oaks. There was only one tree they could've belonged to: Kalpavriksha, the wish-granting tree. Aru touched a branch cautiously, feeling the rough-cut crystals that were embedded in the wood. She felt a muted pulse of magic under her fingertips and drew back her hand.

"Wow," breathed Brynne, pointing at the massive structures haphazardly surrounding them. It looked as if someone had chopped up the Great Wall of China and scattered it across the sand. "It's Vasuki's *skin!*"

Gross, thought Aru.

Vasuki was the naga king who had allowed his body to be used as a rope when the ocean was churned—after that, he lived as a necklace on the god Shiva. Now that Aru looked closely, she could make out the pattern of iridescent scales, bright as peacock feathers, on the pieces of snake skin.

Everything was so . . . massive.

It made sense—these were the treasures of gods. Seeing Agni change in size had reminded her that whenever gods fit in her field of vision, they were just humoring her.

Aru had never felt smaller in her life.

There was no sound except the gentle *swish* of the ocean above and the constant *click* of Aiden's camera.

Mini said, "I thought it would smell different. Like cereal or something."

"Yeah, me too," said Aiden. He sniffed the air. "Kinda smells like an ice cream truck parked outside of a Hindu temple."

Yup, thought Aru, *that*. The smell of cold and cream and wafting incense.

"And I didn't think it would be quite as see-through," added Aru, glancing up at the milk/ocean/sky. "Looks like skim milk up there."

"At least I don't have to worry about lactose," Mini said with much relief.

"I don't know why there can't be an Ocean of Cookies if

there's an Ocean of Milk," reasoned Brynne. "I feel like that should be illegal."

"Truth," said Aiden.

Of all the kinds of oceans they could be walking under, Aru was glad it was an Ocean of Milk and not something weirder, like an Ocean of Kombucha, which tasted like stewed socks and soy sauce.

The broken tree branches and huge pieces of treasure cast long shadows that threw them into darkness. Mini's Night Flame barrette now looked like a lilac halo around her head. Off to the right of them, Aru could just make out a faint golden glow.

"Look!" said Aru, pointing at the glimmer. "Do you think that's the dome of the labyrinth?"

"Must be," said Brynne. "But we don't know who's guarding the outside.... I'm going to scope it out."

In a flash of blue light, Brynne changed into a sapphire-colored hunting dog. She snuffled the ground.

"Follow me!" she said, pointing her paw to the left. "I can smell stronger magic about five kilometers southeast—"

Mini gasped. "You're so *cute* as a dog!"

Aiden snapped a photo.

Brynne growled at them all before bounding off into the shadows.

Mini put her arm across her nose. "I hope I'm not allergic to her. I'm out of tissues, and I don't want to have a runny nose when we fight!" She raced after Brynne, calling over her shoulder, "We'll take the front, you guys patrol the rear!"

"Got it!" said Aru.

The whole place felt a lot quieter without Brynne and Mini, and Aru's thoughts wandered back to what Agni had said. *See well.*

He wasn't the first person to say that to her. The first was Varuni, the goddess of wine. Only she'd slurred through a sort of prophecy before she'd given that advice.... Aru pushed herself to remember, until the words floated back to her:

> *The girl with eyes like a fish and a heart snapped in two*
> *will be met in battle by a girl named Aru.*
> *But take care what you do with a heart so broken,*
> *for uglier truths will soon be spoken.*
> *You, daughter of Indra, have a tongue like a whip,*
> *but be wary of those to whom you serve lip,*
> *for there is a tale beyond that soon you shall see . . .*
> *But all that depends on your surviving the sea.*

Who the heck was the girl with eyes like a fish?

Heart snapped in two could mean Uloopi, whose heart jewel had been stolen and hidden by Takshaka all these years. Or maybe it was Surpanakha?

And that last part . . . *surviving the sea.* That gave Aru chills.

"Is an ocean the same thing as a sea?" she asked Aiden.

He didn't say anything.

"Wait, was that a really dumb question?" asked Aru.

"Huh, what?"

Aru took Vajra out of her pocket and held it up to Aiden's face. Even though the ball's glow was weak compared to Mini's Night Flame, she could see him clearly. And he was clearly upset. His mouth was pulled down, and he was gripping his camera so tight that his knuckles had turned white.

All thoughts of the ocean disappeared. "You okay?" she asked.

He glanced away from her quickly, but not before she'd scanned the rest of his face. He still had soot marks on his cheeks and nose from when he'd run into the fires of Agni, but otherwise he didn't appear... badly off. Then again, he was the son of a famously beautiful apsara. And it showed. Aru felt her face turning red and quickly looked elsewhere.

"Yeah," he said finally. "Kinda wish I'd had Agni's eternal memory stick before now. I could've used it at home."

"Oh, for like... taking pictures of stuff around the house?"

"Yeah, and, um, my parents. We used to have a lot of family photos, but Mom put them away. I don't know where."

Aru remembered how stricken Aiden had looked when Agni mentioned his mom. Because she married a mortal man, she'd given up all connection to the Otherworld.

Hope it was worth it for her.

Aru understood how awful that felt. Like it was somehow *his* fault that his own mom wouldn't get to be part of the world she grew up in... And Aru hadn't forgotten the nightmares that plagued Aiden because of his parents' divorce. His mom wondering if having him was what caused the breakup...

"Aiden?"

He looked up from his camera. "Yeah?"

"Are you okay? Like, really okay? It's fine if you're not...."

Aiden took a deep breath. Then he said quietly, "It's my mom.... What if she regrets her life? She gave up everything for my dad. And then he leaves her to marry a girlfriend he met *while* he was still with my mom. And—"

His voice broke, and it took him a moment to speak again. "What'd she get out of it?"

Aru put her hand his shoulder. "You."

She thought of all the times she'd seen Mrs. Acharya with Aiden. She was always protective of him, always brushing the hair out of his eyes, and smiling at him even when he didn't see it. Aru knew that the next thing she said was not a lie. "And she'd say you're worth it."

Aiden really looked at her then. His eyes were wide and dark, but not pure black. There were flashes of blue iridescence in them, like in Urvashi's eyes. Maybe it was an apsara trait. It made sense to Aru. Apsaras spent so much time dancing in the night skies that maybe their eyes eventually mirrored them.

Aiden took a deep breath, and Aru drew back her hand.

"I like you, Shah."

Aru's eyebrows shot up. Her heartbeat jittered and she felt a not unpleasant *swoosh* low in her stomach, like butterflies taking wing.

Aiden panicked. "But not like, uh—"

Aaaand all the butterflies died.

"Like friends," finished Aru, her voice sounding a touch too bright.

"Yeah," he said, smiling. "Like friends."

Aru would never say no to having more friends, even if she thought, for a second... Well, it didn't matter.

"Just so you know," she said, "being friends with me means that on Wednesdays we wear pink."

Aiden sighed and muttered something under his breath. It sounded a lot like *I need to get more guy friends.*

By now, the landscape had shifted. A tunnel made of pale-green sea glass rose out of the sand. Beyond it appeared a flat, shimmering wall of magic. It looked like a recent addition to the Ocean of Milk, something intended to hide activities from sight. Aru and Aiden saw someone racing toward them from inside the tunnel. They instinctively held out their weapons, but it was just Mini.

"Guys!" said Mini, heaving. "Oh my gods, my dyspnea is out of control. I think I'm dying."

"Dip-what?" asked Aiden.

"*Dyspnea,*" corrected Mini, adjusting her glasses. "It's when you have labored breathing."

"Right. Obviously."

"You guys don't have it because you've been walking so slow," grumbled Mini. She pointed toward the tunnel. "C'mon. You're going to want to see this. Luckily, Brynne turned into a gnat right before they saw her."

"Who's *they*?" asked Aru.

Mini just shook her head. "You'll see." She held her finger up to her mouth as they walked briskly into the tunnel. Inside, the Ocean of Milk and the treasures pushing out of the seabed were still visible, but they looked hazier through the sea glass.

The farther they went, the darker the glass became, until it was pitch-black and they had to rely on Mini's Night Flame. The floor changed from soft white sand to slippery gray rock. The passage veered to the right, and Brynne was waiting for them at the turn, her mace up and powering a vortex of air. "The wind is white noise—it covers other sounds," she explained loudly. She pointed down to the right. "That way we can talk to each other without them hearing us."

Mini turned off her Night Flame and, using Dee Dee, surrounded them all with an invisibility shield. "Or seeing us," she added. "But we still have to move really carefully."

"I know, I know," said Aru impatiently. "I'm, like, the definition of stealth."

She took a step down the passage, slipped on the slick rock, and skidded forward, straight through the barrier Mini had put up. Aru went sprawling. Brynne must have dropped her vortex defenses in surprise, because Aru heard the unmistakable sound of Aiden's camera clicking.

She didn't even have time to properly nurse her bruised nose or ego, because Mini darted forward and quickly cast another shield to make them all invisible again. The end of the black rock passage opened up to a vista the size of three football fields placed together. Gone were the bits of treasure and snake skin. Instead, looming out of the sand was the legendary golden dome—the labyrinth that protected the amrita. Aru felt a quick thrill—they'd found it! Now they just had to find Surpanakha and jab her with an arrow, and they'd be out of here!

Then her gaze fell from the top of the golden dome to its base. There, surrounding it like a terrible army, were thousands of Heartless lined up in neat rows.

Technically, all that separated them from the dome and the Heartless army was a pair of glass double doors at the end of the tunnel. But there was one problem: in an alcove right next to those doors were two naga guards wearing helmets and carrying sharp tridents. Their muscular serpent tails were painted, one with a red stripe, the other a yellow one.

The red-striped guard slashed his trident toward Aru and sneered, "Got any last words?"

THIRTY-FOUR

Oh No! Oh No! Oh, Wait a Minute....

Cue the world's worst five seconds.

Aru froze. Mini had her hands up trying to keep the shield strong. How could the guards have seen them? Were their helmets magic or something? Brynne and Aiden moved to the front of the shield, weapons out...

...and the guard lowered his trident, turning to the other guard to say, "See? *That* is how to sound menacing." He stepped back into the alcove.

The yellow-striped naga guard's shoulders drooped. "I mean, when *you* do it, it seems so easy, but I just can't."

"Hey," said the red-striped guard gently. "Remember what you said yesterday?"

"Oh. About the yellow?"

"Yes."

The naga with the yellow stripe gestured to his tail. "I was nervous it wouldn't go with my complexion."

"Exactly, and now look! The yellow brings out the golden undertones of your skin! It's effortlessly trendy."

The other naga beamed. *"Really?"*

"Really," said Red Stripe. "A pop of color always adds pizzazz."

Yellow Stripe agreed, his tail whipping happily across the gray stone. Then they started discussing the new organic sea-farm-to-jellyfish-table restaurant in Naga-Loka.

Aru turned to Mini, expecting her sister to be just as confused as she was, but instead, she was looking at the underside of her wrist.

"Do you think *I* could pull off yellow?" Mini asked.

Brynne crouched between the two of them and pointed to the glass doors. "They're so distracted we could slip right past them," she said.

"And yes, Mini, you can pull off yellow," added Aiden.

Mini did a delighted preen.

"Are you guys going to be okay, though?" asked Aru. "Mini, you're going to have to keep up your shield, and Brynne, that vortex you're casting might make things tricky."

Brynne squeezed her right shoulder, which was probably beginning to get tired from the weight of the mace. "I'll be okay for a while longer."

"Me too," said Mini, even though her smile looked a little forced. "Let's do this."

Aru focused on changing Vajra into a bright sword. It wasn't a flaming sword, like she'd been hoping for from Agni, but it was still ridiculously cool. Beside her, Aiden brought out his scimitars.

The four of them tiptoed down the passage. The closer they got to the doors, the larger the naga guards appeared. Their torsos were nearly seven feet tall, *way* bigger than a normal naga's, and that wasn't even counting the lengths of their coiled tails.

"Be honest," said Yellow Stripe. "Does this helmet make my head look fat?"

"*Fat* is not bad," said Red Stripe, rolling his eyes. "Stop looking at those magazine covers. They're totally enchanted."

Brynne paused to raise her left fist in solidarity and kept moving.

"I know, I know...but the covers are so shiny..." said Yellow Stripe.

By now, Aru and the others were less than five feet away from the glass doors. There was a clear path before them, and just on the other side was the army of Heartless. All the zombies were standing still, facing the golden dome. The fact that they were outside instead of inside the labyrinth was probably a good sign—they were the only way Surpanakha could retrieve the nectar of immortality, because they couldn't be incinerated. But where *was* Surpanakha?

Mini's shield trembled. Aru could tell that the effort of keeping it up was beginning to strain her. Even Brynne, the strongest out of all of them, had a hard set to her mouth. Aiden wiped Brynne's forehead with his sleeve, and she shot him a thankful smile. Aru offered her sleeve to Mini, only to see her career backward. "The *germs*, Aru!" she hissed. "Get that plague-infested polyester away from me!"

Aru shrugged and kept moving. Aiden got to the doors first. Carefully, he turned the knob.

"Go ahead, Aiden," urged Brynne.

He took a deep breath, then stepped across the threshold.

"Aru, you go next," said Brynne.

Just as Aru prepared to move, one of the naga guards started shifting from side to side. Aru hadn't been listening to their conversation, but she caught bits and pieces about a new club opening up in the naga realm.

"I really cannot dance bhangra," said Yellow Stripe. "What is it again?"

"Pat the dog, screw in the lightbulb, and just sorta bob around—"

"Like this?"

His tail whipped across the floor, catching Aru, Brynne, and Mini. They all tripped and fell. The wind mace faltered. Mini scrambled to hold on to Dee Dee, but the shield shattered. From the other side, Aiden tried to jostle the door and get back to the others, but he couldn't.

"WHAT THE—?" screamed Red Stripe.

He and the other guard swung their tridents.

"Ew, ew, ew!" whined Yellow Stripe. "Human girls!"

"Remember our training," said Red Stripe. "When confronted with unsavory individuals—"

"Who are you calling *unsavory?*" demanded Brynne, swinging her mace. "We're not the bad guys here—*you* are!"

"Bad? *Us?*"

"Look at this sporty red stripe!" said the first naga, pointing at his luxurious tail. "Does that say *evil* to you?"

Mini raised Dee Dee, as if to create another shield, but she was too tired to do it again. Even Brynne's wind mace did little more than blow hot air in one of the nagas' faces. It was up to Aru.

She threw Vajra like a Frisbee. Lightning and thunder crackled loudly, and the two naga guards drew back. Still, they got stung.

"Owee! Ow! Ow!" they said.

Aru tried to get through the glass door, but the nagas recovered quickly. Their two tridents clashed down, blocking the exit with an X. Vajra boomeranged back to Aru, who caught it one-handed, and the lightning bolt shifted into a sword. She gripped its hilt with both hands and swung it, but the nagas moved aside in sync. Each of their tails lashed out, grabbed her wrists, and pulled them apart until Vajra dropped to the ground. It turned into a Ping-Pong ball and bounced back into her pocket, but the nagas didn't notice. They were too busy high-fiving each other.

"You remembered our choreography!" Red Stripe said to his comrade excitedly.

Aru thought it couldn't possibly get worse, but the universe felt otherwise. Because who should come strolling into the passage right then but...

Surpanakha herself, glossy black hair, golden skin, and all.

The demoness held out her hand, her long red nails flashing in the dim light. "Release her," she ordered the nagas. "I will deal with them myself. After that, leave your station at once and investigate the outside of the sea-glass tunnel. I believe I'm being followed."

"Of course, Admiral," said the nagas immediately.

They dropped their tails, but before Aru could pull out Vajra, a pair of magical handcuffs clapped onto her wrists. Vajra remained in her pocket and tried to comfort Aru with a burst of warmth.

Brynne and Mini had also been cuffed, and they wore matching expressions of fury as Surpanakha walked toward them. She pushed open the door, shoving the three of them through it.

Aiden was waiting for them on the other side, breathless and red-faced from trying to get back to them. Out of the corner of her eye, Aru saw the naga guards slithering away down the passage where Surpanakha had appeared.

"Get her, Aiden!" called Aru.

But Aiden didn't move.

"Whoa!" said Mini.

Aru turned just in time to see Surpanakha transforming. Where the demon princess had once stood was Hira, the rakshasi girl from the nature preserve. She tucked her hair behind her ear and waved at them shyly.

"I . . . I thought you could use some help."

THIRTY-FIVE

Hello, New Friend!

Hira looked like she was drowning in her sweatshirt and jeans. They must have been borrowed. Aru remembered what Navdeep had said to her... that she had no family to go home to.

"I'm sorry I followed you," Hira said. The magical handcuffs she had conjured disappeared from their wrists. "I just wanted to get away from those guys for a while....I thought maybe I could be helpful...and then you'd let me stay?"

Brynne took a step toward her, her mace out to the side. For a moment, Aru thought she was going to blast the rakshasi back to the Great Swamp. But instead, she switched her mace to her left hand and held out her right one.

"Thanks, Hira," she said. "You don't have to worry about those pigs anymore. You're safe with us."

Hira's smile totally transformed her face.

"Although, *statistically*, it's probably not true that you're safe with us," said Mini. "We get attacked all the time. But you can totally hang with us!"

Hira's smile faltered only a little. "Okay?"

Wow, thought Aru, *her old friends must have really sucked.*

"Wait a second," said Aiden. He looked at Hira closely. Aru saw that one of his hands was on his scimitar bracelet. "Thanks for everything you did back there, but why were you even with those guys in the first place? Why should we trust you?"

Vajra buzzed sharply in her pocket, and Aru imagined the lightning bolt was grumbling, *Why is Aiden such a momma bear?*

"I didn't really have a choice," said Hira. "I'm part of the Otherworld Foster Care System."

Aru didn't even know that the Otherworld had such a thing, but it made sense.

When Hira spoke, Brynne's face paled, and Aru wondered if she was thinking of her own mother, who had given her up. Aru knew that not all parents stick around—not all can, for whatever reason. It isn't the kid's fault, and sometimes it isn't even the parent's, either. As her own mom always said, there are two sides of every tale, and no decision like that could ever come easy....

Still, that didn't take away the pain of being left behind.

"Navdeep is my foster brother—his family took me in. He's not that bad," said Hira, looking at her feet. "He just acts like that whenever he's with a group of his friends. Sometimes he's really nice—he lets me have the bigger piece of dessert and stuff."

Aiden's suspicions seemed to have melted away, because he uncrossed his arms.

"Stick with us, and we'll make sure you're always treated right. I'll tell my uncles, and we'll set something up for you," Brynne said loftily.

"How—?"

"My uncles know everyone," said Brynne.

Aru, having spent enough time around elite prep-school kids, knew that was code for *I'm ridiculously rich*. Which, of course, Brynne was.

"Ever heard of the architect Mayasura?" asked Brynne. "That's my great-great-great—like, a lot of greats—grandfather on my mother's side. My uncle inherited his talent and runs a firm in New York City. He's got tons of connections in the human and Otherworld."

Mayasura . . . Aru remembered that name! He was the architect who had built the Palace of Illusions for the Pandavas. Aru and Mini had briefly visited it on their last quest, and they'd become friends. Aru hoped the palace wasn't lonely. She often thought of visiting it, but things got in the way, like the fact that it was located in the realm of the dead.

Out the corner of her eye, Aru saw Mini touch her heart as if she were remembering and thinking of the palace, too.

Hira smiled, then looked over at the utterly still and silent horde of Heartless fanned out around the golden dome. They hadn't moved.

"It's like they're asleep," whispered Hira.

Aiden tapped his camera. "I zoomed in on their faces earlier. . . . Their eyes are totally blank—no pupils, even."

"They're under Surpanakha's control," said Brynne.

"We have to find her and finish this thing," said Aiden. "We only have a few hours left." He turned to Hira. "Do you know where she is?"

Hira blanched. "What do you want with Lady M? It's best to stay far away from—"

"We don't have that option," Brynne cut in. "She's our

key to getting the . . ." She stopped herself, thinking better of revealing everything about their mission. "To getting something important back to where it belongs."

"What about you?" Aru asked Hira. "Did she put a spell on you and the guys to make you work for her?"

Hira shook her head. "She . . . she's just convincing."

Brynne grunted. "And evil. Look at all those poor men!"

Mini nodded in agreement.

"Our best bet is to search the perimeter of the dome for her," said Brynne. "Mini, can you shield us again? I'll create another soundproofing vortex. The Heartless probably won't attack without Surpanakha's command. But just to be on the safe side, I wouldn't get too close to them."

"What if we end up having to fight?" asked Mini. She held Dee Dee close. "Our weapons won't be effective in hurting them, because the Heartless have technically been changed by the act of a god, and godly weapons don't work against each other."

"Then we'll just have to use our weapons defensively—to stall," said Aiden. "Until we can turn the arrow against Surpanakha."

Aru grimaced. Kamadeva had said that once they had the arrow, they had to plunge it through the heart of the thief. Only then would the Heartless be restored to their human selves, and the arrow cleansed of its dark power.

Aru swallowed nervously. So little time left to fix the Heartless, to free Boo from imprisonment, and to clear their names. She steeled herself, then nodded.

"Let's do this."

They took out their weapons. With Vajra in her hand, Aru felt a bit better, but she still didn't have a clear sense of what lay ahead. It wasn't like when she'd fought the Sleeper…knowing exactly where he'd show up and what he wanted.

"You with us, Hira?" asked Brynne.

The rakshasi spread her hands. "I don't have any weapons."

"You have intel about the enemy," said Brynne, "and that's just as good."

"Yeah," said Aru. "What's Surpanakha like?"

Hira didn't hesitate. "She's beautiful."

The five of them snuck among the army of Heartless, which was downright terrifying. Brynne took the lead, guiding them through the thicket of men, making sure no one touched any of them by accident. Hira stuck close to her. Mini flanked them on the right, her shield cast like a sort of mirror camouflage. When Mini had used it in the past, because it required less magical energy, the only thing Aru could detect was a slight warp to the air, as if the image had been stretched over a convex surface. Aiden was on the left flank, his scimitars flashing, while Aru had control of the rear.

Vajra buzzed with anxious energy.

"Chill," whispered Aru. "You're freaking me out!"

The lightning bolt sent a pinch of electricity, as if saying *THAT'S BECAUSE I AM FREAKED OUT!*

They made it safely to the edge of the large golden dome. Somewhere inside, protected by every enchantment the gods could think of, was amrita. The nectar of immortality. Aru raised a hand to touch the metal side, then hesitated. It seemed to pulse with warning.

"No sign of Surpanakha on this side," said Brynne. "She's must be trying to get in from the other side."

"What are we going to do when we find her, though?" Aru asked. "What if she doesn't have the bow and arrow on her?"

"She will," said Brynne. "She can't control the Heartless without them."

"She doesn't like fighting," said Hira quietly. "She told us herself."

"Bam!" said Brynne. "We show her our weapons, then she'll stand down."

Aru wasn't too convinced, and when she looked at Aiden and Mini, they didn't seem too confident, either.

Everything was silent....

"Mini, switch places with Aru," said Brynne. "Dee Dee can give us more cover from the rear."

"I think we're *fine*, Brynne," said Aru. "There's no one behind us, and if Mini moves, there's a higher chance that someone will spot us. I say we stay put."

"I say we switch!" said Brynne.

"Aru, Brynne, let's not fight," said Aiden. "We need to stay focused."

"Okay, fine," said Brynne, stopping and holding out a fist. "How about we rock, paper, scissors it?"

Aru crossed her arms. "I am *not* risking my life on a game of rock, paper, scissors."

"Ooh, I love that game!" said Mini.

Something happened at that moment. Aru could sense it even before she realized what it was. In her excitement, Mini had moved too fast, and Dee Dee must have touched the metal wall of the dome.

Their magic shorted out. It was just as Agni had said: the dome rendered celestial weapons powerless. Instantly, Aiden's scimitars stopped glowing, and Vajra transformed into a lifeless ball in Aru's hand. She stashed it in her pocket.

Worst of all, Dee Dee's shield melted, leaving them completely exposed.

"What was—?" started Aru, but before she could finish, Aiden clapped his hand over her mouth and pulled her backward.

Just as Aru was ready to bite him, Aiden lifted his hand and silently pointed at the Heartless.

Before, the eyes of the Heartless had been blank, their bodies still as statues. Now, their pupils—a furious, inhuman red—fixated on Aru and the others. The army took a step forward in perfect unison.

"I was wondering when you'd show up," all the Heartless said at the same time in different voices.

The hairs on Aru's arms prickled....

The crowd of zombies parted as two figures walked—well, one slithered—toward them:

Takshaka, the naga who had betrayed Queen Uloopi.

And Surpanakha, the rakshasi princess. Strapped across her back was a heavy bow, and dangling loosely from her hand was a long golden arrow. It was so bright that it looked like a shard of sunlight.

"I've been waiting a long time to meet you," she said.

"Meet you, meet you, meet you..." the Heartless echoed.

THIRTY-SIX

The Tale of the Demon Princess

A rakshasa or asura didn't start off evil, unless they cultivated their dark arts . . . then they became demonic. But that inner darkness didn't always show up on their faces. Aru had to remind herself of that fact, because Surpanakha wasn't anything like what she expected.

She had gleaming golden-brown skin, and her hair was a mass of dark ringlets studded with small jewels. Her eyes were almond-shaped and tapered to a point. She wasn't dressed in skulls or blood-spattered clothes like Aru had imagined, but in a pair of dark jeans and a long-sleeved golden silk blouse. She didn't look like a demoness at all, except that her bottom canines were a tad longer and sharper than most people's, and her irises were red. But not scary red. More like warmed-up cherries drizzled in chocolate. Her nails were definitely long, but in a fashionable way—not like "sharp bladed fans" or whatever it was her name meant. As for her nose, it was there, and it looked normal. The only sign of her long-ago scuffle with Laxmana was a faint scar across her cheek.

"Sorry about that," said Surpanakha, gently. She twisted

the arrow in her hands, and the army of Heartless went slack behind her, no longer repeating her words.

The arrow worked a bit like a remote control, Aru noted, which had to be somewhat frustrating. Imagine every time you flopped on the couch, not realizing the remote is under the seat cushion, the TV creepily turned on. Except in this case, hundreds of kidnapped people started shouting the latest infomercial.

"I thought having them echo me would make for a dramatic effect," Surpanakha said, "but that was a bit frightening."

"Sur—" started Brynne.

"Oh, please don't call me that," said the demon princess with a sheepish smile. "That's not even my real name. If you want to call me something, call me Lady M."

M? What *was* her real name?

Aru had been expecting lots of things, but not this. She wanted—no, *needed*—to fight. They were running out of time to keep their spots in the Otherworld, and Lady M—or Surpanakha, or whatever her name was—had started all the trouble. But she wasn't threatening them. She was just smiling and being agreeable, and it made Aru want to scream.

Takshaka slithered forward, but Lady M held up a hand. "Leave us, please? I need some time alone with the girls." At Aiden's snort of protest, she added, "And our handsome gentleman."

Takshaka lingered, his milky eyes looking somewhere above Aru's head. He flicked out his tongue, tasting the air. "I would not trussst them. They are on the side of the devas. They have no reason to join our cause."

"*Cause?*" echoed Aiden.

Aru and the others startled. Aiden wasn't usually the one who spoke up first. But when it came to Takshaka, anger vibrated off him. He gripped his camera tightly, and a faint red glow lit the air around it.

"What *cause*? You swore to protect Queen Uloopi, and instead you went behind her back and betrayed her," said Aiden. "Didn't you?"

"I am not ashamed to admit it," said Takshaka, whipping his tail. "I had my reasons. I thought Uloopi was wise, but her judgment became compromised once she fell in love with Arjuna. It was pathetic."

"You hid her heart jewel," said Aiden. "You took her eternal youth. You made her weak on purpose."

"She couldn't be trusted," said Takshaka.

"That wasn't your choice to make," said Aiden darkly.

For the first time, Takshaka looked ancient as grief pulled down his face. "I had to do it, for the greater good. Uloopi would not lisssten."

Aiden dropped his hand from Shadowfax but didn't respond.

"What you did was a noble act," Lady M said to Takshaka with a sad smile. "Let me talk to them, my friend. Allow me to show them the truth, and perhaps I can change their minds, just as I changed yours all those years ago."

Takshaka nodded, then slithered away between a row of Heartless.

Lady M walked over to the metal dome and patted its side. Touching it had no effect on her. "Do you know what's in here?"

"The nectar of immortality," said Mini immediately. "And you want it to—to . . ."

Come to think of it, they didn't actually *know* what she wanted with it. She'd existed for this long, so it's not like she needed immortality. She was already stunning, so she didn't need it for eternal youth. And she had enough power as it was.

"Answer me this," said Lady M. "What is something that never dies but lives a thousand lives at once?"

Now she was asking them *riddles*? They looked at each other for a moment, before hesitantly answering.

"Gods?" asked Mini.

"Demons?" asked Brynne.

Hira shook her head, but didn't answer. Aiden stayed silent, watching all of them.

Aru loved riddles, and so when she heard Lady M's words, a different answer came to her mind:

"Stories?"

It was the only answer that made sense to her. True, gods and demons were immortal, but they didn't live a thousand lives at once. Only stories fit that description. Aru's mom had taught her that many tales from around the world were similar. That didn't make them unoriginal or bad, but rather proof that people cared about and were frightened of the same things no matter where they lived. Each culture put their own spin on the same universal story, keeping it alive in many different versions.

Lady M's eyes snapped to Aru's. "That's right," she said softly, stroking the metal dome like it was a large cat. "Stories. Legends. *Myths*. Once a story stops being told, it dies. Unless people find pieces of it later, polish them up, and breathe new life into them...I need the nectar of immortality not for my body, but for my story."

Lady M stretched out her hands and Aru watched as her

previously smooth, golden-brown skin turned rough and gray. Her once polished red nails grew sharper, deadlier. Even her bottom canine teeth had grown and were now jutting against her top lip. And her nose ... it was fading away.

"It's happening more and more," Lady M went on, her voice breaking. "I am beginning to lose my true self. In the end, all we are is the version of ourselves that others choose to remember."

Wariness prickled through Aru....

"You must have found my soul song in the treasury," said Lady M. "I'm sure you know by now that if you wish to reverse what I've done, you'll have to plunge this arrow through my heart. But did they tell you what would happen to me? To the song left in my soul?"

At their silence, she answered:

"You would kill the truth of my story. My soul would become a song of death."

Brynne was getting impatient and flustered. "We're not here to talk," she said gruffly. "We're here to get back what was wrongfully stolen. Hand over the bow and arrow."

Lady M looked at them with tears in her eyes. "Pandavas ... I accept that you wish to fight me. I understand and would even forgive you if it came to that. But before we draw our weapons, may I tell you my tale?"

Brynne looked unsure, but Mini's face was calm—she was probably relieved not to be fighting. Aru didn't know how to read Hira yet. Aiden looked suspicious, his dark eyes pinned to Lady M.

Aru had never considered herself the *Let's go attack things!* type, but she didn't want to hear Lady M's sob story. She was already torn about fighting Takshaka because she was sorry for his suffering, and now *this*? Aru didn't want to see all those gray spaces between good and bad—she just wanted things to be easy.

But then Lady M asked, "Pandavas, will you see my truth?"

See well. Those words, uttered by Varuni, Sage Durvasa, Ratri, and Agni, echoed back to her. Aru's jaw clenched, but she nodded. She owed it to all of them, and, a small part of her said, she owed it to herself.

Lady M cast out her hands and an illusion flew forth from her fingertips. . . .

"When I was born, my parents named me Meenakshi . . . the girl with fish-shaped eyes."

So she's the girl with eyes like a fish! Aru thought. All this time she'd pictured someone with a flat head and a big round eye on either side. . . .

Meenakshi's story rippled out like a scroll of silver against the metal dome, and in it, Aru saw the image of a happy little rakshasi playing with her big brothers.

"I grew up and got married, and I was content."

The image sped up to show an adult Lady M with flowers in her hair, her hands painted for her wedding day. The scene changed again to display her sitting on a golden throne, dispensing orders and proclamations.

"But my husband was a greedy rakshasa, and so my brother, Ravana, slew him. I was devastated and searched the world for a cure for my sorrow."

The picture expanded to reveal the god king Rama, his wife, Sita, and his brother, Laxmana, moving through the forest. But unlike the vision Aru had seen in Kamadeva's floor, this one showed Lady M's perspective as she walked through the woods, her head bowed, her hand to her heart as if it were so broken she was trying to keep it from falling out of her. The sight made Aru flinch.

She knew what happened next. Lady M fell in love with Rama, who rejected her; then she went to Laxmana, who rejected her; and then she attacked Sita and had her nose cut off.

And Aru saw that the story was true...but it was not the whole truth.

"I was too forthcoming, perhaps, in my affection," said Lady M. "I had never learned to be shy about asking for what I wanted, and I saw no reason to start then."

In the vision, Aru heard Lady M say that if Rama would take her for his wife, she could keep him safe from her brother. But Rama did not want another wife, and though he was kind in his rejection...his brother was not. Laxmana ridiculed her for even thinking that one of them would ever want her as a bride. Lady M's face went from stricken and full of grief to full of fury.

"I regret that I attacked Sita," said Lady M, "but my pride was wounded and my fury demanded release."

Aru didn't think it was right that she lashed out at Rama's wife, because it wasn't Sita's fault. But Aru understood Lady M's hurt feelings. She'd been humiliated.

The whole scenario reminded Aru of a girl in her class who'd gotten bullied. Someone had pretended to be the girl's secret admirer online, then took a screenshot of all their direct messages and sent them in an email blast to every student at Augustus Day. Aru remembered seeing the girl in the hallway afterward and noticing how small she seemed...how alone. It was so bad that the girl's parents pulled her out of school. A week later, the bully was expelled, but no one forgot what had happened.

"Despite the outcome, I do not regret my boldness," said Lady M.

In the vision she knelt alone in the forest, stanching the flow of blood from her face.

"But I am more than my moment of anger."

The Lady M in the scene looked up, and Aru saw her eyes lit by vengeance. For the first time, she seemed demonic.

"In the tales, I am nothing but a monstrous footnote in an epic about gods and men," she said as the images faded. "But in reality, I was so much more. My brother was never punished for killing my husband, yet I am blamed for starting a war. When I dared to express my feelings to two gods, I suffered not only dishonor but also disfigurement. Forevermore I would live with that mistake—it was as plain as the nose removed from my face. But I also had triumphs and joys. I was a daughter, and I was a sister, and I was a wife, and I was a princess . . . and I deserve to be remembered for all those things, too. Do you deny me that?"

THIRTY-SEVEN

Lady M Makes a Request

Aru wished Vajra would snake through her fingers and send her a little shock, something that would clear her mind and help her sort out her feelings. But her lightning bolt had remained a dead weight in her pocket ever since Mini had touched the metal dome covering the nectar of immortality. Aru was on her own.

Her friends' reactions to Lady M's tale were mixed. Mini appeared to be frustrated, like she couldn't decide whether Lady M was telling the truth or lying. Brynne looked angry (which, Aru knew by now, was her usual expression). Aiden's face was strangely blank, as if he were trying to hide his thoughts.

As for Hira, she was entranced. She kept nodding, encouraging Lady M to continue with the story.

"Now do you understand why I need the amrita?" said Lady M, her hands joining together. "The stories about me do not resemble my truth. As a result, my outer appearance no longer reflects my inner soul."

She held up gnarled hands, which now had claws at the end.

Her fish-shaped eyes had a sallow look to them, and her skin was paunchy.

"If my true tale is never told again, I will suffer a fate worse than death. I will have to live out my days as nothing more than the worst that others believe of me."

"But...I still don't understand how the nectar will help you," said Aru. "Couldn't you just write down your story?"

A flicker of impatience crossed Lady M's face before she collected herself again. "This is bigger than just me, child. You think this army is the only one preparing to storm the world? There are many of us who feel we do not deserve the treatment we received from the gods." Her eyes penetrated Aru. "Your father being one of them."

She didn't mean Indra....She meant the Sleeper.

"We find ourselves on the same side," said Lady M. She gestured at the golden dome. "This was all his idea. His way of allowing us to take back what was stolen from us." She gave Aru a doleful look. "He misses you, you know."

Aru's jaw clenched and she gripped Vajra tighter in her pocket. "Yeah, well, considering he tried to kill me, I doubt that's true. He's really not that great. Trust me."

"He reacted in fury as I once did," said Lady M. "You mustn't—"

"You attacked Sita even though she did nothing to you!" Aru blurted. "And you let your brother Ravana abduct her! Just because you feel bad about it now doesn't mean you're not guilty."

"I apologized to her later, when she was exiled to an ashram," said Lady M. "We both found it in our hearts to let go of our anger, and eventually we became friends."

That knocked the breath out of Aru's lungs.

"You...you were *f-friends?*" sputtered Brynne, her eyes narrowing.

"Rama abandoned Sita," said Lady M, unable to hide a little vicious glee. "After he fought to steal her back from my brother, the god king banished her. His people thought she was impure despite her faithfulness. Rama believed her, but he didn't defend her, and he sent her away when she was pregnant with his children. She even walked across open flames to prove her fidelity, but it wasn't enough."

That... *sucked.*

Did any girl in these stories enjoy a happy ending where she didn't a) get her nose chopped off, b) get turned into a rock, or c) get barbecued? It was bad enough that Sita had married a god king only to have him say, *JK! We're going to live in exile and wander through forests for a billion years!*

No thank you.

"I leave you to confer among yourselves for five minutes, Pandavas," said Lady M. "After that, you must choose your side. Help us become as powerful as the gods, or...well, I'm afraid you'll find I also fight hard for what I believe in."

She turned away then, gliding toward the row of Heartless. As she walked, Aru saw that she was changing even more. Her once lovely hair had now become wild and brittle. Two knobs protruded from her forehead...the beginnings of horns. And her skin had turned ashen.

Once again, she was turning into the story people told about her.

"Is anyone's weapon working yet?" asked Mini. She shook

Dee Dee, but the Death Danda currently had all the personality of a pencil.

"Nope," said Brynne.

"Me either," said Aru.

"What are we going to do about Lady M?" asked Aiden.

Hira, who had been silent until then, pulled her ragged sweatshirt around her body. "I feel really bad for her."

Once she said that, some of the tension fled out of Aru's bones. She'd been worried that she was the only one who felt any pity for Lady M.

"Hira," said Aru, "could you stand over there and keep watch? Let us know when you see Lady M coming back."

Aru didn't want Hira to overhear their conversation. She was a little too sympathetic to the rakshasi.

Aru pulled Brynne, Mini, and Aiden into a huddle. "We can't let Lady M—or anyone else—get the nectar," she said.

Lady M was working with the Sleeper, and Aru knew all too well the kind of beings the Sleeper kept in his company. Demons dripping in shadows. Foul-smelling asuras with blood on their hands. Those who'd lost out on the nectar of immortality the first time it was pulled from the Ocean of Milk, and couldn't let go of the grudge.

All of this made Aru's head hurt.

Brynne nodded. "So we fight."

"We fight," echoed Mini.

"Yeah," said Aiden, resigned.

Aru couldn't take it anymore. She blurted out the doubt inside her:

"This is the right thing to do, isn't it?" she asked. Then,

in a quieter voice: "I feel bad for her. But then...look at what she did."

The four of them surveyed the vast army of Heartless. People stolen from their lives, their free will yanked from them.

"Answering a wrong with a wrong doesn't make it right," said Aiden.

"If we don't fight her, *all* those people and *we* are going to pay for it," said Brynne. "We have to fight."

She said this last part more to herself than to anyone else.

Aru agreed, and yet...what Lady M had said made her think of the Sleeper. If everyone had gotten her story wrong, what about...*his*? Aru shook her head. It felt dangerous to even have that thought.

"Is there something else, Aru?" asked Mini quietly.

Aru realized the three of them had been watching her.

"No," Aru lied. "Nothing at all."

If she said it enough times, maybe it would become true.

Aiden looked over his shoulder toward Lady M. "The second we give her that answer, she's going to want to take our heads off."

"I know," said Aru.

"And none of our weapons are working," said Mini, fear edging into her voice.

"*Yet*," said Brynne. "It's like our weapons called a temporary truce."

"Plus, all the nagas and Heartless are on her side."

A thought snuck into Aru's brain.

The nagas at the entrance to the ramp hadn't been able to tell the difference between Hira and Lady M. If the nagas couldn't distinguish between them, then maybe Takshaka wouldn't be able to, either.

"Uh-oh," said Aiden. "Shah's making that face."

"What? What face?" asked Aru.

"That's, like, your signature *I've-got-a-plan* face," said Brynne excitedly.

Aru liked the sound of that. She had a *signature face*? Excellent.

"Does it make me seem really suave, like George Clooney in *Ocean's 11*? Or tough, like Marlon Brando in *The Godfather*?"

"More like a toad that's thinking about a fly it wants to eat," said Mini thoughtfully.

"Wow. Awesome."

"So what've you got, Shah?" asked Brynne. "Tell us what to do."

In that second, Aru realized they weren't just looking at her . . . they were looking *to* her. Like they trusted her. Pride flared through Aru. So what if she couldn't shoot an arrow through a fish eye or whatever it was that Arjuna had done? She had her imagination and three sets of eyes that trusted her, and, honestly, it was enough.

Aru checked to make sure Lady M was still far away. The demon princess was pacing back and forth slowly, almost sorrowfully, in front of her rows of Heartless troops.

"We've got something the other side doesn't have," said Aru.

The others looked at her blankly.

"Well, it's definitely not weapons, brainpower, or looks," said Mini.

"Speak for yourself," said Brynne.

"So, what is it?"

"It's a *who*," said Aru. Her gaze slid to the rakshasi girl a few feet away. "Hira."

Aru motioned to her to join them.

"I thought you wanted me to watch out for Lady M," Hira said.

"Change of plans," said Byrnne. "Tell her, Shah."

"You're going to be our secret weapon," said Aru.

The rakshasi paled. *"Me?"*

"Yup," said Aru. "You're going to—"

But she couldn't share the strategy just then, because Lady M was on her way back over.

"Aiden, Hira," Aru said hurriedly, "I'll explain later. Just make sure you're beside one of us at all times."

Hira nodded, unsure.

Lady M walked over. She looked demonic now, her pupils slitted like a cat's, and she was turning the golden arrow slowly in her hand, like a baton . . . or a sword. "I assume you have made up your minds, Pandavas," she said, her voice rasping.

"We have," said Aru. "We are here to retrieve the bow and arrow of Kamadeva. Turn them over to us, or we'll have to take them by force."

Lady M's bottom jaw jutted out, showing her now-much-larger lower canines. "Very well. All things happen for a reason, and I shall respect the outcome, regardless of who wins. Shall we begin?" A ripple of energy coursed through the army behind Lady M.

Aru didn't know what was going to transpire next. Would some pretty naga girl slither forward holding checkered flags and count them down to battle? Would there be jousting?

Would Aru have to channel Rocky Balboa and start boxing with Lady M?

But it wasn't any of those things.

As one, Aru and her friends said *yes*. It was totally synchronized and totally eerie. At once, Vajra came to life in Aru's pocket, electricity buzzing through the Ping-Pong ball. She pulled it out and it grew into a glowing bolt. She was willing to bet everyone else's weapons reactivated immediately, too.

But even that wasn't the reason they started fighting.

Lady M raised the bow and arrow, aimed it at Aru, and let loose. A lot of things happened simultaneously, but to Aru, it seemed like time slowed to a crawl. She was gradually bringing up Vajra, sluggishly stepping aside. Mini and Brynne got into formation—it must have been superfast, but at that moment, they could've been swimming through thick honey. Brynne swung her mace. Mini aimed her shield. Hira darted back and forth uselessly.

But Aiden . . .

Aiden dove in front of her. And it was only a split second later, when Aru saw the terrible smile on Lady M's face, that she realized Aiden had done exactly as the demoness wanted.

The arrow hit him with full force. Aiden crumpled to the ground.

"No!" screamed Brynne.

She dropped her mace and ran to him.

Lady M picked up the bow again, and plucked the string. Before Aru realized what was happening, the arrow flew back into the demoness's waiting hand.

Terrible guilt pressed down on Aru's lungs. *She* had let all this happen. And now . . .

"Take care of them," she heard Lady M command her troops.

The Heartless turned as one toward Aru, Mini, Hira, and Brynne.

Then, miraculously, Aiden pushed himself off the ground, knocking Brynne onto her butt.

"Hey!" she said.

Aru started breathing again. There was a second when Aru thought Aiden would brush himself off and whirl his scimitars against Lady M.

Instead, he snarled at Aru, his hands raised threateningly.

Aiden had gone Heartless.

THIRTY-EIGHT

Who's the Heartless One Now?

Aru wanted to give up right then, but she knew she couldn't.

Takshaka slithered through the ranks of the Heartless to stand by Lady M's side. She tilted her head, and the army of zombies began to move.

They marched toward the girls, stopping only when they were about twenty feet away to flank them in a semicircle, trapping them against the metal dome. Aru and Mini and Brynne faced them, hiding Hira behind their backs.

The only way to win would be to wrest control of the Heartless from Lady M. The arrow was in her right hand, glinting brighter now that it was being used. Lady M's appearance had continued to become more monstrous, as if she were turning just as Heartless as the men she'd abducted and dragged to the floor of the Ocean of Milk.

Aiden now stood with the rest of the zombies, staring straight through Brynne, who looked like she was going to cry.

"I didn't protect him," she said, her voice breaking.

"Then we'll just have to save him to make up for it," said Aru. "Do your thing, Mini."

Mini aimed Dee Dee at the first line of Heartless, which included Aiden. A burst of violet light blasted them, and they fell to either side. Almost immediately, they started to get back up, unharmed.

Aru tossed Vajra at Aiden while he was down, and the lightning bolt covered him in its net form. He fought it, growling. The net wouldn't last forever, but Aru didn't need forever.

"Hira?" she asked, turning.

The rakshasi raised a timid hand. She had been crouching on the ground, her arms wrapped around her knees. "I don't know what you want from me," she said. "I can't do anything right. I can't help!"

Aru grabbed her by the shoulders. "That's not true. You're the key to all this. Here's what we need...."

Takshaka gloated loudly. "*Told* you they would never come around."

"So be it," said Lady M. "I tried to convince them. My conscience is appeased."

They were now standing within the half circle of Heartless, talking in front of the girls as though they weren't even there.

Brynne's chest was heaving, her eyes red. She turned to Aru, her face grim. Then she shouted, "Lady M!"

The demon princess whirled around. "I am sorry about your friend, but it had to be done," she said. "We need as many soldiers as possible to defend us against the gods. But first, we have to take care of you, Pandavas."

Her voice had changed. Now it was screechy, a horrible

sound that made Aru want to clap her hands over her ears. Lady M shouldered the bow and raised the arrow, preparing to set the Heartless on them once and for all.

Brynne charged, pointing her wind mace. Not once did she take her eyes off Aiden. She'd powered wind channels before, but nothing like *this*, like a tornado full of rage. Lady M braced herself, yet she wasn't the target....

Takshaka went sprawling. His tail whipped forward, knocking Lady M off her feet. The arrow flew out of her hands, as if desperately happy to be free of her. The Heartless instantly froze in place.

"Now!" cried Aru.

Mini turned her shield into a mirror dome and tossed it on top of Lady M, covering her completely.

As Aru had hoped, Takshaka dove for the arrow. He caught it before it hit the ground. He didn't bother picking up the bow.

"A foolish move, Pandavasss," he hissed. "But what did I expect?"

Just keep talking, thought Aru. She called Vajra back into her hands.

A part of her still felt bad for Takshaka, but it was eclipsed by a greater fury. He'd tried to kill them in the treasury. And he'd tricked Uloopi. As for Lady M, her thirst for vengeance had caused her to enslave hundreds of people...including Aiden. The terrible things that had happened to Takshaka and Uloopi weren't right, but neither were their actions.

Through the Pandava mind link, Aru sent a message to Brynne: *Go.*

Takshaka raised the arrow and the Heartless stormed forward. It was absolutely terrifying...and absolutely what Aru had expected. The zombie army surged like a tidal wave, swallowing Lady M. Brynne sent a fire-laced windstorm their way, careful to avoid Aiden.

Heartless-Aiden, now free from the net, kept lunging at Aru, his scimitars whirling menacingly.

"So *rude!*" said Aru, blocking him with Vajra. "We're supposed to be on the same side."

Heartless-Aiden made a weird grunt, which Aru took to mean *My bad. Can't really help it.*

Aru steadied herself, preparing for his next blow. When it came, Aru fell to the ground, just like Hanuman had taught her in combat practice. Aiden roared, ready himself to plunge his blades straight through her. At the last second, Aru rolled out of the way. Aiden snarled. He tried to lift the scimitars to strike again, but they were stuck in the damp sand.

"I want you to know we're still friends," she told him.

Then she whacked him on the head with the lightning bolt and Aiden slumped over, unconscious.

Takshaka was struggling to control the arrow. Brynne had picked up the bow and was holding it behind her back.

"Meenakshi!" he yelled. "Where are you?"

The Heartless were going haywire. Hundreds swarmed in all directions. Aru extended Vajra in front of her and sent out pulses of lightning to confuse the zombies. Mini cast an invisibility shield over them, and a fiery tornado—courtesy of Brynne—flashed in a wide circle around Mini, Hira, Aiden, and Aru. Anyone who got too close received the heel end of the magic sneakers Brynne had chosen at the Warehouse of Quest Materials.

"Now?" she asked Aru.

Aru nodded, breathless. In a rush, the fiery tornado collapsed. Lady M stormed out from behind Brynne, her face a mask of fury as she shoved past the confused Heartless.

"There you are!" said Takshaka, relieved. He bowed his head a little and held out the arrow. "Please, take it."

She grabbed it from him and nocked it on her bow. "It's about time!" she snapped.

"Make them obey!" Takshaka pleaded.

Lady M held the arrow up in the air, and the Heartless froze in place. Then she pointed it in front of her, in the direction *away* from the dome over the labyrinth. As one, the Heartless turned and began marching.

"What's going on?" Takshaka asked, panicking. The scales on his tail flashed a vivid red.

Lady M's eyes widened as she shook the arrow, which sent the Heartless scattering in all directions. "I don't know! Th-they must have tampered with it!"

"Duck!" shouted Mini.

Aru and Brynne crouched down as Mini's mirror dome spun back to her hand, now flat as a discus.

A new shriek joined the din. "Impostor! Thief!"

Another Lady M—this one truly monstrous, bent-over and bloodied, with huge tusks protruding from her bottom lip—pushed her way through the drifting zombies.

Takshaka, thoroughly confused, looked back and forth between the two demonesses. "H-how?" he stammered.

"You fool!" rasped Lady M. "They had a shape-shifting rakshasi working with them!"

Hira had started transforming back to her real self: a frightened rakshasi clutching the bow and arrow.

Aru had to act quickly. This was the final part....

The last step.

The cruelest step.

Aru glanced at Aiden still unconsciously slumped next to his stuck scimitar. He—and all the others—would stay that way if she didn't finish this.

Lady M now looked exactly like the monster from the stories. Aru wished that the sight of her this way made things easier, but it didn't.

Mini reached out and grabbed Aru's hand, as if she knew exactly what Aru was thinking. Brynne knocked Takshaka back with a blast from her wind mace. Hira threw the arrow to Aru, who caught it one-handed. At her feet, Vajra transformed into a hoverboard, and Aru zoomed fast, holding out the arrow. Lady M's eyes widened. At the last second, Aru turned her face away....

But her arm kept moving.

She plunged the arrow into Lady M's chest.

Lady M let out a terrible scream. A wave of energy roiled the seascape. Above them, shock rippled the Ocean of Milk.

Aru didn't need to *see* that the arrow had hit its mark, because she heard it. *My soul will become a song of death,* Lady M had said. Aru would never forget the sound. The song of death was like ice creeping across a windowpane, and a warning shout unleashed a second too late, and water closing over your head, and the silent chime of a moment that has been forgotten forever. It was impossible and painful and, ultimately, inevitable.

When Aru finally opened her eyes again, Lady M was crumpled at their feet, the arrow sticking out of her chest. Dimly,

Aru felt Brynne's and Mini's hands on her shoulder. She must have fallen off Vajra, but she didn't remember that.

All around them, the Heartless stopped and clutched their chests. Then they looked around at one another, wide-eyed.

"What was in my burrito?" asked one guy, turning in a circle.

"Where am I?" asked another.

Aru heard the sound of approaching hoofbeats. The celestial mounts! The Council of Guardians must have sensed that the bow and arrow were recovered. Which meant that help was on the way.

Takshaka hissed, then opened a portal in the middle of the sand. He made to depart, but not before viciously saying, "This changes nothing, Pandavas. By my count, you took too long. You may have changed these Heartless back to mortal men, but you'll still be exiled."

He disappeared, leaving Aru feeling as if she'd swallowed a pound of rocks.

She heard a groan behind her. Aiden was sitting up and rubbing his head. Aru and Mini raced over to him. He stared up in wonder at Mini, but his eyes narrowed when he saw Aru.

"Did you hit me with a lightning bolt?" he asked.

"Yup."

"Did I deserve it?"

"I mean, you *were* trying to attack me."

"You'd gone Heartless," added Mini.

"In that case, I guess we can still be friends." He palmed his chest as if making sure everything was still intact. Then he held out his hands, and Aru and Mini hauled him upright.

"Where's—?" he started to say, but then his eyes went straight to Brynne.

She was kneeling beside the fallen Lady M. Hira stood behind her, hands shoved deep in her pockets. Lady M was glowing. Her monstrous appearance had been replaced by her former beautiful self. Her breathing was shallow, and from the wound where the arrow had pierced her, a bright light shone.

"You are worthy adversaries," she said when they had all gathered around.

Aru knelt beside her. She wasn't sure what to say... or do. She'd taken the advice of the gods—to *see well*. But it hadn't made her *feel* well.

"I will fade from here, and my tale will be what it will be," Lady M said with a sigh. "Will you remember all of it, at least?"

Aiden nodded, his jaw tight. Brynne and Mini and Hira did the same. Aru hesitated... not because she wouldn't remember, but because no one should fade from the world like this. She reached out and held Lady M's hand in hers.

And when she did, a name sprang to her lips. "We'll remember... Meenakshi."

Lady M smiled wide, and she disappeared, leaving behind nothing but the golden arrow.

THIRTY-NINE

Shadowfax Saves the Day

There's a reason movies don't always show what happens immediately after a battle ends.

Because it's really boring.

The cured Heartless collected themselves, shouting things like "DOES ANYONE KNOW WHERE MY OTHER SHOE WENT?" as they lined up to be whisked back home by the celestial mounts. Ever since one of the men had mentioned a burrito, all Aru could think of and all Brynne could talk about was food.

Mini had fished out hand sanitizer from the depths of her backpack and was doling it out to the men. "Just because you were undead doesn't mean you should be unclean," she said.

Aiden held up his camera, and all four girls shrieked at him.

Aru: "No! Look at my hair!"

Brynne: "Do not document my hunger or I will eat you."

Mini: "I'll get a headache from the flash!"

Hira: "If anyone finds out I was here, I'll be in big trouble...."

Aiden rolled his eyes. "I'm not taking a picture of *any* of you."

Brynne put her hands on her hips. "Wait, why not?"

"Rude," said Aru.

"Then why do you even have it out?" asked Mini.

"Just in case," said Aiden cryptically. He looked around the ocean. "I bet that two-faced serpent king will come back any second now."

Right on schedule, a portal opened in the middle of the sand, and up through it slithered Takshaka, dressed in the full regalia of the naga court and acting as if he hadn't been at the Ocean of Milk mere minutes ago. Behind him came Uloopi. And that wasn't all. Urvashi danced out of the portal, her silks waving behind her, and Hanuman jumped into view. Today he was wearing a faded Nirvana T-shirt under a velvet tuxedo jacket.

"The bow and arrow!" said Uloopi, gliding forward.

Brynne held the weapon out to her. Since Meenakshi's disappearance, the arrow had changed. The celestial weapon's former luster had been replaced with a dull sheen.

Urvashi surveyed the torn-up seabed and the great golden tank protecting the nectar of immortality. "But where is the thief?" she demanded.

"You should ask Takshaka," said Aru coldly.

Uloopi's cobra hood flared behind her. "What are you presuming to tell me, girl?"

"Takshaka was just here!" said Brynne.

"And he and Lady M—but everyone called her Surpanakha—were trying to get the amrita, because they thought they'd been dissed by the gods," said Mini, crossing her arms. "Which I think is kinda true, but that doesn't mean they—"

"Enough of this tripe!" interrupted Takshaka.

"I would like to hear them out," said Hanuman. He eyed

Takshaka, his fur bristling slightly. "It is when we stop listening that we commit the greatest wrongs."

The serpent king's tail lashed angrily.

"The Pandavas are acquitted of the charges against them," pronounced Urvashi.

Aru's heart soared, but then it crashed with the next words:

"That," snapped Uloopi, "requires a unanimous vote. Don't forget that they had ten days to complete their task. They failed to meet the deadline."

"But we saved the Heartless!" said Aru. "And we were never guilty in the first place—we were forced to do all this because you didn't believe us."

"And what about Boo?" asked Mini. "Are you just going to keep him imprisoned?"

"No," said Hanuman. "Boo will be freed."

"But not *us*?" asked Brynne. "How does that make any sense?"

Uloopi held out her hand. "Our rules are in place for good reason. The accused will be heard in the Court of the Sky."

Takshaka smiled smugly.

Aru snuck a glance at Aiden. He had always been more of an observer, but she was surprised he hadn't said a word in their defense. He was supposed to be their witness, after all.

But, wait . . . Where was Shadowfax?

She scanned the space around them, but there was no sign of Aiden's camera. What had he done with it? Aiden caught her looking and winked.

"Come, Pandavas," said Urvashi, gesturing to the portal. "State your case before us."

Hira tried to come with them, but Hanuman gently told

her no. "Only the accused or apsaras can go to the Court of the Sky," he said, opening a different portal for her and Aiden to use. "You two wait in the Night Bazaar, and we'll send word to your families—"

"Just my mom," said Aiden. "My dad won't notice."

"Very well."

And with that, Aiden and Hira disappeared through the portal.

"Come on, Shah," said Brynne, jerking her chin at the other portal. "Let's go prove them wrong."

The Court of the Sky felt like an actual courtroom. The dusky purple clouds looked solemn and serious. A half ring of golden thrones surrounded the square of flat clouds where Aru, Brynne, and Mini stood in their cloud slippers, their hands clasped respectfully behind their backs. Far below them, the Night Bazaar twinkled, and Aru felt her heart lurch a little … wondering if this might be the last time she ever saw it.

In a blink, many members of the Council of Guardians— those tasked with overseeing heroes' quests and keeping the world in balance—appeared in their thrones. But not Boo.

"Begin your account," said Queen Uloopi.

Beside her, Aru noticed, Takshaka squirmed a little.

The Pandavas related all that had happened since they left the Night Bazaar. They told them about the terrible swan that Kamadeva kept as a guard pet. They described the monstrous blue crab that couldn't sing. But when they got to the part where they'd fought Takshaka, the serpent king interrupted.

"You *lie!*" he declared, laughing. "I understand these children are known for ly—"

"I never lie!" said Mini. "I actually don't think I can....It makes me nauseated, and then my skin gets all hot—"

"Take back your foolish tale, and we might consider our options," said Takshaka smoothly. "But persist in this fantasy, and you will force our hand, Pandavas. The Council will be unable to reverse your sssentence."

Brynne looked angry enough to tear a hole in the cloud carpet beneath them.

Easy, Brynne, thought Aru to her sisters. *We've got a secret weapon.*

They revealed everything except the fact that Uloopi's heart jewel lay at the bottom of Aru's backpack. Aru planned on returning it to the queen, but she couldn't just *toss* it at her like, *HERE YA GO! HAVE A NICE LIFE!* She couldn't wait much longer, though, since she was secretly hoping that once Uloopi saw the jewel that Takshaka had kept from her, the queen would know they were telling the truth about him. Letting the naga go *on and on* about how innocent he was would only make him look worse in the end. Aru grinned.

"They must cast the final votesss," said Takshaka.

Now can we show them the heart jewel? thought Brynne impatiently.

Aru reached around for her backpack and Hanuman launched out of his seat, ready to argue, when the sight of a portal opening overhead made everyone look up at the same time. Out of a thin beam of light, a boy stumbled into the middle of the court. He had been reunited with his camera, Aru was glad to see.

"Aiden!" said Urvashi, shocked. "You're not supposed to be here!"

"How did he get in?" demanded Uloopi.

"Apsara blood," said Aiden, looking at Urvashi. "There's

something you need to see, Masi. Please. And you, too, Queen Uloopi."

"Get this boy out of here!" snarled Takshaka.

Urvashi drew herself up, her face imperious and full of deadly beauty.

"You do *not* talk to my nephew like that," she said coldly. "Share what you must, Aiden. But don't think you're getting out of trouble."

Aiden looked over at Aru, Mini, and Brynne. A weak smile flickered on his face before he handed his camera to Uloopi. The moment she touched it, images and sounds burst forth, and a hologram appeared in the middle of the Council of Guardians. It showed Takshaka in the Ocean of Milk, scowling at the Pandavas. The perspective was low, as if someone was looking up at him.

"Shadowfax!" whispered Brynne excitedly.

"What cause? *You swore to protect Queen Uloopi, and instead you went behind her back and betrayed her,"* said hologram-Aiden. *"Didn't you?"*

"I am not ashamed to admit it," said Takshaka. *"I had my reasons. I thought Uloopi was wise, but her judgment became compromised once she fell in love with Arjuna. It was pathetic."*

"You hid her heart jewel," said Aiden. *"You took her eternal youth. You made her weak on purpose."*

"She couldn't be trusted," said Takshaka.

"That wasn't your choice to make," said Aiden darkly.

Aru wanted to high-five the whole sky. She had to hand it to Aiden—he was as sneaky as she was, waiting for the moment when Takshaka was surrounded by the Guardians in a place where he couldn't destroy the evidence.

"Is this true?" asked Uloopi quietly. She seemed even more menacing at this volume.

Takshaka paled. He started to stammer, but then Aru reached into her backpack and drew out the heart jewel. She walked up to Uloopi.

Only then did Aru realize she didn't know very much about the naga queen. She knew that she'd loved Arjuna and...that was it. Just like how Aru had only known that Surpanakha—Meenakshi—was scorned and had her nose cut off. It wasn't a complete picture. It would be like if someone only recorded the moments when Aru was fast asleep and then called it a documentary of her whole life.

"This belongs to you," said Aru, laying the jewel at her feet. "And...I really hope that you let us stay in the Otherworld. If you do, maybe sometime you can tell us what happened to you after the great war. Because we'd like to know."

Uloopi stared at the heart jewel. She picked it up in her withered hands. A bright light washed over her, and Uloopi was transformed.... Her wrinkled skin glowed, and the gray in her hair shone like silver. Her eyes sparkled. Uloopi took a deep breath, and the air shimmered around her. When Uloopi closed her eyes, Aru could still see them moving back and forth beneath her eyelids, as if she were catching up on all the things she hadn't properly seen. When she opened her eyes again, her mouth curled down in shame.

"Thank you, Pandavas," Uloopi said. She pressed the jewel to her heart, then touched her forehead. When she removed her hand, the emerald was securely centered there. "I owe you my deepest apologies."

Then she turned to Takshaka. "As for you, *snake*, you have dishonored your house and your name." Her voice trembled with fury and pain. "You broke the vows of friendship and loyalty sworn to me. And this I will never forgive." She shook her head. "How *could* you?"

At the snap of her fingers, a retinue of naga guards appeared and dragged the serpent king away even as he hissed and thrashed against their hold.

For the first time in days, Aru felt like she could breathe easy. Aiden took back his camera and walked over to them. Brynne was beaming. Mini had tears in her eyes. Aru wanted to shout with joy, but then her gaze fell on an empty golden throne, the one marked SUBALA. Mini caught her looking, and she was about to say something when her eyes flew to the sky beyond the Guardians. A wide grin spread across her face. Aru turned just in time to see a blur of gray feathers diving toward them.

"Boo!" she screamed.

He landed on her hair and immediately pecked her. "You look pale! You have to take vitamin D! Pandavas *always* take vitamin D. And what is this scratch on your arm? *Who scratched you?* And what took you so long?"

Aru just laughed. Boo huffed and fluttered over to Mini. He huddled under her ear, as if it were an umbrella and he was trying to stay out of the rain. "Do you know how worried I was? Do you have *any* idea what that does to my plumage?"

He raised a wing, which, to Aru, looked exactly the same. Not that she said anything to him.

"Stress shortens one's life span," he said.

Brynne frowned. "But aren't you immortal?"

Boo jerked up his head, just now bothering to notice Aiden and Brynne.

"Ugh," he groaned, flopping into Mini's hands. "*More* of you? I can't. I just can't."

"I'm not?" said Aiden, raising his hand.

Boo gave him a beady look, then placed his wing over his eyes.

"We missed you, too," said Mini, smiling.

FORTY

Well, This Is Awkward

Boo sat on a stack of books piled on top of Aru's head. "Balaaaaance!" he shrieked. "A Pandava always has immaculate form. A Pandava should be so precise that he—"

"Or *she*," added Aru.

"Or *they*!" chimed in Brynne from a distance.

"Whatever pronoun you so choose!" snapped Boo. Even though she couldn't see him, Aru could imagine him ruffling his feathers.

Aru and her soul sisters were standing on a floor of gold, surrounded by different weapons, various illusion dummies, and posters of demons taped awkwardly to the transparent walls of Boo's floating-bubble classroom.

A warm and fuzzy learning environment it was not.

"A Pandava must be so precise and so skilled that they can separate a shadow from its host! They can grab the wind! They are as swift as—"

"A river!" shouted Aru.

Mini hollered, *"With all the force of a great typhoon!"*

"With all the strength of a raging fiiiiire—" sang Brynne.

"STOP SINGING *MULAN!*" shouted Boo.

Aru laughed so hard that the books fell from her head and toppled to the ground.

Boo squawked and pecked her ear. "Concentrate!"

"I *am*," said Aru.

But that was a bit of a lie. Two weeks had passed since they'd been cleared of stealing the bow and arrow of Kamadeva, and yet they hadn't been able to return the weapon to the god of love until today. It was going to happen in exactly one hour. Which meant that everything still felt strangely up in the air, even as life calmed down.

When Boo had been released from his holding cell, he'd been so shocked and skittish that the three of them had all chipped in part of their weekly allowance to get him a family-size box of Oreos from Costco. But after that, he'd only gotten more vigilant about training the three of them. Aiden joined in sometimes, but he and Hira took most of their magical classes with the kids who had Otherworldly ancestry. Mini's family had asked to foster Hira, and now she lived in their spare bedroom. Even though it'd only been a few days, Aru thought she noticed a huge difference in Hira already. She smiled a lot more . . . and she finally had clothes that fit.

"What happened under the Ocean of Milk was only the beginning," said Boo. He started marching back and forth. He did that a lot when he got nervous. "There's going to be an uprising! A *war!* You have to be ready to face the Sleeper again. Don't forget that misguided intentions are often the most dangerous."

He quieted down when he said that. A week ago, after the girls had told him about Surpanakha, he'd confided that he, too, had once gone down a dark path.

"Way back when, everything I did was to avenge what I thought was an insult to my sister," he'd said. "I was wrong."

Mini had comforted him. "It's okay, Boo."

Boo sniffed. "I thought that by only teaching you the good stories about the Pandavas, you'd feel more inspired."

Aru shook her head. "We deserve to know the bad stuff too, Boo."

"It's not balanced otherwise," pointed out Brynne.

Boo had agreed. From then on, when he told them his daily stories, he didn't shy away from the ugly parts...but that also made him that much more anxious when it came to talks about the great war ahead.

"If you're not ready, you'll die!" he said, squawking at them. "And I will kill you if you die! How dare you!"

"Cheer up, Boo," said Aru. "We're working on our own moves!"

Brynne frowned. "We are?"

"Yeah! We can improvise. Check it out." Aru pointed at Mini and yelled, "Shield!"

Mini looked confused but dutifully created a shield.

"All right, Brynne, blast me forward!"

"Uh...okay..."

Brynne hit Aru with a wind gust just as she ran toward Mini's shield and jumped on it. In her head, Aru had envisioned this epic leap where she soared through the air on the shield and pinned someone with her lightning bolt. In reality, she just slid forward and crashed into the back wall with a loud *thud*. Mini dropped her shield and Brynne ran to her.

"What the heck was *that*?" demanded Boo.

Aru groaned. "I don't know.... It worked in *Wonder Woman*."

"Are you Wonder Woman?"

"I...am facedown in a pile of shame."

Not too far from where Aru was sprawled out, Aiden appeared from a portal. She rolled onto her back only to hear the familiar *click* of Aiden's camera. She blinked open her eyes and there he was, waving down at her.

"Why are you here now?" she demanded. "You're not supposed to be here for another hour."

Aiden shrugged. "Got bored. Decided to record a behind-the-scenes look at the intense lives of Pandavas."

"And?"

"And I may have to change the title of the documentary."

"Go away."

"Not a chance, Shah," said Aiden with a wide grin, and then he helped her up.

An hour later, Aru, Mini, Brynne, and Aiden stood in front of the entrance to the Soul Exchange. Aiden was carrying the bow and arrow. They were encased in an enchanted box carved out of ice to prevent the weapon from feeling the pulse of human hands. Apparently, the bow and arrow couldn't help but want to shoot every time they sensed a heartbeat.

Fortunately, the monstrous guard swan was nowhere to be seen. When the door swung open, they entered not a pristine office building like last time, but a beautiful palace. The floors were made of interlocking golden tiles with rubies at the center. Above them, the ceiling was the actual night sky, and Kamadeva didn't need a chandelier, because constellations twisted in the air, casting silvery light. All along the walls were images of famous couples throughout history and legends: Tristan and Isolde; Héloïse and Abelard; Nala and Damayanti; and even the five Pandavas and their wife, the beautiful and wise Princess Draupadi. Aru scanned the statue of Arjuna. She didn't look anything like him. She had no muscles. And no mustache (thankfully). But Draupadi looked familiar. Something about her eyes...

"So, you survived!" said Kamadeva, appearing before them. He clapped, and Aru looked away from the statues. "Oh. Excellent. I love it when stories don't end in dismemberment!"

Mini's eyes widened. "Me too?"

Aiden offered the box nervously, shifting back and forth on his feet.... After all, Kamadeva had promised him an arrow of love. And Aru knew exactly what Aiden was going to use it for. Brynne had told her that Aiden's dad was stopping by tomorrow to pick up the last of his stuff. His parents would be seeing each other for the first time in months....

"He's going to *Parent Trap* them?" Aru had asked.

"That's the plan," Brynne said. "But, if you ask me, I don't think it's a good one."

When Kamadeva reached for the bow and arrow, the ice case turned to vapor. He beamed as he caught the weapons and lifted them up into the air.

"Hello, old friends," he said, before swinging the bow over his shoulder. He slid the arrow into a quiver hanging on his other shoulder. "You did well by defeating Surpanakha—"

"That's not her name," said Mini quietly.

Kamadeva startled. "Pardon?"

Mini turned bright red, and Aru jumped in. "She didn't like to be called Surpanakha. She preferred Meenakshi. Or Lady M."

Kamadeva looked at them thoughtfully. "And this is the name you wish me to use?"

All four of them nodded.

"Then I will," he said.

"We'd also like to tell you her side of the story sometime," Aru pressed.

"When you're not too busy," added Mini.

"All right then, Pandavas. So you shall."

Somewhere, Aru thought she heard the faintest sigh on the wind...a breath held too long and suddenly exhaled.

"And as a reward for bringing back my bow and arrow, I also have a boon for each of you."

Aru's ears perked up. *Woo-hoo! Boon!* She just hoped this wasn't going to be like Agni's boon, which, no offense, was basically just a divine IOU. What was she going to do with *that*?

"For the daughter of the god of death," said Kamadeva, handing her a small golden box, "I grant you a single minute of time, which can erase a full minute of words you didn't mean to say. Very handy for first-time crushes."

Mini blushed. "Thank you."

Kamadeva held out a slim red book to Brynne. "For the daughter of the god of the wind, I present you with my favorite recipe book! Soul food is delicious, of course, but heart-food?! Ah. It brings you kindness for days."

Brynne grinned and took it eagerly. "Yay! Cookbook!"

"For the daughter of the god of thunder, I give you this"—Kamadeva handed her a silver lipstick tube—"a celestial spotlight made of crushed stars and aged moonbeams. Use it when you feel like the world should see you in a different light."

Smolder power! thought Aru as she thanked the god of love.

"And for you, Aiden Acharya," said Kamadeva, holding out a single golden arrow no bigger than Aru's palm, "an enchanted arrow from my own collection, to do with as you wish. But know that you cannot change someone's free will. And there is no magical cure for grief. All this arrow can do is open the pathway for love. It doesn't make someone smitten, and the love doesn't necessarily have to be romantic. It simply makes them *aware* of love where perhaps they might not have been beforehand."

Kamadeva's words were cryptic, but Aiden smiled anyway. He took the arrow carefully and stuffed it in his pocket.

"Don't put it *there!*" said Aru.

"Yeah," said Brynne. "What if you fall and land on your butt?"

"And then the first thing you see is the floor. Or a lamp," said Mini. "Then you'd be in love with a lamp. Er, super *aware* of a lamp."

"Fine! Fine!" said Aiden, sliding the arrow over his left ear like a pencil. "Better?"

"Sure," said Brynne.

Kamadeva opened the door for them. "I wish you well, Pandavas."

Aiden sighed. "Honestly, I'm really not a Pandava."

"Maybe not by blood. But certainly by marriage," said

Kamadeva. "After all, in another life, you were Queen Draupadi, the wife of the five Pandava brothers."

There are certain horrific moments in life when the only way to fix an awkward situation is to *be* awkward.

Kamadeva had vanished, along with his extravagant palace, leaving the four of them staring at one another in the middle of the forest.

"So..." said Aru. "Should we call you Wifey?"

Aiden—who looked as if he'd been hit by a train—managed a weak laugh.

"Go away, Shah," he said.

"You're my friend, but the thought of being married to you makes me nauseated," said Mini. "No offense."

"None taken."

Brynne shuddered. "You're my best friend, but I would *never* like you. One, because you're basically my brother. Two, I prefer boys who can beat me in a wrestling contest." She thought about this and added, "Or girls."

"You've beaten me a thousand times at wrestling," said Aiden.

"Exactly," said Brynne.

Aiden rubbed his temples. "Okay, I get it. You know, you guys could just say, *Cool story, let's never discuss it again.* Besides, it's not like you're anything like your Pandava souls. I mean, look at Aru."

"HEY!"

"Just saying," said Aiden. "I'd never like you that way. We're only friends."

He was looking at her when he said that, and her face turned hot. He didn't have to make it so obvious he'd never like her that way. Aru told herself she didn't care. At all. She told herself it didn't hurt her feelings.

Maybe if she said it enough times it would be true.

Aru faked a grin and said, "Cool. So, all in favor of Aiden's new name being Wifey, keeping in mind that it's only a name, and he's his own person, blah, blah, blah...."

Mini and Brynne raised their hand. So did Aru.

Aiden looked horrified. "Wait a second! Don't I even get to vote? I don't want to be called *Wifey*!"

"Rules are rules, Wifey," said Mini, laughing.

And that was that.

FORTY-ONE

You Shall Not Pass!

Aru stroked her beard. It was, she thought, an excellent beard. Nice and soft and gray, and perfect for plucking at pensively.

"*Fly, you fools!*" she said, scowling at her reflection in the window.

"Aru, the movie hasn't even started yet!" groaned Mini. "You can't quote Gandalf until halfway through!"

"It's *my* birthday, I'll do what I want!" she said with a cackle.

Aru's birthday was February 15. Otherwise known as the day when all the unsold Valentine's Day candy went on sale and the world smelled like sugar and despair. But this year she was determined to make it a perfect day. She'd invited her friends over to the museum to binge-watch the Lord of the Rings movies. In costume. Mini had dressed up as a hobbit because she liked that their houses had curved walls. "Living in the forest as an elf is way too much pressure to appreciate the outdoors," Mini had said. Hira, on the other hand, had no problem with the elf lifestyle. She had dressed up as one, and every now and then would dramatically shape-shift into Arwen, the elf princess, which made Aru ridiculously jealous. Brynne had dressed up as an orc. As a present, she was baking lembas bread and decorating a birthday cake with Legolas's face.

Aru's mother had refused to dress up. But she had let them use the big panorama room in the museum, which was like an actual movie theater. And as a present, she'd booked two tickets to Paris, where she was going to give a lecture on bronze pieces of Lord Shiva.

It was, Aru thought, the best birthday she'd ever had, and it had barely started.

"Aru, I'll be upstairs reading," said her mom, pausing to kiss her on the head. "When I come downstairs, I do *not* want to see your Gandalf beard on the stone elephant."

Well, there went that idea.

"And do not croak *'my precious'* in my ear at two a.m., like last time."

This was turning into the worst birthday.

"I love you. Have fun."

All right, fine, it wasn't that bad.

Aru waved good-bye to her mom. Outside the museum windows, a layer of frost clung to the trees. Boo had decided to take the evening off. But he didn't fly away before leaving instructions:

"Because it's your birthday, I will refrain from lecturing you about the dangers of sugar, and also, I moved the weekend training session from eight thirty a.m. to eight forty-five a.m., so that you may sleep in," Boo had said. "Happy birthday."

"What? That's only fifteen more minutes!"

"Fifteen more minutes in which the enemy may advance!"

The enemy, in this case, could be the Sleeper, who still

hadn't been found, or Takshaka, who had managed to escape his jailers and disappear. Though Aru didn't like to think about it, she knew that somewhere in the dark, a massive army was being cobbled together. They may not have succeeded in getting the nectar of immortality this time, but both the Sleeper and Takshaka were clever....Soon, they'd find another way.

Already, Aru had begun to hear rumors whipping through the Council of Guardians....Something about Kalpavriksha, the wish-granting tree. After all, the amrita wasn't the only thing that had sprung out of the Ocean of Milk when the devas and asuras churned its waters. There were treasures still left to uncover...treasures that might make all the difference when the next great war finally came.

For now, though, Aru was going to savor tonight. Who knew when she'd have another chance to relax and have fun like this?

"Do you think his dad is there already?" asked Mini, next to her, also looking out the window.

"I don't know. But I hope Aiden is okay."

Wifey hadn't come to Aru's party because his dad was coming over today, and he planned to use his love arrow to get them back together. None of the girls thought this was a good idea, but the boy was stubborn.

"Mini!" hollered Brynne from the tiny kitchen. "I need help! Legolas is melting!"

"Oh no," said Mini.

"I can help—" started Aru, but Hira blocked off the entrance. "You're not allowed!"

"Hira, that was a *perfect* opportunity to say 'You shall not pass!'"

"Oops."

"Fine, fine," said Aru. "I'll stay out here. Holler when I can come back in to *my* party."

"Will do!" said Mini, and she jogged off after Hira and Brynne.

Not knowing what else to do, Aru looked out the window again.

And saw Aiden...

He was pacing his front lawn, Shadowfax around his neck. Kamadeva's arrow poked out of his hoodie pocket. He had the hood pulled up over his head, but still, it obviously wasn't enough to keep him warm outside in this weather. He hadn't asked any of his friends to be there with him when his dad came over. But just because someone doesn't ask for help doesn't mean they don't need it.

Aru stroked her fake beard thoughtfully...and slipped out the front door.

Across the street, Aiden's head snapped up the second the museum entrance closed behind her.

"Why are you dressed like an old man?"

"Old *wizard*," she corrected. "It's for my party."

"Oh." Aiden shoved his hands in his hoodie pocket, then glanced over his shoulder to the windows of his house. Aru wasn't sure, but she thought she could make out the shadow of Mrs. Acharya inside.

"You should go back and have fun," he said. "You don't have to be out here."

"Well, Legolas is melting, so I can't go in yet."

Aiden accepted this without comment, which was proof of their friendship.

"He's coming soon," said Aiden, his words rushing out. "And I don't know what to do. I just want her to be happy."

Mrs. Acharya was now at the window. She didn't even seem to register that Aru was outside with Aiden. Her face looked gaunt and sad, but also . . . determined. The way someone looks when they're going into battle and they don't have any regrets.

"Do you think she'd be happy if she was back with your dad?"

Aiden tugged on his black hair, twisting his curls into bizarre-looking horns.

"I dunno. I *thought* so, but now I just don't know. I just . . . You don't know what she was like before all this."

That much was true, but Aru could take a guess. Since their quest, she'd seen old photos of Mrs. Acharya, the former apsara celebrity. It wasn't so much that that she was supremely attractive, but that she was *happy*. Confident. As though she liked herself more than anyone else and that was all that mattered. In that way, she reminded Aru of Brynne.

These days Mrs. Acharya looked different . . . more caved-in.

"And then I keep thinking about what Kamadeva said," Aiden went on. "That it's not really an arrow of love, but *aware-ness*, and I don't even know what that means!"

He tugged harder at his hair. Aru swatted at his hand. "Stop that or you're gonna go bald!"

Aiden glared at her. The headlights of an approaching car flashed down the street.

"He's almost here," said Aiden. He grabbed her hand. "C'mon!"

Aiden dragged her along as they crossed the lawn and slipped through the front door.

"What are we *doing*?" hissed Aru.

"Just hold on, Shah. Two seconds. Please."

It was the *please* that got her, whether she liked it or not.

"Aiden?" his mom called. "Is that you?"

He held his finger to his lips. Together they crawled past the front door, then took a left into the den, where they hid behind the sofa. In the front hall, Aru saw a long mirror on the wall. Framed photographs (all taken by Aiden) lined both sides of it. The foyer of the Acharya home split off into two rooms. The one on the right was the dining area, where Mrs. Acharya was staring out the window, her arms wrapped around her slender body.

Aiden pulled a small glass bubble-like charm from his jeans pocket and blew it into the air. Instantly, it expanded into a giant translucent sphere that surrounded them.

"Silence charm," explained Aiden. "Now she can't hear us."

Aru poked at the bubble. "Where'd you get this?"

"Night Bazaar. This yaksha merchant gave it to me after I took some headshots for him. He said he wants to be a Tollywood star."

"Huh. Cool. So . . . why the bubble? I mean, I'm totally here for moral support and all that, but . . . what are we supposed to do from inside a bubble?"

Aiden was quiet for a long moment, and then he said, "You know the best thing about taking photos?"

Aru shook her head.

"I can show people what I see," said Aiden in a low voice. "I can show them how *I* see them. I wish I could show my mom. Maybe then she'd see that I think she's . . . perfect."

Aru plucked at her beard. Across the hall, Mrs. Acharya went to the long mirror. Her hair was in a low ponytail, which made her eyes look too big for her face. She smoothed her cheeks in an upward motion, the way Aru's mom did whenever she had a hard day.

"So then why don't you do that?" asked Aru.

Aiden's eyes widened. His gaze went to his mom, looking at herself in the mirror. Outside, a car door slammed shut. Aiden pulled the arrow from his pocket. And then, as if it were just a simple dart, he threw it at his mom, where it hit her on the side of her leg. Aru held her breath, thinking Mrs. Acharya might scream or something, but she didn't. She just shook herself, glancing once more in the mirror. This time, she didn't look away as fast, and she didn't frown. She reached out and touched her reflection. Then she looked beyond it, to the photos Aiden had taken over the years. Pride bloomed across her face. And then, slowly, she smiled.

It might not have seemed like a big deal to anyone else, but it made Aru feel insanely happy. Kamadeva had said there was no magical cure for grief. The arrow only opened a pathway for love, but that didn't mean it had to be romantic. Sometimes the best kind of love was just loving yourself.

"Aiden!" called his mom, a lighter note to her voice. "Where are you? Come on, Ace-Cakes."

Ace-Cakes? mouthed Aru.

"Don't even think about repeating that," said Aiden, scowling.

When his mom went to answer the front door to meet his dad, Aiden gestured for Aru to follow him. She crept after him to the back door, and they snuck out. Aiden walked her across the street and stopped on the sidewalk.

Less than ten minutes had passed since Aru left her party, but it felt a lot longer than that.

"I gotta go," said Aru, tugging her beard.

"Happy birthday, Shah," said Aiden. "And um, thanks. A lot. I mean it."

"You can join in whenever? If you want?"

Aiden brightened for a moment, but then shook his head. "I should stay with my mom. But thanks again. I didn't know what to do back there."

"Decisions are hard," said Aru, thinking of every battle they'd gone through in the past few weeks. "But the biggest one is deciding what to do with the time that is given to us."

Aiden frowned. "Did you just make that up?"

"Nah. Stole it from Gandalf."

FORTY-TWO

There and Back Again, an Aru Tale

The night of her thirteenth birthday, Aru Shah fell asleep in a beard and a wizard robe, and honestly, she had never been more comfortable. Brynne had fallen asleep next to a plate of cookies. Mini and Hira were curled up on the couch.

It had been a very good birthday.

It might have even been the best birthday Aru could remember...if it weren't for that strange text message she'd received around midnight. She hadn't recognized the number, and it had come in when they were *right* in the middle of watching her favorite battle scene, so she hadn't said anything to anyone.

The message was short. Just two emojis—a snake and the smiley face wearing sunglasses—and one sentence:

I'm going to call in that favor soon, Aru Shah.

What was *that* about?

The snake and the sunglasses should have tipped her off immediately, but it wasn't until right before she fell asleep that she remembered the boy who had saved them from Takshaka. Part of her had wanted to shake everyone awake, but . . . it could wait until morning. With pancakes. And turkey bacon. Mmmm.

In her dreams, Aru was walking through a huge forest. At her side, a huge, fluffy white dog that looked a lot like the dream dog from the Grove of Ratri bounded along, occasionally snuffling her hand and woofing happily. Aru was still in a wizard robe, but she didn't have a beard anymore.

It was a totally perfect dream until two loud voices disturbed it:

"That's *her*?" said one.

Aru whirled around and came face-to-face with a pair of girls. *Twins.* They were short and looked younger than her, with deep brown skin. One wore a fashionable hair wrap. The other wore her hair in a series of intricate braids. Their eyes were a blue so pale they looked like chips of ice.

"What are you doing in my dream?" demanded Aru.

"What are you doing in *our* dream?" said one of the twins. "We got here first!"

"Did not!"

"Did too!"

"R-2!"

"D—" started one of the girls before she scowled. "No fair."

Aru grinned. There was something strangely familiar about the twins, but she didn't know why.

One of the girls touched her fingers to her temple, squeezing her eyes shut.

"What is it?" asked her twin. "Is it another vision?"

"Whoa. *Vision*?" asked Aru. "Can you see the future? Can I see it, too?"

The other twin opened her eyes, then raised her hand and pointed to Aru.

"That's her," said the girl. "Next year, she's going to save us."

"Save you?" asked Aru, looking around. "From what?"

The twins answered in unison. "You'll find out soon enough, Aru Shah."

Glossary

I see you're back for more. Ah well, can't say I didn't warn you. Once again, I'd like to preface this glossary by saying that this is by no means exhaustive or attentive to the nuances of mythology. India is GINORMOUS, and these myths and legends vary from state to state. What you read here is merely a slice of what *I* understand from the stories *I* was told and the research *I* conducted. The wonderful thing about mythology is that its arms are wide enough to embrace many traditions from many regions. My hope is that this glossary gives you context for Aru's world, and perhaps nudges you to do some research of your own. ☺

Adrishya (UH-drish-yah) Hindi for *invisible* or *disappear*.

Agni (UHG-nee) The Hindu god of fire. He's also the guardian of the southeast direction. Fire is deeply important to many Hindu rituals, and there are a lot of fun myths about Agni's direction and role. For example, one sage cursed Agni to become the devourer of all things on earth (No one ever told me *why* the sage was mad. . . . Did Agni burn a hole in his favorite sweatshirt? Overcook the popcorn?), but then Brahma, the creator god, fixed it so that Agni became the *purifier* of all he touched. That said, Agni definitely had an appetite. Once, he'd eaten so much clarified butter (often used in religious rituals) from the priests that nothing would fix his terrible stomachache except, well, *an entire forest.* That happened to be the Khandava Forest. Small problem, though. Indra, the god of thunder, protected that forest, because it was where the family of his friend Takshaka lived.

Amaravati (uh-MAR-uh-vah-tee) So, I have suffered the great misfortune of never having visited this legendary city, but I hear it's, like, *amazing.* It has to be, considering it's where Lord Indra lives. It's draped in gold palaces and has celestial gardens full of a thousand wonders that even include a wish-granting tree. I wonder what the flowers smell like there. I imagine like birthday cake, because it's basically heaven.

Ammamma (UH-muh-mah) *Grandmother* in Telugu, one of the many languages spoken in India, most commonly in the southern area.

Amrita (am-REE-tuh) The immortal drink of the gods. According to the legends, Sage Durvasa once cursed the gods to lose their immortality. To get it back, they had to churn the celestial Ocean of Milk. But in order to accomplish this feat, they had to seek assistance from the asuras, another semi-divine race of beings who were constantly at war with the devas. In return for their help, the asuras demanded that the devas share a taste of the amrita. Which, you know, *fair.* But to gods, *fair* is just another word. So they tricked the asuras. The supreme god Vishnu, also known as the preserver, took the form of Mohini, a beautiful enchantress. The asuras and devas lined up in two rows. While Mohini poured the amrita, the asuras were so mesmerized by her beauty they didn't realize she was giving *all* the immortality nectar to the gods and not them. Rude! By the way, I have no idea what amrita tastes like. Probably birthday cake.

Apsara (AHP-sah-rah) Apsaras are beautiful, heavenly dancers who entertain in the Court of the Heavens. They're often the wives of heavenly musicians. In Hindu myths, apsaras are usually sent on errands by Lord Indra to break the meditation of sages who are getting a little too powerful. It's pretty hard to keep meditating when a celestial nymph starts dancing in front of you. And if you scorn her affection (as Arjuna did in the *Mahabharata*), she might just curse you. Just sayin'.

Asura (AH-soo-rah) A sometimes good, sometimes bad race of semidivine beings. They're most popularly known from the story about the churning of the Ocean of Milk.

Bhai (BHAI) "Brother" in Hindi.

Bhangra (BAHN-grah) One of several popular Punjabi-style dances. The technique is quite simple: "pat the dog" and "screw in a lightbulb" AT. THE. SAME. TIME. This is critical. And then you must hop back and forth. Many Indian men think they're very good at this. They are usually not. Like my father.

Bollywood (BALL-ee-wood) India's version of Hollywood. They produce tons of movies a year. You can always recognize a Bollywood movie, because somebody gets fake-slapped at least once, and every time a musical number starts, the setting changes *drastically*. (How did they start off dancing in the streets of India and end up in Switzerland by the end of the song?) One of Bollywood's most enduring celebrities is

Shah Rukh Khan. (Yours truly did *not* have the most giant crush on him and keep his picture in her locker.... You have *no* proof, go away.)

Chaat (CHAHT) Not to be mistaken for a quick phone call, chaat is a yummy savory snack found all over India. My grandmother makes it with fried pieces of gram flour smothered in spiced potatoes, chopped onions, pomegranate seeds, yogurt sauce, and OH MY GOD I'M HUNGRY!

Chakora (CHUH-kor-uh) A mythical bird that is said to live off moonbeams. Imagine a really pretty chicken that shuns corn kernels in favor of moondust, which, to be honest, sounds way yummier anyway.

Dada-ji (DAH-dah-jee) *Grandfather* in Hindi.

Danda (DAHN-duh) A giant punishing rod that is often considered the symbol of the Dharma Raja, the god of the dead.

Devas (DEH-vahz) The Sanskrit term for the race of gods.

Dharma Raja (DAR-mah RAH-jah) The Lord of Death and Justice, and the father of the oldest Pandava brother, Yudhistira. His mount is a water buffalo.

Dosa (DOE-sah) A savory crepe-like dish that is a large part of South Indian cuisine. My best friend's mom used to make them for us every day after school with fish tikka masala. They're delicious.

Draupadi (DROH-puh-dee) Princess Draupadi was the wife of the five Pandava brothers. Yup, you read that right—all five. See, once upon a time, her hand was offered in marriage to whoever could do this great archery feat, etc.... and Arjuna won because Arjuna. When he came home, he jokingly told his mom (who had her back to him and was praying), "I won something!" To which his mother said, "Share equally with your brothers." The rest must've been an awkward convo. Anyway. Draupadi was famously outspoken and independent, and she condemned those who wronged her family. In some places she is revered as a goddess in her own right. When the Pandavas eventually made their journey to heaven, Draupadi was the first to fall down and die in response (PS: She loved Arjuna more than her other husbands). Mythology is harsh.

Drona (DRONE-ah) The famous warrior teacher of the Pandavas. He promised to make Arjuna the best archer in the world and therefore shunned Ekalavya, the son of a tribal chieftain, who had the same ambition.

Durvasa (dur-VAH-suh) An ancient and powerful sage so infamous for his short temper that his name literally translates to *one who is difficult to live with*. Legend has it that the reason he is commanding and grumpy is because he was born out of Shiva's anger. Go figure. It was Durvasa who ended up cursing the gods to lose their immortality, all because of a flower wreath. Yup. Once, Durvasa was wandering the world in a (shocker) *ridiculously good mood*. He came across a beautiful nymph, saw her flower garland, and was like, "OMG that's adorable. Gimme." The nymph, probably aware of what happened when Durvasa *didn't* get his way, respectfully gave him her crown. While wearing the flower garland, Durvasa ran into Indra. He tossed the garland to the god, who caught it and placed it on the head of his cloud-spinning elephant. The elephant was like, "Ugh! My allergies!" and threw the wreath on the ground. Durvasa was like, "How *dare* you!" and placed a curse on Indra that, just like the flower garland, he and the rest of the devas would be cast down from their positions.

And that, children, is why you should always ask an elephant permission before you put any flowers on its head.

Ekalavya (eh-KUH-lav-yah) A skilled warrior who trained himself in the art of archery after he was rejected by the legendary teacher Drona on account of his lower status. Drona's favorite student just so happened to be Arjuna. One day, Arjuna saw Ekalavya perform an incredible feat of archery and got distressed that someone was actually better than him (cue hair flip). This made Drona nervous, because he had promised Arjuna that he would be the best archer who ever lived. Drona demanded to know who Ekalavya's teacher (guru) was. Ekalavya said, "You." As it turned out, the archer had made a symbolic statue of Drona and meditated on it to guide him in his self-teaching. When Ekalavya offered Drona *guru daksina*, an act of respect to teachers, Drona responded with "Give me your right thumb." At this point of the story, I just get angry. Why should Ekalavya be punished for achieving something on his own merits? GRUMP. But respect, especially to one's elders, is critical in many Hindu legends. And so Ekalavya cut off his thumb and was no longer better than Arjuna.

Gali (GAH-lee) *Air* or *wind* in Telugu.

Gandharva (gun-DAR-ruh-vuh) A semidivine race of heavenly beings known for their cosmic musical skills.

Ghee (GHEE) Clarified butter, often used in Hindu rituals.

Gulab jamun (GOO-lab jah-MOON) A delicious dessert made with milk, dripping in warm syrup. Most commonly found in my belly.

Guru daksina (GOO-roo DUCK-shee-nah) An offering to one's spiritual guide or teacher.

Halwa (HUHL-wah) A catchall term for desserts. It literally means *sweet*.

Hanuman (HUH-noo-mahn) One of the main figures in the Indian epic the *Ramayana*, who was known for his devotion to the god king Rama and Rama's wife, Sita. Hanuman is the son of Vayu, the god of the wind, and Anjana, an apsara. He had lots of mischievous exploits as a kid, including mistaking the sun for a mango and trying to eat it. There are still temples and shrines dedicated to Hanuman, and he's often worshipped by wrestlers because of his incredible strength. He's the half brother of Bhima, the second-oldest Pandava brother.

Idli (IHD-lee) A type of savory rice cake popular in South India.

Indra (IN-druh) The king of heaven, and the god of thunder and lightning. He is the father of Arjuna, the third-oldest Pandava brother. His main weapon is Vajra, a lightning bolt. He has two vahanas: Airavata, the white elephant who spins clouds, and Uchchaihshravas, the seven-headed white horse. I've got a pretty good guess what his favorite color is....

Jaani (JAH-nee) A term of endearment that means *life* or *sweetheart*.

Jaya and Vijaya (JAY-uh and vee-JAY-uh) The two gatekeepers of the abode of Vishnu. Think divine club bouncers. One time, they refused to let a group of powerful sages in to see Vishnu because they thought the sages looked like kids. Who knows what they said? Probably "Ha! Imma need to see some ID, infants." And then they laughed. I bet they stopped laughing pretty quick when the sages cursed them to lose their divinity and be born as mortals on earth. (Sometimes I'm offended that this is the worst curse possible. "OH GOD, NOT A MERE MORTAL, A SLAVE TO INTERNET SUBSCRIPTION

SERVICES AND SUBJECT TO TAXES! ALAS!") The god Vishnu gave them a choice. Jaya and Vijaya could either take seven births on Earth as pious devotees of Vishnu, or they could take three births as his sworn enemies. They chose the shorter option. One of their reincarnations turned out to be as the most popular villain of them all: Ravana—the ten-headed demon king who kidnapped Vishnu's wife—and his brother. Makes you wonder about the real nature of villains, huh?

Kalpavriksha (kuhl-PUHV-rik-shaw) A divine wish-fulfilling tree. It is said to have roots of gold and silver, with boughs encased in costly jewels, and to reside in the paradise gardens of the god Indra. Sounds like a pretty useful thing to steal. Or protect. Just saying.

Kamadeva (KAH-mah-deh-vuh) Hindu god of human love or desire, often portrayed along with his wife, Rati. One time, the gods needed Kamadeva's help to get Shiva and Parvati back together after Parvati had been reborn on earth. The problem was that Shiva, devastated over her loss, had been in deep meditation and pretty much refused to open his eyes to anything. Enter Kamadeva, armed to the teeth with the stuff of crushes: funny memes, spaghetti noodles for that iconic *Lady and the Tramp* moment, same Hogwarts houses, etc., etc. But Shiva was having *none* of it. Furious at being manipulated, he opened his third eye on poor Kamadeva, incinerating him on the spot. But don't worry, Shiva and Parvati got back together! And Kamadeva was eventually fine, but perhaps a little less eager to jump into the games of celestial match-making after that.

Kauravas (KORE-aw-vuhz) The famous cousins of the Pandava brothers and, later, their sworn enemies.

Khandava Forest (KUHN-duh-vuh) An ancient forest, once home to many creatures (both good and bad), including Takshaka, a naga king. On the advice of Lord Krishna, the Pandavas burned the entire forest for Agni, the god of fire, to consume. One of the inhabitants they spared was Mayasura, the great demon king architect, who built them the beautiful Palace of Illusions on top of the ashes.

Krishna (KRISH-nah) A major Hindu deity. He is worshipped as the eighth reincarnation of the god Vishnu and also as a surpreme ruler in his own right. He is the god of compassion, tenderness, and love, and is popular for his charmingly mischievous personality.

Lassi (LUH-see) Lassi is a blend of yogurt, water, spices, and sometimes fruit. In my opinion, nothing beats a tall glass of mango lassi on the hottest day of summer.

Laxmana (LUCK-shman-ah) The younger brother of Rama and his aide in the Hindu epic the *Ramayana*. Sometimes he's considered a quarter of Lord Vishnu. Other times, he's considered the reincarnation of Shesha, the thousand-headed serpent and king of all nagas, devotee of Vishnu.

Mahabharata (MAH-hah-BAR-ah-tah) One of two Sanskrit epic poems of ancient India (the other being the *Ramayana*). It is an important source of information about the development of Hinduism between 400 BCE and 200 CE and tells the story of the struggle between two groups of cousins, the Kauravas and the Pandavas.

Mahabharata War The war fought between the Pandavas and the Kauravas over the throne of Hastinapura. Lots of ancient kingdoms were torn apart as they picked which side to support.

Makara (MAH-kar-ah) A mythical creature that's usually depicted as half crocodile and half fish. Makara statues are often seen at temple entrances, because makaras are the guardians of thresholds. Ganga, the river goddess, uses a makara as her vahana.

Masi (MAH-see) *Aunt* in Gujarati, specifically a way of addressing one's maternal relation.

Mayasura (MAI-ah-SOO-rah) The demon king and architect who built the Pandavas' Palace of Illusions.

Meenakshi (mee-NAHK-shee) Another name for the goddess Parvati, but it also means *the one with fish-shaped eyes*. I assume it must be a very attractive fish, because imagine if they were talking about one of those deep-sea anglers with the light attached to its forehead. Nope.

Naan (NAHN) A leavened oven-baked flatbread. Sometimes people say *naan bread*, which is as redundant as saying "ATM machine."

Naga (**nagas**, pl.) (NAG-uh) A naga (male) or nagini (female) is one of a group of serpentine beings who are magical and, depending on the region in India, considered divine. Among the most famous nagas is Vasuki, one of the king serpents who was used as a rope when the gods and asuras churned the Ocean of Milk to get the elixir of life. Another is Uloopi, a nagini princess who fell in love with Arjuna, married him, and used a magical gem to save his life.

Pachadi (puh-CHAH-dee) A traditional South Indian *raita*, or condiment, served as a side dish. Broadly translated, it refers to food that has been pounded.

Pandava brothers (Arjuna, Yudhistira, Bhima, Nakula, and Sahadeva) (PAN-dah-vah, ar-JOO-nah, yoo-diss-TEE-ruh,

BEE-muh, nuh-KOO-luh, saw-hah-DAY-vuh) Demigod warrior princes, and the heroes of the epic *Mahabharata* poem. Arjuna, Yudhistira, and Bhima were born to Queen Kunti, the first wife of King Pandu. Nakula and Sahadeva were born to Queen Madri, the second wife of King Pandu.

Parvati (par-VAH-tee) The Hindu goddess of fertility, love, and devotion, as well as divine strength and power. Known by many other names, she is the gentle and nurturing aspect of the Hindu goddess Shakti and one of the central deities of the goddess-oriented Shakta sect. Her consort is Shiva, the god of cosmic destruction.

Pranama (PRAH-nuh-mah) A bow to touch the feet of a respected person, e.g., a teacher, grandparent, or other elder. It makes family reunions particularly treacherous, because your back ends up hurting from having to bend down so often.

Rakshasa (RUCK-shaw-sah) A rakshasa (male) or rakshasi (female) is a mythological being, like a demigod. Sometimes good and sometimes bad, they are powerful sorcerers, and can change shape to take on any form.

Rama (RAH-mah) The hero of the epic poem the *Ramayana*. He was the seventh incarnation of the god Vishnu.

Ramayana (RAH-mah-YAWN-uh) One of two great Sanskrit epic poems (the other being the *Mahabharata*), it describes how the god king Rama, aided by his brother and the monkey-faced demigod Hanuman, rescue his wife, Sita, from the ten-headed demon king, Ravana.

Rambha (RAHM-bah) One of the most beautiful apsaras, often sent on assignment by Lord Indra to break the meditation of various sages and also test them against temptation. This is all well and good, except for that *one* time when

Rambha (doing her job, mind you) disturbed a sage who then cursed her to become a rock for ten thousand years. TEN. THOUSAND. YEARS.

Rati (RAH-tee) The Hindu goddess of love and carnal desire and other stuff that Aru is too young to know about, so move along.

Ratri (RAH-tree) The goddess of the night. Her sister, Ushas, is the goddess of the dawn.

Ravana (RAH-vah-nah) A character in the Hindu epic the *Ramayana*, where he is depicted as the ten-headed demon king who stole Rama's wife, Sita. Ravana is described as having once been a follower of Shiva. He was also a great scholar, a capable ruler, a master of the *veena* (a musical instrument), and someone who wished to overpower the gods. He's one of my favorite antagonists, to be honest, because it just goes to show that the line between heroism and villainy can be a bit murky.

Rishi (REE-shee) A great sage, usually someone who has meditated intensely and attained supreme truth and knowledge.

Salwar kameez (SAL-vahr kah-MEEZ) A traditional Indian outfit, basically translating to *pants and shirt*. (A little disappointing, I know.) A salwar kameez can be fancy or basic, depending on the occasion. In my childhood experience, the fancier the garment, the itchier it is to wear.

Samosa (SAM-oh-sah) A fried or baked pastry with a savory filling, such as spiced potatoes, onions, peas, or lentils. It's like a Hot Pocket, but 1000x better.

Sanskrit (SAHN-skrit) An ancient language of India. Many Hindu scriptures and epic poems are written in Sanskrit.

Shakhuni (SHAW-koo-nee) One of the antagonists of the *Mahabharata*. Shakhuni was the king of Subala, and the brother of the blind queen Gandhari. He is best known for orchestrating the infamous game of dice between the Pandavas and the Kauravas that led to the Pandavas' twelve-year exile and, ultimately, the epic war.

Shakuntula (shah-KOON-tuh-luh) A famously beautiful woman and one of the many victims of Sage Durvasa's infamous curses. Once, Shakuntula fell in love with, and secretly married, a neighboring king. He went back home to tell his parents the good news, and promised to come back for her. Shakuntula, pining and lovesick, spent a lot of that time sighing and listening to Ed Sheeran, etc., etc., which means that she was too distracted to notice Sage Durvasa when he visited the ashram where she lived. Angry about going unnoticed, Sage Durvasa placed her under a curse that the person she was thinking of would immediately forget her. Yikes. Shakuntula was heartbroken, but Sage Durvasa softened the curse a bit, saying that if she showed her king the ring he'd given her, he would remember her. So Shakuntula set out to do that, but as she crossed a river, her ring fell in the water and was swallowed by a fish. Lo and behold, the king was all "new number who dis" when Shakuntula showed up.... It could've been downright tragic, but then a fisherman caught the fish, sliced it open, found the ring, and showed it to the king. Maybe the fisherman guy was expecting a great reward, but the king just jumped up and yelled, "OH CRAP! I TOTALLY FORGOT I HAD A WIFE!" and ran off to go apologize to Shakuntula and ride off into the sunset with her, etc., etc. I wonder if the fisherman ever got a thank-you gift. I doubt it.

Sherwani (share-VAH-nee) A knee-length coat worn by men in South Asia.

Shiva (SHEE-vuh) One of the three main gods in the Hindu pantheon, often associated with destruction. He is also known as the Lord of Cosmic Dance. His consort is Parvati.

Sita (SEE-tuh) The consort of the god Rama, and a reincarnation of the goddess of wealth and fortune, Lakshmi. Her abduction by the demon king Ravana and subsequent rescue are the central incidents in the *Ramayana*.

Surpanakha (SOOR-pah-nah-kuh) The sister of Ravana, the demon king in the *Ramayana*. Surpanakha was once taken with the beauty of the god king Rama and and his younger brother, Laxmana. Rama explained that he had a wife already and wasn't interested in another, so Surpanakha asked Laxmana, who also rejected her, but not nearly as kindly. Things went downhill from there, with Surpanakha not only getting humiliated, but also getting her nose cut off after trying to attack Sita, the god king's wife. Not a great day, all in all. After that happened, she ran to her brother and sought vengeance, but once Ravana heard how beautiful Sita was, he had other plans.

Takshaka (TAHK-shah-kah) A naga king and former friend of Indra who once lived in the Khandava Forest before Arjuna helped burn it down, killing most of Takshaka's family. He has sworn vengeance on all the Pandavas ever since. Wonder why…

Uloopi (OOH-loo-pee) A nagini princess who was the second of Arjuna's four wives. A practitioner of magic, Uloopi was responsible for saving Arjuna's life on the battlefield after he was killed by his own son (though he didn't know it at the time).

Urvashi (OOR-vah-shee) A famous apsara, considered the most beautiful of all the apsaras. Her name literally means *she who can control the hearts of others.* Girl also had a *temper.* In the *Mahabharata,* when Arjuna was chilling in heaven with his dad, Indra, Urvashi made it known that she thought the Pandava was pretty cute. But Arjuna wasn't having it. Instead, he respectfully called her *Mother,* because Urvashi had once been the wife of King Pururavas, an ancestor of the Pandavas. Scorned, Urvashi cursed him to lose his manhood for a year. (Rude!) In that year, Arjuna posed as a eunuch, took the name Brihannala, and taught song and dance to the princess of the kingdom of Virata.

Ushas (OOH-shahs) A Vedic (ancient Hindu) goddess of the dawn, who pulled the sun into the sky with the help of her bright red cows. They must have been very strong cows. Her sister is Ratri, goddess of the night.

Varuna (VAH-roo-nuh) The god of the ocean and seas.

Varuni (VAH-roo-nee) The goddess of transcendent wisdom and wine. She is the consort of Lord Varuna.

Vasuki (VAH-soo-key) A naga king who played a major role in the churning of the Ocean of Milk when the gods and asuras needed help. He basically got wrapped around a mountain and was used as a churning rope. It's a good thing he wasn't ticklish. After the Ocean was churned, Lord Shiva blessed him and he is often depicted coiled around the god's neck.

Vayu (VAH-yoo) The god of the wind and the father of Bhima, the second-oldest Pandava brother. Vayu is also the father of Hanuman, the monkey-faced demigod. His mount is a gazelle.

Vishnu (VISH-noo) The second god in the Hindu triumvirate (also known as the Trimurti). These three gods are responsible for the creation, upkeep, and destruction of the world. The other two gods are Brahma and Shiva. Brahma is the creator of the universe and Shiva is the destroyer. Vishnu is worshipped as the preserver. He has taken many forms on earth in various avatars, most notably as Krishna, Mohini, and Rama.

Yaksha (YAK-sha) A yaksha (male) or yakshini (female) is a supernatural being from Hindu, Buddhist, and Jain mythology. Yakshas are attendees of Kubera, the Hindu god of wealth, who rules in the mythical Himalayan kingdom of Alaka.

If you made it to the end of this glossary, you deserve a wish from a wish-granting tree! Or at least a big ole glass of mango lassi. Yum.

About the Author

Roshani Chokshi is the author of the instant *New York Times* best seller *Aru Shah and the End of Time*, the first book in a series for middle grade readers about the adventures of five Pandava sisters. Her acclaimed novels for young adults include *The Star-Touched Queen* and its companion, *A Crown of Wishes*, and *The Gilded Wolves*. The Pandava series was inspired by the stories her grandmother told her, as well as Roshani's all-consuming love for *Sailor Moon*. Rosh lives in Georgia and says "y'all," but she doesn't really have a Southern accent, alas.